A TIME FOR LOVE

The bright rays of the morning sun crept across Summer's face, tickling her eyes with light. She opened them, drowsily at first, then wider, seeing John standing at the foot of the bed.

"So . . . it wasn't a dream. You are truly here."

His velvet voice worked its magic. "Yes, I'm here." He took a step toward her. "You've come to me a thousand times in the night. Now you're here, where I can touch you . . ." His hand reached out slowly to caress her cheek. "Feel the heat of your body."

Summer shivered at his touch, then pushed his hand away. "No! Don't! Let me go back . . . back to my own time. To my own life." After all, she thought, she was an intelligent, twentieth-century woman, and he was just a primitive eighteenth-century man. He would be no match for her! "This is your world," she said, "not mine."

John put his hand under her chin and tilted her head up to look at him. "It could be yours."

He pulled her into his arms and kissed her gently. She struggled for a moment, but her body betrayed her and she gave in to the passion that surged within her . . .

SANDRA DAVIDSON

A LOVE FOR ALL TIME

ZEBRA BOOKS
KENSINGTON PUBLISHING CORP.

To my children:
William, Erin, Scott, and Michael,
who are not afraid of ghosts.

And to Elizabeth Hawks,
the lady who started it all
two hundred and fifty years ago.

ZEBRA BOOKS

are published by

Kensington Publishing Corp.
475 Park Avenue South
New York, NY 10016

First printing: January, 1993

Printed in the United States of America

Prologue

Her fingers slowly traced the words etched into the ancient tombstone. Worn by the ravages of wind and time, they were barely decipherable, but it didn't matter, for she knew them by heart; so many times had she stood at this very spot, so many times had she read this haunting verse. Speaking softly, her voice released the words from their stone bondage, commending them to the autumn air.

> Pray Kind Reader, lend an ear
> As you are now so once was I
> As I am now so you shall be
> Prepare for death and follow me

She knew, no matter how many times she had been told to the contrary, that the words were meant for her alone. It didn't matter that the stone had been standing two hundred years before she was born, or that her reasoning was totally irrational, the shiver that crawled along the surface of her skin each time she read the frightening epitaph confirmed that it was so.

A mournful cry drifted to her ears, piercing her

troubled reverie. Shielding her eyes with her hand, she looked up at the bright morning sky to the bird of prey circling overhead.

Her eyes tracked the raptor as it glided lower and lower, then seemed to stop dead in the air before plummeting, and with a flurry of wings landed on the tombstone that bore the disturbing message.

Gazing into the unblinking eyes of the majestic hawk, she was mesmerized by the golden light emanating from their fathomless depths. Slowly, she extended her arm, offering it to the bird who hopped onto it as if it had done so countless times before.

"Well, my beautiful, feathered friend, what strange fortune has brought you to me?"

As if the sound of her voice had broken some ancient spell, the hawk let out a wild cry, then took flight, a sharp talon piercing the delicate tissue of her wrist in its hasty departure. Startled, her gaze shifted from the vanishing hawk to her wounded arm, watching as a crimson ribbon of blood welled up, then streamed down her hand to the grass-covered grave below.

Chapter One

Summer Winslow breathed a sigh of relief as the last tour group of the day walked out the door of the Wells-Thorne house. The beautiful fall weather had brought droves of people to historic Deerfield, keeping her too busy to think of anything but the job at hand. She was grateful for that, for it had kept her mind off the sword.

Her heart began to beat faster now, as she thought of what she would be doing in a few short moments. Hurriedly, she locked up and ran around the corner to Memorial Hall, praying Janet would be there as she'd promised. Making her way around the museum to a private entrance, Summer knocked on the door, waiting for what seemed like an eternity before it was finally opened.

"What took you so long?" Summer said. "I was afraid you'd changed your mind."

"Shhh!" Janet whispered. "I had to wait until everyone left, didn't I? Now get in here, before I do change my mind."

"What are you whispering for?" Summer asked, speaking in a hushed tone herself.

"I don't know. This sneaking around has turned

me into a ball of nerves, and I don't like it one little bit."

"For pete's sake, Janet, it's not as if we're master criminals or jewel thieves. Relax. I'm only going to hold the sword for a few moments, examine it, then put it back. What could go wrong?"

"What could go wrong? I could lose my job, that's what could go wrong. And for what? So your obsession can grow even stronger."

Summer's brow crinkled. "Obsession is a pretty strong word, Janet. Research. That's all it is. Research for my book."

"Research? Ha! You've been obsessed with Elizabeth Hawke ever since you read her spooky epitaph, and if that's not bad enough, you're in love with her husband, a man who's been dead for two hundred years. But even *that's* not creepy enough for you. No. Now you have a sick fascination for the man's *sword*. Or hasn't it occurred to you that swords are considered phallic symbols?"

Summer rolled her eyes, groaning loudly. "I don't believe this conversation. Listen, Dr. Freud. You know very well how I feel about John Hawke's sword, and it has nothing to do with phallic symbols. I just want to hold it in my hands for a minute, that's all. What's wrong with that? Any historical writer worth her salt would kill for the opportunity to touch a personal possession of the person she's writing about. It's as simple and as uncomplicated as that."

Janet shook her head in disbelief. "Why do I bother trying to reason with you?"

"Darn it all, Janet, I wouldn't ask you, but the glass case is always locked; and I don't have access to the keys like you do. Your transfer to Memorial Hall has given me the only chance I might ever have to touch it."

Brushing a strand of wavy black hair from her eyes, Janet replied, "Why do I always let you talk me into these things? All right. You win. But I'm staying with you as long as you're in the museum. I want to make sure nothing goes wrong."

Summer threw her arms around her friend, hugging her tight. "Thanks, Janet. You're a good friend. I promise nothing will go wrong."

In a moment they were in the small windowless room that held the sword and a portrait of its owner, Col. John Hawke. Military apparatus and uniforms were displayed in tall glass cases on one side of the room, and eighteenth-century women's clothing and accessories on another.

Summer stood in front of the portrait, gazing up at John's face as she had done so often, drawn back time after time until his face had become as familiar to her as her own, engraved in her heart as well as on her brain.

The painting, done in rich, dark oils, showed John to be handsome in a rugged way, with hair a deep sable brown and compelling green eyes that mesmerized her, following her wherever she moved. His nose was straight and masculine, his lips extremely sensuous, with the slightest of smiles touching his mouth as if he shared a special secret with her.

He was posed in a chair, his sword strapped to his side, with his right hand resting lightly on the hilt. It thrilled her to think that in a few short moments, her own hand would rest on that same hilt.

"Janet, do you mind leaving the room until I've finished?"

Janet sighed deeply. Summer was really losing her marbles. Why in the world would anyone need to be alone with an old sword? "All right, I'm going, but I think devoting your life to studying dead people like this is downright creepy. What a waste of prime womanhood. With that strawberry mane of yours, and a figure that could bring your Colonel Hawke back from the dead, you could have any man you want. You should be out in the world, dating, having fun—not cooped up in a musty old museum, mooning over a man dead two hundred years."

Seeing her words were having no effect, she threw her hands up, saying, "Okay, I give up. You've got ten minutes, then we've got to get out of here."

"That's all the time I need," Summer said, still staring at John's portrait. "Do you have the keys to the case?"

"I unlocked it before you got here," Janet said, then walked out of the room, shaking her head in frustration.

The sudden quiet of the room was overwhelming, making Summer feel uneasy, though she didn't know why; but then everything that had happened to her since she first laid eyes on Elizabeth Hawke's tombstone had been disquieting.

Closing her eyes, she thought back to the day when fate—in the guise of Brian Jameson—had brought her to Deerfield and to Elizabeth's grave.

They had been on a Sunday drive, exploring the back roads of western Massachusetts, when they saw the road sign for Historic Deerfield. On a whim they had stopped, and had been enchanted by the lovely old buildings. They would have toured them, but it had been too late in the day. Instead, Summer talked Brian into exploring the burial ground, one of the oldest in America.

When Summer discovered Elizabeth's stone, her only thought had been that it might prove to be an interesting one to do an oil rubbing of. She loved transferring epitaphs and artwork from dull gray stones onto pellum cloth in vibrant oil colors, especially the really old stones. They had much more character than modern ones, and the artwork etched into them was more intricate in design.

She still remembered the feeling that had swept over her when she had read the name engraved on the stone. Elizabeth Hawke! The name echoed wildly through the cells of her brain, then careened through the chambers of her heart like an electric shock. She stood there, stunned by the strong emotion she felt, wondering what could have caused it. Then her eyes had been drawn to the epitaph, and she had read the haunting words.

She tried to put it out of her mind, but more and more she had been drawn back to the stone, each time feeling the same strange sensation. She felt, in some inexplicable way, that she was connected to Elizabeth, and she wanted—no, *needed*—to know how.

Then she found the tombstone of Col. John Hawke, a silent sentinel next to Elizabeth's. His name conveyed a feeling of masculinity and strength, and she vowed to find out everything she could about the man who had been Elizabeth's husband.

In the ensuing months, committed to researching their lives, she had undergone intense training to be a guide in Deerfield, so that she would have access to documents and artifacts denied the general public. It turned out to be a most effective way to do research, and it had paid off handsomely.

John, she discovered, had been a hero, rescuing his wife and daughter from the French and Abenaki Indians, as they were being force-marched to Canada. But a piece of important information was missing. There had been another female captive on the march, but according to the available information, that young woman had died before the colonel could rescue her. No mention of her name had been made, nor the date of the rescue, which frustrated Summer no end. But then, research could be very frustrating.

Inconsistencies and fractured pieces of information abounded, making for long, often dreary hours of work to piece it all together. But every time she discovered some new artifact, or bit of pertinent data, it made up for everything.

Like John Hawke's sword.

She remembered how elated she had been to discover it. The weapon was a silver-mounted small sword popular with militia officers of the time, only much fancier than most. The pommel was fashioned in the shape of a hawk's head, with emeralds set in the eyes. From her first glimpse, she felt a strong compulsion to touch it, and now . . . now she would have her chance!

Her heart pounded as she opened the door, breathing deeply as she stared at the sword, as if seeing it for the first time. The sword's blade was dulled by time, and the silver hilt tarnished, but it still retained its primitive beauty.

An immense sense of euphoria swept over her as her hand moved slowly toward the weapon, changing to concern when her fingertips began to tingle with electricity. She hesitated, unnerved by the strange sensation, but her eagerness overcame her fear, and her fingers moved closer. The tingling sensation grew, and the baby-fine hair on her arm stood on end; but still she inched her fingers closer, closer, until—at last—she touched the cold steel.

Instantly, a brilliant light blinded her, and a strange sensation rolled over her, compressing her body as if she were plunging through a tight hole made solely of light. When she could see again, she was astonished to find that she was standing under a huge tree.

What was happening to her?

She closed her eyes for a second, hoping it would correct her vision, but when she opened them again, the tree was still there, and the sword too, propped up against it, only now . . . now . . . it was shiny and new.

A flash of blue caught her eye, a jacket draped over a limb of the tree. She recognized it as a man's garment from the seventeen hundreds, but how could that be? How could any of this be?

Dazed and bewildered, her gaze shifted from the tree and the sword to the sound of splashing water, startled to see a man standing in a river, the water swirling around his naked hips.

She gasped.

The man raised his head and looked straight at her.

Without thinking, she instinctively reached for the sword. With a blinding flash, she found herself back in Memorial Hall.

She breathed deeply of the musty-smelling room, taking comfort in the familiar odor and in the walls that clothed her in normalcy. It had been an hallucination. That was the only reasonable explanation.

Unless . . . unless . . . Janet was right, and she was going crazy. But it had seemed so real, so vivid. How could she have imagined it? She had to know the truth. She could never breathe an easy breath again, until she knew what had caused the incredible illusion.

And there was only one way to find out.

Swallowing hard, she braced herself and reached for the sword once more. With trembling fingers she touched the metal blade, ignoring the tingling sensation in her fingers. The light hit her again, sending her back to the tree and the sword and the naked man in the water, who was clearly disturbed at seeing her appear from nowhere.

"What manner of apparition are you, woman?"

His voice, so deep, so velvety, sent shivers up her spine. If this was an hallucination, it was a darn good one. Not only could she see him in all his glory, and hear him speak, but she could feel the gentle breeze through her long, waist-length hair, and smell the earthy verdant vegetation.

"Must you haunt me in the light of day, too?"

What was he talking about? She wanted to answer him, but couldn't; afraid if she spoke it would break the spell she was under, and send her away from the magnificent sight of him, wet and glistening in the golden light. Send her away from the river, sparkling in the afternoon sun that sent shimmering waves of light rippling around him, as if paying homage to some magical water god.

"Speak, woman. Have you no shame standing there staring at a naked man? Well then, if you have not, shall I come closer so you can get a better look?"

With that, he started toward her, kicking up sprays of water as he moved. Summer stood frozen, unable to move, unable to take her eyes off his glorious body.

He started up the embankment and drew uncomfortably close before she panicked and moved toward the sword, a spray of water sprinkling her face as he reached out to grab her. For a few desperate seconds, she feared she wouldn't reach the sword in time, but then her fingers found the steel, and the flash of light transported her back to the museum.

"That was no hallucinaton!" she cried, then touching her cheek with the tip of her fingers, she felt the drops of water and fainted dead away.

14

From a great distance she heard her name being called, and opened her eyes to find Janet leaning over her.

"Summer. What happened? Are you all right?"

Her mind awhirl, Summer struggled with an explanation. "I . . . I guess I, uh, fainted from the excitement of actually touching the sword." *That was no lie.* "I'll be all right. I just need to go to the bathroom, splash cold water on my face. I'll be right back."

Before Janet could protest, Summer headed down the hall to the bathroom, a tingle of excitement coursing through her. The man in the water was *John Hawke!* She was certain of it. There was no mistaking the green eyes and sable hair, no mistaking the arrogant manner so evident in his portrait. But the painting she knew so well didn't do him justice. No artist, living or dead, could ever have captured the wild untamed, sensual look she had seen in his eyes, as he moved toward her.

A look that made her want to propel herself back to him—now, this very moment!

Thank goodness Janet's presence made that impossible. It would be foolhardy. John might well be waiting for her to put in another appearance at the river. She had no idea what his intentions had been when he came after her, and she couldn't afford to find out.

Moving to the sink, she turned on the faucet and splashed water on her face. She had to pull herself together, had to think with a clear head. The cool water felt good against her skin.

Somehow, incredible though it seemed, she had gone back in time, propelled there by John Hawke's sword. The shiny, new-looking sword she had seen propped against the tree was undeniably the same

15

time-worn sword here in the case.

When she touched the sword here, it sent her back to the exact spot it happened to be in the eighteenth century. But why? How? It was too much to take in all at once. She knew only one thing for sure. She felt a terrible fear, and at the same time an overwhelming joy at the prospect of touching the sword again.

And she would.

But not until late evening when the darkness would give her cover and when—she hoped—Col. John Hawke would be asleep. Her heart pounded wildly at the thought of seeing him up close, so close she could reach out and touch him, so close she could smell the masculine scent of his body.

She ached to tell Janet what had happened, but she was afraid that if she spoke about it, the spell would be broken, and she would never be able to go back in time again. More than anything, she wanted to do that. To see John one more time. That's all, just one more time.

Her mind raced, thinking of a way to get back into the museum tonight. Asking Janet was out of the question. There had to be another way. Her eyes scanned the room, lighting on the bathroom window. Of course!

Moving swiftly to the small window by the sink, she opened it a crack, praying the alarm wasn't set. Then she remembered: it couldn't be set until they were outside. Good—no problem. As calmly as she could manage, she walked back to the room and stopped short.

Janet was reaching for the sword!

"Good thing I noticed the sword wasn't in the exact position as before, or we could have been found out."

Summer held her breath.

Would Janet disappear before her eyes?

She watched intently as Janet's hand moved closer to the sword. Watched as her friend's hand closed around the steel, moving it back in place, then sighed deeply when she saw Janet was still there.

Whatever magic had sent her back in time was hers alone. She wanted to laugh and cry at the same time, but one look at Janet's scowling face forced her to compose herself. In a lilting voice, she called out, "Why don't you take a look outside, make sure no one sees us leaving."

Perplexed by Summer's exuberance, Janet shrugged and walked out the door. Summer was getting crazier and crazier.

Summer turned off the lights and opened the door, a deep sense of satisfaction filling her. Soon she would be in the same century, the same room, as John Hawke.

In her excitement, it completely slipped her mind that he had a wife named Elizabeth.

Chapter Two

Summer didn't remember driving home, didn't remember climbing the stairs to her apartment. She had accomplished something so amazing, so fantastic, that she wanted to shout it to the world, but she couldn't. It might break the spell and prevent her from seeing John again, and she wouldn't let anything prevent her from doing that.

Unlocking the door, she entered her cheerful living room, decorated in tranquil hues of peach and cream. She had always felt refreshed and contented coming home to her cozy apartment, but not today. Now she felt disoriented, as if she didn't belong. Or was it just the great impatience she felt to go back to John Hawke's world?

She ate, then showered, hardly aware of what she was doing, restlessly waiting for the hours and minutes to tick by; for the time to come when she could go back to the museum. She hadn't wanted to leave before midnight—when John was sure to be asleep and out of harm's way—but by ten she was pacing the floor, too anxious to wait any longer.

Pulling on leather jeans, the only black pants she owned, she struggled with the zipper, cursing at the tight fit, then slipped into a black silk shirt. Dressed as she was, she hoped to blend into the shadows. Rummaging in the back of her closet, she found the hooded black cape she had worn in the play *The Crucible,* and draped it over her shoulders, feeling foolish at all the skullduggery. Ironically, she had played the part of a woman accused of being a witch. Déjà vu? She certainly hoped not.

Pulling the hood over her bright hair, she addressed her black-clad image in the mirror. "You look like a cross between Cat Woman and Darth Vader." Laughing to relieve the tension building inside of her, she grabbed her shoulder bag and headed for the door.

The highway was deserted this time of night, and it gave her an eerie feeling to know that after she touched the sword the road would disappear, and in its place would be virgin forest. Turning down Memorial Street, she parked by the side of the road and peered out the car window.

A lump formed in her throat as she gazed at the ancient brick building. It looked so dark, so forbidding, or was it just her guilty conscience that made it seem that way? Was she actually going to go through with this? This wasn't a game. She could go to jail for this. What was it called? Breaking and entering? But she was so near, so close to the sword with the power to send her to John Hawke's world, how could she stop now? Clenching her teeth, she turned off the ignition and slid out of the car, locking it behind her. *Ready or not, here I come.*

She walked across the lawn, her shoulders tight with anxiety, shivering when a sudden breeze kicked up and rustled the leaves on the trees. She wanted to turn and run back to the safety of her car, but she couldn't. There was the open window just inches away. A window that would bring her closer to John.

Pushing it up as far as she could reach, she grabbed the sill and tried boosting herself up, a task made infinitely more difficult by the tight confines of her pants. After a few tries, she hooked her leg over the sill and pulled herself over the top.

Sliding through the window, she landed on the bathroom floor. The eerie silence was broken by the faint steady drip of a leaky faucet. Taking a few timid steps in the dark room, she bumped into the sink.

Her adrenaline was pumping now.

Adjusting to the gloominess, she made her way to the door, and crept down the hall to the curator's office. Janet had let it slip that an extra key ring to the exhibits was kept in a drawer of the desk, and Summer prayed that was true. Sliding the drawer open, a rush of blood entered her head at the welcome sight of the keys. Grasping them tightly in her hand, she made her way to the room where the sword lay waiting for her touch.

Scant light penetrated the small room, but it didn't matter; she could find her way blindfolded, if she had to. Feeling her way to the case, she unlocked the door, dropping the museum's keys along with her own car keys on a shelf, and jumping at the loud clanging noise they made in the silent room.

She reached for the sword, then hesitated, her hand hovering over it while she gathered her courage. She could stop now, turn back to the world she knew, and be safe. She could stop now, forget about John Hawke and the ancient world he belonged to, and get on with her life. Through the darkness that hugged her, she knew John was smiling down at her from his portrait on the wall, urging her on. She couldn't stop now. She had come too far.

Bracing herself, she touched the sword.

Immediately, powerful smells assaulted her nostrils, and she knew she was no longer in the museum. The aroma of burnt wood and melted wax could be easily detected, along with another familiar smell. What was it? Beer? No. Something else alcoholic. A small point of light caught her eye. A candle, burning low on the mantel of a fireplace. The flame danced wildly, as a strong breeze from an open window somewhere behind her played with it, causing eerie images to flash on the wall, enlarged to monstrous size. She shuddered, and sought the means of her escape. John's sword.

It was sheathed in its scabbard, hanging over the arm of a roundabout chair, a blue wool jacket thrown carelessly over the chair as well. Good . . . she was safe as long as the sword was nearby.

As her eyes adjusted to the dim room, she made out more shapes, seeing the outline of a tall canopied bed against the far wall. She drew in her breath. Were John and Elizabeth asleep there? She listened for the sound of steady breathing that would give her the answer, but heard nothing but the plaintive cry of a night bird calling to its mate. Her eyes strained to see, but the bed was veiled in darkness.

She would have to move closer.

Gathering all her courage, she inched forward, afraid with each step she took that the creaking of a floorboard would give her away. But there was no sound. She moved boldly, until suddenly her foot struck something hard.

An empty bottle clattered across the bare wood floor, making a loud racket in the too-silent room. She stopped dead, sucking in her breath, as she waited to be discovered, her heart in her throat, her fingernails digging into the palms of her hands.

The silence of the room bore down heavily on her,

as if it were a tangible, living thing, making her skin crawl with fright. Why didn't John and Elizabeth stir? Why didn't they call out, demanding to know who she was?

She had to know.

Forcing herself to lift one foot and then the other, she walked the rest of the way to the bed.

It was empty, but crumpled bedding showed it had been recently occupied. Damn! Where were they? She couldn't afford to stick around to find out. It was much too dangerous. With a heavy heart, she turned . . .

. . . And walked right into the arms of John Hawke.

Chapter Three

For a few frozen seconds, Summer stared into John Hawke's eyes, her mind trying to grasp the reality of his presence just a heartbeat away. Then, acknowledging he was truly there, her knees buckled and she began to fall.

John's arms tightened around her. "Whoa there! Steady now, Will-o'-the-wisp. It seems I'm not the only one who's drunk too much rum this night."

The smell of liquor was strong on his breath, and his eyes were drowsy with drunkenness, yet he still held her with a steady grip. She tried to call out, but her throat was tight with fear.

"Methinks you're no wispy will-o'-the-wisp after all," he said, pulling her tighter against his chest. "For you have substance, and what tantalizing substance it is."

Summer felt as if her ribs were about to cave in, but she was too stunned to do anything about it. This was John Hawke, who held her so tightly. John Hawke!

"Or, are you a succubus, come to entice me into sinful acts of fornication, so you may steal my soul for the devil? Pastor Bradford did warn me of such as

23

you. Well, by God's blood, you'll find me an easy mark. Come—do with me what you will." With that, he started dragging her toward the bed.

Summer came to her senses, struggling hard to free herself from his drunken hold, but his grip was too strong. In a voice barely more than a whisper, she cried, "Let me go!"

The sound of her voice surprised him, as if he had thought her incapable of speech, but he quickly regained his composure.

"She speaks, and with an angel's voice. 'Tis a clever disguise for a witch, methinks. I could almost believe you human, if I hadn't seen you disappear before my very eyes more than once this day. 'Tis no wonder I'm drunk. It would be unnatural to be in any other condition, considering the circumstances."

"Let me go. I'm no witch, or, or, succubus, or any other imaginary thing. I'm a real woman."

"Aye, you have the body of a woman, that's certain. But a witch you be. Instead of a broom, you ride a sword. My sword, by God! But tonight, the only thing you shall ride is this." With one strong arm, he forced her hand down to touch the hardness between his legs.

Summer was filled with rage. Was this the man she had dreamed of so long? This crude, barbaric *drunk?* She struggled harder to free herself, and when that didn't work, she tried words. "Colonel Hawke, where is Elizabeth?"

John stopped struggling with her, but held her wrist tight so she couldn't escape. He looked at her with a curious expression. "What do you know of Elizabeth? And why do you address me as Colonel? It's common knowledge I'm a captain in the Hampshire Regiment."

"Captain?" Summer was confused a moment, then

it came to her. She had come back to a time before he became a colonel. "Well, *Captain* Hawke, you'll be a colonel someday. I know, because I'm from your future."

As she said the words, she knew how foolish they sounded. She saw the amusement in his eyes and couldn't blame him. It was hard enough for her to believe.

"My future?" John's laughter filled the dimly lit room. "You must be as drunk as I to tell such a tale."

"Go ahead. Laugh if it makes you feel better. But I am telling the truth."

Summer saw the smirk that crossed his face and tried harder to convince him. "I know a lot about you, Captain. I know when you were born, and when you will die. I know how many children you'll have and their names. I even know the exact dates of their births."

The infuriating smile still lingered on his face.

"Your first child will be a girl, Alisha. She—"

John interrupted her. "You say my first child is Alisha? Ha! Your knowledge is awesome, witch."

Summer was unnerved by his reaction. Why was he being so sarcastic? Hadn't Alisha been born yet?

As if reading her mind, he answered scornfully. "Alisha was born five years ago. What more *truths* do you know?"

"Five years ago?" She counted quickly in her head. "Then this must be 1744. Could this be September 21, 1744?"

"You have that right, at least, though a fool would know what day and year this is. I'm weary of talk, witch. Come—lay with me. Steal my immortal soul. God knows I've been told often enough I was in danger of losing it."

Laughing coarsely, he pulled her to his chest

again, forcing his lips on hers. Summer struggled futilely for a moment, then went limp. His drunken strength was too much for her. His lips became more demanding, shocking her with the intensity of feeling he expressed as his mouth ground into hers.

Against her will, she felt a tightening in her belly. It grew, compelling her to respond to his fervent kiss. Here was the John Hawke she had dreamed of so long, this passion-filled man who belonged to another time, another woman.

Knowing this one kiss was all she could ever have of him, Summer gave herself up to the sensual pleasure that snaked through her body.

John was surprised at the witch's response. Her body melted into his own, flaming his desire to greater heights. This woman, brought to him by his own sword, was destined to be his. He knew it as surely as he knew his own name. For this was the woman who had haunted his dreams every night for the past year, teasing him with the promise of her rapturous body, until he thought he'd go mad.

When she appeared to him this morning at the river, he thought he was hallucinating, that he had truly gone mad from wanting her. But now, she was truly here, a flesh and blood woman. He would finally feel her under him. Finally find release from the torment that had tortured him so long.

As the kiss drew to a close, he released his tight hold on her, confident that she was his for the taking.

Summer felt his arms loosen and pulled herself free. She ran toward the sword, her fingers reaching out to grasp it. But before she could touch it, John grabbed her. Holding her with one strong arm, he used the other to send the sword soaring out the window.

"Methinks you'll stay awhile now, witch."

Summer watched in shock as the sword disappeared. She was trapped. My God, she never expected any of this to happen. She was totally unprepared for a man such as this. His actions were bold, and uninhibited, and very primitive. Could there be such a drastic difference between men of the eighteenth and twentieth centuries? "Captain Hawke, I . . . I appeal to your chivalry. Surely men of your century are chivalrous to women?"

"You must truly come from another time, if you believe that! I tell you what. Since you are so eager to leave my company, I'll make a covenant with you. Give me an hour's pleasure in bed, and I'll let you touch my sword and be on your witch's way. You owe me that much, woman, after teasing me so relentlessly in my dreams each night. Do you agree? Shall we seal it with a kiss?"

Summer couldn't believe she'd heard him right. He couldn't be serious. But as he lowered his head to kiss her, she realized he was, and her hand moved quickly, striking him hard across the face.

Fire danced in his eyes as he spoke. "'Twill be all the sweeter when you lay under me."

The fire in Summer's eyes matched his own. "You'll have to let me go sooner or later. I don't think your wife will approve of this ridiculous covenant of yours."

"Elizabeth will be gone a fortnight."

Summer's heart sank.

"She left this morning for her sister's house in Northampton. What say you now?"

"I say, go to hell! I'll just take refuge with someone more hospitable than you."

"By your leave then," he said, bowing low in a mocking gesture." I'm eager to see how you explain your strange appearance to these superstitious folk."

To make his point, John removed the black velour cape from her shoulders. It fell to the floor along with her shoulder strap purse, and his eyes moved over her shapely form, outlined so seductively in the strange leather breeches she wore.

"Women here do not dress so strangely, or provocatively. Your clothing will be of much interest to them. Then there is the slight matter of your sudden appearance in town. No carriage delivered you, no one saw you come. I'll wager they'll not hesitate to call you witch and cry out for your burning."

Witches were hanged in Massachusetts, Summer knew from her studies, not burned, but what difference, the result would be the same. She couldn't take a chance on being seen. Certainly, she hadn't intended on being seen by anyone, including this insufferably arrogant man, who stood looking down at her with such confidence, so sure he would have his way with her.

John mistook her silence for acquiescence. "Come, witch," he commanded, grabbing her long hair in his hand. "I'll not have you burned, but would set a fire in your belly that can be quenched only in my bed." With a slow, deliberate movement, he tangled his hand in her long hair, drawing her closer and closer.

Summer felt panic rise in her throat. What could she do? She hadn't come back in time to be raped by a drunken colonial. Instinctively, she used the only weapon available, slamming her knee in his groin. John roared, then doubled over in agony, his hand still caught in her hair.

Summer cried out as his arm jerked, pulling her down with him. She landed on top of him, her scalp aching from the sharp pain. Wincing, she set about untangling her hair from his hand, prying his fingers loose one at a time, afraid at any second that he would recover and take his revenge on her.

When she was free of him, she ran to the nearest door, shutting it hard behind her. Spying the heavy metal bolt, she slammed it home, comforted by the secure sound it made. That had been too close for comfort.

She put her ear to the rugged wooden door, listening for sounds from the other side. It was deadly quiet. What was he doing?

She waited a long time before she was convinced that she wasn't being pursued, then relaxed a little. Evidently, she was safe in this room. But that was little comfort, since the sword—her only means of escape—was somewhere outside in the dark.

Moving away from the door, she explored her surroundings as best she could, and discovered she was in another bedroom, a decidedly feminine room from what she could make of it. Did John and Elizabeth have separate bedrooms? It seems there was more to be learned about the Hawkes; things no history or genealogy books would have knowledge of.

Drawn to the only source of illumination in the room, Summer walked over to the window, where a soft beam of light drifted in from the moon overhead. Good. She could crawl out the window and search for the sword. It couldn't have gone very far.

She opened the window slowly, so John wouldn't hear, and peered out. Oh, no! She was on the second floor. A very high second floor. Did she dare jump? And if she did, then what? Was John waiting down there, ready to pounce on her? Was that the reason for the deadly quiet on the other side of the door?

No! She couldn't risk it, not as long as she was safe

29

where she was. Her only hope was that in the morning, when John sobered up, he would be more civilized and would let her touch the sword. At least, when he was sober, she would be able to reason with him. But how did she reason with herself? How did she reason with the fact that she had responded to John's kiss with such passion, her lips still tingling from his touch.

He had awakened in her a strong, sexual urge she hadn't known existed, and it frightened her to think how easily she had been aroused. But she mustn't think of that. She mustn't think about how it felt to be in his arms. She had to leave here, go back to her own world, where she belonged. In the morning, she would face him and demand he let her go. By then he would feel foolish about his so-called covenant, or better yet, not remember it at all.

Having decided on a course of action, she stretched out on Elizabeth's bed. It felt strange, being there. She had once stood on the woman's grave, and here she was seeking refuge on her bed. *A bed the woman had slept in just one night ago.*

Inhaling the faint, lingering odor of lily of the valley that still clung to the pillow, she shuddered. Elizabeth's scent. Elizabeth was no ghost, no phantom of her dreams. She was a living, breathing woman, and would soon be back to claim her home, her bed, and her husband.

Chapter Four

The bright rays of the morning sun crept across Summer's face, tickling her eyes with light. She opened them, drowsily at first, then wider, seeing John standing at the foot of the bed. He was staring at her with the same mesmerizing gaze she had seen in the eyes of the hawk, that once perched so boldly on her arm.

She lay there, hardly breathing, hardly believing what she saw, taking in every masculine detail of his handsome face. Never had she felt such intense emotion as at this moment, seeing him in the light of day, a living, breathing man. She wanted him. More than she had ever wanted anything in her life.

How much more pleasurable it was looking at the real thing than at an ancient canvas in Memorial Hall, but painful, too, knowing she could never have him. For the first time in her life, she knew the true meaning of the word heartache.

John gazed at her a long time without speaking, his mind sorting through all the conflicting emotions that rushed through his head at the sight of this exciting woman, part will-o'-the-wisp, part enchantress. He was lost, completely; he would never be the same again. Not as long as he could picture her in his mind as she was now, hair tousled, lips parted, eyes gazing up at him with such strong yearning glistening in them, that it filled his heart with hope. "So . . . it wasn't a dream. You are truly here."

His velvet voice worked its magic, sending feathery chills to her stomach and below. "Yes, I'm here," she answered, swinging her legs over the side of the bed and sitting up, her body trembling at his nearness.

He took a step toward her, his eyes never wavering from her face. "You've come to me a thousand times in the night."

She clutched at the bedcovers.

He took another step. "Yet I despaired of ever seeing you as you are now . . . in the flesh."

"I . . . don't know what you're talking about."

He was in front of her now, and she could barely breathe. How could one man have such a powerful effect on her?

"No matter. You're here now, where I can smell you, touch you . . ." His hand reached out slowly to caress her cheek. "Feel the heat of your body."

Summer shivered at his touch, then drawing on every bit of willpower she possessed, pushed his hand away. "No! Don't! Let me go back to my own time."

"To whom? A lover? Husband?"

"To my own life. This is your world, not mine."

John put his hand under her chin and tilted her head up to look at him. "It could be yours."

Summer stared into his wonderful green eyes, wanting to believe, but Elizabeth's name kept echoing through her brain. "It can never be."

"It can! Why else would you have been sent here by my sword? There has to be a purpose to it. You didn't go hurtling through time on a whim."

Summer's eyes opened wide. "John! You know! How?"

"I found this on the floor this morning," he said, holding up her purse. "It contains objects so strange, so fanciful, they could only have come from another world, though, in truth, I hardly believe it even now."

Summer couldn't imagine what strange things he was talking about, but it didn't matter, the only thing that mattered was he finally believed her. Everything would be all right. "Now that you know, surely you'll let me go."

John ignored her words. Rummaging through her purse, he found what he was looking for, and his voice took on a different timbre. "I figured out what this strange device is for," he said, pulling out her ballpoint pen. "Truly a worthwhile invention. No dipping, or blotting, no need of bothersome ink-wells. Marvelous! And what of these? I cannot fathom what they be. The substance they are made from is foreign to the touch. The little cards are stiff like wood or glass, but they *bend!* Quite extraordinary."

He held up Summer's plastic credit cards, and she had a hard time suppressing her laughter.

John's excitement became more pronounced with each sentence, each word that he spoke. "And this," he said, taking out her driver's license. "The artist who painted this miniature of you is a master indeed! Such detail on so small a painting can hardly be believed. Tell me, what is a motor vee hick all? Oh, and I saw the date on your strange card—1993—truly amazing!"

It was funny seeing how excited John was over objects she had always taken for granted. She relaxed, forgetting for the moment that she was still his prisoner, and dumped the contents of her purse on the bed.

One by one, she picked up her things, explaining them to him, and enjoying the astonishment so evident on his face. She found things she hadn't realized were in her purse—an unopened package of Advil, a pack of spearmint gum, and a prescription bottle of penicillin. She had had a strep throat a few weeks earlier, developed an allergy to penicillin, and had been given another antibiotic to take in its place. It seems she hadn't gotten around to cleaning out her purse since then.

When she was done with her explaining, she put everything back in her bag, thinking of the furor the discovery of a plastic bottle could cause in some future archaeological dig. But wait, something was missing. "John, do you have my little notebook?"

"This?" he answered, taking it from his jacket pocket. "It seems to be a book of the future. My future, that is."

"Book of the future? Yes, I suppose it is." Searching his face, she continued. "I'm sorry. It must be terrible knowing the exact date of your death."

"My death?" He laughed heartily. "Don't concern yourself over that. According to your little book, I'll live much longer than I could have hoped for. But alas, much as I'd like to believe, I hold no credence with your book. The facts concerning my children are wrong, and probably everything else as well."

"What do you mean? You told me yourself Alisha was born five years ago."

"'Tis true. But Alisha is not my child."

Summer's eyes opened wide. "But—"

"Elizabeth and I share the same house, but as you can see, we don't share the same bed. We never have. So . . . it is quite impossible for these future sons of

34

mine to be born."

Summer couldn't believe what she heard. It was as if John was the one who had traveled from the future, so incredible was his story. Adam and Aaron Hawke would be born. She knew of their lineage. They would live to have children of their own, and their children would have children, and so on all the way up to the twentieth century. Those facts couldn't be denied. "I don't believe that for a moment."

"It matters not what you believe. It is the truth."

His arrogant manner reminded her of the previous evening and something occurred to her. "How did you get in here? I bolted the door last night."

"The back stairs. You failed to notice them last night."

Summer looked back to where he pointed. She had seen the bannister in the dark, and mistook it for a piece of furniture. "Well, you failed to notice them, too, when you were bent on raping me."

"In truth, I was in no condition to think about stairs. God knows I couldn't have climbed them, drunk as I was. But what is this talk of rape? You were never in danger of being violated. As I recall, we have an agreement."

"As I recall," she answered, standing up to face him, "we have no such thing. Even if I were tempted, which I most assuredly am not, it would be out of the question. You're married to Elizabeth, and will continue to be married to her the rest of your life." Summer grabbed the notebook from his hand and waved it in his face. "This proves it. Surely, now that you're sober, you'll do the right thing, and let me go."

"You know the terms, woman." John's voice was cold, but his eyes sparked fire. Didn't she know her destiny lay with him?

Summer was dumbfounded. This couldn't be happening. She had been so sure he would let her go, once he was sober. "John, you can't—"

John heard the door downstairs close and put a finger to his mouth. "Shhh!"

Moving to the stairwell, he peered down, then a smile crossed his face and he spoke in a low voice. "'Tis Hannah, my brother Caleb's housekeeper. I forgot I arranged to have her come over every morning to cook for me while Elizabeth is away. Let me think. Ah, yes, I have a scheme to get us both out of an embarrassing situation."

John moved back to Summer, looking her over provocatively. "I know naught of your time, but here, unmarried women, especially women of your obvious charms, do not spend time alone with men, particularly not in their bedchamber. I'm afraid Hannah is an uncommonly moral person, holding with the old Puritan ways, though they've been out of vogue for some years now. She'd never understand. We'll tell her you're my cousin Summer; isn't that the name on your little cards? Summer Winslow?"

"Yes, that's my name."

"Aye, Cousin Summer from Boston. You were on your way here for a visit, when you were waylaid by Indians. You managed to escape, but your poor driver was taken. I found you wandering outside of town and brought you here. Naturally, all your things were stolen by the savages. That explains your lack of clothing and other belongings, and why your escort is absent. Now quickly, get out of those strange garments. Hannah mustn't see them."

"Take off my clothes? Certainly not! And I'm not going to pretend to be your cousin either. If you think—"

"I don't think you realize what a superstitious lot

the people of Deerfield are. If Hannah sees your strange garments, she'll doubt our story. She may even suspect you of being a witch.''

The frightening stories of the Salem witch trials flashed through her head. The witch scare had been in 1692. It was conceivable that many people living in Deerfield now, could have been alive then. And, too, Salem was not all that far from Deerfield. Probably no more than a hundred miles. It was possible they still believed in witchcraft. John certainly seemed to believe it last night, when he called her a witch and a succubus. She could hardly blame him for that though, considering the circumstances. ''All right. You win . . . for now. But if you think I'm going to keep up this charade, you're crazy. What do you want me to do?''

''Help yourself to my wife's clothing.'' He nodded his head toward a large wooden wardrobe in the corner. ''They'll fit well enough, though I warrant they'll be snug in the bosom. You're considerably more endowed than Elizabeth.'' His gaze drifted over her breasts, lingering while he thought of all the pleasurable things his mouth and hands could do with them, and his fingers flexed, impatient to be started. ''I, um . . . I'll send Hannah to lace you up.''

Summer felt uneasy as he descended the stairs, leaving her alone to face this Hannah person. How was she ever going to pull it off?

She listened at the stairs as John related the story he had just made up. She had only a moment to compose herself before she had to face Hannah. Stripping off her clothes, she threw them under the bed, then climbed under the covers, pulling them up around her neck. Her heart pounded, hearing the woman's slow steps on the stairs.

At her first glimpse of Hannah, Summer relaxed.

The woman had the friendliest face she had ever seen. She was short, middle-aged, and roly-poly, with breasts large enough to hide a small dog. Her hair was carrot red, braided and pinned to the top of her head. She wore a plain gray dress of homespun with an immaculate apron over it.

Hannah wobbled as she made her way over to where Summer lay, her chest heaving, short of breath from her journey up the stairs. "Poor little lamb," she murmured between labored breaths. "Don't you worry none. Hannah will take good care of you. Captain Hawke told me of your unfortunate misadventure, and of losing all your belongings. Well, don't you worry. I'll pick out something real pretty for you to wear. I know Mistress Elizabeth's wardrobe well. 'Twill take but a moment."

Summer watched spellbound as Hannah bustled around the room chattering away incessantly. She opened a large ornate chest of drawers, pulling out a contraption Summer recognized from her research as a pannier hoop, the kind that made you stick out on the sides, rather than all around. Then she moved to the tall wardrobe, rummaging through it until she found what she was looking for, a hunter green bodice, with separate matching skirts, or petticoats as they were called now. Hannah drew Summer out of bed, paying no heed to her nakedness, and proceeded to dress her.

The décolletage of the bodice was extreme, revealing much more of her breasts than she wanted, but when she looked into the mirror—no, she must remember to call it a looking glass—she discovered that the green highlighted the red gold of her hair, and made her eyes even bluer by contrast.

"My, my, but you're a pretty thing; tall, too, compared to Mistress Elizabeth. That one's a delicate

38

little creature, though you'd never know by the way she mucks about in the forest. We'll have to take the hem down on the petticoats, but 'twill do for now.''

Hannah prattled on about Elizabeth while she dressed her, then began brushing Summer's long hair. "'Tis a pity such beautiful hair must be pinned up, but it would be considered vainglorious to flaunt such abundantly long hair."

Summer hadn't known that. What else didn't she know? She had thought her knowledge of colonial life extensive, but obviously there was a lot she didn't know. She was sure to trip up on something important. How did she think she could get away with it? Unfortunately, she had no choice in the matter. She had to go along with this crazy scheme, until she could get her hands on the sword. Damn John Hawke, why wouldn't he let her go?

Hannah's plump little hands worked skillfully at pinning up Summer's hair, while they stood in front of the looking glass. Summer was fascinated with the transformation. She felt extremely feminine in the beautiful gown, and comfortable, too, despite the cumbersome hoop. She was surprised at the softness of the fabric, a sharp contrast to the rough feel of Hannah's dress, and wondered what it was. But she couldn't ask; she was expected to know that kind of thing.

"There you be, my pretty lamb. All finished. My, my, what a rare beauty you are."

Summer gazed at her reflection, as if she were staring at a stranger. With her hair pinned up, the last trace of twentieth-century woman was erased. No one looking at her could ever tell she came from another time. It felt strange, staring at herself in the glass, but in a nice sort of way. She was amazed at the feeling of self-assurance that swept over her now that she was dressed in colonial garb, and she liked it. Considering the predicament she was in, she would need every ounce of confidence she could muster to get through this day.

Turning around, she glanced over her shoulder to look at her back reflected in the glass, noting the large gap between each lacing. "I see what you mean. I must be much larger than Elizabeth."

Hannah nodded, but her attention was on something else. Picking up Summer's hand, she inspected it. "Not married are you, love? I don't see no ring on your finger. 'Course those Injuns could have took it?"

"No, I'm not married. Why do you ask?"

"Well, no offense, Mistress Summer, but I can tell by your face and form, you be past marriageable age, and bless my soul if there isn't an abundance of unmarried men in this community. Why, they outnumber the women greatly."

"Do they really?"

"That's a fact. Too far out in the wilderness here. Not many women willing to come out this far. Don't you worry though, Captain Hawke and all the men in these parts are brave lads. They'll keep us from harm, that they will. And you'll have a husband in no time a'tall. Why, they'll be beating the door down trying to get to you."

That last statement was not particularly comforting to Summer. If the men in town were anything like John Hawke, she'd have her hands full indeed. And what was this obsession Hannah had about age? She acted as if it were indecent for Summer to be unmarried at her age. Maybe she was just an incurable romantic, and couldn't stand to see anyone without a mate. She had her job cut out for her if that was the case, since the only man Summer wanted

40

was already taken.

Hannah took her hand again and started pulling her toward the stairs. "Come, lamby, we'll show your cousin how beauteous you look. I wager you must have looked an awful sight after your terrible ordeal." A puzzled expression crossed Hannah's face, and she looked around the room bewildered. "Where is the clothing you were wearing? I'll launder them this afternoon."

Summer's heart raced. "Ah, they are . . . were . . . too badly damaged. John, uh, burned them."

"Just as well. They'd be a terrible reminder to you, best put it all behind you." Peering down the stairs, Hannah laughed. "I see your cousin Nathaniel has arrived. Won't he be surprised to see you!"

That's for sure, Summer thought, following Hannah down the stairs. All the self-assurance she had a moment ago had disappeared at the thought of meeting yet another member of the Hawke family. It had gone well with Hannah, but then Hannah had done most of the talking, and she had a way of making Summer feel right at home.

She glanced down the stairs, hoping for a peek at Nathaniel before she had to face him, and was rewarded with a glimpse of him standing at the open door with John. He was holding a sword in his hand. A very familiar sword. John's. It was John's sword! Her heart jolted. Here was her chance to touch it. But, if she did, Hannah would see her disappear. That couldn't be helped. She had to leave now, before something happened to prevent it.

Hannah's stout body blocked her from moving down the stairs quickly, and Summer grew more and more anxious with each agonizingly slow step the housekeeper took. She had to reach the sword before John realized what she was up to.

41

Nathaniel's voice carried up to her on the stairs. "John, I saw the damndest thing outside. Your sword was stuck in the ground, right under your bedroom window. Were you trying to spear that polecat that's been plaguing us lately? I don't think Father would have approved of that particular use of the swords he gave us."

John was about to answer when he heard the women on the stairs. Looking up, he saw Summer's eyes locked onto the sword, and grabbing it from Nathaniel's hand, he threw it out the door. He slammed the door hard, then bolted it for good measure.

Nathaniel started to say something about John's crazy behavior, but lost interest when he glanced up to where John was staring so intently. His mouth dropped open as he watched the vision in green descend the stairs.

John, too, was staggered by what he saw. He had thought Summer incredibly sensual in her strange breeches, but in the familiar, feminine apparel of his time, he couldn't take his eyes from her. She no longer looked strange or foreign, but as glorious a creature as he had ever seen.

He reveled at her tiny waist and voluptuous breasts that seemed ready to burst from the top of her bodice, and yes, her hair, her fabulous hair done up in soft curls. Who could blame him for wanting to keep her? He had wanted her ever since his first glimpse of her at the river, had wanted her every night when she came to him in his dreams. And now she was here, truly here, to fulfill the promise she had whispered to him during those long lonely nights.

He watched as she glided down the stairs, then pulling himself together, cleared his throat and introduced her to his wide-eyed brother.

42

It took a moment for Nathaniel to recover from the shock of seeing this angel in his brother's house, but he soon made up for it, taking her hand in his and raising it to his lips.

"Enchanted, Cousin Summer. Your name fits you well, for your hair rivals the color of the setting sun on a hot summer evening."

John listened in disbelief. His little brother, his shy, awkward little brother, was speaking with a sophistication he had never witnessed before. And was showing an interest in the distaff side he had never revealed before.

Summer gave Nathaniel a dazzling smile. He would be no threat to her. Nathaniel was as genial as his brother was intense. She liked him already. Her gaze swept over him in interest, guessing his age at about twenty. She noted he wasn't quite as tall as John, but every bit as good-looking, with sandy brown hair and eyes as blue as her own.

She threw herself into the part she was playing, knowing her performance was more of Scarlett O'Hara than of an eighteenth century woman. But she didn't care. She was enjoying herself too much.

Batting her eyelashes, she cooed. "Thank you, Cousin. I'm most happy to meet you at long last. I dare say you must be surprised to find we're related. A cousin twice-removed, I do believe. Isn't that right, *Cousin John?*"

"That's right, *Cousin Summer.*" John thought her performance entrancing, though entirely deceitful. He would have to watch himself around her. It seems she knew how to bend a man to his will with very little effort. A twinge of jealousy hit him as he watched her flirting outrageously with Nat, but he hid it, knowing her performance was for his benefit.

Summer watched Nathaniel's face while John related his story of her miraculous escape from the Indians, reassured that he believed every word. Even Hannah listened with rapt attention, though she had heard the story just a few minutes earlier.

"I'm sorry for your ordeal, Summer, but I must confess, I'm happy you made the trip. Had I known such a charming relative lived in Boston, I would have visited long ago. How long do you expect to be staying?"

"I really can't stay. It depends on the kindness of my cousin John." Her words dripped honey.

"Then, no doubt, you'll be here for some time. 'Tis unlikely John would let so precious a jewel escape his hospitality."

"Hmph!" Hannah snorted, taking it all in. "One thing is certain, this little *jewel* won't be staying in this house. Not as long as Mistress Elizabeth is out of town. There be talk enough in town of the eccentric Hawke women, no need to add to it, I say. No, Mistress Summer will be staying with me and Charles in your brother Caleb's house. He won't be back for awhile, and by then Mistress Elizabeth will have returned."

John started to protest, then thought better of it. Hannah was right. What had he been thinking of? Things had been happening so swiftly since her sudden appearance, he hadn't had time to think it all through. "Very well, Hannah. You've made your point. Mistress Summer will stay with you." Turning to Summer, he added. "You'll be in good hands, Cousin."

"She surely will," Hannah replied, wrapping her arms around Summer's shoulder. "I'll take good care of this poor orphan lamb. She'll forget all about her ordeal in no time a'tall. Then, when she's feeling spritely again, why, we'll find her a suitable husband."

Orphan lamb? Had John told Hannah that she was an orphan? No wonder Hannah was mothering her so much. Summer stared daggers at John, and watched as he smiled sheepishly, shrugging his shoulders. She felt like slapping the silly grin off his face. Thank goodness she would be out of his clutches soon, thanks to Hannah. That woman was a marvel. John had backed right down to her.

"Well then," Hannah declared, clapping her hands together. "Since that's settled, I'll make you all a nice hot meal to break the fast. Then, we'll get Mistress Summer settled in her new home. You must be weary, Lamby, but don't you worry none. I have just the thing for you. I'm putting you in the room overlooking the river. 'Tis bright and cheery, the perfect place to forget all about them savages."

"And I'll do my part, Hannah," John said all too agreeably. "I'll go to town for the mantua-maker, and bring her to Caleb's this very day. Our cousin has need of a new wardrobe."

Summer was stunned by this turn of events. "No, really, I must insist—"

"I must insist, Cousin. We cannot have a relative of ours with but one dress to her name, like a bound servant. You'll have clothing to fit your station in life, and . . . ah, an idea has struck me. I'm going to have a particularly beautiful gown made up first, for my mother's birthday ball next week. It'll be a most opportune time to introduce you to the town." His eyes traveled over her in an intimate caress. "You'll make quite an impression, my dear, quite an impression."

Summer fought down the panic she felt. What was John up to? How could she face a whole town full of

45

superstitious colonials? Was he trying to frighten her deliberately? Damn him, he was doing a good job of it. And what was all this talk of a ball? How long did he intend to keep her here, anyway?

Her face flushed with anger, as she realized she was at the mercy of his whims until she could get her hands on the sword. He would have his way, but only for the moment, if she had anything to say about it. After all, she was an intelligent, twentieth-century woman and he was just a primitive eighteenth-century man. He would be no match for her.

Chapter Five

Summer hadn't realized how hungry she was, until the tantalizing aroma of Hannah's cooking teased her nostrils. She ate, relishing every morsel of the eighteenth-century cooking. The bread, hot and crispy on the outside, soft and chewy on the inside, was without a doubt the best she had ever tasted. The butter spread lavishly over it, creamy and delicious, though it looked very different from the butter she was used to, almost white in color. She drank an amber liquid from a pewter mug, having no idea what it was, but could taste a hint of ginger and nutmeg, and was sure it had an alcoholic content. Could it be mead, she wondered?

All through breakfast, Nathaniel and Hannah chattered away, while she sat, nodding her head at appropriate moments, trying to say as little as possible, even though she had picked up their jargon quite easily. Her acting background helped there. She loved listening to Hannah and Nathaniel. Their speech pattern was much smoother than modern day lauguage, not as abrupt, and strangely, it sounded more southern in flavor than New England. It was fascinating, listening to them.

John sat across the table from her, saying nothing, his eyes never wavering from her face. She could feel his warm gaze and the sexual tension it aroused in her, and was glad when the meal ended and he rose from the table, excused himself, then walked out the kitchen door. Curious, she turned her attention to the window in time to see him walking into the barn, sword in hand. It was obvious he was going to hide it. Good. It shouldn't be too difficult to find there.

Feeling better, she took a good look around her surroundings for the first time. The kitchen was much like the ones she was familiar with in the restored homes, only warmer to the eye and cozier: a room that was truly lived in.

A trestle table stood in the center of the long narrow room, with a bench on either side of it. Dried herbs hung from overhead beams, adding to the pungent smell of the room. Baskets and strings of vegetables hung from the beam, too, to keep them from rotting, she imagined, or to keep rodents away, or maybe simply because there was no other place to store them. There were no countertops or cabinets, as there were in the world she came from.

A huge fire-blackened, fieldstone fireplace dominated the inside wall, a rugged plank mounted over it as a mantel. Black iron pots with long handles hung on hooks in the fireplace, or rested on warming shelves or trivets on the floor, and a big pot of stew simmered over the glowing embers, adding its own special aroma to the room.

It was thrilling to see how life had been—no—*is* lived in the seventeen hundreds, and she hugged herself with joy as her eyes continued their journey around the room. She noticed a wooden cupboard standing in the corner, filled with pewter chargers, wooden trenchers, tankards, and even crystal goblets, a sure sign the Hawkes were well off. She took in every interesting detail to take back with her to the twentieth century.

She offered to help Hannah clean up, but the cheerful woman wouldn't hear of it. "You sit and rest, Lamby, I'll be done in no time a'tall, then we'll take you to your new home."

Summer watched, fascinated at the amount of work involved in cleaning up the breakfast things without running water or electricity, but Hannah tackled her chore without complaint and was soon finished.

When John strode back into the room, Summer could tell by the look on his face that it wouldn't be as easy to find the sword as she had thought. He couldn't hide the smug look of satisfaction on his handsome face, but she consoled herself with the thought that she would find it. She would steal over whenever she had the opportunity and search for it.

"Ready to go, Cousin? Elizabeth has the carriage, so you'll have to share my horse."

"We have to ride there?"

John laughed. "Far easier to ride than to waste good shoe leather. Cal's property abuts mine, but a pasture several cow commons wide separates our two houses. Come, I won't bite you, and neither will Shadow."

Taking her arm, John led her outside where a sleek black stallion was tied to a post. Summer looked around in eager anticipation of seeing Deerfield as it was in the seventeen hundreds, and a look of confusion crossed her face. Where were all the other houses? "John, how far are we from town?"

"No more than a league."

League? How strange to hear that term. What was that? About three miles? "Isn't it dangerous living so far from town?"

"In truth, there is some danger, but we're not without ways of protecting ourselves, and we're certainly not the only foolhardy ones. Pastor Bradford lives another half league beyond Cal's. His father, Martin has a profitable fur trading business there. Fear not, Will-o'-the-wisp, the militia patrols the area each day, and oftentimes camp in our pasture. We manage quite well here, as you will soon see for yourself."

A shiver went through Summer at his words. He was dead serious about keeping her here. This was no game. *She was really a captive.* She became light-headed as that knowledge sank in. What had she gotten herself into?

John offered his knee to her and she obliged, putting her foot on it for a boost onto the horse, her long petticoats and pannier hoop making the move extremely difficult. John swung up behind her, and his hands came around her to grasp the reins. His closeness sent her heart beating erratically. She felt a strong desire to lean into him, feel him up against her hard and strong. This is madness. She had to take her mind off him. She would concentrate on her surroundings. Yes, concentrate on anything but the feel of him, the smell of him, the . . . Stop it!

Summer turned her head to glance back at John's house. You could tell a lot about a man by the house he lived in. One glimpse, and she fell in love with it. It was a gambrel-roofed house, painted brown with rust red shutters and trim, a cozy warm-looking house.

They rode to Caleb's in silence, with Nathaniel and Hannah riding beside them on their own horses. Hannah bounced up and down her horse's back, her huge breasts moving like a pendulum as she rode. "I don't mind telling you, I cannot abide horses. I prefer to keep my two feet planted on the earth, where the good Lord intended them to be." Summer smiled sympathetically, but John and Nathaniel ignored her, having heard it all before.

As they rode down the road, Summer found it harder and harder to forget about the strong arms that circled her. John's nearness was affecting her ability to breathe, and the feel of his breath on the back of her neck was excruciating. An intense excitement was building inside her. Every touch of his skin on hers sent tiny electric shocks through her, and she wondered again at his ability to affect her that way.

Nothing in life had prepared her for this sexy eighteenth-century man. He seemed infinitely larger than life, and she felt overwhelmed by his intense and sensual nature. Were all the men of this century so exciting? She certainly doubted it.

John had a hard time concentrating on the ride. Fragrant strands of Summer's hair blew in his face, teasing him with their silkiness, and her soft body, so close, so warm, excited him beyond belief. What was it about this woman that bewitched him so? Were all women of the twentieth century so enticing?

No, he decided. This one was special. And he would make sure that it was *his* century that she lived in. As long as he kept the sword from her, she would belong to him.

As they drew close to Caleb's house, Summer could see it was a replica of John's, painted a dark brown like his, with shutters rosy pink instead of rusty red. It stood to the left of the narrow road, with outcroppings of smaller buildings and a barn behind and to the right of it. The same river that traveled behind John's house, where she had seen him bathing yesterday, (*was* it yesterday?) meandered through Caleb's property. Remembering John's hard-muscled, naked body brought a flush to her cheeks, and she pushed that dangerous image from her mind, concentrating once more on Caleb's property.

Beyond the pasture she could see a steep hill with a path wending its way to the top. The shape of the hill looked familiar. Could it be the same hill she had so often climbed in her own time? It was impossible to tell for sure; everything looked so different now, without streets and houses to give her bearings, but the hill did look like the same one.

The hill she was familiar with had an ancient apple orchard at the top, where she always went when she felt the need to be alone. It was her sanctuary, a place where she felt serene; no, more than that, comforted, though she couldn't explain why. She often rode to the top of the hill on a rented horse, or hiked up on foot, and sat with her back up against the trunk of one of the gnarled old trees and read or daydreamed. She drew comfort from the thought that it might truly be her hill, her sanctuary, for she needed all the comfort she could get right now.

John jumped down from Shadow and held his arms out to her. How easily he lifted her down, as if she weighed no more than a child. At such close range she could see the yellow specks in his vibrant green eyes. Eyes that danced as he held her close, releasing her only when he felt Hannah's eyes on him.

Tipping his tricorn hat to Hannah, then to Summer, he mounted his horse again. "Expect me back this afternoon. The mantua-maker shall come out here today, if I have to snatch her bodily."

Summer didn't doubt that at all. She had never met such a forceful man in her life. She watched as he rode out of sight, and wondered if he knew how masculine and appealing he looked on his fine stallion.

Turning back to the house, she saw Nathaniel leading the horses to the barn, and Hannah standing with a man who could be none other than her husband, for he matched her so well. He was big and burly, with a weatherbeaten red face and features as open and friendly as Hannah's.

"Lamby, come and meet my big galoot here. He's big as ary horse, and strong as ary bull, but don't let his looks fool you, for he's gentle as a newborn babe. Charles, this be Mistress Summer Winslow, cousin to the Hawkes. She'll be staying with us awhile."

"Happy to make your acquaintance, Mistress," Charles said in a raspy voice. "Hannah and meself will do our very best to make ye comfortable. 'Twill be right nice having a young face around here."

"That it will. Come, Lamby, I'll show you to your bedchamber now, and leave ye be to rest awhile, before that callous cousin of yours returns with the dressmaker. Believe you me, you'll be needing all your strength for that."

Hannah led the way up the central staircase to the second floor, then down the hall to the last room. Summer entered and looked around. A canopied bed edged in delicate cream lace stood kitty-cornered between two windows, covered with a patchwork quilt done in shades of mauve, slate blue, and cream; Rose-colored curtains billowed out gently from the breeze that blew through the open window. "It's lovely, Hannah. Whose room is it?"

"Why, no one's, Mistress. It's been used only on the rare occasion when we have overnight guests. With

Master Caleb away so much, it's little entertaining we do. 'Twill be a rare treat having you to fuss over."

"Tell me about Caleb. What does he look like? Is he as good-looking as his brothers? I swear, I've never seen two men so handsome." Summer sat on the bed and patted the cover with her hand, indicating Hannah should sit down, too.

Hannah looked uncomfortable for a second, then shrugged her shoulders and sat down next to Summer. "Yes, Lamby, he's every bit as handsome, but in a different sort of way. He's the same age as John, you know. Though they had the same father, their mothers were different."

"Oh? Was his father married more than once?"

"No, Caleb was, uh . . . born on the other side of the blanket, so to speak. But Jessica did raise him like her own."

"Oh, I see." Summer could see Hannah was uncomfortable talking about Caleb's illegitimacy and changed the subject. "What about Jessica? What is she like? You mentioned earlier that the Hawke women were eccentric. What did you mean by that?"

"A peculiar lot they be, never seeming to fit in with the other women in town. Minds of their own, too. They let no man dictate to them how they should live. Now, Jessica, she minds her own business, keeping mostly to herself. Doesn't even attend meeting, which is most peculiar. But the townfolk respect her even so, and she raised her sons to be fine men. There's not a man more looked up to than John Hawke."

Hmph! Summer thought. Probably out of fear. The big bully. "Where does Jessica live?"

"In town, right next to the burial ground. She has a colored man, Otis, to attend her. Used to be a slave, he did, but Jessica don't hold with slavery, and she gived him his freedom. A fine woman, she be."

"Tell me about Elizabeth. What kind of woman is she?"

"Elizabeth? She's a wild little thing, a creature of the forest. Too many restrictions in town for the likes of her. If you ask me, she'd have made a good Injun. Knows all the herbs and medicines, she does, and when folk are ailing, why they seek her out for her special remedies. Just the other day, I called on her m'self. Had a terrible toothache. She fixed me right up, with some oil of cloves and other secret ingredients I dast not ask about."

"Wild, you say?" Summer said, excited at finally finding something out about the woman who had haunted her for so long.

"That's a fact. Spent her childhood following after John and Caleb. Many folk complained at such improper behavior for a female, but it didn't do no good. You see, she was an only child, the other babes died before they marked their first birthday. The Nims spoiled her rotten, they did.

"When she growed up, she favored Caleb over John and was heartbroken when he left town after the death of their father, and she married John soon after that. What a surprise that was, for they always acted more like brother and sister than man and wife."

That information fit right in with what John had told her, and they did have separate bedrooms. Was it possible he was telling the truth?

"I can tell you, marriage has changed her not a whit. Why she would still rather traipse around in the woods, gathering herbs and roots, than to sit at ladies' tea parties, gossiping with the other women."

Summer was surprised at this description. She

hadn't pictured Elizabeth like that at all. "Is she very beautiful?"

"That she is, and more. When she walks into a room, all stop and stare, that commanding she is. Hair as black as a raven, eyes as silver as the crescent moon, and she carries a hawk on her shoulder at times, a strange sight to behold."

A hawk! Summer suddenly remembered the hawk that had come to her in the graveyard. It couldn't be the same one, that had been in the twentieth century! It was one more thing to wonder about. One more reason to think about the strange bond she felt with Elizabeth.

Hannah noticed that Summer had turned pale. "I think mayhap it's time you rested. We'll have many a time to talk of the Hawke women, and you'll soon see for yourself just how they be. But don't you worry none, I'm sure they'll take to you right enough, and make you feel at home."

Summer was thankful to be left alone for awhile. She *was* tired. It had been an incredible night and morning. She needed time to assimilate all that had happened to her, and she would need all the strength she could muster for what was yet to come. She would be meeting Jessica, Caleb, and most importantly, Elizabeth, if she had to stay here any length of time. The thought of meeting Elizabeth face to face frightened her. How could she look into the eyes of the woman whose husband she desired so much that she couldn't remain in the same *century* as he, without wanting to be in his arms?

It was imperative that she find the sword and return to her own time, for if John and Elizabeth hadn't consummated their marriage yet, they soon would. They were destined to have two more children. In fact, Adam Hawke would be born in just nine months, so obviously, something would happen soon to bring them together.

As much as she desired John Hawke, she would never be his mistress. She couldn't bear to share only bits and pieces of his life. But, oh, how she wanted him. She doubted men such as he even existed in the twentieth century. Civilization had changed men too much. They no longer had to defend their homesteads against raiding Indians, no longer had to know how to survive in a hostile environment that nudged at them every day of their lives. Sitting at a desk all day was certainly not an activity designed to make men more masculine. The thought of John Hawke sitting behind a desk brought a smile to her face. She had been born in the wrong century, it seemed, for she much preferred colonial men. But, if that were true, if indeed she had been born in the wrong century, hadn't the mistake been rectified? She was now in the *right* century. But what good was it doing her, when she loved a man she could never have? It was too painful to think of.

And then another even more painful thought came to her. What if she could never return to her own time again? What if she had to stay here where she would see John every day, desiring him, but never having the right to lie in his arms. Could fate be so cruel?

Chapter Six

Summer drifted off to sleep with the image of John's face before her. She dreamt of him naked in the river, the sun glistening on his wet body. She was naked, too, standing on the riverbank, her waist-length hair swirling around her, stirred by a caressing breeze.

John opened his arms, beckoning her to come to him, and she moved into the water, drawn to him as a moth is to flame. His arms closed around her and he drew her out to deeper water, until only their heads and shoulders were above the surface.

She felt the sensuous touch of his skin on hers, and a thrill of ecstasy coursed through her. Circling his neck with her arms, she slid up and down his body in a seductive manner, the buoyancy of the water making the provocative move so easy.

"Summer," he called to her in his velvet voice. "Will-o'-the-wisp, wake up."

She opened her eyes dreamily, then wider upon seeing John standing by the bed. John looked at her strangely, as if he could read her mind and knew she had been having an erotic dream about him.

"I hated to wake you, for it seems you were having

a pleasant dream. Was it of me?"

Her face flushed crimson. He could read her thoughts. Visibly flustered, she knew the only way to deal with him was in anger. Jumping from the bed, she said, "Captain Hawke, I resent your cavalier treatment of me, and I resent your trying to control my life like this. I have no intention of staying here long enough to get any use out of a new wardrobe, so you might as well send the dressmaker home."

One eyebrow raised. "Oh? Does that mean you plan on giving me that hour's pleasure so soon? I had thought you'd hold out much longer than this. Very well, I'll have the dressmaker sent away, then we can—"

Summer grabbed his arm. "Don't you dare. I didn't mean I was going to give in to you. I only meant I was going to find a way to make you send me back."

"That's more like it. I knew you had more spirit than that. Think how much more pleasurable it will be, when we finally do come together. We'll—"

Summer raised her hand to slap him, but John anticipated the move and grabbed her hand, raising it to his mouth. He turned her hand over, kissing the palm, his green eyes flashing a message she understood all too well. Releasing her hand finally, he strode over to the stairwell and called down to Hannah to send up Tess, the mantua-maker.

Summer was furious at John's treatment of her, and at herself for being so attracted to him despite it. But she held it in. She would have to endure being measured for clothes she had no intention of wearing, but that was all right, John would be wasting valuable money, and it served him right.

When they were through, and all the fabric samples carried back to the dressmaker's gig, Tess and her assistant left looking even more tired than when they came. John walked out with the two women, saying something about a special gown he wanted made first, for his mother's ball. He helped the women into the gig, then watched as it jostled down the road, content with his day's work.

His eyes grazed over the land he loved, taking in a rider cantering toward him. Damn! It was the preacher, Bradford. John's brow knitted. His dislike for the man was intense, though he couldn't quite put his finger on why. But it was a feeling that wouldn't go away. His instincts had always proved to be reliable before, and he had no reason to doubt them now. A man didn't live long in this wilderness without good instincts. He was sure it was only a matter of time before he discovered what it was about the preacher that rankled him so.

Daniel Bradford greeted John cheerfully, reining in his horse near him. "The Lord has sent us favorable weather this day, Captain. Yes, yes, fine weather indeed." Getting no response from John, he continued. "Wasn't that Tess Warner and her slave that just left here? Having new garments made for your unfortunate cousin, I warrant. Which comes to the reason for my visit. I've come to call on this mysterious cousin of yours, who has so unexpectedly shown up on your doorstep."

Damn his overcurious hide! John had a good mind to send the preacher on his way, but knew it would cause more trouble than it was worth. The preacher held an important position in the community. "Methinks you are overly devoted to your pastoral duties, Preacher, since my cousin has not yet had time to rest from her ordeal. But, if you insist, then I'll see if she'll receive you."

John led Daniel into the keeping room, then sent Hannah upstairs to fetch Summer. The two men sat facing each other over tankards of hard cider, waiting in awkward silence.

When Daniel could stand it no longer, he attempted a conversation. "I've not seen you at meeting, Captain. Not since the death of your father. Let me see, how long has—"

"And you're not likely to, Preacher. I'm content to be as I am, so save your preaching for the poor misguided souls who have need of—"

Summer walked into the room, saving John from having to insult Bradford further. She smiled timidly, and looked to John for reassurance.

"Ah, Summer, you are most timely in your appearance. Come. Meet Pastor Daniel Bradford. He's come to welcome you to our little community."

Summer looked at the tall, blond man, and extended her hand. "How do you do, Pastor. Forgive me, but I'm most curious to know how you found out about my, uh, visit so quickly."

"My dear, news travels swiftly in small towns such as ours. Everyone is buzzing about your sudden appearance. A most curious appearance, it would seem."

Summer froze at his words, then realized he was talking of her supposed escape from the Indians.

"You'll be the talk of the town for many a day, I fear, and find the townfolk most eager to meet you."

Summer looked to John again for support.

"And they shall, next week at Mother's ball," he said, then proceeded to tell the preacher the story he had concocted about Summer. Daniel seemed to believe him, and Summer relaxed a little, appraising the blond preacher. Daniel was good-looking, in a smooth sort of way, but he didn't seem the type to be a preacher. In fact, he seemed more like a strutting peacock bent on impressing the newest hen in his domain. His lecherous stares made Summer very uncomfortable. The man couldn't take his eyes off her breasts. His gaze kept shifting to her low-cut neckline as he talked. She was sorry she wasn't wearing a modesty piece over her bodice, as Hannah did.

"Will you save a dance for me? It would please me much to dance with the most beautiful woman at the ball."

"Why, thank you, Pastor, I'll be sure to save you a dance, since you asked so graciously." Dance! She didn't have the foggiest notion how to do the minuet, or whatever it was they danced now. What was she going to do? Damn John for insisting she meet the townfolk at the ball. She was sure to make a complete fool of herself.

"Please, call me me Daniel, and if I may be so bold as to call you by your given name?"

"By all means," she answered sweetly, glancing over at a scowling John. He obviously disliked Daniel, which could prove interesting. "I never expected the town's preacher to be as young and handsome as you. How long have you had your calling?"

Daniel's chest expanded, and his face took on a pleased look. "Why, uh, these past five years. 'Tis quite an awesome responsibility, as you might imagine. But I am devoted to my work. Mayhap you'll be here long enough to come to meeting, see firsthand how I conduct myself at the pulpit."

"Why, to be sure, I'd like that. If my cousin will bring me."

John was livid. What game was she playing now? "Yes, yes," he said impatiently. "Come, sit, and serve our guest some tea."

"I'm afraid I can't stay. My mother is expecting

me. Bedridden, you know," he said, staring at Summer's breasts again. I do hope you'll be kind enough to come visit her. She gets very little company."

"Oh, I'm sorry to hear that. Of course, I'd be delighted."

"Good." Bowing deeply, he took her hand in his and brushed it lightly with his lips. "Until then," he said and swept out of the room.

Summer looked at John. Could he be jealous of Daniel's attention to her? If she had to stay here awhile, she was going to take full advantage of that jealousy. "Daniel is a handsome man. Is he married?"

"Married? No, Bradford isn't married." He paused, wrinkling his brow, then spoke again, his voice taking on an edge. "Summer, a word of advice. I wouldn't get too friendly with that man. There's something decidedly furtive about him. It would be unwise to put your trust in him."

Summer laughed. "Really, John. If you can't trust a preacher, whom can you trust?"

John ignored her comment, his manner becoming brusque. "I have business in town. We'll continue this conversation in the morning. Expect me at breakfast." He glared at her a second, as if trying to make up his mind about something, then strode out of the room, his face like a thundercloud.

Summer was pleased with herself. She had cleared an important hurdle. The town preacher seemed to have accepted her story. There was no reason to think the rest of the town wouldn't follow suit. Barring any stupid blunder on her part, she was safe for the time being. And . . . she had succeeded in making John angry and jealous. That gave her a remnant of satisfaction, and eased her feeling of helplessness. He

63

would see that keeping her here against her will was a very big mistake.

She sought out Hannah, finding her in the kitchen. "Hannah, do you have any soap? I'm going down to the river to bathe."

Hannah looked at her dumbfounded. "Bathe? In the river? Why . . . yes, I do have some soap, but . . ."

"Good. Is it safe to bathe there? What I mean is, I wouldn't want anyone to wander down there while I'm in the water."

"That would be the least of your worries, Lamby, if some savage happens upon you. Here, better take the bell to ring in case of trouble. And . . . Summer, take this knife. It's the custom in these parts for women to carry a knife at all times."

Armed with knife, bell, soap, and toweling, she made her way down to the river and waded in. The water was cold, but refreshing, clearing her head and making her feel much better. She soaped her hair with the funny-smelling soap, then ducked under the water to rinse it off.

Paddling about, she thought about the day's events and of their outcome. She had gotten through them much better than she could have hoped for, and was certainly coping with being held captive much better than she would have thought possible. Her will to survive was strong, and it would help her to prevail.

She was John's prisoner for the time being, but she wouldn't make it easy for him. He seemed to think he could do whatever he pleased with her, as if she had no will of her own. Well, she would show him. It was time to put that arrogant man in his place. He said he would see her at breakfast; well, she would just plan on being somewhere else instead. He would soon find out she wasn't a rag doll, but a woman with a mind of her own. And when he got that message, he would soon tire of her and be happy to send her back to her own time.

Having decided on that, she felt much better, and emerged from the water more confident than she had been since she first glimpsed the indomitable, Captain Hawke.

Hannah, Charles, and Nathaniel gave her curious glances when she returned from her bath, shiny and clean. It was obvious they thought her action strange, but she didn't care. Her new confidence gave her the courage of her convictions. Joining them at the trestle table, she held her head high and her eyes sparkled with life.

Supper turned out to be very pleasant without John's disturbing presence and she relaxed, enjoying Nathaniel's jovial company. He was nothing like his brother, thank goodness. She felt completely at ease with him. She liked his easygoing manner and quiet charm, and listened as he talked all through supper about the house he wanted to build on the hill behind the house. The three brothers owned the land jointly, but had agreed Nathaniel could build his home there when he took a bride.

"You should see the view from up there, Summer. 'Tis breathtaking. You can see down the valley in all directions."

That gave Summer an idea. "Nathaniel, why don't we ride up there in the morning? I'd love to see your beautiful view." That way she could check out the hill, see if it was her sanctuary. At the same time, it would serve to put John in his place, when he came in the morning and found her gone.

Nathaniel was taken aback by her boldness, but recovered swiftly. "I . . . I would like that very much. I didn't know you could ride."

"I can. If you'll lend me a pair of your breeches and

one of your shirts, I'll show you just how good a rider I am."

Hannah gasped, Charles choked on his drink, and Nathaniel's mouth hung open, as it had been wont to do since his first glimpse of Summer a few hours ago.

"Mistress Summer, it would be unseemly to dress in men's garments," Hannah said indignantly. "I don't know how the women of Boston behave, but here, it would be unthinkable."

"I don't see the harm in it, Hannah," Nat said in her defense. "I'll gladly lend you my clothing. Shall we ride first thing in the morning then? I can't think of a pleasanter way to start the day."

Looking at the bewildered faces around the table, Summer laughed. "Hannah, don't look so shocked. Jessica and Elizabeth aren't the only eccentric women in these parts."

The sight of Summer descending the stairs in Nathaniel's black breeches and mustard yellow shirt, was too much for Hannah's delicate sensibilities. She clucked her tongue and shook her head in dismay. "The sight of women in men's clothing is offensive to Almighty God. Nothing good will come of this folly, Mistress, mark me well."

Nathaniel thought the sight not offensive at all, but rather tantalizing. "Who would have thought a woman could look so, um . . . interesting, in men's breeches. 'Tis a marvel. Turn around. Let me have a good look at you."

Summer pirouetted for her audience, setting Hannah's tongue clucking even louder at the shameless sight of the snug-fitting breeches from the rear.

Nathaniel enjoyed the view from behind even

more. He had never seen a woman's hips and buttocks outlined before, at least, not to this exciting extent. The voluminous petticoats women wore obscured such a delightful sight as he was gazing at this minute. "Cousin, the only thing lacking is a hat, but that's easily remedied. Here. Wear mine."

Summer caught the tricorn as it sailed toward her, then plopped it on her head, tilting it down as if it were a stetson.

"That's an unusual way to wear a tricorn, but most appealing. I think I'm going to enjoy this ride. Shall we go? The horses are tied out front. I saddled a mare I'm sure you'll like. She's gentle, sound of foot, and has a gait as smooth as silk."

"Good. I'm eager to get started." Summer wanted to leave before John showed up, and spoiled her plan to put him in his place.

Nathaniel watched as Summer walked out of the room, her hips swaying provocatively with each step she took. Yes, he was going to enjoy this very much.

Hannah didn't miss Nat's attention to Mistress Summer's tight breeches. "No good will come out of this, Miss. Mark my words."

Hannah followed Summer and Nat out to the horses, and watched as Nat helped Summer into the saddle. "What is the world coming to when women dress as men? Why, next thing you know, they'll be drinking and smoking in public!"

If Hannah only knew, Summer thought, smiling to herself as she waved goodbye to the plump little woman. She followed Nat up the path, delighting in the white mare beneath her. The animal's gait was smooth, its step sure. It was going to be a pleasant ride. Horseback riding was one of her favorite things to do. She loved feeling the power of the animal beneath her. Somehow, it imbued a feeling of power in her, too, and riding up hills was the best way to feel it.

It was exhilarating the way the horses seemed to make the steep incline so effortlessly. She could only imagine the strength they possessed in their sleek bodies, a strength she had always admired and envied in men, too. She often wondered what it must feel like to have the strength of a man. Such a useful thing to have!

When they reached the top of the hill, they sat quietly on their mounts, scanning the wide valley below. Summer was almost certain now that it was the same hill that had been her sanctuary in her own time, but the landscape was so drastically changed. Where was her ancient apple orchard? Of course, it wouldn't be ancient in this time, might not even exist yet. But it was so beautiful here! If it wasn't her sanctuary, she would soon make it so. "You're right, Nathaniel, the view is spectacular. You can see for miles in every direction. What a wonderful spot to build your home. Your wife will be lucky, indeed, to live here. Have you met her yet—your future wife, I mean?"

Nathaniel gazed at Summer with a fervent expression. "I do think so."

Summer realized he was referring to her, but she pretended ignorance. This impressionable young man would make some young girl a wonderful husband, but not her. "You'll have to introduce her to me, so I might pass judgement. Make sure she's worthy of you." Laughing, she slid off her horse. "Shall we pick wildflowers for Hannah? Poor woman, I fear I've scandalized her, dressed as I am."

Nat jumped off his horse and held the reins of both animals, as Summer picked the Black-eyed Susans and Queen Anne's Lace that dotted the hillside.

"Nat, tie the horses. I have need of your arms. These are the last flowers of summer, so we must gather a big bouquet."

"Not too big a bunch, I pray, else we won't be able to carry them back with us."

"Neve fear. We'll find a way. I hope Hannah isn't allergic to goldenrod," she said, adding a clump of the golden stalks.

"Allergic? In truth, I have never heard that strange word before. What is its meaning?"

Summer struggled for an explanation, mortified she had used a word not in usage in 1744. Evidently, allergies were still unknown. "I meant, I hope the goldenrod is agreeable to her."

Nathaniel accepted her answer, thinking that Boston women were more knowledgeable and worldly than the women of the Pocumtuck Valley. For only such a worldly woman as Summer would be brave enough to wear men's clothing, and with such aplomb. One would think she was used to wearing such unfeminine attire.

John rode Shadow up the steep incline faster than the stallion was used to, but he was too angry to care. What kind of game was Summer playing, riding off with his brother Nat, when she knew that he wanted to see her this morning? The little witch. When he got his hands on her, he'd . . . he'd . . . He crested the hill and saw two men standing with their arms full of flowers. What the . . . Where the devil was Summer? If anything had happened to her, Nat would answer to his fist.

As he drew closer, he sat that one of the figures was not a man at all. Even with her hair pulled up into a tricorn, he knew it had to be Summer. No man looked like that in breeches. Summer waved to him as he approached and he calmed himself, knowing it would be unwise to let her see she had gotten his dander up. He slid off Shadow and greeted them casually.

"How did you know where to find us, John?" Nat asked.

"Hannah told me where you were headed, though she failed to mention the unique riding habit Cousin Summer is wearing. Quite fetching, I must say."

"Yes, yes, quite fetching," Nat answered, wondering why John spoke so calmly, yet had a glint of steel in his eyes. A look Nat hadn't seen many times in his life, but a look that always forewarned a blowup of some kind.

"Did you forget I wanted to meet with you this morning, Summer?" A little edge crept into his voice.

Uh, oh, Nat thought, here it comes.

"No!" Summer said, defiantly. "I didn't forget. I chose not to be there. Horseback riding was more to my liking."

The glint of steel in John's eyes widened. Nathaniel could see the current building between John and Summer. "Here, let me take those flowers, Summer. I'm going to ride ahead a bit." Nat took the flowers from Summer and walked to his horse in deadly silence. Sticking the flowers in his saddlebag, he rode off quickly, glad to get away from the awkward scene.

"Why didn't you tell me you wanted to ride this morning? I would have gladly accompanied you."

"Hasn't it occurred to you yet, that I don't want your company? You may be able to keep me prisoner in this century, but you can't force me into wanting to be with you."

"I don't believe that for a moment. You want me as much as I want you. I can see it in your eyes. I can feel

70

it in the very air that surrounds us. It is thick between us."

John pulled her into his arms and kissed her roughly. She struggled for a moment, but her body betrayed her, and she gave in to the passion that surged within her. The feel of his lips on hers was compelling. She could never, would never, get enough of them. And when his tongue thrust into her mouth, probing, searching, her body turned to liquid heat, and she suddenly became too weak to stand.

John felt the sudden weight in his arms and drew her down to the ground, never taking his lips from hers. His hands moved over her body, eager to know every part of her, and a moan escaped his lips. "Summer, I want you so much."

Summer felt his hardness press into her through her clothing, and tried to push him away. "John— no—we have no right."

John's lips trailed down to her neck, nuzzling her behind her ear. "Summer, Will-o'-the-wisp, I've waited so long for this. Come to me tonight. Be with me. My need for you is more than I can bear."

Tears sprang to Summer's eyes. Oh God, how she wanted him! "Please, John, I beg of you. Don't do this to me. Let me go back to my time, before it's too late."

John pushed her away. Standing up, he raised his fists to the sky. "Dear God in heaven, what have you done to me? I did the Christian thing, I married Elizabeth to give her unborn child a name, and this is how I'm rewarded? You send me the creature I desire most in this world, through two hundred years of time, and by my own sword, then you deny me her love. What have I done to offend you so, that you punish me so cruelly?"

71

Summer sat up, staring at John with wide eyes. Never had she seen a man act in such an uninhibited and extraordinary way.

Nathaniel heard the commotion and rode back, an anxious look creasing his young face. "What's the matter?" Dismounting, he strode over to Summer, still sitting on the ground. "John, if you've hurt her, I'll lay your skull open."

Blinking her tears away, Summer forced a smile to her face. "Nat, I'm fine. John didn't harm me, but it would be nice if one of you gentlemen helped me to my feet. The ground is very damp."

John reached down and pulled her up. "There's much that isn't written in your book of the future." Letting her go, he strode to his horse and rode away at a furious gallop.

Summer stood watching, her heart full of pain. She wanted him with a fierceness that couldn't be tamed. She had never felt so out of control. If she didn't leave soon, she would give him what he wanted, what she wanted and needed so much.

Nathaniel gazed at Summer as his brother rode off. He saw the love shining in her vivid blue eyes and the pain that accompanied it. A tinge of sadness pierced his heart, as he realized that this woman would never be his.

Chapter Seven

Summer tossed and turned in bed, the image of John standing on the hill with his fists raised to the sky engraved on her mind. She had been shocked, yet at the same time, thrilled by his uninhibited display of emotion. *She loved him.* She couldn't help it. But what chance did she ever have, where he was concerned?

She was drowning in emotion. With each new day, new sensations engulfed her. Adding to the trauma was the knowledge that she might never see her family or friends again. How could she deal with the fact that by a touch of the sword, all she held dear was taken away from her, every familiar thing in her life gone? It wasn't as if she could pick up a telephone to call her family and reassure them she was all right.

When sleep overcame her at last, she slept deeply and dreamlessly, awakening in the morning eager to face John, to deal with the things she could do something about, instead of paralyzing herself with worry. If Alisha wasn't John's child, whose was she? If he and Elizabeth had never consummated their marriage, then . . . Summer could go no further.

How could she possibly believe they hadn't made love; in nine months, Elizabeth would be giving birth to Adam Hawke, and in another two years, to yet another son? Either John was lying to her, or something would bring them together in the next few days. But she didn't want to think about that now, didn't want to think about John and Elizabeth making love.

Dressing quickly, she went downstairs, the smell of Hannah's cooking greeting her as she made her way to the cozy kitchen. Hannah looked up from the pot she was stirring, a large wooden ladle in her hand, and brushed a strand of carrot red hair from her face. "Good morrow, Lamby. Did you have a restful night?"

"Yes, thank you. Breakfast smells wonderful, Hannah."

"Well, then, come along and eat. Charles has long since et and is out in the fields." Hannah's eyes swept over Summer's feminine attire, and her mouth curled up in a satisfied smile.

Summer sat quietly while Hannah served her, waiting awhile before she dared ask, "When do you expect Elizabeth back?"

"Don't rightly know. The captain and Nat headed out for Northampton at first light. Mayhap she will return with them." Hannah watched Summer's reaction, knowing in advance what it would be. Unhappiness was written all over her young face. "Then again, mayhap she won't. This is Captain Hawke's usual day for going to Northampton to tend to business interests."

"Oh. When do you expect him back?"

"He usually spends the night at his uncle's, then returns the next morning."

74

"Oh," a disappointed Summer murmured again, lonely already at the thought of not seeing John all day. Well, she would have to find something to occupy her mind. She knew she should take this opportunity to search for the sword, with John out of the way. But she wanted so much to go to the ball, to drink in the atmosphere, so she could engrave it deeply in her mind. What harm could there be in waiting a few more days? It would be a wonderful memory to bring back home with her!

Besides, what if she actually found the sword? If she touched it, she would never see John again, and she wanted to see him one more time. Just one more time. Then she would gladly return to her own time. And when she was gone, why then, John could explain her sudden disappearance as blithely as he had her arrival. There would be other chances to search for the sword. Hadn't Hannah said John went to Northampton on a regular basis?

After breakfast, she went outdoors for a walk around the property, too restless to just sit and worry. Hannah had made it clear that she wanted no help with the chores, telling Summer she was being well paid for those services. Summer certainly wasn't going to argue about that. Housework had never been her forte. It was nice having Hannah to care for her. Her own mother, although loving in every way, had never been the type to stay at home and play housewife.

Summer strolled around to the back of the house, admiring the autumn splendor of trees beginning to turn colors. Breathing deeply of the cool air, she thought it wouldn't be long before it was too cold to bathe in the river.

"Enjoying the Lord's glory, I see."

Summer whirled around to find Daniel Bradford studying her.

"You startled me, Pastor. I'm afraid I was deep in thought. Yes, the trees are truly glorious. I'm looking forward to seeing them at their peak of color."

"They are not the only glorious forms hereabouts. Whilst you were admiring the trees, I have been admiring God's loveliest creation—woman, and my dear, you fill that position well."

Summer was eager to change the subject. It was disconcerting to have him stare at her so openly. "What brings you out so early in the morning?"

"You, my dear. I'm on my way to town, and thought you might like to make the trip with me. I could introduce you to some of our more worthy citizens."

"It's kind of you to offer, but my cousin wants to keep me under wraps, so to speak, until the ball. He thought that would be the best way to meet everyone."

"So I heard. And it will be a most impressive introduction. He's hired the best mantua-maker in the area to make your ballgown, spared no expense, I understand."

"You do know everything that goes on in town, don't you, Pastor?"

"Please, I thought we agreed to call each other by our given names. If I cannot convince you to come to town, mayhap you would consider taking tea this afternoon at my father's house. As I mentioned, my mother is bedridden. She'll be unable to meet you at the ball."

Summer wanted to say no. She was uncomfortable around Daniel, but how could she refuse to take tea with his bedridden mother? Damn him. He knew she couldn't refuse. "Yes, of course."

"Good. Will three o'clock be satisfactory?"

"Quite satisfactory."

"Until then," he said, bending to kiss her hand.

Summer fought the compulsion to wipe her hand on her skirt. John was right. There was something about the man. Oh, well, what harm could it do? It was an opportunity to show John Hawke that she wasn't sitting around waiting for him to return.

In hopes of finding out more about Daniel, Summer went in search of Hannah, finding her scraping ashes from the fireplace. "Hannah, Daniel Bradford was just here, and it seems I'm to take tea with his mother this afternoon."

"That's nice, Lamby. She could use the company, poor little thing."

"What do you mean?"

"Sarah took sickly a couple years ago. Just gave up living. Waiting for the Lord to take her from a life of pain. Her husband Martin owns a fur trading business. The Pastor was a part of it, 'til he up and got the calling. Surprised folk, to be sure. No one suspected he was pious enough to do the Lord's work."

"What happened to make Sarah give up on life?"

"All I know is two years ago she had two grown daughters. Real beauties, too. Them rotten Frenchies stole down from New France with their savage friends and took them away. Lordy, how I fear them Injuns. Seen many a scalped head in my day. Don't mind telling you my greatest fear is of getting scalped. I hear tell they love hair the color of mine, hang it from their wigwams. Gives me the chills just thinking 'bout it."

Hannah shuddered as if someone was walking

across her grave, and folded her arms across her chest to comfort herself. "Anyway, as I was saying. I hear tell them Frenchies sold the girls to some wealthy Frenchmen. Just about broke Sarah's heart. She blamed her husband, though I can't fathom why. Unless there be something more she hasn't told me. My heart goes out to the poor lost soul. 'Twill do her good to have a visit from you."

Riding in Daniel's two-wheeled gig was exceedingly bumpy on the dusty road fraught with ruts and ridges, but thankfully, in a short time they were turning into the tree-lined entry road to the Bradford place. The narrow road led to a clearing where the Bradford house stood, along with a small rugged cabin that sat on the other side of the clearing. No one was about, except for a husky blond man bent over a pile of wolf skins.

He looked up briefly as they rode by, staring at her with the coldest blue eyes she had ever seen; she was glad when he went back to counting skins. If that was Sarah's husband, it was no wonder the poor woman had taken to her bed.

Drawing to a halt in front of the dingy white house in a state of disrepair, Daniel helped her out and led her to the doorway, where a young Indian woman stood.

"Summer, this is Asperensah, our housekeeper." He spoke a few words to the woman in her native tongue and she nodded and went into the house, sashaying in a manner that told Summer she was more than just a housekeeper.

"Asperensah is fixing us some tea. If you'll have a seat, I'll go upstairs and tell Mother she has company. Then, if you don't mind, we'll take tea upstairs with her."

Hannah was right, Summer decided upon meeting Sarah Bradford. Tiny and fragile-looking, she seemed too delicate for the rough world of fur trading and savages. The little woman seemed happy to meet her guest, but Summer couldn't get over the feeling that Sarah was afraid of something. Fear shone in her pale blue eyes, and she jumped whenever her son spoke. It seemed all the Bradfords were strange.

Aside from Sarah's obvious nervousness, the visit turned out to be pleasant enough. Asperensah set a plate of flat biscuits in front of them, which to Summer's surprise turned out to be quite tasty. Much like Scottish shortbread.

Daniel juggled his teacup on his saucer like an expert, which, of course, he was, but Sarah's cup rattled terribly in her hands, reminding Summer of a small injured bird she had once held in her hands. Its tiny heart fluttered so rapidly she feared it would die of exhaustion.

Suddenly, a bloodcurdling war whoop split the air, and the pounding of hooves drummed on the ground below. Summer's heart was in her throat, but Sarah and Asperensah remained calm.

"Don't be frightened, my dear, 'tis but some overzealous Indians here to do business. If you'll excuse me, I'll attend to them, and be back in a moment." Daniel left the room quickly, followed by the Indian woman, who smiled at her like a cat with a mouse in her claws.

Summer ran to the window in time to see a small band of Indians ride up to the cabin across the way, and was surprised to see a white man riding with them. He was impossible to miss, sitting his saddle as if he were born to it. Dressed in buckskin, he wore a hat with a flamboyant purple plume and, curiously, had a patch over one eye.

She watched entranced, as the cocky man dismounted and walked over to Daniel with an arrogant strut, slapping him on the back in a rough, but friendly manner. This man was no trapper. This was a man used to being in command. Daniel talked with him a few moments, then started back toward the house.

Summer quickly moved away from the window, not wanting Daniel to know she had been watching, and sat back down next to Sarah's bed. Sarah's eyes were wide with fright.

Taking her tiny, ice-cold hand in hers, Summer patted it reassuringly. "Would you like more tea, Sarah?"

Sarah's eyes searched Summer's and saw the sympathy there. "No, thank you, Summer dear. It was so nice of you to come out here to visit me, but as you just heard, it can be quite . . . unsettling here, sometimes."

"It was a bit scary listening to those awful war whoops. Do they do that often? And who is the white man with the patch over his eye? He made quite an entrance on his horse."

Sarah opened her mouth to speak, but Daniel came into the room just then, followed by Asperensah.

"I'm afraid I'll have to take you home now. Something has come up."

Summer wasn't sorry about that. Leaning over the bed, she said, "I've had a lovely visit. I hope you'll be feeling better soon." She kissed the tiny woman on the cheek and Sarah's eyes became shiny and wet, her hand clinging to Summer's for an embarrassingly long moment. Yes, the Bradfords were strange people indeed.

Summer slept fitfully that night, waking to the thought that John would be back in the morning. And he might not be alone. Knowing that, she dressed carefully for the occasion, taking particular care with her hair. If she was going to meet Elizabeth, she wanted to look her best. Thanks to Hannah's patient tutelage, she was learning how to groom herself as well as any woman born to the eighteenth century.

A strange musical sound greeted her as she walked into the parlor, and found Hannah and Charles standing over a small harpsichord. "What in the world is going on, Hannah? Where did that come from?"

Hannah's cheery face lit up. "Captain Hawke sent it over this morn. Isn't it a beauty? I've yearned sorely for such an instrument as this, but never hoped to have so dear a thing. 'Twill cheer us all up on long winter nights, that's a fact."

"Whatever possessed him to do that?" Summer asked, looking around the room eagerly. "And where is my extravagant cousin?"

"He returned last evening and came straight over here to see you, but I told him it was no decent hour to be calling on a respectable woman and sent him home."

"Oh," Summer sighed, disappointed. "Will he be coming back today? And Elizabeth. Is she home?"

"Didn't say, and I didn't ask. But we will be having company. The captain is sending over the dance master. That man thinks of everything, he does. He's instructed that you learn all the latest dances, so you'll be ready for the ball. Master Thaddeus Broom

81

is to come at two, and again every afternoon until the ball. Can you imagine that? The captain wants me and Charles, and Nat, too, to learn all them fancy dances. What a rare treat it shall be! The dance master is in great demand this time of year. We're fortunate indeed to be getting private lessons."

He certainly does think of everything, Summer thought, relieved and excited at the prospect of learning the dances of the seventeen hundreds. At least she wouldn't appear a complete fool at the ball.

The dance master was tall and spindly-looking, and gave the appearance of walking on his toes; though on closer inspection, Summer saw it was his exceptionally high-heeled shoes that gave him that effect. He was dressed in a green brocade jacket, gold velvet breeches, and his linen shirt was layered in lace ruffles, though from the look of it, it had seen better days. His most prominent feature was a huge Adam's apple that bobbed up and down conspicuously when he spoke. But the man could dance. And dance he did, with energy that seemed boundless. It was no wonder he was so thin. He must dance off everything but skin and bones.

The dance steps turned out to be complicated, though Master Broom made them look easy, but after awhile, Summer had them all memorized. Nathaniel had a natural grace and took to the dances easily. Charles, on the other hand, was obviously uncomfortable dancing, but good-naturedly went along with the lessons for Hannah's benefit. The plump little woman adored dancing, and was in complete awe of the scrawny dance master.

Hannah and Charles, unused to such goings-on, became winded and sat watching as Summer and Nat continued to dance. In a sudden move, Nat twirled her around, and the next thing she knew, she was in John Hawke's arms.

Her heart raced as she gazed into his eyes and felt his strong arms tighten around her. Oh, how good it felt to be held by him again! She lowered her eyes, hoping he wouldn't know how happy she was to see him.

John was an excellent dancer, moving her around the room gracefully, while she tried desperately to compose herself. When she dared to gaze into his eyes once more, he stared down at her with such longing that a hard lump came to her throat, and her heart filled with the same fierce emotion. They danced silently, unaware of anyone else in the room, the electricity powerful between them. When the music stopped, John broke the silence with his velvet voice, sending shards of heat through her body.

"You learn fast, Will-o'-the-wisp. Methinks you must do well at everything you choose to do."

She knew the hidden meaning of the words and blushed a crimson red.

"Are you well pleased with her progress, dance master?"

"Indeed, I am, sir. So much so, that dare I ask if Mistress Summer will favor me with a dance at the ball?"

"Do you hear, Summer? It seems you'll be in great demand at Mother's birthday ball. You must be sure and save me the first dance."

When it was time for Thaddeus Broom to leave, John and Summer walked him to his horse. Guiding her out the door, John touched her arm lightly, sending sparks flying between them. The next thing she knew, the dance master was gone, and she and John were walking behind the house to the flower garden. She looked up at him with a bewildered look.

"We must talk," he said softly, leading her to a garden bench. "I want to apologize for my action the other morning on the hill. I'm afraid I must have seemed a madman to you."

"It's forgotten, John, but I think it's time you told me the truth about your marriage to Elizabeth."

"There's nothing to talk of. My feelings for her are as a brother toward a sister, nothing more. That's what I've been trying to make you understand."

"If that's true, then who is Alisha's father?"

"My brother, Caleb."

"Caleb?"

"As I told you before, Caleb, Elizabeth, and I grew up together. Although she was a girl, we allowed her to tag along. She was such a wild little thing, knowing much about the things we were most interested in. We treated her like a boy, until we grew up . . . and she fell in love with Caleb. The two of them spent a lot of time alone, with the inevitable result. She became pregnant. Unfortunately, she didn't know this until after Caleb left town, or he would certainly have married her.

"You see, after my father's death, Cal seemed confused as to where he belonged. He went to live with his mother's people. When Elizabeth came to me and told me she was pregnant, she was desperate. If I hadn't married her, I don't know what she would have done. She talked wildly of going off to live alone in the forest. If you knew her, you would know that wasn't an empty threat. She would have done so. I couldn't help feeling partially responsible for her dilemma, because I had covered for them so no one would know they were unchaperoned.

"Believe me, Summer, I have always treated

Elizabeth as a sister, and she was more than happy with that arrangement. She had no desire to share my bed. We married soon after, and Alisha was born.''

Summer wanted desperately to believe him. If what he said was true, would it be so wrong to love him? "What happened when Caleb found out you two were married? He couldn't have been happy about that, if he truly loved Elizabeth.''

"He was away for almost a year. By the time he came back, Alisha was a few months old. Elizabeth and I agreed it would be best if Cal never knew he fathered Alisha. What earthly good would it have served? The deed was done. Elizabeth was married to me. For the sake of the child, the townfolk must believe Alisha is mine. There's still a remnant of Puritanism left in the souls of the people hereabouts.

"Cal seemed to take the news of our marriage well, but 'tis hard to tell with him. He's very stoic. Comes from his mother's blood. Never shows his feelings, nor his pain. To this day, I cannot say for sure how he feels about my marriage to Elizabeth, for the subject has never been mentioned between us.''

John leaned down to kiss Summer lightly on the lips. "Summer, darling, don't you see, there's no reason why we can't be together. We would be hurting no one.''

Summer looked up at him with shiny eyes. "John, I can't believe that. You'll have a son by Elizabeth in just nine months. How can you say we won't be hurting anyone?''

"Blast your damn historical research. It was wrong about Alisha. She's not my child, and it is wrong about the next child, too.''

"Don't you see, it *wasn't* wrong about Alisha. As far as the world is concerned, she *is* your child.''

"No, I don't see that. All I see is that we belong together. How can you deny it?"

Tears sprang to Summer's eyes. How *could* she deny it? She did belong to him, for he owned her heart and soul. "Maybe my being here has acted as a catalyst, John. Maybe, somehow, it will bring you and Elizabeth together, and she'll conceive the child destined to be born. I don't know. I only know what must be."

"Summer, I cannot argue with your infernal research. I don't know how or why you managed to come here, 'tis beyond my ken, but you are here, and I want you. Look at me, Summer," he said tilting her chin up. "Somehow, we'll be together. Fate has decreed it." He would have spoken further, but saw Charles and Nat walking toward them. "Now, smile. We have company."

"That was some dancing lesson, was it not? Why, Charles, I do believe you have the makings of a master of the dance, yourself. Think you the same, Nat?"

There he goes again, Nat thought. His face is smiling, but that dangerous glint is back in his eyes. What is it about Summer that provokes him so? "Aye, John. Charles shall capture the attention of all who see him dance."

"Leave the poor man be," Summer scolded. "I thought he did an admirable job of learning the dance steps. By the end of the week, he'll be kicking up his heels as well as you and Nat."

"Thank ye, for defending me, Mistress Summer, you have a kind heart indeed, but I know my failings. Best I stick to growing crops and grooming horses."

"Ah, that reminds me, Summer. I was thinking we

86

should take another gallop up the hill in the morning."

"Wonderful idea, Nat. But perhaps we should sneak out without Hannah seeing us. She hates for me to wear your clothes, but I must confess, I love to. They're more suited to riding than petticoats. Will you join us, John?"

"I'm afraid I have business to attend to in town on the morrow. Now, if you'll excuse me, I have things to do."

Summer watched as John walked away. It seems she was destined to anger him, destined to watch him ride off. But hadn't destiny also made her touch the sword? Hadn't destiny brought her into John's arms? Was it possible, in some unfathomable way, that they were destined to be together?

Chapter Eight

The day of Jessica Hawke's ball finally arrived, sending Summer into a frenzy of activity. Tonight she would meet the citizens of Deerfield, and she had no idea how she would be accepted. Would they know at a glance that she was different? Would they treat her an unwelcome outsider? Only Hannah's continuous assurance that all would be well kept her from total despair.

Then, too, John had chosen to stay away the past five days. She had no idea if he was angry with her, or if it was business interests that kept him away. She knew only that his absence made the days agonizingly long. If it hadn't been for the daily horseback rides with Nat and the dance lessons from Thaddeus Broom, she would not have been able to bear it.

She tried to keep her mind occupied every waking moment, so she wouldn't think about John, and used her free time to practice eighteenth century manners. She curtsied in front of the looking glass until her back and legs ached, and worked at handling a fan gracefully. She practiced walking in her cumbersome gown, until she was able to glide across the floor in her hooped skirts easily. Going through narrow doors proved to be a challenge; the hoop made her skirts exceedingly wide on each side. But she soon mastered her movements, so that no one could tell she hadn't been wearing the strange apparatus all her life.

The packages that came each day from the dressmakers, or shoemaker, or milliners, always held some new article of clothing to intrigue her, and her wardrobe grew larger each day. Except for the most important thing of all—her ballgown. What would she do if it wasn't finished in time or—heaven forbid—it didn't fit?

She wanted to look beautiful when John saw her, after so many days away. That is, if he showed up at all. Of course, he would show up! It was his mother's birthday, wasn't it? His mother! What if Jessica Hawke didn't like her? More importantly, what if she pronounced her a fake right in front of the whole town? Summer was driving herself crazy with worry. She must concentrate on getting ready for the ball and push everything else from her mind.

Let's see, she could wash her hair, then Hannah could set it in rags. Then, she would . . . what? There was nothing else she could do until the gown arrived. Grabbing her bath things, she headed for the river.

The water was cold, but thank goodness, the air was warmed by the bright autumn sun. Dipping her big toe into the water, she cringed, then bracing herself, waded out into the river. She washed her hair quickly, it was too cold to dally long, then rinsed the soap out of it, and was starting out of the water, when she heard someone walking down the path. Her heart stopped, until she saw the flash of blue skirt and realized it was only Hannah.

"Lamby, best make it quick if you want me to get your hair curled before the men return. I sent them on an errand, but they'll be back soon."

"Thanks, Hannah. I'll be right there." Stepping out of the water, she dried herself and dressed quickly, following Hannah back to the house. It amused Summer that Hannah still couldn't understand her need to bathe so often. Hannah actually thought bathing was bad for your health. She did notice, however, that Hannah's face and hands seemed much cleaner lately. Was it possible that she was having a good effect on her?

They sat in the sun, while Hannah brushed out Summer's long hair, then rolled it up on thin rag strips. When she was finished, Hannah's frequent giggles turned to full-blown laughter at the sight of Summer with rags tied all over her head.

"Come inside and see yourself in the looking glass." Hannah grabbed her hand and pulled her playfully into the house to the looking glass in the hallway.

Summer looked at herself and burst out laughing. She looked like a comic version of Medusa. "Hannah, I have only your word that this . . . this . . . raggedy head of mine is going to turn out with beautiful curls. If it doesn't, I shall have to wrap my head in a turban, or better yet, wear a powdered wig."

"Fear not, Lamby. You'll look fine. As for wearing a wig, not many folk in these parts wear them. They're exceedingly hot and uncomfortable, and do itch the scalp something fierce."

"But, Hannah, this is a special dress-up occasion, surely John will wear one tonight?"

"Him? Never! He cannot abide them, and since he does not, why then, not many men would think to do so."

Returning to the bright sunlight, Summer sat basking in the warm air as her hair dried, while Hannah puttered around the kitchen garden. She enjoyed the older woman's company. The plump little woman was like a mother to her, although at times Hannah drove her mad with her straightlaced ideas of right and wrong. But Summer didn't know what she would do without her.

In this strange, foreign world, Hannah was the one steady influence, the one person she could count on always. She watched Hannah's movements through lazy, contented eyes, as the sun made her drowsy with sleep, and for the moment, she forgot her worries and fears.

The sound of hooves pounding on the road pulled her out of her contented little cocoon. Could it be the men returning so soon? Her heart stopped when she heard John's voice. He mustn't see her like this, not with her head all bound up in rags!

Jumping up, she ran for the house, just as the men turned the corner. They stopped dead at the sight of Summer's rag-clad head and burst out laughing. Humiliated, she kept running until she was in the house, away from their mirth and ridicule. She had wanted John to be devastated by her looks; well, she had certainly succeeded! Tears scalded her eyes as she ran upstairs to the refuge of her room and threw herself on the bed.

Hannah couldn't believe the men had acted so callously toward Summer. "Shame on you for laughing at Mistress Summer. You've hurt her feelings. She's skittish enough about meeting all them folks at the ball tonight, without having to endure—"

"Hannah," John interrupted. "We weren't ridiculing your little lamb. It's just the sight was so unexpected, so . . . so . . . never mind. Here, take this gown up to her. It's the reason for my visit. Nat, Charles, it seems we're not wanted here, so we shall retire to my place. I'm sure Hannah won't mind if we get ready for the ball there. Now, stop scowling at me, Hannah, 'tis most unbecoming. Go to Mistress Summer.''

Hannah took the exquisite gown in her arms and carried it gently up the stairs, holding it as if it were made of delicate china. "This will perk you up, Lamby. Just take a gander at this gown." Hannah held it in front of her. "Ain't it a beauty? A gown fit for a fairy princess, in truth.''

Summer looked at the gown through tear-stained eyes, and her heart melted. It was the most beautiful thing she had ever seen. Made of white satin, it had huge, butterfly-ruffled sleeves and a plunging, heart-shaped neckline. The fitted bodice was covered with irridescent beads that shimmered like a thousand little lights, and the skirt was heavy with yards and yards of satin, overlaid with some kind of gauzy material. She couldn't help thinking what a perfect wedding gown it would make. Stop it, she chided herself. Stop thinking of what can never be.

"I can't believe that rough warrior designed such a delicate gown," Hannah declared, shaking her head. She wondered if Summer realized that the captain was hopelessly in love with her. Hannah's heart went out to John and Summer for the heartbreaking situation they were in. If ever two people were meant for each other, it was these two. Why had John married Elizabeth, when any fool could see they didn't love each other. Young uns. They surely didn't use the brains the good Lord gave em.

With the men safely out of the house, Hannah and Summer took their time getting ready for the ball.

Happily, the gown wasn't designed for a pannier hoop; it would be much easier dancing without that cumbersome obstruction.

At last, it was time to try on the gown. If it didn't fit, she was doomed. She would stay home and lock herself in her room. But, as it fell into place, and Hannah laced it up in back, Summer could see that it did fit, beautifully. Gazing into the looking glass, she gasped, "Oh, Hannah, have you ever seen such a gown in your whole life?"

"No, Lamby, nor a woman to wear it so well. Why, there won't be a man there tonight that won't get weak in the knees looking at you. I swear, I wouldn't miss this ball for all the tea in China. Oh my, I do believe I hear the men returning. Now, you must stay up here a spell, keep them waiting. It'll do them good. Anticipation is half the pleasure, I always say."

Summer waited until Hannah left, then ran down the hall to the front of the house and looked out the window. John was just getting out of a carriage. Her heart swelled with pride as she gazed down at him, resplendent in a brown velvet, tight-fitting jacket and brown satin breeches. Nathaniel was dressed in slate blue velvet and looked marvelous, too; she was sure the young girls in town would find him irresistible.

Running back to her room, she took one last peek in the looking glass. Her long, golden red hair was pulled to one side, and entwined with white satin ribbons and pink silk roses, that Hannah had made for her.

On the floor below, John paced the length of the narrow hallway, the muscles of his face taut with tension. Nat and Charles stood nearby, watching and pitying him.

"What is keeping the infernal woman? Hasn't she

had all day to get ready?"

Then, hearing the swish of satin, the three men looked up to the top of the staircase. Summer glided down the stairs, her gown alive with iridescent fire as she moved, her hand trailed gracefully along the bannister railing.

Nat didn't realize he had been holding his breath until he gasped. Charles accompanied him with a gasp of his own, while John still held his breath, mesmerized by the enchanting creature before him. She was truly his will-o'-the-wisp tonight. His throat grew tight with emotion, as he watched her descend the stairs like a princess.

Nat broke the silence with, "God's blood, Summer, but you look like an angel come to earth. Don't you agree, John?"

John's answer was a short, gruff grunt.

Summer couldn't believe it. Didn't he like the way she looked? After all the trouble she had gone through—allowing Hannah to lace her bodice so tight she could barely breathe—this was the way he reacted? Her tight bodice pushed her breasts incredibly high, and made her waist look as tiny as Scarlett O'Hara's, and all he could do was grunt? She had worked on her hair until her arms ached, and all he could do was stand there like an idiot?

She was getting angrier by the second, her heart beating faster, and with her heart beating faster, she became short of breath in her too tight bodice. She knew if she didn't calm herself immediately, she might pass out.

Nathaniel held out a white rose. "Here, let me pin this on your gown for accent."

In a voice much gruffer than usual, John said, "No—don't change a thing."

Summer's anger melted and her heart soared. He

did think she looked beautiful.

The ride in the open carriage was magical. She sat in back with John, while Nat sat in the front driving the white mare. Hannah and Charles rode ahead of them in a borrowed gig.

The last roses of summer were blooming, their heady fragrance carrying on the night wind, adding their own magic to the night. A night she would never forget.

Summer was entranced by the sight of candlelight flickering in the windows of the houses on the street, a sight so beautiful it took her breath away. Here it was at last. The street she had walked on so often in a different time. But never had it looked so warm, so inviting. She absorbed all she saw, storing the magical sight away for when she could no longer be here.

Lanterns and candles set on the ground lighted the way to the tavern door, giving the street a festive atmosphere, while music drifted from the window and high-spirited voices echoed on the night air. This was it. This was where the eighteenth century would begin for her in earnest.

An excitement filled her as the carriage pulled in front of the building, and she stepped out with the assistance of both her handsome escorts. What an entrance this will be, she thought. In one fell swoop, she would be meeting all the people she had been reading about for the past year, all the people whose names she had seen engraved on bleak stones in an ancient burial ground. She swallowed hard.

John spoke, breaking through her eerie reverie. "What an entrance you will make, Will-o'-the-wisp. They'll talk of this night for a long time to come. Are you ready?"

Summer nodded mutely, suddenly afraid, not only

95

of all the familiar ghosts she would soon meet, but especially afraid of Jessica Hawke. Her well-being would soon be in her hands. If Jessica accepted her, all would be well; if she denounced her as a phony, Summer would be in a precarious position. Taking a deep breath, she held on tight to her escorts and moved toward the door . . . and her destiny.

Chapter Nine

Hannah dashed ahead as fast as her plump little legs could carry her, her heart pumping hard with excitement. She found a spot just inside the door, where she would have an unobstructed view of Mistress Summer's entrance, and signaled Charles to join her there. She had been looking forward to this night for over a week, and wanted to make sure she didn't miss a thing.

Summer started through the door, her back rigid with tension, until the gentle pressure of John's hand on her back gave her the reassurance she so desperately needed. With head held high, she smiled her most radiant smile and entered the room.

The entire ballroom became still at her entrance, even the musicians, who put down their instruments and peered down at her from their lofty perch in a small balcony. Taking a deep breath, she looked around her at the sea of strange faces. She felt as if she were dreaming, for the moment held no sense of reality. These people, all of them, had been long dead before she was even born, but here she was in their midst, staring into their faces, so full of life.

"Summer," John said, in a voice loud enough for

97

everyone to hear. "Let me introduce you to everyone as we make our way around the room."

In a sweet, but equally loud voice, she answered. "Cousin, take me to your mother first. After all, this is her birthday ball. I would like to pay my respects."

John looked at her with new regard, and steered her toward the chair his mother sat in, then bent over to kiss his mother on the cheek. "Mother, you're looking exceptionally well tonight. Methinks you grow lovelier each new year."

"Enough of this frivolity. Introduce me to your lady. Let's get the amenities over with, so our friends and neighbors can get back to their dancing."

"Your wish is ever my command. Mother, this is your niece from Boston, Summer Winslow."

Summer looked down at the woman who had the power to make life very uncomfortable for her, and fought the urge to turn and run. Jessica was petite, with well-groomed, snow white hair, and wore her gunmetal gray gown with an air of aristocratic elegance. But behind her eyes that were the same shade green as John's, Summer saw intelligence and steel. Jessica didn't look like the sort of woman who could be easily fooled. She would have to know Summer was no real relation. They had been fools to think otherwise.

"How do you do, Aunt Jessica? It's a pleasure to meet you." Summer curtsied as she had practiced in front of the looking glass, her knees shaking violently.

Jessica's gaze was frank and discerning. She took her time looking Summer over, while Summer became increasingly more nervous, holding her breath as she waited for the verdict.

Finally, when Summer was about to break, Jessica crooked her little finger, indicating that Summer should lean closer. Summer's heart beat like a trap drum, but her face stayed composed as she leaned down and was promptly kissed on the cheek.

"Welcome to our little village, Summer dear. I trust your visit is a pleasant one? I've been unwell of late, else I would have invited you to stay with me in town, but I shall endeavor to make up for that. You must come to supper soon. Otis will prepare a sumptuous meal, worthy of my beautiful young niece."

Summer's gasp of relief mingled with those of the people standing close enough to hear. Jessica was not known for her hospitality. Her acceptance of Summer would pave the way for Summer's acceptance by the whole town.

"Have my sons been treating you properly, my dear? If not, I shall severely reprimand them. I fear they're not used to entertaining young ladies."

"I've been well treated, Aunt Jessica. Nat and John have been very kind and gracious."

"As is only right. After all, you are close kin, are you not?"

Summer was flustered. Jessica's words were said with sincerity, but she could swear that behind her green eyes was an awareness that Summer was not her kin. But, if that was so, why would she pretend that she was, and go along with the sham? What reason could she possibly have?

"And now, please enjoy yourselves, and let an old lady sit and reminisce of the days when she, too, was young and almost as beautiful as you, my dear." Jessica waved her hand toward the balcony, and the music began.

Stunned that she had been accepted by Jessica, she let John move her from group to group, introducing her to the curious townfolk. Her head was soon reeling, trying to remember faces and match them to their names. But the names were all familiar to her. Sheldon, Nims, Wells, Smead—she knew them well from her research. And she did recognize two people in the crowd. The dance master, Thaddeus Broom, who bowed to her in a theatrical manner that had her smiling, and the preacher, Daniel Bradford, who pushed his way to her side.

"You are looking exceptionally lovely tonight, Summer. Would you honor me with the first dance?"

"I'm sorry, Daniel, but you see, I've promised the first dance to my cousin."

John started to smile, but Summer pushed past him, taking Nat's arm instead. Nathaniel was as surprised at her move as John, and looked over his shoulder to see how his brother was reacting to the snub. The dangerous glint was once again burning in John's eyes.

Nat was confused. Why had Summer deliberately set out to snub John, after all the effort and labor he had invested in her for this evening? He would never understand women.

Summer glanced at John as she walked by him to the dance floor. His face was expressionless, but she knew what he must be feeling. She hadn't intended to dance with Nat first, but something came over her, and suddenly, she wanted John to feel the hurt she felt every time she was in his presence. But, instead, it was she that was hurting now, for she wanted nothing more than to be in his arms right this minute.

Nat moved her around the floor in an easy manner. After all the practice sessions they had had, she was very much at ease with him. At least there would be no tongue-wagging about her and Nat, since he was so much younger than she. If she had danced with

John first, there would be talk of John having a fling with her, while Elizabeth was out of town. She told herself that was reason enough to be dancing with Nat first, but it didn't help to ease her feelings of guilt; and when the dance ended, she looked around for John.

He stood talking with an attractive young brunette and made no move to claim her for the next dance, so she reluctantly consented to dance with the overeager preacher. They moved into line for a longways dance, and when it was finished, Daniel steered her over to a quiet corner of the room.

"I know I speak boldly, and with much haste, but I want my intentions known to you as soon as possible."

"What intentions are you speaking of, Daniel?" Summer asked absentmindedly, gazing over his shoulder at John still talking to the young woman. She felt a twinge of jealousy watching him, so handsome in brown velvet, so sexy, damn it all. She hated the way the young woman smiled up to him, as if he were the most fascinating man in the universe.

"My intentions of courting you with the purpose of marriage."

"Marriage?" Summer almost choked on the word.

"I know I speak hastily, but I fear you'll not be on the marriage market long. You will be pursued, I'm certain, by many suitors."

"Daniel, I think you should know, I have no intentions of making Deerfield my home. So it would be futile to pursue the subject any further." Her brow crinkled. Daniel was obnoxious. Why didn't he go pick on that woman John was talking to? She seemed more his type.

"I was given to understand your move here was permanent. Even so, perhaps you'll change your

101

mind. My prospects are very good, as you might already know. I'll be inheriting my father's business, am much esteemed in the community, and am considered quite the most eligible bachelor around. You could do much worse than to marry me."

Didn't he ever give up. "I'm honored you should want me as your wife, but I'm not in the market to marry anyone."

Daniel's disappointment was obvious. "May I see you anyway from time to time? You may change your mind. It's a woman's prerogative, after all."

Over Daniel's shoulder, Summer could see John heading her way with a grim look on his face. Her heart started pounding, but she smiled sweetly at Daniel, batting her eyelashes at him for John's benefit. "Yes, Daniel, I'd be delighted to have you call."

Daniel was stunned at this unexpected turn of events, and took Summer's hand in his, kissing it fervently.

The glint in John's eyes was flaming as he grabbed Summer's arm with a steel grip and steered her toward the dance floor, while Daniel stood there too stunned to protest. "I do believe this is our dance, Cousin."

Summer was shocked that John would behave so in public. Was there no end to his aggressive behavior? It angered her to think that once again he would have his way with her. As her anger built, she became short of breath in her tight bodice, and could breathe only in shallow little breaths.

John circled her waist with his arms, and it was too much for her. She became dizzy, her body swayed, and she raised her hand to her forehead. John realized what was happening and steadied her with his arm. Just as quickly, her head cleared and she announced.

"I . . . I'm all right now, you may remove your hands from my body."

"I think not. I'm taking you home. It's obvious you're in no condition to dance."

Summer was outraged and pulled away from him, her breath coming in short little spurts. Through gritted teeth, she hissed, "I'm staying right here. Go back to that, that, woman you were talking with and leave me alone."

She started to walk away when the dizziness returned even stronger. Trying to ignore it, she continued on until a curtain of darkness descended and she knew no more.

John caught her easily, scooping her up in his arms. With long strides, he carried her limp body off the dance floor and out of the ballroom, to the astonishment of all in the room.

Amidst the flurry of excited voices, Hannah's voice rang out, "Charles, we must see our poor little lamb home and to bed. It seems she's not recuperated fully from her ordeal with the Indians. But, 'twas very brave of her to try and see it through." Hannah then marched out of the room, head held high, followed by Charles and Nat, their faces creased with worry.

With the satin-clad bundle still in his arms, John climbed into the back of the carriage, calling out to the three figures that made their way over to him. "Good. Hannah, Charles, will you ride ahead and make ready Summer's bed? Nat, drive me and our poor delicate cousin home?"

"You'll not be going anywhere, sir, until I've loosened Mistress Summer's bodice. I fear I laced her too tightly." Hannah leaned over Summer and untied the lacing at the back of her gown, pulling it loose. "There. She'll be fine now, but take care she doesn't bump her head on the ride home."

"Don't worry about your little lamb, Hannah. I'll hold her in my arms like a newborn babe."

The carriage rumbled down the street, then through the wilderness that separated the Hawkes' property from town. The night was pitch-black now, except when the moon peeked out from behind thick clouds that blanketed the sky. The white mare, unused to riding in such darkness, balked. Nat had his hands full keeping her moving, soothing her with his voice.

The jerky movements of the carriage, combined with the cool night air caressing her cheeks, woke Summer gently. She opened her eyes to see the face she loved most staring down at her. Nestled in John's arms, she wished she could stay there forever. Tears fell silently down her cheek, as she realized she would never have that right.

John felt her wet face with his fingers. "Hey, what is all this? You have nothing to cry about. Your grand entrance was matched only by your equally grand exit. You've given the townfolk much to talk of through the long, dreary, winter months ahead."

Summer cried all the harder.

John responded by holding her tighter and lowering his head to hers. He kissed her softly on the lips, crooning, "I was right that first night. You are a witch. How else could you put such a powerful spell on me?"

He kissed her again, more demanding this time, and Summer responded with the same eagerness. What harm could it do? They were in an open carriage driven by Nat. Hannah and Charles were just a few feet ahead in the gig. Nothing could possibly happen, except, she could experience the touch of John's lips on hers without fearing the consequences.

Her arms went around his neck, and her lips responded passionately to his mouth. The feel of his lips on hers was so good, so right, so incredibly sensuous, she couldn't get enough of them. And when John's tongue broke through her lips and searched her mouth urgently, a surge of desire swept through her, so strong she couldn't breathe.

John moaned, unprepared for the passionate response from Summer. It took him unaware, kindling the excitement he felt into a raging flame, and the desire so long held in check became too much to bear.

"Summer," he cried, and with trembling fingers reached down to pull her breasts free of their scanty covering. Before she had time to protest, his rugged hands moved over her breasts, caressing them roughly, and his lips sought a pink, rigid nipple, taking it in his mouth, and sucking on it as if he could derive nourishment from it.

"John! What are you doing? We can't do—"

His lips moved up to hers, stopping further speech.

Hearing noises from behind, Nat inquired, "Is everything all right? Is Summer feeling better?"

"Yes, Summer is feeling much better," John assured him, as he cupped her soft and silky breasts with his hands.

Summer couldn't believe how fast John had moved. How could she be so foolish as to think she was safe in an open carriage, or anywhere else with John Hawke? She tried to move away, to no avail. She was pushed up against the seat of the carriage.

"John, please," she whispered, so Nat couldn't hear. "You can't do this. I . . ."

"Hush, darling, you're safe enough. Trust me. I just want to touch you, feel your beautiful body. I've dreamed of this, waited for this, so long."

John moved away from her a little so his view of her naked breasts would not be hindered, and a moan escaped his throat as the moon came out from behind a cloud, giving him a splendid view of her milky white breasts and delicate pink nipples.

He caressed them gently now, with both hands, wondering at the soft, sensuous feel of them, and of the strong feelings of desire and love that swept over him. He ached to possess her, to brand her inside with the heat of his hardened shaft. This woman— witch—Will-o'-the-wisp, was chosen to be his, sent through endless time to be with him here, in his life, in his bed, and he would make it so.

Nathaniel spotted the outline of a house in the distance, and shouted back to John and Summer. "We're almost home."

Gazing fervently into Summer's eyes, John smiled as his hands continued to stroke her glorious breasts. "Yes, we're almost home."

Chapter Ten

Summer's face flushed, remembering the carriage ride home last night, and the feel of John's hands on her breasts. It was dangerous being near the man, for obviously she couldn't trust herself. If it hadn't been for Nat's presence in the carriage, she was certain she would have surrendered to him.

And when the carriage had pulled up to the house, and when he had carried her upstairs to her room and closed the door behind him, why, she was sure he was going to continue where he had left off, despite Hannah and Charles downstairs. But, he had only kissed her longingly, and asked her to meet him in the morning on the hill—alone.

Alone. She knew what that meant, but she had been so weak with desire for him last night, she had agreed to the rendezvous. Now she was faced with the decision of whether to meet him or not. If she did, it would be going against everything she believed in, and it would change nothing. John would still be married to Elizabeth, and she would have to settle for stolen moments with him, something she was unwilling to do for anyone.

If she chose not to meet him, she would have to go

on aching for him, desiring a man she could never have. She had to find a way out of this dilemma, once and for all. But how? She had searched for the sword two days ago with the idea of using it whenever she decided to go back to her own time, but had found nothing. John had obviously moved it to a new hiding place. The chances of finding it now were nil. Even so, touching the sword was her only way out. She had to find a way.

The answer came to her then: the solution to her problem was obvious. There was only one way he would give in to her demand to touch the sword, and that was if she agreed to his covenant. If she met him on the hill as planned, if she gave herself to him, then he would have to keep up his end of the bargain and let her go. It was a way out, and God forgive her, she would take it. She couldn't go on like this much longer.

Filled with resolve, she jumped from bed and dressed in her riding clothes, then tiptoed downstairs. She ran out to the barn, saddled the white mare, and rode up the hill, her heart beating in anticipation, her body taut with excitement. Cresting the hill, she saw he wasn't there yet, but then, he had farther to travel than she. She slid off the mare, let the animal graze in the tall grass, and wandered the hilltop restless and impatient. Where was he?

Time passed, but still he didn't come. She was starting to worry. Where could he be? Why wasn't he here? Didn't he want her anymore? Wasn't that just like a man. He had pursued her hotly, then when she was ready to give him what he wanted, he doesn't show.

She turned back to the panoramic view and saw a rider coming up the path. Relief flooded her until she realized the rider was Nat. She hid her disappointment as he rode up to her.

"I thought I'd find you up here, when I saw the mare was missing. You know you shouldn't ride alone. Those damn Frenchies are everywhere these days. There's been another flare-up of the endless wars between the French and English. They'd like nothing better than to steal a beautiful young damsel like yourself, and carry her off to New France. It wouldn't be the first time such a thing happened."

Summer laughed nervously. "I knew a handsome young man would find me and keep me from harm, and I was right, for here you are."

Nathaniel saw the tinge of sadness in Summer's eyes. "We were all worried about you last night. Are you all right?"

"I'm fine, Nat, really. I'm just sorry I spoiled your fun."

"You spoiled nothing. I returned to the ball after I saw you safely home."

"Oh? Did John return to the ball, too?" Summer waited with trepidation for the answer. Could that be the reason he didn't show up this morning? Had he found a woman more willing at the ball? Perhaps the brunette he was talking with.

"No. I took him home on my way back to town, and I must say he was in quite a state. I've never seen my brother so happy."

"Happy? Why do you suppose that was?"

Nat looked at her solemnly. "You know the answer to that far better than I. The man is in love with you, Summer. And who could blame him? I was a little in love with you myself, but I knew the first time I saw the two of you together, I never stood a chance."

"I'm sorry, Nat. If I could have chosen who to be in love with, I would surely have chosen you. You're so much kinder, gentler, than your brother. But, please, you must believe that John and I are not . . . we're not . . ."

"Summer, you needn't say anything. I know you're not the sort of woman to fall easily into a man's bed. I know what you feel for him. You can't hide it. John's marriage to Elizabeth has never been more than a marriage of convenience. There isn't a soul in town who isn't aware of that. I'm amazed he never found someone to love before this. But then, it seems he's been waiting for you. And Summer, you're well worth the wait. Don't worry over me. Last night I met the most delightful creature at the ball. Her name is Charity Osborne. Lives with her family even farther from town than we do. They've only just moved here."

"Nat. I'm happy for you. Tell me about her. Is she pretty?"

"That she is. With hair so light, it looks like molten silver, and huge green eyes you could drown in. She's my age, strong-looking, too, but very shapely, with nice wide hips to carry babies."

"Nat, already talking of babies and you've just met. It must be love." Summer took his hand and squeezed it. "When will you see her again?"

"I thought I'd ride out there tomorrow. You don't think that's pushing too fast, do you? I don't want to scare her away."

Summer laughed. "You're a Hawke for certain. The Hawke men see what they want and go after it. Don't worry, I'm sure she won't be able to resist you. There's not a woman alive who can resist the charm of the Hawke men for very long."

Nat's face beamed. "I pray you're right. And if everything works out, I'll be building that house up here sooner than I planned."

Summer wished she had researched Nat, so she

110

would know if he wins his silver-haired girl. She had seen his tombstone in the old burial ground, knew it was John's brother, but she hadn't done any further research on him. The same with Caleb. She knew even less about him. There wasn't even a tombstone in the burial ground to mark his grave, that is, if he was even buried there.

The old burial ground! It seemed such a long time ago that she had stood at Elizabeth's stone. Suddenly, she wanted to see the graveyard as it looked now. Wanted to stand at the exact spot Elizabeth's grave would someday be. That spot held the key to the strange feelings she had in her own century. "Nat, if you're not doing anything today, why don't you ride with me into town? I want to see it in the light of day. And I want to visit the burial ground."

Nat looked puzzled. "Why would you want to visit a graveyard? I can think of pleasanter things to do."

"Will you come with me? I don't want to go to town alone. I was expecting to go . . . riding with John this morning, but evidently he's found more important things to do with his time. I can't bear to be alone today, Nat, please?"

Nat gave her a funny look. "I'm sure whatever kept John away was important, or he would be here. From what I saw of him last night, it would take the very devil himself to keep him away from you. But, since he isn't here—I am at your service."

"Thanks, Nat. But I think I better change into more suitable clothing first, don't you?"

"After last night, I don't think the townfolk would be surprised at anything you did, but, yes, it would be wise to change your clothing. You've given them enough to talk of."

Back at the house, she dressed quickly in a new gown of dusty rose that made her look feminine and vulnerable, a look she was glad to portray. The more helpless she seemed, the kinder she hoped people would treat her. She still felt afraid of meeting the colonials. If she tripped up, or acted strange to them, she could still be accused of being a witch. That thought was never far from her mind. She couldn't help it, this was still an alien world to her.

They rode to town in the carriage from the night before, and thoughts of her passionate, moonlight ride with John filled her head. At least she would have that memory to take back to her own time.

As they approached the town, she became more and more nervous. This would be her first trip in broad daylight, and she wasn't sure what to expect.

The town in the light of day was not the magical place it had been the night before, but then she hadn't expected it to be. The houses were painted in bright colors, much gayer than she would have expected for this time period, and they looked warm and inviting. But on closer inspection, she could see garbage lying in piles under the windows it had been thrown from. Chickens and geese wandered freely around the houses, and on the road, scattering noisily when the carriage rode by. Horse dung littered the dusty, gouged-out road, the smell lingering heavily on the air; and flies and gnats swarmed around the garbage and dung in droves. No, the town in the hard light of day was not the magic kingdom of the night before, but she loved it all the same.

As they rode down the street, people gaped openly at her. Perhaps coming to town wasn't such a good idea after all. She felt vulnerable without John's reassuring and masculine presence. Not that Nat wasn't a masculine young man, for he certainly was, it was just that John was older, more experienced, and exuded masculinity from every pore of his body.

When they neared the burial ground, Summer's fears evaporated in the excitement of actually seeing where it had all begun. Nat dropped her off at the gate, then went next door to visit his mother, which pleased Summer, for she preferred being alone when she searched for the site of Elizabeth's future grave.

The grounds were barely recognizable now, with but a handful of tombstones where she was used to seeing so many. But as she glanced around, trying to get her bearings, she spotted a young oak tree, remembered a giant, gnarled one, and knew exactly where to go.

She strode over and gazed down at the grass-covered spot, now naked without the familiar tombstone, and stared down at it a long time, deep in thought.

A movement caught her eye, a shadow slowly moving across the gravesite. Summer's eyes opened wide in fright, and she looked up . . . into the eyes of a raven-haired woman.

Her heart stopped.

The woman looked at her with interest, the skirt of her midnight blue gown moving around her in the stiff breeze that suddenly blew up from the river. Her scarlet cape folded lovingly around her in the wind, then unfurled like a flower, revealing her small, shapely form. Long, wildly tangled, raven curls swirled around her beautiful face in abandon, as the wind kissed them with a passionate display. And, in sharp contrast, a red-tailed hawk perched on her shoulder, unmoving, its unblinking eyes locked onto Summer's as intensely as its mistress's were. Summer knew it could be only one woman, and her face turned white.

"My dear, did I startle you? You look as if you've seen a ghost."

I have seen a ghost, Summer thought, her wide eyes taking in the wild-looking beauty who stood looking at her with such self-assurance.

"I am Elizabeth Hawke," the woman said, in a deep, throaty voice that belied her small frame. She extended her hand to Summer.

Summer watched, transfixed, as the shadow of her own hand moved across the gravesite toward the shadow of Elizabeth's hand. In shock, she felt the cool touch of Elizabeth's skin on hers, and a shiver went through her.

Elizabeth noticed the shiver. "Are you chilled? Mayhap you're not feeling well?"

"No, I . . . I'm fine, really. I . . . I wasn't expecting anyone to be here, especially you. What I mean is, I knew you were away."

"Well, as you can see, I have returned, and not a moment too soon, it seems. I was just visiting with Jessica, when Nat told me of you. I understand you were welcomed to Deerfield most graciously last evening. I'm sorry to have missed it. I understand it was quite an exciting ball, thanks to my husband's unusual manner of escorting you from the ballroom."

Summer's face became crimson at Elizabeth's words. "I'm afraid my bodice was laced too tightly, and I fainted. Your, ah, your husband had to carry me off the dance floor. And he was kind enough to see me home. Poor man, I'm sure I spoiled the evening for him. We had been there such a short time, you see, before it happened." Summer hated herself for being so flustered, and for rambling on like an idiot before this confident, cool woman.

Elizabeth was a paradox. So composed and beautiful, and yet at the same time, so wild-looking and earthy. Summer had never seen hair quite like

114

Elizabeth's, reaching halfway down her back in marvelous disarray. And the woman was so commanding, despite her delicate frame. How could Summer hope to compete with such a woman; how could John be immune to such untamed beauty?

Elizabeth raised one perfect eyebrow. "Yes, so I heard. Though after seeing you, I doubt that John's evening was ruined. 'Tis strange, I never heard of a cousin from Boston before this very day. Why do you suppose that is?"

Summer's face reddened again, and she sought to change the subject. "Of course, I would have known you anywhere with that hawk on your shoulder. She's quite beautiful. May I?" Without waiting for an answer, Summer offered her arm to the hawk.

"I wouldn't do that, if I were you. Beauty is wild to all but me." As she spoke, Beauty made a liar of her by hopping from Elizabeth's shoulder onto Summer's arm, as if it had done so a thousand times before. It was Elizabeth's turn to be startled.

Nat chose that moment to greet the two women. He had been watching from a distance, more than curious about the first meeting between Elizabeth and Summer. "How did you do that, Summer? I've never been able to get close to Beauty. You are truly a sorceress."

Angrily, Elizabeth held her arm out to the bird, giving it the signal to perch. The hawk, instead, pecked her viciously on the arm, drawing blood. Summer watched in horrible fascination as the blood welled up, trickling down Elizabeth's hand, then fell to the earth. Yet another shiver escaped her, and she unconsciously rubbed her own wrist, and the small triangular scar there.

"I'm sorry, Elizabeth. I didn't mean for that to happen. Are you all right?"

Anger burned in Elizabeth's silver eyes as she called the hawk once more. The bird responded this time, flying onto her shoulder.

"I see you know how to get what you want, Summer. But heed my warning. Be careful of what you ask, for some things come with a heavy price." Whirling around, Elizabeth stormed off, her cape swirling around her in a furious flurry of red.

Summer fought the tears that threatened, and lost. They streamed down her face, glistening like dew in the morning light. In a voice choked with emotion, she said, "Nat, please take me home."

Chapter Eleven

The fire was almost out, but Summer didn't notice. She sat staring at the glowing embers in the fireplace, her mind a million miles away, or, Hannah thought, was it just down the road at Captain Hawke's place? She had tried to interest Summer in quilting, to take her mind off Elizabeth and the dreadful encounter in the burial ground, but the poor little lamb had soon lost interest, and now just sat staring into the fire.

She didn't understand any of it, only knew that Summer was hurting. It weren't an easy problem to solve, this business of loving a married man, but the good Lord willing, she'd find another man to love and get over this terrible heartbreak.

A light rapping on the door sent Hannah's heart racing, and brought Summer out of her melancholy trance. Who could be calling so late at night?

Hannah tiptoed over to the door. "Who's there?"

"John Hawke."

With a quick glance at Summer, Hannah threw open the door. "Captain, what brings you out so late?" As if she didn't know the answer to that already.

With a sheepish grin, he answered, "I . . . I found I

couldn't sleep and decided to take a walk. Next thing I knew, I was standing outside your door. I noticed the light and thought I'd stop in for a moment."

"Well, come in, sir, out of the damp night air. I'll get us all a brandy," Hannah made her way to the kitchen, knowing it was a private word the captain wanted with Summer.

John sought Summer's eyes. "In truth, I couldn't sleep until I talked to you. I want to explain why—"

"Please, John, don't try to explain. Your wife and child are with you now; you're a family again, that's the way it should be."

John strode across the room and grabbed Summer by the shoulders. "That's not the way it is at all. I couldn't meet you this morning, because Elizabeth was escorted home by some of my militia. They stayed the morning. How would it have looked if I had left upon my wife's homecoming? It would have been a slap in her face, and I wouldn't do that to her. Can you understand that, Summer?" His fingers dug in her shoulders.

"Let go of me."

"Not until you say you understand, and forgive me for leaving you to wait on the hill. You did go up there . . . didn't you?"

Summer looked into his eyes with longing and hurt.

"Ah, lass, I'm sorry you spent such a lonely morning."

"Well, don't be. I'm not. After meeting Elizabeth today, I realized all the more that I have to leave—now—before we become embroiled in a desperate situation."

John gripped her shoulders even tighter. "I'll never let you go. We'll work it out. Say you'll meet me on the hill in the morning. I promise you, I'll

118

make up for today. I thought . . . after the ball . . . we've come so close, Will-o'-the-wisp, you can't give up now."

"John, don't do this. I have no intentions of ever being alone with you again. And . . . and . . . if you won't let me go back to my own time, then I'll make a life of my own here—without you. As it so happens, I've already had an offer of marriage."

"What? Who?"

"The pastor, Daniel Bradford."

The dangerous glint lit John's eyes. "Mark me well, if you marry Daniel Bradford, you shall be a widow on your wedding night. No man will ever have you, but me. Be sure of that."

"Here we are, children," Hannah said, appearing in the doorway carrying a tray with goblets filled with an amber liquid. "I warrant we shall all sleep better after a taste of this ambrosia."

John and Summer moved apart, but not before Hannah saw the look that passed between them. Oh my, oh my, she thought, it is certainly getting interesting around here. Hannah watched as John gulped down the brandy, then strode angrily to the door.

"Good night, Hannah," he mumbled as he strode out, closing the door noisily behind him.

Hannah opened her mouth to speak, when the door was flung open again. "I almost forgot. Caleb sent word he'll be home in time for evening meal tomorrow." Then, having dropped that bomb, he turned and left again.

Summer collapsed into a chair. "Oh, no, this is more than I can bear. Yesterday, I met Jessica Hawke, today, Elizabeth, and it seems tomorrow, I'll met yet another Hawke. I don't know if I can handle this. These Hawkes are wearing me out. Hannah, tell me

Caleb is nothing like his brother John. I don't think I can deal with another John Hawke."

"Poor Lamby, it's been a busy life ye've led since your stay here. But fear not, Caleb is nothing like John. He's as gentle as a lamb. Oh, dear, if he's coming tomorrow, I'll have to ready his room. I'll cook a special meal with all his favorites, and, oh my, it will be good to have him home. Just think how surprised he'll be to find his Cousin Summer here."

"That's what I'm afraid of. Mayhap he won't be happy with me usurping his home. Mayhap he'll throw me out."

"Where would you be getting such a fool notion as that, child? Family is always welcome. Is it so different where you come from?"

"I guess I'm weary. Don't mind me."

"Here, Lamby, take another glass of brandy. I do believe you need it."

It was pleasantly warm the next day, and Summer decided to take one of her notorious baths, knowing it might well be her last one. The weather was getting increasingly cooler. But if Caleb Hawke was coming home today, she wanted to look her best. Calling out to Hannah that she was going down to the river, she made her way down the path. The water was moving swiftly and looked colder than usual. That wasn't surprising, considering it was the first week of October already. But she had swum well into October many a year, and wasn't going to chicken out now.

She stripped off her clothes and quickly dove under, not wanting to prolong the agony. The shock of cold hit her as she submerged. She swam vigorously, trying to get the circulation going, then lathered her hair and body, rinsing it out right away, anxious to get out of the water as soon as she could.

Glancing up to the log where her towel lay along with her bell and knife, she was jolted by the sight of an Indian brave standing by the log. He stared down at her with unblinking eyes, and a face that showed no emotion at all.

Her heart raced, flashes of western movies filling her head, pictures of women being scalped and raped. Stop it! This wasn't the wild west of the eighteen hundreds. Noooo, it was an even more primitive time, and she knew for a fact women were scalped in the seventeen hundreds. Hannah had painted an all too vivid picture for her.

Calm yourself, he must be from a friendly tribe or he wouldn't be so close to town. Whatever happens, she mustn't show fear. Indians admired brave people, or at least they always did in the movies she went to. "Sir, would you please leave, so I can get out of the water in privacy?" She took pride in her well-modulated voice and civil manner. The savage would never know how frightened or upset she was.

The Indian's face remained expressionless. He seemed not to have heard her. *Maybe he doesn't understand English.* She gestured broadly with her hands, making motions for him to leave. He didn't move. *Now what?*

In a much louder and demanding voice, she repeated, "Sir, I ask you to leave—now."

Still nothing. She looked at his body, and saw no sign of a weapon, but that was not very reassuring, knowing her own weapon was doing little good at the moment, lying on the log under her towel. The Indian, naturally, was standing between her and it. And the bell. If only she could reach it, she could ring it and bring someone to her rescue.

"Scat! Shoo!" she shouted, all signs of civility

gone, her arms motioning wildly to him. But still he just stood there.

When it dawned on her that he was not about to leave, she studied him as she tread water, sizing him up. Was he a good guy or a bad guy? How in the world could she tell? He did make an impressive sight though, dressed in leather leggings that hugged his legs, and a little leather breechcloth that covered only the essentials. He was naked to the waist, with skin an attractive reddish tan, a chest rippling with muscles, and long black hair reaching to his chest. If she hadn't been so frightened, she would have enjoyed looking at him immensely. She had never seen such a striking figure before, his looks rivaling those of John Hawke.

Damn! How did she get into these situations? She was beginning to shiver violently from the cold, and knew if she stayed in the water much longer, she could die of hypothermia. But if she did get out she could very well be attacked by the savage. What was she to do?

She thought of moving downstream, but knew it would be useless. Besides, her knife and bell were here. If she could reach them before he came at her, she would have a chance. Anger flared in her eyes. Even a savage should realize the rules of propriety and leave.

She tried to outwait him, but before long was numb with cold. She had no choice. She would have to leave the water. Gathering her courage, she steeled herself and started out, her eyes locked onto those of the tall, regal-looking savage. She was damned if he was going to see her cringe in fear. Holding her head high, she boldly waded toward shore.

Only the slightest of changes could be discerned on the Indian's chiseled face as she moved out of the water; his eyes narrowed slightly, and a corner of his mouth curled up just the slightest bit.

Summer emerged from the river, long beads of water running down her ivory skin, as she neared the log that held her knife. She fought the urge to run every step of the way, and expected at any second to feel the rough hands of the savage on her body. She grasped her knife, relieved to feel the cold steel in her hand, and spun around, holding the weapon in a position to defend herself.

He was gone. How could he have disappeared so fast? True, the woods were thick here, but she hadn't even heard a leaf crunch. Shaking all over, she grabbed the bell and started ringing it furiously. Then wrapping herself in the towel, she waited for the help she knew would come.

In a few seconds, she heard movement through the woods, and heard Charles calling out to her.

"Over here," she shouted, and in a moment, Charles appeared carrying his flintlock. He quickly averted his eyes, seeing her wrapped in nothing but the towel. His embarrassment disappeared instantly when Summer told him about the Indian, his eyes searched the surrounding woods while she talked.

Hannah came bursting through the trees anxious with fear, a pitchfork held tight in her hands, expelling a loud sound of relief when she saw Summer was not harmed. "I knew no good would come of you being stark naked in the woods. Thanks be to God, you're not hurt."

Summer described the Indian to Hannah and Charles, remembering something odd about him. Something she had been too frightened to think about before. As she had gotten closer to him, she had noticed he had blue eyes. Hannah and Charles exchanged bewildered glances, then Hannah put a protective arm around Summer and led her back to the house. She was shivering violently now, and not just from the cold.

Hannah put her straight to bed, and fetched the brandy bottle. "Here, Lamby, this will warm you up and calm your nerves, too. Now, I want you to stay under the covers until supper time, and I pray you don't catch your death from that freezing water! The very idea, bathing this time of year. I warned you it was unhealthy."

Summer smiled to herself. Getting scalped by a savage would have been unhealthy indeed. What a strange thing to have happened. She was amazed at how boldly she had marched out of the water to confront the Indian. He had probably been too stunned at her audacity to do anything more than just stare at her. In any case, she was glad the incident had ended on a happy note.

The brandy warmed her stomach, and she burrowed down into the covers. It felt good to be warm again. She soon became drowsy, and giving in to the feeling, slept.

When she awoke, she slipped out of bed and dressed carefully for her meeting with Caleb Hawke. Would he show up as his message had said, at supper time? He might as well. She had met every other Hawke in town, including the one that perched on her arm. She couldn't help wondering though, how her comfortable lifestyle would change with the master of the house underfoot. She had almost come to think of this as her home.

Choosing the dusty rose dress to wear again, she brushed her hair until it dried, letting it hang long and lustrous down to her waist. Hannah would probably cluck her tongue at that impropriety, but she didn't care. She knew she looked best with her red gold hair framing her face. Besides, Elizabeth wore *her* hair loose, so why couldn't Summer?

When she walked into the kitchen, Hannah was bent over a large pot, stirring the delicious-smelling contents with a wooden ladle. Hannah looked up at her, smiling, and didn't seem to notice her hair. Probably still too shaken over Summer's encounter with the blue-eyed Indian.

Summer sensed another presence in the room, and turning, saw a man step out of the shadows. He was dressed elegantly in a rust-colored velvet jacket, matching breeches, and a lace ruffled shirt, his long hair pulled back in a well-groomed ponytail.

As he moved closer, Hannah spoke. "Summer, dear, this is the master of the house, your cousin, Caleb. Caleb, this is Summer Winslow who I've been telling you about."

Caleb held out his hand to Summer, and as she reached out to shake it, she got a better look at his face as it emerged fully from the shadows. Raising her already extended arm, she slapped him soundly across the face.

Hannah gasped and clutched at her heart, but Caleb hardly changed expressions. Summer could see a twinkle in his bright blue eyes.

"Mistress Summer!" Hannah cried in horror. "What devil possesses you to act so to your cousin? Please forgive her Cal, for believe me, she is truly a sweet-tempered, virtuous woman. I don't understand."

"It's quite all right, Hannah. Don't fret." Caleb's voice was as deep and velvety as his brother's. "I well deserved the blow."

Hannah plopped down on the bench, stunned.

Summer was furious. "How dare you put me through that today! Standing there like a wild

125

savage, frightening me to death. Letting me freeze in the water, until I had no choice but to get out and subject myself to your stares. You, you, you—"

"I most humbly apologize for that, Summer, but you must believe me, I didn't expect you to take such bold action. I was ready to turn my back so you could come out, when you chose to do that very thing right in front of my eyes. You astonished me with your courage."

Understanding, at last, what it was all about, Hannah cried, "'Twas you, Caleb Hawke, that had us all in such a dither!" She shook her finger at him. "Shame on you."

"I'm truly sorry, but I must admit my curiosity got the better of me. Summer, when you emerged from the water like Venus rising from the sea, and more beautiful even, than that fabled beauty, I'm afraid I became rooted to the spot."

"Rooted, you say? Well, you became quickly unrooted when I reached for my knife."

"Ah, yes, I felt the sudden need to make a hasty exit, else the sight of your beauty might be the last thing I saw ere you thrust that deadly weapon into my heart. And, gladly would I have died after such a splendid sight, but I hoped for yet another glimpse of your charming self another time. Will you accept my apology, and take supper with me? Hannah has prepared all my favorite foods."

Summer was speechless. This half-breed Hawke spoke with the eloquence of Shakespeare, and yet, just a few hours ago had looked for all the world like a wild savage. Why hadn't she been told Caleb was half-Indian? A million questions raced through her mind.

Caleb saw the confusion in her bright eyes. "I see no one has told you that you have a half-breed cousin."

"No, they didn't. Although, dressed as you are now, you don't look much like an Indian."

"Which do you prefer, I wonder, the savage of this afternoon, or the civilized gentleman of this evening?"

"Since they are one and the same, it would be hard to separate the two. Would you have acted differently this afternoon, if you had been dressed as you are now? I think not."

"Quite right. Any man with blood running through his veins would have acted exactly as I did today."

Summer blushed and sought to change the subject. "Tell me how you come by your Indian blood."

"My mother is a Pocumtuck Indian, one of the few remaining ones, I might add. Our tribe has been all but wiped out by the white man's diseases, and from war with the Mohawks."

While they ate, Caleb filled her in on his background. "Nenepownam, my mother, was deep in the forest when she came across Zebulon Hawke near death. He had been hunting, and was mauled by a bear. She had her people bring him back to her village, where she nursed him back to health.

"In simple terms, they fell in love, and I was conceived. Mind you, it would be hard for any man to resist my mother's charms, for even today she is a handsome woman. But, she knew the love they shared would end when Zebulon recuperated, for he did not belong in her world. And for that reason, she never told my father of my conception. She intended that he should never know, but fate had other plans.

"When Zebulon returned home, he resumed relations with his wife, Jessica, who became pregnant right away. One day, after John's birth, Nenepownam showed up on Jessica's doorstep, carrying me in her arms. Her milk had dried up, and she decided I had a better chance of survival living with my father. Jessica took the news in stride, taking me in, and suckling me along with her own child. My father loved Jessica all the more for her acceptance and love for me."

Summer was touched by the story. "Jessica must be a remarkable woman to accept another woman's child like that, and your mother, too. It must have been hard for her to give you up."

"They are both truly remarkable women, and I have been greatly influenced by them both. You see, it was decided that I would spend my summers with Nenepownam, once I was old enough. Jessica and Zebulon wanted me to know my Indian heritage. They understood how important it would be for me to take pride in that. They knew pride would help me over the rough spots, the jeers and taunts from other children, and the frowns from adults because of my Indian blood.

"Each summer Nenepownam would set up camp in the woods nearby, and I would be sent to her. Those summers meant a great deal to me. She taught me the way of the Pocumtuck, and I came to know and love their uncomplicated and spiritual life, and their great love of the forest and streams. John and Elizabeth were allowed to accompany me at times, and they, too, learned the Indian ways. Nenepownam became quite attached to Elizabeth, seeing the wild spirit that lay just beneath the surface. She taught her the Indian way of healing and Elizabeth was an apt student, becoming an expert on herbs and other medicines. The townfolk were not pleased with this arrangement, as you can well imagine, but the Hawkes and the Nims, Elizabeth's family, were too powerful to be influenced by them."

"Did the people of Deerfield ever accept you as a Hawke?"

"On the surface, yes, but I was always very much an outsider. After my father died, I felt it would be best to live with my mother's people. Jessica was against it, as were John and Nat, but I left anyway. But before long I was drawn back to life here in Deerfield. I had ties here that could not be broken, and now spend my time in both worlds. Had I known such a beautiful sight would greet me this time, I would have returned sooner."

Summer blushed again, knowing he was referring to her earlier nudity. Caleb was as straightforward as his brother, and his sexuality as apparent. The family resemblance was strong, too, despite his Indian blood. No doubt about it, Caleb Hawke was a good-looking man. She sighed. Life was getting very complicated.

Hannah sighed, too, thinking the same thing. She envied Summer the attention she was receiving from the handsome young brothers, and she got a vicarious thrill watching them court Summer. For that was what they were truly doing, whether they knew it or not. There was a spring to her step as she cleared the table telling Summer and Caleb to leave her to her work.

Caleb escorted Summer into the parlor, where a cheery fire burned brightly in the fireplace. "I was quite astonished to find I had a cousin from Boston, whom I had never heard of before. Tell me, just how are we related? Not too closely, I pray."

Summer was saved from answering that awkward question by the arrival of John and Nat.

"Cal," John shouted, "I'm glad you're back. It's been too long." The two men embraced, patting each other on the back roughly. Nat joined in, and soon all three men were embracing.

"My, my," Caleb said, "Is this little Nat? I do believe you've grown six inches since last I saw you."

Summer gazed at the three brothers with admiration. What a sight they made. Tall, well-formed, and handsome, their masculinity was overpowering, almost taking her breath away.

"I see you've met our cousin, Summer Winslow. Quite a pleasant surprise, what?"

"Ah, yes, she most certainly is. You'll never know just how much."

Summer turned crimson at his words.

"I was just asking her about her blood link to us, when you came in."

"Ah, well, that will have to wait. We have urgent business to discuss. That French bastard, Robillard, is up to his old tricks, I'm afraid. We've got to do something to stop him, before he has the territory in flames again. I thought you might have some ideas about where he is, since you've just come from your Indian friends. I've brought some maps." John indicated the rolls of oiled cloth under his arm. "Thought we could map out a strategy. Summer, sweeting, fetch Charles for us. He should be sitting in on this, too."

Feeling lonely and left out of the warmth and camaraderie that surrounded the three brothers, Summer left the room as she was told, fetching Charles to join the other men.

So much for all the attention she had been getting. It seems that when the Hawke brothers got together, they forgot women even existed. Summer went to the kitchen seeking Hannah's cheerful and comforting presence.

Chapter Twelve

The next few days continued to be lonely for Summer. John and Cal spent hours pouring over maps and meeting with militia officers at the house, or out at the pasture where the militia was now camped. And Nat had all but disappeared. Summer knew he must be spending time with his new love, Charity Osborne.

At least each evening she had Cal's company for supper, and she was grateful for that. She was getting to know and like him very much. He had a way of cheering her up without even seeming to try.

In the evening they played cards by the fire, or sat around the harpsichord, listening while Hannah played. The little woman spent every available moment learning new tunes, and seemed obsessed by the instrument. It was a source of amusement to Charles and Summer to see her practice so diligently, a frown of concentration creasing her face.

But try as she might, Summer could not get John out of her heart, or her mind. Each new day brought her closer to the edge of despair. She walked sometimes for hours trying to sort things out, to wear herself out until she was too tired to think about him, but it never worked.

She stood now by the pasture fence, gazing in the direction of John's house, as if doing so would bring him closer to her. Turning back to the house, she saw a horse and buggy approaching. Damn! It was Daniel.

After his feverish declaration to court her at the ball, she was not at all eager to see him again. Why had she batted her eyelashes at him so shamelessly, when she had only wanted to make John jealous? She was being punished now for that impulsive act.

"Good morrow, Summer. I was on my way to town, when I thought to stop and ask you to join me. Several of the female children are gathered in the meetinghouse this morning to receive instructions from me, and I thought you might like to meet . . ."

Summer started to mouth the word no, when Daniel added, "Your little cousin, Alisha will be one of them. Have you met her yet? I thought not. It would be a most opportune time to do so. She is quite a lovely child, though I fear she is too strong-willed to be truly pious."

Alisha! How could she pass up a chance to meet Elizabeth and Caleb's child? She hadn't seen Elizabeth since their disturbing meeting in the burial ground. This was a chance to make things right between them. Besides, she was well acquainted with the male members of the family, but knew nothing of the female members, and she wanted to rectify that.

"Daniel, how thoughtful of you. I would indeed like to accompany you. If you'll give me a moment, I'll let Hannah know where I'm going."

Daniel sat back in the gig, a smug smile on his face. There was more than one way to win Mistress Summer Winslow over. It wouldn't be long before he was courting her. After all, he was the most eligible bachelor and the most persuasive talker in town. It would be quite a feather in his cap to have her as his wife.

Summer was an intriguing woman, and quite the most stunning one he had ever seen. It was strange though, that she stayed at Caleb's instead of in town with Jessica, where she could be more comfortable. Of course, Jessica hadn't been well, and the woman did cherish her privacy more than anyone he knew. But she had seemed so taken with Summer at the ball. He would have bet money on Jessica taking Summer under her maternal wing. Hmmm, there was something afoot there.

The ride into town was pleasant enough, though Summer had to put up with Daniel's incessant chatter. Heavens, the man could talk. When they rode by John's house, her eyes scanned the property looking for any sign of him, but there was no one to be seen except a few men working the fields. Oh, well, maybe he was in town. It would serve him right to see her riding into town with Bradford.

The words he had threatened her with came back to haunt her. *If you marry Daniel Bradford, you shall be a widow on your wedding night.* Did he mean them? She believed he did. Smiling, she thought, if only he knew how much she disliked this pompous preacher.

The meetinghouse stood on the town common, and was more elaborate than she had expected. It was quite large, with a tall steeple, and an entrance made up of ornately paneled, double doors. When they pulled up in front, a rugged man of about thirty came over to help her alight from the gig.

"Mistress Winslow, I'm happy to see you've recovered admirably from your fainting spell the other night."

Summer looked to Daniel for introductions, but he stood stone-faced and silent. She was amused at his attitude, knowing that he most likely thought of this man as yet another candidate as a suitor for her hand in marriage.

"Forgive me, Mistress, for being so forward. I am Sergeant Josiah Davidson of your cousin John Hawke's militia unit."

"Oh? How interesting." Seeing Daniel's scowling face, she couldn't help making him more jealous. "You must come to tea soon, Sergeant, and tell me of your duties with my cousin. I suspect he is a hard taskmaster."

Josiah's face lit up. "That he is, Mistress, but he's also fair-minded, a virtue much needed to govern men properly."

"Davidson, you'll have to save your philosophy for another time. Mistress Winslow and I are late for a lesson inside."

Summer was irritated at Daniel's unpleasant behavior, but she let him steer her inside the building. Now was not the time to tell him off. She couldn't help being a little afraid of the man. He held such power in town, and she was sure he wasn't above using it for his own personal gain.

The interior of the meetinghouse was as elaborate as the outside, thanks to the stained-glass window that dominated the wall behind the pulpit. It was certainly an unusual and rare sight for a building from such an early period. The window depicted Adam and Eve in a lush garden of Eden with animals of many species at their feet.

She sat in an inconspicuous spot, admiring the window, then—remembering her purpose for being there—looked around the room for Alisha Hawke. It wasn't hard to pick her out from the other little girls in the room. She had the same ethereal beauty, the same enormous gray eyes, as her mother. A lump came to Summer's throat, as she thought about the cold, but very beautiful Elizabeth Hawke.

When the meeting was over, Alisha hurried over to where Summer sat and curtsied to her. "You must be Cousin Summer from Boston, are you not? My mother told me you were visiting at my Uncle Caleb's."

Summer was enchanted with the child. "And you must be my Cousin Alisha, I would know you anywhere. You look just like your mother."

Alisha's little face beamed. "Thank you. I am happy to look like my mother. She is very beautiful, isn't she?"

Summer laughed. "She certainly is."

Daniel looked down at Alisha with a frown on his face. "Alisha, I seem to recall that not five minutes ago we had a discussion about the sin of vanity. It would do well for you to remember."

Summer bristled. He was a fine one to talk about vanity. The pompous ass.

Alisha looked properly contrite, but her eyes sparkled with life. "Yes, sir." Turning to Summer, she said. "I'm to go to Grandmother's now. Mama is waiting there for me. Would you like to come with me? I'm sure Mama and Grandmother would love to take tea with you. Especially Grandmother. She talks of you often."

"Is that so? I'm sorry, Alisha, but I don't believe this would be a good day to visit, but I'd like to walk you home. You don't mind do you, Daniel?"

"No, certainly not. I shall be happy to walk with you."

Damn. She was hoping Daniel wouldn't be interested in the walk. She wanted to get rid of him, but obviously it wasn't going to be that easy.

They walked the short distance to Jessica's house, Alisha holding tightly to Summer's hand. She was such an affectionate little thing. Elizabeth was lucky to have such a sweet little daughter, but then, she was lucky to have John, too.

When they reached the house, the door was immediately thrown open and Elizabeth appeared in the doorway.

"Alisha, your grandmother and I have been waiting tea on you. What kept you?" Elizabeth's eyes traveled over Summer's form in an accusing manner.

Alisha ran up to her mother. "Mama, can Cousin Summer come to tea with us? I'm sure Grandmother won't mind."

Elizabeth stared into Summer's eyes with a coldness that made her shiver. "I'm sure Cousin Summer has other plans. We mustn't press her, Alisha."

Hearing a horse's whinny, Summer turned to look at the approaching rider, grateful for the distraction from the awkward situation. John sat astride Shadow, his eyes traveling intensely from Summer to Daniel, then back to Summer.

"How fortuitous I came along just now, Summer. I was on my way back to Caleb's to talk with him and can give you a ride home."

Elizabeth made a strange strangling noise, and Summer looked over at her, startled.

Elizabeth's face was suddenly animated, her eyes shiny and bright. "John, you didn't tell me Caleb was back!"

Summer was stunned. After all these years, Elizabeth was still in love with Cal. It was written all over her face. What an interesting turn of events. Did

John know? How could he not?

"Didn't I tell you, Elizabeth? It must have slipped my mind. I'm afraid I've been preoccupied of late." He looked directly at Summer.

Daniel was not pleased with the way things were progressing. He had counted on stopping with Summer somewhere along the road home to plead his case once more. "I brought Summer to town, and I shall see that she returns safely."

John's brow furrowed. "Since she is my cousin, and since I'm going there anyway, I'll bring her home myself. Attend to your pastoral duties, Preacher, and do not concern yourself with my family."

Daniel could see there was no use arguing with such a pigheaded man. "Very well, but it seems foolish for Summer to have to ride uncomfortably on your horse, when she could ride in my gig."

Summer was glad not to have to spend any more time with Daniel, but it was irritating that once again John was being overbearing. Why hadn't he first asked her if she wanted a ride? Putting on a smile she didn't feel, she said, "Really, Daniel, I don't mind at all. Shadow has a broad and comfortable backside."

Triumphant, John reached down, and Summer put her foot on top of his in the stirrup, and was pulled up behind him.

Elizabeth didn't miss the way John looked at his cousin. There was something between the two of them, she was certain of it. She had sensed it since her first glimpse of Summer in the graveyard. In a perverse way she was relieved, for it meant that Summer wouldn't be setting her cap for Caleb. Oh, Caleb, how long had he been back? Why had no one told her of his return? She fought the urge to ride out there this very moment. She must bide her time. No one must know how she still felt about him.

Elizabeth looked down at her small daughter, her little hand waving goodbye to John and Summer. She couldn't bear it if Alisha was hurt by careless talk from the townfolk. Her daughter was the one precious thing in her life, and she was a part of Caleb, the only man Elizabeth would ever love. "Come, Alisha, Grandmother is waiting. How did your lesson go?" Taking her small hand in hers, Elizabeth led her daughter into the house.

Summer embraced John tightly around the waist, loving the feel of his hard strong body. She tried to stay angry with him, knowing it was the only way she could combat her strong attraction to him, but it was hard to stay angry long.

As they bounced along the road, John could feel the softness of Summer's breasts pressing into his back. His manhood swelled, hardening uncomfortably, and making for a painful ride. His need of her grew with each touch of her skin, each whiff of her feminine fragrance.

As they moved to the horse's rhythm, the ride became more unbearable as he imagined the two of them locked together, moving in an erotic rhythm of passionate lovemaking. He had dreamt each night of such a union, dreamt of her long before she came. She had haunted his dreams for over a year, and now, she haunted his every waking moment, too. God forgive him, if she didn't come to him soon, willingly, he was afraid his need of her would become so great he would take her by force.

Summer was deep in erotic thoughts of her own. She wanted to be with John, feel his closeness, but, as usual, the feelings that surfaced whenever she was close to him became too much for her. Would she always feel so intensely aroused in his presence? It was unbearable. And it was all his fault. If he would only let her go back to her own time, she could get over this fierce longing.

Anger began to build once more, as it had to, to keep from hurting so. Why had he insisted on taking her home on Shadow? He was so damn aggressive and domineering. Just once she'd like to get the best of him, let him have a taste of what it felt like to be controlled and dominated. An idea came to her then, a way to beat him, and she moaned out loud, setting her plan in motion. "John, could you stop a moment? I have a cramp in my leg. I need to get down and rub it."

John laughed as he dismounted, "Shall I rub it for you?"

As soon as his feet touched ground, Summer lifted herself forward onto the seat of the saddle, and taking the reins, dug her legs into Shadow's sides, galloping off.

John stood there with an open mouth. "What the—"

He watched as she rode Shadow down the road like a whirlwind, the animal's powerful hooves kicking up a cloud of dust. Looking around, he saw that she had left him near the entrance to his own house. He wasn't going to let her get away with this. He would take her over his knee and spank her, no matter if Hannah and Charles were there.

Summer couldn't believe she had pulled it off so easily. It felt good to get the best of John Hawke. That would teach him to be so arrogant. Feeling high with victory, she couldn't bear to go home yet. Instead, she rode through the pasture and up the path to the top of the hill, glorying in the surge of power that swept over her.

Jumping down from Shadow, she tied him to a tree, and twirled around in glee. She couldn't keep from laughing out loud. He would be so angry. But hopefully, not too angry. After all, she *had* waited until they were near his house, before she left him. It was too bad she couldn't have seen the expression on his face as she rode off.

She lay down in the tall grass, giggling to herself, and feeling very smug. It served him right. Looking up at the clouds overhead, she wondered what John would do when he saw her next. She would make sure she wasn't alone with him when that happened, just in case he didn't have a sense of humor.

Deep in thought, she didn't hear the riders approaching at first, then realizing that she wasn't alone, peered through the tall, golden autumn stalks. John? How did he get here so fast?

But it wasn't John. Two strangers were riding toward her in a furtive manner. Who could they be, and why were they acting so strangely? The hair on the back of her neck stood on end, and she wished fervently that she was back at the house safe and secure with Hannah.

She watched, frozen, as the two men slid off their horses, and walked slowly toward her as if stalking an animal. She looked around wildly, but it was useless. There was no one to help her. Nowhere to run.

"What have we here?"

The words were spoken with a French accent. Oh God! She was in terrible danger. The men circled her, speaking to each other in French, but she didn't need to know their language to know with a dead certainty what they wanted.

"No!" she cried, out, standing up to run.

Laughing, they grabbed her roughly and pushed her back on the ground. "We shall soon see just what we do have, hah, *mon ami?*"

The bigger man grabbed her breasts, pulling them free of her low-cut bodice, his ragged fingernails scratching the delicate tissue.

The shock of pain brought her alive, and it registered on her brain that she was about to be raped. This couldn't be happening. Not to her. She struggled fiercely, kicking and scratching, but the men were too powerful for her.

"Hold the firebrand, whilst I show her how the French do it." The huge brute unbuckled his breeches, and his red, swollen member was thrust out.

She struggled all the harder at the sight of him, more frightened than if he were wielding a knife, but the other man brutally pinned her shoulders to the ground with his knees, holding her down with the full weight of his body.

The half-naked man grabbed her flailing legs, and pulled them savagely apart, moving between them with urgency.

"Noooooo," she cried in a high, keening voice.

Suddenly, the man froze, and Summer wondered what had caused her reprieve. Then she heard it. The sound of thundering hooves.

John came riding over the crest of the hill and immediately took in the situation. Blind with rage, he reined in his horse a hundred feet away, and pulled out his flintlock pistol. He aimed it at the Frenchman, praying it would not misfire, and was rewarded with a loud report. The Frenchman fell to his knees, wounded in the chest.

The other man released Summer, and to her

horror, reached for his pistol. Flintlocks had only one shot. John would have no time to reload before the man shot him. Crying out in fear, she leapt onto the man's back, her fingernails digging into his face. He flung her off violently, and as her head hit the hard ground, she heard the shot ring out. Blackness closed in on her.

Chapter Thirteen

From a great distance, Summer heard her name being called. Dizzy with pain, she opened her eyes, focussing on brilliant green ones above her. "John! Oh, John, I thought you were dead. I heard—"

"Shhh, darling, I'm fine. I pretended to be hit, so that I might have time to load my pistol again. Your flinging yourself on him distracted the bastard enough to make his aim go wrong. I owe you my life, my brave little Will-o'-the-wisp."

Summer sat up suddenly. "Where are they?" Pain knifed through her head, and she sank into John's arms.

"Gone. They managed to get to their horses, when I ran to see if you were injured. But don't worry. They won't get far. I wounded them both. The bastards! I'd like to kill them with my bare hands. Are you all right? Did they hurt you?"

Summer touched the back of her head with her fingers. "Ow! It hurts here."

John's fingers gently probed through her hair, seeking the injury, and felt the hard lump that protruded. "The size of a goose egg, I warrant, but the skin is unbroken. You'll be fine in a few days."

His eyes traveled down to her face, then farther to her naked breasts, seeing the ugly red scratch mark. Wincing, he reached for the canteen attached to his belt, dribbling water on the inflamed area, then tore a piece of ruffle from his sleeve, and blotted on the scratch gently. Lowering his head, he brushed his lips over the wound.

John's tender touch coming so soon after the brutal touch of the two Frenchmen brought tears streaming down her face. She had come so close to being savaged by those horrible men. She began to shake all over and, seeking comfort, wound her arms around his neck.

John held her tenderly, caressing her back gently with his hands while he soothed her with his voice. "There, there, you're safe now. I'll not let anyone hurt you, my darling."

His gentle strokes calmed her and her shaking subsided as she let out a deep shuddering sigh. It was so good to be in the circle of his arms. Soon, his hands had a different effect on her body, and she trembled once again, the heat emanating from his body and the feel of his wonderful hands combining and multiplying her desire.

His gentle strokes became more intense as his hands moved up and down her back, taking on an urgency as they strayed farther and farther around her sides, until they came into contact with the soft, silky mounds that he could never resist. The sweet agonizing touch of her breasts sent an exquisite knife of pain through his loins and, unable to control his longing, he kissed her hungrily, his tongue darting between her lips, sending shards of heat throughout his body. She was here, as warm and as willing as he had dreamed so often.

His kiss released Summer from the bondage her

heart had endured, and she responded to his touch with all the pent-up emotion that had been restrained too long. She wanted him. Wanted him inside her, hard and velvety, like the tongue that probed her mouth so urgently. Desire flared hot within her, and she drew her teeth along the length of his tongue, sucking on it gently, then harder, as her desire demanded. She delighted in the taste of him, in the feel of him; her own tongue flicked between his lips, needing to pleasure him as much as he pleasured her.

John felt her teeth and tongue, and his desire rose beyond the limit. Moaning, he laid her down gently, his husky voice pleading as he pushed her skirts up around her waist. "Summer, Will-o'-the-wisp, don't deny me, my need is too great."

His words were unnecessary, for her need was as great as his own. She opened her heart to him, and then her arms, and then her thighs.

He moved between them with one fervent glance at the golden mound that shielded the warm, moist treasure he sought and entered her, reveling in the hot, wet cocoon that surrounded his shaft. She took him fully, thrusting her hips to meet him.

Suddenly he became still, gazing into her eyes with the same intense desire and overwhelming love that showed on her face. This was it. What they had waited for so long. What they had dreamed of each day since their first meeting, and before. They laughed joyously, then became serious as they moved together slowly, deliberately at first, then harder, faster, in a rhythm that sent them soaring into ecstasy, eyes open, not wanting to miss one second of intense lovemaking.

As their bodies came together over and over in the ancient dance of lovers, they climbed higher and higher into a sensual world that belonged to them alone. Each deep thrust, each silky, sliding retreat of his shaft, brought intense pleasure, intense craving for more, until, at last, they clung together as one powerful explosion after another racked their bodies; and they cried out their pleasure, filling the air with their sensual music.

They lay spent for a time, breathing raggedly. And when John could breathe normally again, he kissed her gently on the lips, then her forehead, and the tip of her nose, telling her over and over, "You're mine, mine, mine." His kisses reached her delicate ears, and the nape of her neck, then moved down to her throbbing nipples, sucking each before continuing his journey. He moved past the bunched-up petticoats at her waist, to the silken mound between her legs, his tongue darting into her before trailing down her leg to her foot. Taking off her shoe, he took her big toe in his mouth, wetting it thoroughly.

"What are you doing?" she laughed, as his wet tongue tickled her.

"Marking my territory," he answered gruffly, rolling her off the spot where they had made love.

She protested mildly, curious to what he was up to, and watched in astonishment as he started pulling out the brittle autumn grass from the earth by the roots, working industriously until he had cleared an area a foot in diameter.

"What are you doing? Have you gone crazy?" She watched as he dug a shallow hole with his bare hands, then, wiping his hands on his breeches, reached into his jacket pocket and pulled out an apple.

"Here—eat it," he said, thrusting it into her hands.

Summer thought he was completely mad now, but did as he asked, her curiosity heightened considerably. She bit into the crisp apple, delighting in the crunchy sound it made, then ate it, relishing every soury bite. Taking chunks from her mouth, she fed them to John, and he devoured them greedily.

When she was down to the core, he took it from her, carefully removed all the seeds, laid them in the hole he had dug, and covered them with the freshly dug earth. Patting the small mound gently, he looked up at her with such love on his face, she wanted to cry.

In a voice filled with emotion, he said, "A tree, heavy with fruit, shall grow here on this site of our first mating. It will grow strong and tall, a tribute to our love. In years to come, our children, born of that love, will eat of its fruit, and play amongst its branches. This is but the first of many apple trees that I shall plant here, and the Hawkes for generations to come will reap the harvest of their crimson fruit."

With eyes glistening with liquid green, he lowered his voice to a husky whisper. "Mayhap a child grows within you even now, from this first fervent mating."

Tears welled Summer's eyes. There was no doubt now. This hill, so familiar, the ancient apple orchard that had once been her sanctuary in a different time, was born but a moment ago.

Chapter Fourteen

Dark clouds rolled overhead, as the three brothers rode up the hill accompanied by men from John's militia unit. John knew that the Frenchmen couldn't have traveled very far in their condition, and had hopes of capturing them before the rains fell. He was surprised, in fact, that the one who had taken the shot in his chest hadn't been found dead already.

Beside the satisfaction of taking the men captive that had almost raped Summer, he hoped for information that would lead to the capture of their leader, Major Phillipe Robillard. He'd torture them if he must for that information, and gladly, too, after their vicious attack on Summer.

He recalled the horror he had felt when he had crested the hill and found that bastard standing over her, his swollen cock pointed at her like a weapon. Praise God, he had made it there before the bastard could touch her. Damn Robillard! There was no doubt in his mind that the major was responsible for the attack on Summer, and every French and Indian attack since his own encounter with the French devil.

What had started as an act of war, was becoming a

personal vendetta to Major Robillard. The Frenchman blamed John for the loss of an eye, and it mattered not that he had been attacking John's property when he confronted him. They had fought hand to hand, before the man had lost his balance and fallen onto an andiron by the fireplace. John cringed at the remembrance of that gory deed, and regretted deeply that the major had gotten away in the confusion that followed—stealing one of John's favorite mares in the process.

Ever since that day, Robillard seemed bent on attacking the settlers of Deerfield, taking delight in every bit of damage he could render. John was determined to get the bastard once and for all. The lives of his family and neighbors depended on it, and after Summer's close call today, he wouldn't rest until the man was dead or in irons.

Caleb's voice broke through his reverie. "Look, they have marked the trail well with their blood. We'll find them soon."

Riding in the lead, Caleb's eyes swept over the hilltop, looking for further signs of the men. The tall dried grass had been pushed aside where the Frenchmen's horse had ridden through, making a trail impossible to miss. They followed, moving down the other side of the hill until the thick grasses gave way to woods too dense to ride through. The Frenchmen's horses grazed on grass at the edge of the woods. Tying his horse to a tree, John proclaimed, "At least we have their horses, to make up for the one Robillard stole from me."

They came across the body of the first man sitting against a tree. He looked like a man resting, until, on closer inspection, his unnatural paleness and the pool of blood he sat in, showed that he was indeed dead. John felt a grim sense of satisfaction looking down at the lifeless body, but Nathaniel was shaken by the sight.

"Shall we bury him, John?"

"No, Nat, let the carrion do their work. We must press on. There's not much daylight left, and it could rain at any time. We must make the most of it." Wiping his forehead with his sleeve, he continued. "Nat, search the body for anything that might lead us to Robillard."

Nat did as he was told. He didn't want to appear squeamish in front of his brothers, but he hated the chore. His stomach lurched at each touch of the man's cold body. When the search revealed nothing, they continued the hunt.

The encounter with the corpse left Nathaniel weak in the knees, and his palms felt cold and clammy. He wanted to immerse his hands in a stream and wipe away every trace of the dead man's touch. Feeling suddenly weak, he stopped for a moment, leaning against a tree to wipe his sweaty forehead with his handkerchief. Something wet dripped onto his cheek from above. Damn! Using his handkerchief, he wiped it off.

Blood! Oh, God! Nat jumped away from the tree and looked up; a man was sprawled across the limb.

"John! Cal! Come quickly. I've found him." Nat raised his flintlock, pointing it at the man in the tree, and waited for his brothers to come.

In short time, the Frenchman was untreed and standing before them. Cal and John fired questions at him, but he seemed not to understand English.

Wondering if it was true, or if the man was just shamming his ignorance of the English language, John said, "Start a fire, Nat. It's going to be a long night."

Nat gave him a funny look. "Don't you think we

150

should bring him back to town? And question him there?"

"No, Nat. What must be done now, is best done away from the women." John looked pointedly at the captive.

The man's face blanched. So—he does understand English and knows what fate awaits him.

The Frenchman silently surveyed the situation, his eyes glazed with fear. He looked from one man to the other, contemplating which would be the weakest adversary. His gaze moved from the grim-faced one to the one with the narrowed blue eyes, then settled on the youngest one, stacking twigs for kindling.

Nathaniel stood up, rubbing bits of dirt and bark from his hands; as the Frenchman grabbed him, pulled a knife from the sheath at Nat's side, and held it to his throat.

Without thinking, Nat reached up and grabbed the knife-wielding hand of the man, struggling with all his strength to wrest it from him. Caleb took the opportunity to get a shot off, hitting the man in the side of the head. The Frenchman dropped to the ground in a heap.

Nat's knees buckled, and he sat down hard on a fallen tree. "Thank you, Cal. I'd be dead now, if you hadn't made that shot."

"Damn!" John cursed. "Now we have no one to lead us to Robillard."

"I'm sorry, John. It's my fault. If I hadn't been so stupid as to let my guard down, he'd still be alive."

John quickly embraced his younger brother. "Nat, don't fret. You're alive, that's all that matters." Turning to Cal, John said, "Nice shot. I knew you were an expert marksman, but I had no idea you were that good. I know I never would have chanced such a tight shot. But then, I'm not as cool-headed as you."

Cal grinned. "I've had plenty of time to practice out in the wilderness. Shall we go back and tell Summer she needn't worry about those bastards again?"

Waiting for the men to return was unbearable. Sitting by the fire, the two women talked in whispers, listening for the sound of thundering hooves that would signal their return. Charles had been sent along with the farm help to the outlying settlements to warn of a possible French and Indian attack, leaving Hannah and Summer alone with nothing but a single flintlock for protection. John had wanted Nat to stay with the women, but Summer had urged him to go. The men were in far greater danger than she and Hannah.

Summer tried to console herself by remembering that according to her notes, John would not be killed, he would live a long, full life. But she couldn't be sure those facts applied any longer. Perhaps her coming had changed the future. That was a terrifying thought, for if it were so, she could count on nothing any longer.

She tried to think in what way she could have changed things by her presence, and could think of nothing except her love for John. It was the only thing, but it was an important consideration. If she kept on as she was, as his lover, it would undoubtedly change everything. Elizabeth would not have John's sons, and that would have terrible repercussions on future generations.

She couldn't take the responsibility. She had to go back to her own time. But how could she leave John? How could she bear never seeing his face, or feeling his arms around her? She couldn't think of that now, or she'd never have the courage to leave. At least she would have one wonderful memory to cherish forever. And John would have to honor his promise to her because of it. She had given him her body; now he must give her the sword to touch.

It wouldn't be easy telling him that, but the picture of Elizabeth that flashed through her head made it easier. She wouldn't take up the leftover bits and pieces of John's life. Would not feel the shame of a clandestine relationship. She would find the courage to tell him.

Hannah watched Summer covertly. She could see the turmoil on the young woman's face, and could only imagine what she must be thinking. "Come, little lamb, let me brush out your hair. 'Tis a soothing exercise, and will calm us both."

Gratefully, Summer allowed her companion to brush her long hair in soothing strokes. Hannah's voice was calming, too. She crooned reassuring words that soon had Summer slipping into tranquility.

Suddenly, there was a loud pounding on the door. The two women looked up, frightened, until they heard John's booming voice. Hannah ran to the door, unbolted it, and threw it open.

John stood framed in the doorway. His eyes sought out Summer, taking in the beautiful sight of her sitting before the fire with her long, silken, sunset hair hanging loose, the wind from the open door moving it softly around her body.

He stepped into the room followed by Nat and Cal, and gazed at the woman he had held in his arms a few hours earlier.

His woman. That thought made him feel very vulnerable, for his future happiness was now in her hands. He had never wanted to love a woman as much as he loved her. But it was done. It couldn't be taken back. God help him, he would love her forever.

Nathaniel spoke first. "Well, Summer, you've nothing to fear any longer. Those Frenchies can never harm you, or any other woman again. They're both dead as doornails." He spoke the words with much cheerfulness, forgetting already how sick he had been at the sight of those lifeless bodies.

Summer looked from one brother to the next, searching for any sign that they were injured, but all seemed fine.

"Good!" Hannah proclaimed. "Now let me get you some supper, and we'll forget all about Summer's terrible ordeal. I've got a rabbit stew simmering on the fire. It won't take but a moment to serve it up."

"Thank you, Hannah. That sounds just right." Caleb said, noticing Summer and John, and the hungry way they looked at each other. "Nat and I will see to the horses."

When they were alone, Summer's gaze turned to one of such sadness that John was immediately afraid. "What is it, Will-o'-the-wisp? Why do you look so sad? Surely you don't feel bad about the dead Frenchmen? They'd have killed you after they—"

"John," Summer said, forcing herself to say the words before she lost the courage. "I hold you to your bargain. The covenant has been kept. You had your hour's pleasure, now you must let me touch your sword. I can't stay here any longer. I want to go home—to my own people—tomorrow."

John couldn't believe what he heard. How could she want to leave, after their glorious union on the hill? Had she made love to him only as a means to leave him? Could she be that cold-blooded? He swallowed hard, as his dreams for the future died. "Very well. As you wish. Far be it from me to go back

154

on our covenant. You fulfilled your end more enthusiastically than ever I could have hoped for. I'm sorry you were subjected to my foolish ramblings of apple trees and children. It seems I got carried away, and made a fool out of myself."

Summer heard the hurt and bitterness in his voice, and it affected her deeply. But she knew it would be easier this way. She answered coldly, while inside her heart was breaking. "Thank you, John. I did have my doubts that you'd live up to your end, but I'm happy to see you will comply. Tomorrow morning then. At your house. Everything should be as it was then."

"Does that mean you want me to be drunk, as well?"

"No. I don't think we have to go that far. What time will be convenient? I mean, we don't want anyone to be around. It could prove embarrassing to you."

"Never fear. I'll see that no one is around. Now, if you'll excuse me, my supper is getting cold."

Summer sat alone, crying silently, until Hannah fetched her. Wiping Summer's tears away with the corner of her apron, she said, "Lamby, it's all over. There's no need for tears. Now, come, you'll feel better after you've eaten."

Yes. It's all over, she thought. All over. She allowed Hannah to steer her into the kitchen, where the men sat. Her eyes were rimmed with red, but the men pretended not to see.

John sat stonily, staring into his pewter bowl with the same wild glint in his eyes that Nat had noticed so often when Summer was present; and Caleb watched quietly, knowing something beside the Frenchies was bothering her. He sensed a deep sadness and that disturbed him, for he was growing fond of his beautiful headstrong cousin.

Summer ate as much as she could bear. Not out of hunger, but to appease Hannah. She didn't want her to see how unhappy she truly was. This was the last night she would ever see these people that she loved so well. Hannah, who had been like a mother to her. Charles, treating her like a daughter. Nat, gentle Nat, like the younger brother she never had, and Cal, so calm, so cool. She had grown to love him. Of course, she had. He looked so much like John, and his sensuality was as strong. Why couldn't she have fallen in love with him, instead of John? Everything would be so different.

She wished also that she had gotten to know the Hawke women. At least she had met them all, and could carry their images with her to the twentieth century. And John, his image would be ingrained in her head forever. How could she ever forget what he looked like? How could she ever be happy again, without him?

She looked over to where he sat, just as he raised his head to look at her. His look conveyed so much. She saw the dangerous glint, but beyond that, she saw something else. He still wanted her. It was evident in his burning gaze. She tore her eyes from him, unable to withstand the desire she saw in them, the desire she, too, felt.

She was glad when the meal ended, and she said her good nights. Then, shielding the flame of a candle with the palm of her hand, she made her way up to her lonely room.

Chapter Fifteen

Too soon the morning light revealed the world she would be leaving. With a heavy heart she readied herself, rolling her leather pants and black silk shirt around her purse to make a small bundle. She would change into the clothes she had been wearing when she came at John's house, having no desire to explain how she came to be dressed in eighteenth-century garb when she returned to 1993. She would have enough to explain as it was.

She went to the wooden wardrobe filled with clothes John had ordered for her, and lovingly examined each beautiful gown, mourning their loss already. Lifting out the white satin ball gown she loved so much, she held it against her body. She longed to take it with her as a remembrance of the night she wore it, but knew the sight of it would be too painful a reminder of John. Better to sever all ties.

"I thought I heard you walking around," Hannah said, when Summer entered the kitchen. "How do you feel this morning? You look a mite peaked."

"I feel just fine, Hannah. What time did Charles get home last night? Poor man, he couldn't have

157

gotten much sleep.''

"He did do a goodly amount of riding last night, but he and the others were able to warn all the settlers that the French might be stirring up things again. They stayed up most of the night planning their strategy. I warrant if things get any worse, we'll all have to move to town, and I don't relish that at all. It would mean moving in with Mistress Jessica, and God love her, she's a hard one to live with. Set in her ways, she is. There be nothing worse than being in another woman's kitchen, and adjusting to her way of doing things. Lordy no.''

Summer laughed, hugging Hannah. "Then for your sake, I hope it doesn't come to that, for I would not wish you unhappy for anything in the world." Summer swallowed hard. This was the last time she would ever see Hannah. She gazed into the woman's warm hazel eyes, drinking in the soul and character so openly displayed there, and the love, too. "Your friendship has meant a lot to me, Hannah. You've made my stay here very happy. I'll never forget that.''

Hannah looked at her funny. "Summer Lamby, what are you trying to say? You aren't planning on going back to Boston, are you? I couldn't bear to see you go.''

Summer pulled herself together. Smiling sadly, she said, "No, of course not, Hannah. I was just feeling a little melancholy, don't mind me. I'm going for a ride now, but don't fret, I'm only going as far as Elizabeth's. I have something to return to her.''

Summer headed for the door quickly, before Hannah could see the tears that sprang to her eyes. She ran out to the barn and mounted the white mare, and without looking back, rode straight for John's house. She couldn't stand the hurt that tugged at her heart over leaving all these people she had grown to love. Galloping at full lope, she wanted the heart-wrenching ordeal to be over with as soon as possible.

Reining in at the fence post in front of John's house, she slid off the mare just as John opened the door. He stood watching as she walked over to him, then, remembering the bundle in her saddlebag, ran back to get it. "The clothes I was wearing, when I came. I'm going to change into them," she explained.

"Not taking any chances, are you? Tell me, is it so hateful here, or am I the only hateful thing in your life?"

"John, please, if you think carefully, you'll realize this is the only thing I can do. Where's Elizabeth?"

"In town, at my mother's. You needn't fear. No one will interfere with your precious journey home."

Standing aside, he watched as Summer entered the house, and with a heavy heart, followed her up the stairs to his bedroom.

His face was sober, his manner cool when he spoke. "There you are," he said, indicating the sword on the bed. "It's ready when you are."

Summer couldn't believe he was going to let her go so easily. Had he ever loved her at all? Or had she just been an amusement that he was tired of? Tears rimmed her eyes. "Can you let me go so easily?"

"Confound it, woman! You hated me when I kept you here. Now will you hate me, because I let you go?"

He pulled her to him roughly. "I'll not beg you to stay, but would say goodbye like this." Grabbing her head in his hands, he kissed her hard. The strength in his arms was powerful, and using it, he pushed her down on the floor, his urgent need pressing into her.

Summer felt herself responding to him, as she always did. What could it matter if she gave in to her lust for this man, just one more time? She was leaving. The sword was there on the bed waiting for her. She could have this one bittersweet moment to add to her memories. One more moment of love before she left his arms forever. Circling his neck with her arms, she responded to his kiss with an urgency that matched his own.

Realizing she was his for the taking, he undressed her, his hands and lips working at the same time to fire the flame in her body. When his anxious fingers fumbled, she helped him, until her clothes lay in a limp bundle on the floor.

Leaning over her, John looked down at her, so soft, so vulnerable. This was the first time he had ever seen her completely naked. His eyes traveled over her, relishing every inch of her femininity.

Her breasts, so perfectly shaped, with delicate pink nipples pointing at him delightfully, urging him to cover them with his mouth. Her small waist, no larger than the span of his hands, waiting to be circled. Wide, sensuous hips that enticed him further, and the golden mound between her legs, demanding his homage. Homage he was happy to give her.

Parting her legs gently, he lowered his head between her velvet thighs, and sent his tongue searching through the golden hair to her secret place. His tongue slid inside her, seeking the sweet nectar of love that could be found nowhere else.

Summer moaned loudly, feeling his tongue inside her, feeling the exquisite, hot touch that sent her soaring on the wings of rapture, her body writhing in the intensity of pleasure no man but John Hawke could ever give her. When she could bear it no longer, she grasped his head, pulling it away from her before it was too late.

Frantically, her hands worked at undressing him, and when their naked bodies came together, and when he slid into her, slowly, enticingly, she cried out her need for him and wrapped her legs around him, holding on tight as they rode together in a rhythm that soon became feverish.

"John, John," she cried, each time he drove into her harder than before, the pleasure becoming more than she could bear. "Oh Johnnnnn." And when her release came, she clung to him, crying out in wonder at the intensity of their lovemaking.

Afterward, they lay in each other's arms for a long time, each lost in thought of what was to take place next. John raised himself up on his elbow, and looked down at her. When he saw the sadness reflected there, he knew she was going to proceed with her plan to leave him. Without speaking, he got up and dressed in silence.

For a minute Summer was afraid he would take the sword away, but he made no move toward it. She stood, wrapping her discarded gown around her body to hide her nakedness, which now embarrassed her under his unblinking stare. When she was finished dressing, she walked over to the bed. In order to touch the sword, she would have to come within inches of his body. Had he done that on purpose, to make her feel uncomfortable? Did he plan on stopping her from touching the sword?

Looking into his eyes, she reached for the sword.

John's expression never changed. He was going to let her go.

Something inside her felt betrayed. Fighting back tears, she touched the cold steel blade.

Nothing happened.

She blinked her eyes, then touched it again.

Still nothing.

How could that be? She looked at John questioningly, but he said nothing. Grasping the sword's hilt with one hand, she ran her fingers down the length of the blade with her other hand. Still nothing. Could it be that the sword had to be in the same position it had been in, when she had come to this time?

Thinking back, she remembered it had been in the scabbard hanging over the arm of the chair. She asked John to move it there, and he did so without so much as blinking an eye.

His face was expressionless, except for the slightest of smiles that flickered across his face when he moved the sword to the chair. A smile that vanished instantly when he turned toward Summer once more.

Summer walked over to the chair, and touched the sword, panic filling her eyes when nothing happened. She looked at John suspiciously, but his face was impassive, though his eyes held that familiar glint.

"I don't understand," she said in a choked voice. "Why isn't it working? Have I stayed in this century too long? Is that it?"

John spoke, his voice barely more than a whisper. "It seems I was right. Destiny *has* decreed that you stay with me."

"I don't believe this is happening. Have you done something to the sword? Is that why you've been so cooperative?" She pulled the sword from its scabbard and looked at it closely. It was the same as before. Nothing had been changed. Filled with anguish she flung it on the bed. "What am I to do? I won't—I can't be your mistress! If I'm forced to stay here, I'll, I'll, have to think of other alternatives?"

John looked at her soberly. "What alternatives?"

Her mind whirled. In desperation, she cried, "Daniel. Yes. Daniel. He wants to marry me."

In a low, cold voice, John said, "I warned you once before that you will be a widow on your wedding night, should you marry that simpering idiot."

Fury, born of desperation, showed in Summer's eyes. "Do you think you can go around murdering everyone who stands in your way?"

From the doorway, a voice answered. "Actually, Summer, he does think so."

Summer whirled to face Caleb.

"I remember well the time he squashed a toad beneath his foot, simply because it peed on him."

John was not happy to see his brother. "What are you doing here?"

"I might ask the same of you. Mother is at my place, and anxious to talk with Summer—immediately. She's in quite a state, I fear, after hearing about Summer's encounter with the Frenchmen. And, by the way, your wife and daughter are there as well." He emphasized the word wife deliberately, his eyes sweeping from John to Summer, to the bed.

Summer saw Cal's eyebrow raise, and the pointed way he looked at John's bed. "Cal, don't go lifting your eyebrow to me. It's not what you think," she proclaimed, trying to hide the feelings of guilt she felt so deeply.

"And what do I think, dear cousin, finding you alone here with John in his bedchamber, dressed in a most provocative garment? I do admit though, that I fail to see the significance of the sword on the bed. That's a new one for me."

"Caleb Hawke. Look carefully before you accuse me of indiscretion. Do you see my dress? I have just changed from it into these riding clothes. That's the only reason I'm in John's chamber. And notice please, that the bed is untouched."

Cal gazed at the strange outfit Summer wore, then

163

looked at the bed again. It *was* untouched, and Summer looked so innocently outraged that she must surely be telling the truth. Still . . . if he hadn't shown up just now, he was sure she would have ended up in John's bed. What was he going to do with this provocative young lady? The attraction between her and John was all too obvious. "Why did you find the need to change here, when you have your own chamber in my house?"

Summer had foreseen that question. "Because, as you very well know, Hannah would have been upset seeing me out riding again, so soon after my incident with those Frenchmen. I thought to spare her the agony by leaving the house in my dress."

That explanation impressed even John, who knew the real truth. He was amazed at the capacity of this woman to talk her way out of tight spots. Women of the future were more than a match for the men of his time, it seemed.

"I'm sorry, Cousin, for having jumped to the wrong conclusion, and now, if you would spare Hannah, you'd better change again before we ride home. They're waiting for us."

Summer closed the door when the men left, feeling relieved that she had gotten out of a sticky situation, but her heart weighed heavy. She hated to lie. It was alien to her nature, but what was that next to the terrible sin she had just committed? But then, if it was true that John had never consummated his marriage to Elizabeth, was it truly a sin? She tried to console herself with the idea that it wasn't.

When she was once again dressed in eighteenth century clothing, she opened the door to face the two men. Gazing into John's green eyes, then Cal's blue ones, she knew with a certainty that one of these men would be deciding her future.

* * *

Elizabeth stood at the window in Caleb's parlor, watching as the three figures rode closer, her eyes singling out Caleb's beloved form. This was her first glimpse of him in months, and her heart beat wildly in anticipation as he drew closer and closer. Cal, sweet Cal, if only she could feel his arms around her once more. It was all she ever dreamed of, all she ever wanted from this life.

It wasn't fair that she was denied his love because of one mistake. She had married John so the people of Deerfield could not condemn her. If she had known Caleb would return, she would have waited. Damn the people of Deerfield for making it impossible to be with Caleb. And damn civilization, too. If she had her way, she would live in the forest away from all these self-righteous and boring people.

She didn't fit in here. She never had. She yearned to be in the forest with Nenepownam and the Pocumtuck Indians. She had been given a taste of that life when she and John and Cal visited Nenepownam each summer. Those blissful visits had left her with a yearning for that way of life that she had never been able to dispel. How she envied the Indians their freedom and their closeness to nature. It seemed a much more natural way to live.

As the figures drew closer, her eyes shifted to the smaller form that rode between the two brothers. Summer, sitting her saddle proudly, her hair blowing loosely like the mane of the horse she rode. How could she ever hope to compete with such a lovely, vital woman. Even now, she saw Cal lean sideways in his saddle toward her, saying something to make her laugh.

Elizabeth watched, sick at heart. Was it Summer's

sole purpose in life to take everything from her that she held dear? She had even tried to take her hawk, that first time they met in the graveyard. And what a strange meeting that had been. Summer had seemed frightened at first. Her face turning white when she looked up at Elizabeth.

Never had she met such a strange woman. What was it about Summer that seemed so foreign, so different from any woman she had ever known?

Hearing the riders, Alisha ran from the house to greet them. "We've been waiting for you such a long time. Where have you been?"

Summer looked to John before speaking. "Why, nowhere, darling. Just for a little ride." Summer slid from the mare and embraced Alisha. "And what about you? What are you doing here? I thought you and your mother were in town visiting your grandmother."

"We were, until grandmother heard about you and the terrible men who attacked you. Then she got very angry, and decided we must all come out and see you right away. Are you all right? Did those bad men hurt you?"

"No, darling, I'm fine." Looking up at John and Cal still mounted on their horses, she said, "Well, gentlemen, shall we go in and face the music?"

When she saw the perplexed look that followed that statement, she continued, "What I mean is, let's face your mother and get it over with." She would have to be more careful of her expressions. Grasping Alisha's hand, she walked into the house.

Elizabeth turned from the window to watch, her cool gaze turning to heat when Cal walked in looking handsomer than ever. She could never get enough of looking at him.

Summer swept over to Jessica, sitting as regally as

she had at the ball, and curtsied. "Aunt Jessica, how good to see you. I've been meaning to call on you, but it seems you've saved me the trip to town."

Jessica silently glanced at the young, vivacious woman, then turned her attention to her sons.

Cal's gaze swept the room, resting on Elizabeth and turning her spine to jelly.

"You're looking well, Elizabeth."

Her lips parted, but she was unable to speak.

Cal brushed her cheek with his lips, then made his way to Jessica's side. Leaning over, he kissed her cheek. "That goes for you, too, Mother."

Patting his cheek, Jessica answered, "'Tis good to see you, Cal, but we'll have to save our greetings for later. Now that everyone is present, we can get down to the business at hand. A report has come to me of Summer's close call. It distressed me deeply. I thought her safe here in the company of my strong sons, but I see that your care has been lacking. Therefore, I propose that Summer move into town with me, where she may be sure of being well taken care of."

Her voice softened when she turned to Summer. "I would have asked you sooner, child, but I admit to an ulterior motive for having you stay here. I had hoped your exposure to my sons would have a beneficial result. Namely, that you would become enamored of one of them, and marry into the family."

Summer was dumbfounded. "Aunt Jessica, do I understand you correctly? You wanted me to stay here, solely for the purpose of marrying me off to one of your sons? Why?"

"Because, my dear, on first glimpse of you at the ball, I knew you would make an excellent wife for a Hawke. And, considering the scarcity of suitable mates in this wilderness community, I deemed it necessary to work on that result swiftly, before you fell for some good-for-nothing popinjay. I know now that it was wrong of me to force the issue, therefore, I shall remedy it by having you live with me. At least then I can vouch for your safety."

"Aunt Jessica, I'm not a possession you may give away to whomever you please. I'm a flesh and blood woman with a mind of my own."

Entering the room, Nat said, "Good for you, Summer. And as for marrying me, a few weeks ago I dreamt of such an alliance, until Summer made it perfectly clear that her feelings for me were as a sister to a brother. She was right. I know that now, for I have found the woman I intend to marry."

Jessica was speechless. She hadn't known of any young woman in town who could strike such powerful feelings in her youngest son.

"Her name is Charity Osborne. You'll meet her soon."

Now that the phantom woman possessed a name, Jessica could once again speak. "Well, I declare. It seems there's to be a wedding after all. Though not the one I planned. Tell me about her, son. I don't remember any Osbornes living in town."

"That's because they don't. Charity lives with her parents at a homestead northwest of here. I met her at your birthday ball."

Jessica was beaming. "Do tell? It seems I've brought you and your lady love together after all. How exciting. We shall have to invite her and her folk over to supper, so we may become acquainted. I'll have Otis fix a grand meal on the morrow. No, wait, I fear it will have to be a full week from now to make all the arrangements." Jessica stood and hugged her son. "Is that satisfactory to you, Nat?"

It was Nat's turn to be dumbfounded. Never in his

life had his mother asked his advice on anything. She always preached, or told him what he should be doing or thinking. His face lit up. "Yes, Mother, that will be quite satisfactory."

"Nat, you know how happy I am for you," Summer said, embracing him and kissing his cheek. "I'm sure I'll love your Charity."

"And I," Elizabeth added. "And now that Nat is spoken for, and John is married to me, that leaves but one son to marry off to Cousin Summer." Her voice sounded bitter. "Tell me, Cal. How do you feel about marrying Summer?"

Caleb was silent a moment. Standing, he looked from John to Summer. In a quiet voice, he said, "I'm not sure where Summer's heart lies. But the idea intrigues me. It would not be difficult to love so fair a lady. What man would object to lying beside her each night? What say you, Summer? Would you find marriage to a half-breed repulsive?"

Summer was stunned by this turn of events. As was everyone else in the room. John stood next to Cal, like a man turned to stone. Elizabeth's face held a look of pure horror. Only Nat and Jessica seemed untouched by Cal's words.

"Cal, surely you know your Indian blood is not the issue here. And Aunt Jessica. I really don't think this is the time or place to be discussing my personal life. Frankly, I resent it. I'm staying here at Caleb's unless, of course, he fears being put in a compromising situation by my presence." With eyes sparking fire, she asked, "What say you, Cal?"

"I say, well done, cousin. You're most welcome in my home, and . . . mayhap it will be your own, for the idea of marrying you has much merit. My heart grows warmer with each glimpse of your fair face."

"Enough talk of marriage," John said, his voice

sounding strained. "The poor woman is in no need of suitors. She has enough already."

Jessica raised an eyebrow. "Oh? Whom are you referring to, John?"

Summer wanted to know the answer to that herself.

"Why, Preacher Bradford. Summer tells me the man has asked permission to court her."

"That pompous ass!" Jessica retorted. "My dear, I hope you haven't seriously considered such a union."

"No. I have not."

"But, Summer," Elizabeth implored. "Daniel Bradford is a man of means. A woman would be foolish not to think of her future comfort."

Bristling, Summer answered. "Is that why you married John? Were you thinking of your comfort?"

Things were getting out of hand. Both Summer and Elizabeth were headstrong women. Jessica tried to defuse the situation by ignoring Summer's attack on Elizabeth. "In any case, I doubt Daniel Bradford capable of giving much comfort in any area, including his bed. The man loves himself far more than he could ever love a woman. But I will say no more. Obviously, it is not the right time to speak of Summer's future husband. Now, come kiss me, child. Say you forgive a meddlesome old woman."

Summer kissed Jessica's cheek. The woman was infuriating, but Summer was fond of her. She gave her a hug, too, to let her know she was forgiven. The atmosphere in the room lightened immediately, and everyone began talking at once, wanting to know more about Nat's new love.

Summer envied Charity. Nat would make a wonderful husband, and marrying into the Hawke family was a definite plus. Summer could never truly belong to the family, unless Jessica had her way and she married Caleb. But by the look on John's face, he would never accept that. She couldn't accept it either. There was only one man she wanted to marry, and it broke her heart looking at him. They had just made love, sharing their bodies in an incredible act, his scent still clinging to her body, and yet, she had no right to even hold his hand.

Watching from across the room, unable to touch him, was painful beyond belief. She was more desperate than ever. Her plans for returning to her own time had ended abruptly when the sword no longer responded to her touch. Could the fact that she didn't really want to leave, because of her love for John, have rendered the sword useless? If that were so, she was doomed to stay a prisoner forever, for she would never stop loving him.

Chapter Sixteen

Four nights later, after Hannah and Charles had retired for the evening, Summer came back downstairs in her flannel nightshift and stood before the fire, warming her hands. She couldn't sleep, worried about John and his brothers out searching for Major Robillard, the Frenchman who was responsible for terrorizing the Deerfield area. This was her first taste of living in a place where war was only a few miles from her doorstep, and it unnerved her.

Hannah heard her stirring and brought down a shawl, wrapping it around Summer's shoulders. Without uttering a word, she went to her favorite chair by the fire and picked up her needlework. Her poor little lamb had need of her company.

Hearing a knock on the door, Hannah peered out the window, then cried, "Praise be! They're back." She unbolted the door and flung it open.

Summer looked up to see the outline of a man in the doorway. The glare of the fire blinded her to all but the glint of silver and emerald from the sword at his waist. John!

He stood gazing at Summer's lovely body, outlined through her nightshift as she stood by the fire, his eyes following every delectable curve. God's blood, but she was desirable.

Suddenly Summer flew across the floor, flinging herself into his arms. "Thank God, you're safe. I've been so worried."

"Cousin, if I'm to get such an enthusiastic reception each time I come home, it shall be well worth the trip."

Summer was shocked to find herself in Caleb's arms. But the sword . . . She had seen the sword.

Grabbing her around the waist, Cal squeezed her tightly and kissed her heartily, and she forgot everything but the situation she was in. She didn't dare push him away or tell him she thought he was John. How could she ever explain? She allowed the kiss to continue, surprised at the pleasant feeling Cal's lips evoked.

When he released his tight hold on her, she looked over his shoulder to see John standing in the doorway, anger showing on his face, and . . . something else . . . fear. But what could John be afraid of?

Though the night was cool, sweat broke out on John's forehead as his eyes darted to the sword at Cal's waist, and to Summer's slim fingers resting just a sparse inch from the blade. In a taut, controlled voice, he said, "Summer, I suggest you get some clothes on. I can see through that cloth. And so can my brothers."

Summer's cheeks flushed pink. She had thought herself decently covered. Why was he acting so strangely? She backed out of Cal's arms and went upstairs to dress, wounded by John's words.

When she returned, Hannah was serving the men trenchers of stew in the kitchen.

"I'm beginning to think Major Robillard has refuge somewhere nearby," John said, filling

173

Charles in on their journey. "How else to explain his bewildering disappearances? That one-eyed bastard may have an ally amongst us. Someone to hide him after each attack."

The talk of a one-eyed man brought a picture to Summer's mind. "John, is this Robillard truly one-eyed?"

John looked at Summer, now dressed in a hunter green dress, his eyes moving over her form with interest. Four long days away from her had been excruciating, his desire for her never stronger. Smiling more confidently than he felt, he answered Summer. "Yes, he wears a patch over his left eye to cover an empty socket. He lost the eye several years ago in hand to hand combat with me, and has been on a personal vendetta against Deerfield, and me in particular, ever since."

"I saw a man with a patch over his eye at Daniel's the other day. Could he be the man you're looking for?"

"Daniel's? What were you doing there? I told you to stay away from that man."

"Summer," Cal said, "don't worry your pretty little head over it. We've already checked into reports of a one-eyed man at the trading post. It was just a fur trader."

The man she had seen didn't look like a fur trader to her. She remembered the haughty way he sat his horse. But it was obvious Cal and John wouldn't take the word of a mere woman. Pretty little head, indeed. She'd just take a look for herself. Surely Sarah would have information about the one-eyed man, and could reassure her if he was truly a fur trader. Then she could dismiss it from her mind.

With morning light, Summer dressed in her favorite riding outfit, made her way to the stable, saddled the mare, and headed down the road toward Daniel's place.

Cal cornered the house in time to see Summer ride away. What was the little vixen up to now? She seemed bent on getting into trouble. It looked like he would have to watch her more carefully, a chore he minded not at all.

The sunset-haired beauty was a joy to look at, and he couldn't help but admire her. He smiled, thinking about the unexpected treat of having her fling herself into his arms the night before, and of the kiss that followed. It stirred up feelings he hadn't had for a long time. Not since the last time he had been with Elizabeth, before her marriage to John.

Saddling his horse, he followed Summer at a safe distance. Using skills he had learned from his Indian friends, he was able to stay just out of her sight, until, riding around a bend in the road, he caught sight of her reining in her horse near another rider. Preacher Bradford.

Was it a rendezvous?

No, Summer seemed genuinely surprised to see him. Cal climbed off his horse and slapped its flank to send it home, then crept closer to hear the conversation between Summer and Daniel.

"I was just on my way to see you, Summer. Hoping I could entice you into visiting Mother again. She enjoyed so having you there. I believe she is quite fond of you."

"What a coincidence. I was just on my way to do that very thing. Is she feeling better?"

"I fear not. But a visit from you would have beneficial results, I'm sure."

Daniel looked at Summer's breasts, outlined seductively in the man's shirt she wore. "Dare I hope your visit today means you have become more amenable to my request to court you?"

Summer wanted to tell Daniel exactly what she thought of him, but she needed to find out about the one-eyed man. But, truth to tell, she was beginning to feel foolish about the whole thing. There were probably more than a few one-eyed men in the territory, as well as men who had lost an arm or leg. After all, they were at war with the French. And the French and Indian Wars had been going on a very long time.

Opening her eyes wide with innocence, she said, "Daniel, there is a saying where I come from. Where there's life, there's hope."

"Hope. That's all I ask for." Daniel looked at Summer's curvaceous body in the tight-fitting breeches, and grabbed her horse's bridle, pulling the animal close to his. He reached out for her, intending to kiss her while she was in such an agreeable mood.

Summer saw it coming, and wanted to slap his face, but she had started all this and couldn't back out now. But as Daniel's lips came closer, she knew she couldn't go through with it. She kneed her horse, moving it out of reach. Daniel missed his mark, kissing the air, and she had a hard time keeping from laughing out loud.

Anger rose in Caleb, watching from the trees. Anger at Summer, as well as Daniel. He remembered what Elizabeth had said about Daniel being a man of means, and wondered if Summer had decided that Daniel was a good catch. That thought disturbed him more than he thought possible.

Stepping out of the woods, he called out, "Ah, Summer, how providential meeting up with you like this. I seem to have lost my mount. Mayhap you could ride me back home. Oh. Is that you, Bradford? Beautiful day, what?"

Summer was relieved to see Cal. Her Mata Hari act was not working out as she planned. She had underestimated the sex drive of the horny preacher. She would have to find another way to find out about the one-eyed man, and the next time she set off to visit Sarah, she would make sure she had a chaperon.

"Sorry, Daniel. It looks as if my visit will have to wait. Give my regards to your mother."

With a tip of his tricorn, Cal climbed up behind Summer, barely hiding the smirk on his face. Bradford was seething, and for some reason Cal took immense pleasure in that.

When they rode around the bend in the road, Summer saw Caleb's horse peacefully grazing on grass. "Providential? Hah! What did you do, follow me from the house?"

Cal jumped off the horse and looked up at her. "You have a way of always getting into trouble, Summer. I was just trying to keep you from harm. It would be wise if in the future you didn't ride alone—ever. One would have thought you'd have learned your lesson by now. Do you have an affinity for being attacked by hot-blooded rogues?"

Summer was feeling reckless. The Hawke men had a way of making her feel that way. "No, Cal. I just have an affinity for being rescued by handsome, hot-blooded men." With that she rode off, leaving Cal standing there with his mouth open.

Cal was intrigued by her words, and by the woman herself. Never had he met a woman so full of life. But, God, she was exasperating. He felt like taking her over his knee and spanking her, but she didn't seem to be the kind of woman who would stand for that. She'd probably fight him tooth and nail. Laughing, he mounted his horse and followed her back home.

When Summer's horse was unsaddled and stabled,

she strode toward the house with Cal following close at her heels. In a haughty voice, she said, "Am I so irresponsible you must follow me, even here?"

Caleb laughed. "Have you forgotten that I live here, too? Or do you mean to keep me out of my own house."

Without answering, Summer opened the door and entered the kitchen. A too quiet kitchen. Where was Hannah? Her eyes swept the room, falling on a note lying on the table. She read the message, written in a childish scrawl. "Charles and me gon to towne bak tonit."

"It seems we're alone. Hannah and Charles have gone to town. Probably to get supplies for the Osborne supper. I know Nat is visiting Charity, so I guess it will be up to me to cook, but I warn you, I have limited knowledge in that area."

"You mean there's something you're not proficient at, my dear? You do everything else so well. Ride like an Indian, swim like a mermaid, and look like an angel. Methinks you would make love like a goddess."

Summer looked at Cal with a solemn expression. "Cal, I'm sorry if my words about hot-blooded men gave you the wrong idea. I was just being playful. I didn't mean for you to take them seriously."

A flicker of pain flashed across Cal's face, then disappeared quickly. "I'm no fool. I know. You needn't explain. And now, since you admit to being a terrible cook, I'll make us something to eat. I'm a superb cook, but I wouldn't tell that to Hannah if I were you. It wouldn't set well with her that a man can cook as well as she."

In leisure, they ate Caleb's meal, talking quietly of small things, laughing and enjoying each other's company. It felt good to Summer to be able to relax with a man, instead of constantly being on guard. Cal was much more casual and easygoing than John. It had to be his Indian blood, because it surely couldn't be the intense Hawke blood. Come to think of it, though, Nat was easygoing, too. Whatever it was, she liked it, and felt more relaxed than she had in a long time.

In the afternoon, they did the chores that Hannah and Charles usually did. Milking the cows, feeding the animals, cleaning the stalls. Then they gathered enough firewood for the night, and water from the well. Every once in a while they would look up from their chores, and their eyes would meet.

Is this what it would be like to be married? Cal mused. Damn it all, that was the third time today he had thought of marrying Summer. It was his mother's fault for bringing it up in the first place. No—that wasn't true. Since that first day, when he had seen her emerging from the river like a goddess, he had thought of little else.

In the evening, he cooked another meal, and afterward they sat in the parlor, talking and drinking rum in front of the fire.

"There must be a full moon tonight," Summer murmured. "It always affects me strangely. Makes me restless and full of energy I can't seem to dissipate. Does the moon affect you, Cal? I've asked others that question, and they never know what I'm talking about. Do you know what I'm talking about, Cal?"

"Mmm, I do. The moon affects me, too. But, then, I always thought it was my Indian blood stirring. Mayhap, you have a touch of Indian blood running through your veins."

"Mayhap I do." Summer stood on wobbly legs and headed for the rum bottle, pouring herself a full mug, then sat down by the fire again.

Cal blinked when he saw how much rum she had poured. "How many of those have you had?"

"Who's counting," she said, then hiccuped loudly. "It's un . . . ungen . . . ungentlemanly for a man to notice how many drinks a lady has."

Summer was a woman of many complications. Warm and soft one minute, self-assured and haughty the next. The mood she was in now was hard for him to figure out. He watched as she downed the drink, then stood up.

"If you'll excuse me, I think I'll go beddy bye. It's been a long and lovely day."

Walking to the window, she blew a kiss to the moon. "Good night, beautiful moon. Good night, beautiful Cal." Blowing him a kiss, too, she left the room, climbing the stairs on unsteady legs while leaning heavily on the bannister.

Alone in her room, the restlessness became unbearable. The room seemed to be closing in on her. She needed to tire herself out, her mind too full of thoughts of John. She felt trapped. Not so much by time, as by the feelings in her heart. She would have to see John, be reminded of her love for him every day of her life, and she couldn't bear it.

Her only option at the moment seemed to be to marry someone. At least, in that way, she would be unattainable to John, and it might ease her heart. She thought about the handsome man downstairs, so much like John in some ways, but so different, too. He was gentle and trusting, two traits John did not possess. He would make a wonderful husband, but she couldn't do that to him. He deserved a woman whose heart belonged to him completely. So what was she to do? Why hadn't the sword worked? She needed to be free of John and the terrible pain of wanting him.

The rum, rather than calming her down, seemed instead to heighten her awareness of everything. She paced the room, looking out the window to keep from feeling closed in. She could see the river sparkling in the light of the moon, beckoning to her.

Quickly, she stripped off her clothes and wrapped a blanket around her naked body. It was chilly outside, and the water would be even colder, but it didn't matter, she would swim away her restlessness, wear herself out so that she no longer minded not being in John's arms.

Only the smallest of sounds gave her away as she moved downstairs and out the door. But Caleb, with his Indian awareness, heard her and once again followed her, wondering what in God's name she was up to now.

At the riverbank, Summer looked up to the full moon overhead, her body weaving slightly from the effects of the rum, and she raised her arms over her head, as if reaching up to touch the orange sphere. The blanket slid from her body, landing in a heap at her feet.

Caleb sucked in his breath as he gazed at her naked form. This goddess come to earth fascinated and aroused him with her pagan performance, which continued as she slowly moved into the water.

Hardly a ripple stirred as she began to swim, moving effortlessly through the water as if she were truly a goddess. Then turning on her back, she exposed her glistening breasts to the moon, and moved so seductively in the moonlit water that his body ached to join her.

Stripping off his clothes, Cal entered the water, oblivious to the cold.

Summer heard the water splash and stopped swimming, listening in fright. Her first thought was that it was one of the militia men stationed in the pasture. They often came to the river to wash their clothes or to get water, but it was too late at night for that.

"Who's there?" she whispered in a small frightened voice.

Cal dove under and emerged inches from her body. She gave out a little cry.

"Summer, goddess of the moon and of my heart, I'm here to do your bidding."

"Cal! You gave me such a fright. I was afraid I was once again in the clutches of some hot-blooded rogue."

"You are," he said huskily, pulling her body through the water until it nestled up against his own. The feel of her skin against his sent a bolt of excitement through him. He wanted her fiercely, but had to control his powerful urge. Had to be gentle, so he wouldn't frighten her away. He kissed her lips softly, sweetly, then feeling no resistance, pulled her hard against his chest and kissed her as his body demanded.

Summer felt his hardened shaft against her body, and decided her future in that one masterful touch. She would marry Cal and he would take care of her, help her to forget John. Her arms wound around Cal's neck and held on tight. He would be her lifeline, her salvation. He would make her forget.

Cal lifted her up in his arms and carried her out of the water. No words were necessary. They both knew something important had been decided. He laid her down on the blanket she had been wrapped in and stood looking down at her in wonder, hardly daring to believe she was waiting for him.

Summer looked up at Cal's naked, hard body, so beautiful in the moonlight, so overwhelmingly masculine. How could she go through with it? Cal was a real man. He expected her to respond like a real woman.

As he lowered himself onto her body, the heavens opened up in a torrent of rain.

"You see, goddess. An omen. The blessed rains have been sent to sanctify our union." With great tenderness, he held her head in his hands, and kissed her with such sweetness that the last shred of doubt and resistance melted away, and she welcomed him.

The rain pelted their naked bodies as Cal's hands moved unhurriedly over her, delighting in the feel of her flesh.

Summer shivered as the warmth of his hands touched her cold, wet skin, exciting her unexpectedly. She responded to his gentle touch, the rum warming her belly, Cal's hands warming her skin; a potent combination that brought her quickly into a state of heightened desire.

When Cal sensed she was ready, he entered her, thrilling to the deep sensuous pleasure it gave him. They moved together slowly, dreamily, in deep contrast to the fast furious rains that pelted them, reveling in the sensuous touch of their wet bodies sliding against each other. His slow deliberate movements sent Summer into a frenzy, and she cried out to him for release. Cal obliged with long, hard strokes, until, at last, the cry she uttered was from bliss.

Looking into her eyes, he whispered. "You'll have to marry me now, else you will be a fallen angel, and I prefer my angels on pedestals."

Summer's heart broke as she answered, "I'll marry you, Cal. For it seems I'm destined to belong to a Hawke." Tears fell from her eyes, but Cal didn't see them, for they mingled quickly with the raindrops that streamed down her face.

"Summer. It isn't the rum talking, or the effects of the full moon? You do want to marry me? You do love me?"

Summer couldn't say the words that belonged to another man. She answered instead, by pulling his head down and kissing him hard.

Cal was relieved. For a moment, he had been afraid she was going to say no. "Won't Jessica be surprised. Two weddings instead of one. She'll be overcome with happiness."

Horror filled Summer as she contemplated telling John and Elizabeth. "There's something you should know before we tell anyone. Something that might alter your mind about marrying me."

Cal's heart became restricted. "If you're going to tell me of a past love—don't! Our lives begin this moment. Nothing else matters. I know you and John are attracted to each other, but our marriage will end that. John will have to reconcile himself to the fact that he can never have you."

Summer winced at Cal's words, but she brushed her guilt aside. She could never tell Cal that she had been John's lover. "There are more people involved than just John. Elizabeth for one. She loves you and always has. Have you been so blind you couldn't see that all these years?"

"Elizabeth in love with me? That's impossible. There was a time when that was true, but no longer. If she loves me, why did she marry my brother?"

His words sounded bitter, and Summer realized that Cal's feelings toward Elizabeth ran deeper than she suspected. "Cal. She married John because you left when she was carrying your child. She had no choice."

Cal was stunned. "That can't be true! Are you

184

saying Alisha is my child?"

"I can't believe you never realized the truth."

"Why did she never tell me?"

"What good would it have done? They were married by then. Alisha was born by then. Cal, now that you know the truth, do you still want to marry me? It will hurt John and Elizabeth gravely."

Cal's face took on a taut, determined look. "They made their choice five years ago. I make mine now. Our bond was sealed here tonight, under the gaze of the full moon. It is a sacred bond, and I hold you to it." His lips came down on hers, harder, rougher than before, as if the pressure of them could wipe away the past and seal their fate forever.

Chapter Seventeen

Brushing a wayward strand of carrot red hair from her face, Hannah smiled at a beaming Caleb. "Sit down, Cal. Breakfast is ready."

"Mmmm, smells like ambrosia from the gods." Grabbing Hannah around her ample middle, he kissed her on the lips. "Ah, Hannah, leave Charles and run away with me. We'll make a new life together in the forest, where you can cook me all my favorite foods, and I can recite romantic sonnets to you."

Hannah giggled. She had never seen Caleb so happy. "'Tis not me you be wanting to run away with, I'll wager, but Mistress Summer. Has she agreed to marry you? Is that what has you so frolicsome?"

Summer entered the room in time to hear Hannah's words. "I thought we agreed not to tell anyone until the proper time."

"Ah, Summer darling." Cal released Hannah and grabbed for Summer, pulling her into his arms. "What harm in telling Hannah? She'll keep the secret for us."

Hannah embraced them both. "Yes, I'll keep your

secret, gladly. Ah, me, it makes me plum happy to see you two together. Wait 'til Jessica finds out. She'll be beside herself with joy."

"Wait 'til Jessica finds out what?" Nat stood in the doorway, watching the goings-on.

"My lips are sealed." Hannah said, laughing.

Nat looked from Summer to Cal. "Don't tell me. Let me guess. You two are going to marry. No! I can't believe it."

Cal whacked Nat on the back. "Do you think you're the only one who can catch a bride?" Then, turning serious, he added, "Nat. You must keep it to yourself. There are people who must be told in a gentle way, understand?"

Nat understood too well. John would not take the news well, no matter how it was presented. "Shall I accompany you when you tell John? You may have need of my strong arms."

"No, little brother. Summer and I will handle it ourselves. You have enough to occupy your time. Is it all set with the Osbornes? Did they agree to come tomorrow for a family supper?"

"Yes, they'll be here. The Osbornes seem happy enough that I'm to marry their daughter. The Hawke name carries much influence around here. Their only concern was that we have known each other such a short time. But then, look at you and Summer. Your acquaintance is as short as mine and Charity's. I'm riding back there tomorrow to escort them to town. Cal, I'm feeling nervous about this supper, and I don't even know why."

"It's only natural, Nat. It's not every day a man finds a bride and introduces her to his family." Cal hugged Summer to his side. "Which reminds me, darling, there is yet another person to be told of our betrothal—my mother. This is the day I am to meet her and my half brother, Pedajah, before they make their journey to winter camp. I was going to make the journey with them until I met you, and now, I must meet them as arranged so they don't worry. Would you like to accompany me, or are you too frightened to meet the savage side of my family?"

"Cal, don't speak so of your family. I'd like very much to meet them, as long as we can be back in time for Nat's supper tomorrow? I wouldn't want to miss that."

"Indeed. The rendezvous spot is a two-hour ride from here. We'll be back this evening." With a twinkle in his eye, he added, "Good thing you are coming along. Otherwise, I'd be worrying about leaving you alone with a pasture full of militia men. You might take it in your head to go dancing naked in the moonlit meadow. After all, there'll be a full moon again this night."

Summer laughed at their private joke, her face flushing a pretty pink. But Hannah was aghast. She clucked her tongue furiously.

"Hannah," Summer said, trying to reassure her, "Cal is being frivolous. Do not take him so seriously." Summer scowled at Caleb, warning him to curb his tongue.

Reassured, Hannah packed them a lunch of bread, goat cheese, and cider to take along, all the while lecturing them on the hazards of traveling through the wilderness.

Summer dressed in Nat's clothing for the arduous journey and decided to take along her shoulder strap purse. Worn across her body, it was a handy knapsack to carry her personal items, and it still held her things from the twentieth century. She had a feeling she would have need of the Advil before the long trip was over.

They rode in silence at first, enjoying each other's company and the crisp fall air, while the countryside became wilder and more beautiful with each passing mile. The trees were at the height of color now, vivid in rich reds and golds, and the sight of them took her breath away. Never had she seen such lovely unspoiled landscape. And what a way to enjoy it, riding through the natural beauty, instead of whizzing by on a highway, as she had done so often in her own time.

She was eager to meet Cal's mother and to see Indians in an environment extinct to the world she came from. Her interest in anthropology was too strong for her not to be curious. Besides, this trip would give her one more day of reprieve before telling John and Elizabeth that she was marrying Cal. She needed that reprieve desperately, for telling them would be the hardest thing she had ever done.

Cal talked about his people after a while, telling her they were Pocumtucks, the few remaining members of a once powerful tribe, now decimated by white man's diseases and war with the Mohawks. The few Pocumtucks left were scattered now, or traveled with other friendly tribes such as the Scatacooks, the tribe his mother and brother had joined.

Summer's bottom was getting sore from the long ride, and her legs chafed from rubbing against the sides of her horse, but Cal assured her that the wilderness path they now followed would take them directly to the Indian camp. The path followed a fast-moving river that wended its way through the forest at the bottom of a steep mountain.

When at last they reached their destination, Summer saw curls of smoke rising lazily above the curtain of trees that hugged the river, and a craggy overhang that jutted out from the bottom of the incline. A group of Indians sat under the overhang, while others gathered around the fires.

It was a tranquil scene, until Caleb let out a bloodcurdling war whoop to greet his people, startling Summer and making her horse rear in fright. She held tight, squeezing her legs together to keep from falling.

Cal's war whoop was answered in kind by the Indians, whereupon Cal jumped from his horse and ran to greet the young brave running toward him.

Summer watched as the men embraced, then were joined by other braves, who all took turns embracing Cal and slapping him heartily on the back. The first Indian that Cal had greeted now turned to look at her with curiosity, and she remembered that she had on Nat's clothes, her long hair hidden under a tricorn hat.

Cal laughed when he saw the brave's curious glance. "Summer, take off your hat so my brother can get a good look."

Summer smiled, sweeping the hat from her head, her hair cascading down to her waist. She ran her fingers through it, shaking it into place. The Indian brave's eyes widened on his otherwise placid face.

"Pedajah, this is Summer Winslow, my betrothed. We are to marry soon."

Pedajah walked over to Summer, still sitting on her horse, and took her hand, shaking it vigorously. "I am happy to meet Cal's woman. It pleases me that his journey through life will no longer be that of the lone wolf." Pedajah turned to his brother. "I am sad, even so, that my brother will no longer walk with the Pocumtucks."

"Pedajah," Cal said, putting his hand on the brave's shoulder. "I'll not forsake my mother's people. We will always be brothers. Nothing can break that bond. Now, tell me. Where is my mother? Why do I not see her beautiful face among my greeters?"

"Caleb, it grieves me to tell you, our mother is not well. A half-day's journey from here she stepped in a metal trap meant for the beaver. Her foot is badly injured. We must pray the gods do not let bad blood possess her foot, for she will surely perish."

"Take me to her."

Leading the way, Pedajah put his arm around Caleb's shoulders. "It is good you are here. She will not take the medicine of the Scatacook shaman."

"Why is that? Surely she wants to get well."

"He is not a Pocumtuck. That is the reason. She grieves for the old days, and for her people who are scattered on the four winds. It is different with me. My father was a Scatacook, my wife and child are of these people. I trust in their ways."

Summer dismounted and followed Cal and his half brother to a pallet of reeds, where Cal's mother lay.

"Mother," Cal said, kneeling to embrace her. "Those damn fur traders and their infernal metal traps! Why do they not hunt the beaver as we do, instead of sitting on their fat rumps, waiting for the trap to do the work for them?"

"Hush, my son, do not blame them for my stupidity. Had I been more careful where I walked, this would not have happened." Nenepownam looked past her son to where Summer stood shyly. "Come closer, child, and let me look at you. Let me see the woman who has lightened my son's steps and put joy in his heart."

Summer stepped closer and knelt beside Cal. She held her hand out to the Indian woman. "I am sorry for your injury, Nenepownam, it must be very painful."

"Yes, it is so. But Pocumtuck women are born to pain. I will survive it."

Summer gazed into Nenepownam's face, beautiful despite the pain etched there. Her eyes were golden brown and fringed with heavy black lashes, and her high, finely shaped cheekbones gave her an exotically beautiful look. No wonder John's father had fallen in love with her.

"Mother, you're coming back to Deerfield with us. There's no way you can make the trip to winter camp on that foot. And I'll not have you dragged on a travois."

Nenepownam looked at him with shiny eyes. "As you say, my son. It will give me a chance to get to know your bride."

Looking at the mangled foot, Summer remembered that she had her purse with her. "Cal, I have medicine in my bag. Very powerful medicine. It will kill any, uh, bad blood in her foot. I have a painkiller, too." She rummaged through her purse searching for the vial of penicillin. She knew it was there, because she remembered telling John what it was the day he had taken such delight in the contents of her purse.

She found the vial and the container of Advil, and sprinkled the right amount in her hand.

Nenepownam looked with suspicion at the little things Summer offered her, then looking into Summer's wide blue eyes and trusting what she saw there, swallowed them with water from Cal's canteen.

After awhile, the Indian woman dozed, and Cal moved to a circle of men by the fire, leaving Summer to her own devices. She turned her attention to a young squaw with a chubby, year-old baby, trying to

Now you can get Heartfire Romances
right at home and save

Heartfire Romance

Get Four Free and Receive A $1.00 Rebate!

Home Subscription Members can enjoy
Heartfire Romances and Save $$$$$
each month.

get the child to walk. He would take a step or two, then fall down.

Summer made her way over to the woman and gestured to her. The woman understood and aimed her wobbly child in her direction. Summer held her arms out to the baby, who walked right into them, attracted by her bright hair. His chubby fingers grasped a handful of hair, pulling hard. The two women laughed, delighting the baby; he let go of Summer's hair and clapped his hands together, victorious at his achievement.

Cal heard the musical laughter and turned to see Summer with the baby in her arms. His love for her grew as he gazed at the beautiful maternal sight, and he envisioned strong, healthy sons and daughters, brought into the world by their love. It pleased him greatly, and pleased him also to see how easily she made herself at home with these people he loved. Not many white women could do that.

Pedajah, too, saw Summer holding the baby, and saw the contented way Cal looked at her. He had hoped Cal would find a woman of the Five Nations to marry, but he could see now that Caleb's fate had been determined. The woman with the sunshine hair owned his heart.

The young squaw steered Summer over to a group of women and, with hand signaling and facial gestures, the women communicated, giggling and laughing over their efforts.

Summer admired the leather dresses they wore, especially the ones made from doeskin. Soft and velvety, they were bleached white and smelled of fine leather. The Indian women, in truth, were fascinated by what Summer wore. They had never seen a white woman wearing breeches before. It was a topic discussed with much interest.

When Summer realized they were talking about her unusual outfit, she posed for them, holding imaginary reins and galloping an imaginary horse. The Indian women laughed, nodding their heads in understanding.

After a while, the men joined the women, and they ate venison cooked over an open fire. Summer thought she had never tasted anything so delicious, and filled her belly with the tasty meat. She liked these people. Cal's people. Loved listening to the low, husky voices of the braves, a genetic trait that would be handed down for generations, for she knew the Native Americans of the twentieth century spoke in the same deep, but gentle tones.

Summer hated to leave the peaceful scene, reluctant to face the turmoil that awaited her back in Deerfield, and her stomach turned over just thinking of it. But all too soon, it was time to go. She mounted her horse, waving goodbye to the Indians gathered around her. Nenepownam was carried to Cal's horse and set up behind him, and her belongings were put in saddlebags and laid over the flank of Summer's mare.

When they had been riding a while, Nenepownam announced that the little white and red things had worked, her pain was greatly relieved. Cal gave Summer a grateful smile.

Summer was surprised at how well Nenepownam spoke English. She supposed that was due to Cal's influence, but also because of John and Elizabeth, who had spent a lot of time with the Indian woman as well. She wondered how Jessica would take the news of Nenepownam moving in with Cal. But then, since Jessica had raised Nenepownam's son, there probably wasn't any animosity between them, unlike herself and Elizabeth. But the animosity was all on Elizabeth's side. Summer had strong feelings about Elizabeth, but none of them hostile. She admired Elizabeth's wild beauty and independent way, and dreaded having to tell her about marrying Cal, every bit as much as she dreaded telling John.

Every mile they rode brought them closer to that confrontation, and her stomach started to act up again. She felt nauseated and light-headed, and had a hard time keeping up with Cal. If just thinking about it could cause her to be sick, how was she going to be when she actually faced them?

She wanted desperately to stop and rest, but one look at Nenepownam's mangled foot put that thought out of her mind. The Indian woman needed to be in bed with her poor foot propped up.

Thankfully, it wasn't long before she could make out the two familiar houses separated by the pasture, now filled with tents of the militia.

In the distance, a figure started out toward them. As it drew closer, Summer saw it was John on Shadow. Her pulse quickened as it always did at the sight of him. He looked so masculine and proud riding his black stallion.

She watched as he galloped up, drawing to a halt abruptly in front of them. The expression on his face was stern, until he saw the small form of Nenepownam and her hurt foot.

John's face softened. "How did it happen?"

"Beaver trap. I'm taking her to my house. There's no way she can make the trip to winter camp."

"Of course," John answered, "I'll bring Elizabeth over with her poultices." Then turning his head toward Summer, he finally acknowledged her presence. In a subdued voice, he said, "Summer, you look tired." Pulling on his reins, he turned Shadow and rode toward his home.

Summer was stunned. Is that all he had to say? And the way he said it, with no feeling! It was not the John Hawke she was used to. Not the fighting man who always got what he wanted, one way or another. Had he finally resigned himself to the fact that he could never have her? She knew she should feel relieved, but instead, she longed for the John who had so fervently pursued her. She was desolate as they rode up to Cal's house, where a very anxious Hannah ran out to greet them.

Cal carried his mother upstairs to his room and gently settled her on his bed, while Hannah clucked around her like a mother hen. In no time, Nenepownam was in one of Hannah's nightgowns, which swam on her small frame, and sitting up in bed.

Elizabeth came flying into the room carrying her medicine bag, greeting Nenepownam warmly. "It has been too long since my eyes have gazed on you. You're as beautiful as I remember." Embracing her, she added, "Let me look at your injury."

Very gently, Elizabeth lifted Nenepownam's foot and looked at the wound with an experienced eye. She felt the woman's forehead, shaking her head. "Cal, your mother has a fever. Not a good sign. My poultices may work, but only time will tell."

"Elizabeth," Summer said hesitantly, "I, uh, I gave Nenepownam some medicine that I had from . . . Boston. It will kill the infection, I'm sure. And I have pain pills, too. She needs to take them every four hours, if they are to do her any good. In fact, she should take some right now."

Elizabeth couldn't believe what she heard. Did this woman dare to interfere with her healing, too? Was there no end to her conceit? "Summer, I think I know best what is right for Nenepownam. It would do well for you to stay out of matters you know nothing of."

196

Summer held back her tears. Elizabeth's ignorance of penicillin could cost Nenepownam her foot. She looked to Cal for guidance.

"Elizabeth," Cal said with authority. "If Summer says her medicine will help Mother's foot, then we are going to use it. There's no reason why your medicine should interfere with Summer's. And, Hannah, see to it she receives it as Summer prescribes."

Elizabeth was furious, but it wouldn't do to show it. Nenepownam needed her. How could Cal be so blinded by that woman? "Very well," she said in an icy voice. "If you'll give me room, I'll apply the poultices."

Cal grabbed Summer's arm and steered her quietly out the door. "You look exhausted, Summer. I think you should go to bed. I'll send Hannah up with some supper for you."

Summer was too tired to argue. "All right, Cal, but no supper. I've been feeling sick since we started our ride home, and it seems to be getting worse. A good night's sleep will do me good."

Cal looked worried. "Why didn't you say something? We could have stopped somewhere, rested for a while 'til you felt better."

"I thought it more important to get your mother home as soon as possible. She was suffering more than I. Please don't worry. I'll be fine."

Cal felt her forehead. In 1744 every sickness was worried over, for too often the mildest cold turned to a raging fever that ravaged the body, the smallest cuts could mean agonizing death. One never knew. Her forehead was cool to the touch. "Mayhap you are overly tired from our long ride."

"Yes, that's all it is. Well, good night then, I had a lovely time today. And Cal . . . I like the savage side of your family."

197

Smiling tiredly, she reached up on her toes and kissed his cheek, then went to her room at the end of the hall.

A candle was lit, and a fire burned invitingly in the fireplace. Hannah was, as always, thoughtful. Summer undressed, slipped into her nightgown, and sank into the luxuriousness of the feather bed. But she was not to rest in peace. Angry voices sounded from the hallway. The door burst open, and an angry John pushed his way in, followed by a solemn-faced Cal.

Striding over to her bed, John shouted, "Look at her. She's exhausted. Whatever possessed you to take her on such a long, dangerous journey? No wonder she's ill."

"John, you should know, Summer is no longer your concern."

Summer's heart raced. Oh, no. Cal was going to tell John right here and now about the betrothal. A surge of nausea swept over her.

"Summer and—" Cal stopped when he saw Summer dash from the bed and over to the chamber pot in the corner. She made it just in time, as her stomach lurched and she spewed her dinner into the ceramic pot.

Chapter Eighteen

John and Cal stood rooted to the spot, helpless and horror-stricken as Summer continued to retch violently. Cal came to his senses first, yelling loudly for Hannah, who came running in, fear showing on her round little face.

Hannah saw her little lamb bent over the chamber pot and drew in her breath sharply. She sent the men from the room with a scalding tongue. "Don't let me see your faces in this room again tonight. The poor child is in need of rest. Now scat!"

Hannah helped Summer back to bed and cleaned her face with a cool cloth. "There, there, Lamby, Hannah is here. She's going to take good care of you."

Summer sank back in the bed, grateful for Hannah's presence, and was soon asleep, reassured that Hannah was there to watch over her. In the morning she felt better, except for a slight nausea when she saw Hannah with a tray of food. "How is Nenepownam? I'm sorry I added to your burden last night. I don't know what came over me. Must have been the venison I ate at the Indian camp."

"'Tis my fault, Lamby. I should have known

better than to let Cal take a delicate creature like you on such a long trip into the wilderness. What was I thinking of? You could have been scalped by bloodthirsty savages."

Summer smiled to herself. She had never considered herself a delicate creature.

"As for Cal's mother, she's improved in great measure. Her forehead is cool this morning. 'Tis certain your medicine be working good. Elizabeth's poultices, too. Drawing the badness right out of her foot, it is. Elizabeth stayed the night. Slept on a pallet in Nenepownam's room. Right fond of that Indian she is. But then, the two of them are so much alike—wild things."

"Where's John? Did he stay the night, too?"

"No, I sent him back to his own home with Alisha. I had my hands full enough. Didn't need another underfoot. Went willing enough, too. Never saw a man look so helpless, as when he saw how ill you be. I don't know what we're going to do with that man. Believe you me, I don't want to be the one who tells him about you and Cal."

Summer's stomach lurched at the mention of telling John. "Hannah, take the food away. I can't eat."

Hannah looked at her closely. "You look a mite peaked, child. Are you sure it's just bad food making you feel poorly?"

"Of course, I'm sure. I'll be fine. Stop worrying."

Once the nausea passed, Summer got dressed and went to Cal's room to check on Nenepownam. The Indian woman was sitting up in bed, working on a deerskin dress. Summer brushed her fingers over the leather, luxuriating in the soft, velvety feel of it. "You must truly feel like a princess wearing such a dress."

Nenepownam smiled warmly. "And you, will you feel like a princess when you wear it? It is my marriage gift to you. The dress is a ceremonial one, like those worn by Pocumtuck women at their marriage ceremony."

Tears came to Summer's eyes. "Nenepownam, how thoughtful of you. I don't know what to say."

"There is nothing to say. It is only fitting for me to make this dress for you, since Hannah tells me your own mother does not live near by."

At that moment, Summer felt an incredible loneliness for her mother. Was she still grieving for her lost daughter?

Nenepownam saw the sorrow on Summer's face, and her hand reached out to touch Summer's. "Do not be sad, Summer. My son loves you very much. He told me so last night, though he didn't have to. I could see it on his face. He will make you happy and will give you many babies to play with. And think of this, your name will be Summer Hawke, an appropriate name for the bride of an Indian prince. Is it not so?"

Summer laughed through her tears. "Yes, it is so."

Elizabeth walked into the room just then, and saw the warm exchange between Summer and Nenepownam. Her eyes narrowed and her heart constricted. Once more, this woman came between her and those she held dear.

Summer exited the room as soon as Elizabeth came in, alarmed by the look on her face, wanting to put distance between them.

Cal was waiting for her down in the parlor. "I was just about to brave Hannah's fortress to see how you were doing." He drew her into his arms and kissed her.

Summer quickly pushed him away. "Cal, don't.

201

Elizabeth might come down and see us."

"And what if she does? Are you afraid of Elizabeth Hawke?"

Summer nodded her head solemnly.

"But why? She is but a small, frail thing next to you. You've faced fiercer creatures than she but a few days ago."

"I know. It's foolish. But she's the one person in the world I am truly frightened of."

Cal shook his head. "Then, darling, I won't let go of your hand for an instant, but I think it's time to tell her of our marriage. Look—I see the fiercesome creature now, coming down the stairs. Be brave, my darling, no harm will befall you while you are with me."

Summer held tight to Cal's hand as Elizabeth walked toward them, her silver eyes locked onto Cal's. Summer could see she was upset.

"Nenepownam tells me the deerskin dress she is making is for Summer. For her wedding to you. Tell me she's mistaken, Cal. Tell me you are not going to marry her."

Summer's hands started shaking, and Cal held her even tighter. "Yes. 'Tis true," he said quietly, his blue eyes shining brightly. "Be happy for us, Elizabeth."

Elizabeth held onto the back of a chair for support. She closed her eyes tightly, then opened them, a strange sad look impressed on her face. "Must I be happy that Summer lay with my husband in carnal sin and, not satisfied with just him, now seeks gratification in your arms as well?"

Caleb's anger flared. "Elizabeth, watch carefully how you speak of my betrothed. Summer has not slept with your husband. You can be assured of that."

"Oh?" Elizabeth's voice was filled with anguish

and pain. "Look to her face, Cal. See the guilt written there."

Cal turned to look at Summer, afraid of what he would find, and under his direct gaze, she turned her head away.

Summer could stand up to anything but Elizabeth, and the guilt she felt over her love for John.

Caleb was stunned by the guilt so naked on her face.

"Cal, oh Cal," she cried, turning her head to look at him once more, her eyes shining bright with tears, her voice choked with emotion. "I'm so sorry, I—"

Pain pierced Cal's heart too strong to bear. He had given freely of his love, thinking her untouched by his brother; had believed her when he had found her that day in John's bedroom. She said she had not bedded him, the lie tripping off her tongue so easily. What kind of a woman was she? "My God, Summer. Who else have you bedded? 'Tis no wonder Daniel is in such a dither over you. Has he sampled your charms, too? And what of Nat? He—"

Summer's hand struck Cal full on the face, the sound echoing flatly in the silent room.

Cal slapped her back, his face turning white when he realized what he had done. But he couldn't apologize, his hurt was too great. Instead, he turned and strode out of the house.

Summer's face stung. She wanted to rub it, but wouldn't give Elizabeth the satisfaction of seeing that. What was a slap compared to the pain Cal must be feeling. He wasn't a violent man. Far from it. He must be hurting deeply to strike out like that. "Well, Elizabeth. You've won this battle. Cal won't marry me now. But your victory is shallow, for you'll never have him either."

Fire shone in Elizabeth's eyes. "I'll at least have the

satisfaction of knowing you will never lie with him again."

"And what about John, Elizabeth? Doesn't it matter to you that I've made love to your husband? Your husband, Elizabeth. Don't you care about that at all?"

The vehemence was stronger now. "My husband? Never my husband, but in name. A woman needs more than that to be a wife." Overcome with sobs, Elizabeth ran from the room in tears.

Summer stood frozen, reliving the terrible scene over and over in her head. Sitting by the window, she stared out at the dreary morning, watching as dark clouds rolled overhead. Indian summer was clearly over, and winter beginning. A distinct chill was in the air. Would she ever feel warm again?

What lay ahead for her? It seemed certain that she would be spending the rest of her life in this century, and it occurred to her, ironically, that that was exactly what she wanted. *She wanted to stay, even though she could never be with John.*

In the few short weeks since she had touched the sword and come to this ancient world, she had been deeply entwined in the eighteenth-century way of life, and had never felt more alive. The people she met here were more dear to her than anyone she had ever known in her other life, with the exception of her own family. It was as if she had been sleepwalking her way through life before, and had not awakened until she came here. That was exactly how she felt, and realizing that, she felt as if a weight had been lifted from her shoulders.

She had no idea what the future would bring. Whom she would marry, or if she would marry at all. But somehow, she would work it out. She was hopelessly in love with one man, betrothed and rejected by another, but she would work it out. She was in almost constant danger of being raped and murdered by marauding Indians and scurrilous Frenchmen, but she still wanted to make a life for herself in this wild, precarious place. Because, for better or worse, this was where she truly belonged.

Chapter Nineteen

Every room in the house smelled deliciously of baked, roasted, and boiled foods, setting Summer's stomach to rumbling with hunger after losing her dinner the night before. Not to mention breakfast this morning. But she didn't dare eat. She couldn't take the chance of being sick again. This was the day of the Osborne supper, and there was still much to do.

Hannah put her to work in the kitchen, after Summer assured her repeatedly that she was feeling up to it. She helped Hannah bake apple and mince pies, and bread enough to feed the entire militia. Other delicious concoctions already cooked sat on the trestle table ready for delivery to Jessica's. No one went hungry when Hannah cooked. It was a matter of pride with her.

When all the food was cooked and the kitchen scrubbed clean, then and only then did Summer turn to thoughts of the long evening ahead of her. She would have to face Cal's look of betrayal and Elizabeth's accusing eyes.

She took special care in getting ready for the supper, dressing in emerald green, a color that set off her red gold hair to perfection, and made her eyes look all the bluer by contrast. Hannah was dressed in her best Sunday-go-to-meeting dress of dark brown, her inevitable apron worn over it. Charles was dressed in slate gray breeches and matching wool jerkin, and looked exceedingly uncomfortable and fidgety. She knew how much he hated the tight confines of jackets of any sort. But Hannah took no pity on him, insisting the Osbornes' first impression would be a favorable one.

Nenepownam wore an elaborately beaded leather dress—much like the one she was making for Summer—and looked every inch the Indian princess. Her injured foot made it impossible for her to walk, so Charles carried her to the wagon and sat her next to him on the seat. The others would have to ride in the carriage, for the wagon was loaded with food dishes, plus a keg of Charles's finest apple jack.

When the wagon pulled up in front of Jessica's house, her black servant came out to help unload the food. Otis was an elderly man, tall, stiff-backed, with pure white hair that curled around his ears, easing the look of austerity that emanated from his every pore.

Jessica, resplendent in lavender silk, embraced everyone as they entered the house. It had been a long time since she had entertained so many, not since her husband had died, in fact, but this was a very special occasion.

The sight of Nenepownam startled Jessica for a moment. Caleb had mentioned his natural mother was staying with him because of some injury, but she had forgotten it in all the excitement of Nat's betrothal. She hid her surprise and greeted Nenepownam warmly, seeing she was comfortably seated with a pillow under her hurt foot.

Nenepownam handled the meeting with Jessica with aplomb. She was a princess to her people, no matter how few of them were left, and she was not easily intimidated. Besides, she had warm feelings for the woman who had raised her son so well. She had always been grateful to Jessica for not preventing her from seeing Cal each summer, as most women would have done.

Summer headed straight for the parlor, eager to meet Charity and her parents. She found Mr. Osborne standing by the fireplace with a very nervous Nathaniel. Charity and her mother sat in chairs that flanked the fireplace.

Nat's fact brightened when Summer walked into the room, and he was quick to introduce her to the Osbornes. They seemed typical of what Summer thought homesteaders should look like, rugged, weatherbeaten, with tanned faces and plain dress. Very much like Hannah and Charles.

Charity was a surprise though, tall, well-formed; she had the face of an angel. Her hair was so light in color it was almost white, shimmering like silver in the light of the fire. No wonder Nat had fallen so fast. Charity's demeanor was friendly, and the light in her eyes whenever she looked Nat's way, matched his own.

Summer was happy for Nat. He and Charity seemed so perfectly matched, and she couldn't help thinking how wonderful it would be if she and John could be together in the same way.

John came in then and her gaze followed him. He was dressed in the brown velvet that he had worn the night of the ball, and seeing him in it brought back a flood of memories of their moonlight ride. He looked her way and caught her staring at him, his face taking on a strange, haunted look, and she turned away, unable to withstand the torment she felt.

Cal walked in; Summer could tell he had been drinking. She hadn't seen him since he slapped her face, and was relieved he hadn't ridden off to join Pedajah at winter camp. When he looked at her she could see the pain in his face and wished, somehow, that she could erase it.

Nat walked over to greet him, and Summer could see Cal struggling to put on a good front for Nat's sake. He needn't have worried. Nat was too nervous to notice anything.

Jessica's eyes didn't miss much though, or Elizabeth's either. Elizabeth was paying close attention to Cal, her eyes darting to him every few seconds. But Cal was oblivious to her glances, or seemed to be. Summer had never seen him so quiet. But when Alisha came into the room dressed prettily in white muslin, Cal became suddenly attentive, staring at the little girl as if he had never seen her before.

Otis announced supper, and they all filed into the dining room, their voices rising in anticipation of the tasty meal. The huge table was loaded with bowls heaped high with food, and each place was set with individual trenchers. No one had to share a trencher in Jessica's house.

The amount of silver cutlery dazzled the Osbornes. The Hawkes must truly be rich to own so many forks, a luxury in this rural community. The Osbornes were impressed by the extravagance, and were puffed with pride that their daughter would be marrying into such a fine family.

Summer no sooner sat down, then the nausea rose in her throat and she felt dizzy. She tried to hide her sickness from the others, not wanting to spoil the supper for Nat and Charity, but Jessica soon noticed how pale she was.

"Summer, dear. What is it? You look white."

Everyone looked at Summer, causing her further discomfort. "I'm sorry, Jessica. It seems I'm indisposed. I'm afraid I'll have to forgo the meal. Mayhap if I lie down awhile, I'll feel better." She stood up unsteadily, holding the table for support.

John and Caleb were instantly on their feet, but they weren't fast enough. Hannah moved swiftly to Summer's side.

"My poor lamb. Still feeling poorly? Let me take ye upstairs. Jessica won't mind if you use her bed a spell."

"Yes, yes, take the child upstairs. I'll be up in a while to look at her. John! Caleb! Sit! We didn't cook all this food to feed the pigs."

The two brothers hesitated, then obeyed their mother's command, but they eyes followed Summer as Hannah helped her from the room.

Summer lay on Jessica's bed, fighting down the increasing nausea. The venison. It had to be that. Surely it wasn't one of the terrible diseases of the eighteenth century, like typhoid, smallpox, or heaven forbid, the plague. She would feel better soon, after all the excitement over Nat and Charity's wedding died down. Not to mention her own wedding to Cal. That is, if he still wanted her. Her stomach churned, as it did every time she thought of marrying Cal. Was that it? Was she sick because she couldn't bear the thought of marrying anyone but John? The one man she couldn't have.

Jessica brought up a charger of cider which went down nicely, and after a while the nausea subsided, and Summer joined the festivities again.

She was surprised to find that the Osbornes would be spending the night at Cal's house. In the morning, Hannah and Charles would accompany them back to their homestead.

It seems the two couples had much in common, and had become fast friends in the course of the evening. Hannah and Charles were going to help the Osbornes pack up their things and move to town. Since the hostilities had heated up, the Osbornes felt uneasy staying so far from town. John had concurred, grateful his militia would have one less outlying family to worry over.

Jessica took the opportunity to convince Charity to stay in town with her, and Charity was all too eager to comply. It would be much easier making wedding plans, if she were at Jessica's.

Alisha, caught up in all the excitement, didn't want to be left out. She begged her mother to let her stay overnight with her grandmother, and Elizabeth readily agreed. Cal looked so forlorn, she wanted to be free to help him if he allowed.

But Cal seemed in no hurry to leave Jessica's. Obviously drunk, he was sprawled out on the floor before the fire, as everyone made ready to leave.

Sleeping arrangements were made for the Osbornes once they returned to Cal's. They would sleep in Summer's room, and she would move in with Nenepownam.

Hannah would gladly have given up her bed for Summer, but Summer wouldn't hear of it. "Hannah, you and Charles have more need of a bed than I. You'll be getting up at the crack of dawn, riding in that bumpy old wagon for miles. Are you sure you're up to this trip?"

"If the truth be known, I'd rather stay here all cozy and warm, but with Charles and meself helping out, the Osbornes will be able to move out of that isolated farm all the sooner. And it won't be soon enough to suit me. I don't trust them French devils, or the savages that do their bidding. I'll rest a lot easier when the Osbornes are back with us. It'll be crowded, until they can find a place of their own in town, but we'll manage just fine. I'm just sorry you have to give up your room."

"Don't be, Hannah. It's the least I can do. I'll move my things in with Nenepownam. It'll give me a chance to get better acquainted. We'll be just fine. Like one big happy family."

Hannah's eyes became shiny and wet. She hugged Summer to her ample bosom. "Yes, Lamby Pie, one big happy family."

By the time Summer got out of bed next morning, Hannah and Charles had left with the Osbornes. She wandered through the house, lonely already for the sound of Hannah's cheerful voice sounding through the rooms, and was glad that Nenepownam was there to keep her from feeling completely desolate.

Summer made the Indian woman some breakfast and chatted with her awhile, careful to avoid any mention of weddings. She didn't want to say anything to Cal's mother about canceling the wedding, until she had talked to Cal. When Nenepownam tired, she went downstairs and sat at the kitchen window sipping hot tea.

It was raining again. The perfect setting for her somber mood. She thought of poor Hannah and Charles, riding through the miserable cold rain in their open wagon, then consoled herself with the thought that by now, it was possible that they had reached the Osborne place, and were being warmed by a cozy fire.

She sat, reflecting on the last tumultuous days. Glad they were behind her. Suddenly, the door was flung open, and a wet and disheveled Caleb stood in the doorway weaving back and forth.

"Cal, you look terrible. Let me help you upstairs. You've got to get out of those wet clothes, before you catch cold." Putting her arm around his waist, she helped him inside, closing the door against the driving rain.

"No! Far better you remove your clothes and get on your hands and knees, so I may service you as you deserve—like a bitch in heat."

Summer was shocked and hurt by Caleb's bitter words, but she swallowed her pride, knowing he was drunk and striking back at her because he hurt so terribly. "Cal, please, let me help you."

"Yes, yes, help me. Give me what I need." Cal grabbed at her, pulling her roughly up against him with one arm, while he hiked up her skirt and groped underneath it with his free hand.

Summer struggled with him unsuccessfully, until the door blew open again and Elizabeth appeared in the doorway, her eyes taking in the sordid scene. Removing the shawl that had been used to shelter her from the rain, she stared at Summer as if it were *she* who was attacking Cal, instead of the other way around.

"Don't just stand there, Elizabeth. Help me with this drunken oaf, since it's your fault he's in this condition. I'm trying to get him upstairs."

Elizabeth glared at Summer, then moved to Cal's side, taking one arm while Summer took the other.

"Ah, another beauty to service," Cal slurred, looking at Elizabeth through bleary eyes. "How lucky can one man be?"

Elizabeth and Summer struggled up the stairs with Cal, and into Summer's room, the journey made more difficult by Cal's wandering hands.

"Help me get him out of these wet clothes," Summer panted, out of breath from lugging Cal up the stairs. "What are you doing here anyway, in this awful rain?"

"To attend to Nenepownam."

Summer started untying Cal's shirt. "Help me undress him. He's too heavy to manage by myself."

"You can't be serious. It would be highly improper."

"Since when have you cared so much about propriety? You'd think you've never seen a naked man before. I dare say you have, else Alisha would not be born."

With Elizabeth's help, Summer undressed Caleb, while he weaved back and forth precariously, his hands groping at the women's clothing.

"Ah, this is the stuff dreams are made of," he proclaimed lustily, hugging the women to his body. "Two luscious women taking me to bed. Do with me what you will, I'll try to endure."

Summer rolled her eyes at Elizabeth, but Elizabeth wasn't amused by any of this. Finally, there was nothing left to remove but Cal's wet breeches.

"Pull his breeches off. I can't hold him much longer."

Elizabeth's fingers were shaking too hard to unbutton him, so Summer took over, impatiently tugging the breeches down around his ankles. Cal lost his balance and toppled backward onto the bed, taking the two women with him. He started laughing, and with his arms still wrapped around them, pulled the women closer.

"Have patience, there's enough of me to content you both."

Summer had a hard time keeping a straight face. He was really quite funny when he was drunk, but when she looked across Cal's body to Elizabeth, she saw Elizabeth staring down at Cal with a strange expression on her face.

Summer sought the spot where Elizabeth's eyes were so fervently locked, and realized that she was staring at Caleb's fully aroused manhood. Understanding flooded her. It was desire written on Elizabeth's face,. That, and so much more.

It had been five years since Elizabeth and Cal had been lovers. Five years since she had seen him naked, or lain in his arms—any man's arms by the look of it.

John had said that they had never consummated their marriage, and she hadn't believed him, until now. Seeing the hunger on Elizabeth's face, she knew it could be true.

That one deep understanding melted Summer's heart. She was no longer afraid of Elizabeth. The silver-eyed, raven-haired beauty held tight in Cal's arms, was not some supernatural being bent on harming her. Elizabeth was a woman, vulnerable in her love for the naked man she looked at with such passion. And, with that understanding, came the knowledge that she could never marry Cal.

Summer suddenly felt lonelier than she had ever been in her life. Extricating herself from Cal, she climbed off the bed and said, "I leave Cal to your tender mercies, Elizabeth."

Walking to the door, she hesitated, then added, "Cal knows the truth about Alisha. I think it's time you two talked."

Summer saw the panic that leapt into Elizabeth's eyes, as she slowly closed the door on the star-crossed lovers.

Chapter Twenty

Summer's parting words stunned Elizabeth. For five years she had lived with the lie of Alisha's birth, and now, in one casual sentence, her secret was revealed. She could only pray that Caleb was too drunk to understand what had been said.

Feeling Caleb's arm loosen around her, she rolled away and climbed out of bed, unnerved by the overpowering sight of Cal's aroused state. Taking a quilt from a nearby chair, she covered his nakedness, unable to focus on anything else as long as he lay there exposed. She started to leave, when Cal called to her.

"Don't go, Elizabeth."

She waited fearfully for Cal to continue, dreading what he would say.

"Is it true? Is Alisha my daughter?"

"Yes," she said, turning to face the only man she had ever loved.

Cal let the information sink in before he spoke, his voice filled with emotion. "We've never spoken of why I left, or how I felt when I came back and found you married to John. But it must be spoken of now, to make things right between us. I did love you—God knows—but when my father died, I didn't know which world I belonged to. I was torn in two, but never by my love for you. I ached to come to you, to ask you to leave with me, but I couldn't. What kind of life could I have offered you in the forest? How could I ask you to give up a comfortable and civilized life here, and trek through the wilderness as the wife of a savage. It was unthinkable."

"Unthinkable?" Elizabeth choked on the words. "Leaving me without a word, without so much as a wave goodbye, *that* was unthinkable! Didn't you know how much I loved you? Didn't you know I would have gladly followed you *anywhere?*"

Cal had never seen Elizabeth so overwrought. This was not the cool, unruffled woman he knew.

"Cal, oh Cal, how could you have thought I would mind leaving here, where I have never fit in? Didn't you know me at all? I have always preferred the open way of your mother's people to the restricted, demanding life here. I am more Indian than you, Caleb Hawke. Your mother taught me well."

"Elizabeth," he said soothingly, hoping to calm her down. "I thought of you as a delicate flower. A lily that thrives as long as it is given special care, is protected from the harsh elements, a flower that would wither and die if transplanted into the wilderness. You are so small, so delicately built, I thought you would never be able to withstand the rigorous life in the wilderness."

"You set me on a pedestal without looking to see if I wanted to be on it. Have you not seen the wild lilies growing by the side of the pond? They come up each spring unattended by anyone, and they are as beautiful, nay, even more beautiful than the ones that grow in Jessica's garden. I would have thrived in the forest, Cal. I would have gloried in being with the man I loved. How could you not know that?"

"I never realized . . . I was a fool. If only you had married anyone but my brother, I would have fought for you. But when I returned and found you married to John, it ended right there."

"Oh, Cal, Cal . . ."

"Don't say it. Don't say anything. It's too late for words. It's too late for us." Caleb turned his face to the wall, hiding his pain.

Elizabeth thought of telling him that her marriage to John was in name only, but it would only humiliate her, and would make no difference to this honorable man. She was defeated.

Raising her hand to open the door, she hesitated, unable to bring herself to give up so easily. She had loved this man all her life. She would fight for the love they once shared. The love she still felt so strongly.

She turned back to Cal once more, finding him still facing the wall, rejecting her as he had five years ago. No! Not this time. Today he would not turn his back on her. With trembling fingers, she removed her clothes, letting them fall in a heap on the floor.

Standing there, naked and vulnerable, with only her love to sheath her, she cried huskily, "Cal. Look at me."

Cal's head turned slowly, his bleary eyes opening wide at the sight of her small, shapely, naked body.

"Elizabeth, in the name of God, don't do this!"

Elizabeth walked over to the bed, and with a slow deliberate movement, removed the cover from Caleb's aroused body. She climbed on the bed, straddling him with her legs, and eased herself over his hardness. Pushing down, she felt the deep piercing, and wondered at the sensation it caused in her. The fit was tight, it had been so long, but the pleasure she felt far outweighed the discomfort.

Caleb moaned, helpless to resist the desire that overcame him. He pulled her down to his chest, then rolled over, until he lay on top.

The feel of Caleb's skin against hers sent a deep sensation through her, a shudder of pure pleasure undulating along her body, as she gave herself up to the wild feelings that possessed her. Her fingernails raked down Cal's back, then held tight to his buttocks, as his strong thrusts drove her crazy with desire. Every move sent her into an agony of pleasure so strong, she cried out over and over like a wounded animal.

Cal responded to Elizabeth's erotic fury with a wildness of his own, sinking his teeth into her silken neck, and sucking on her soft skin hungrily.

His actions made Elizabeth even wilder, and grabbing his head, she pulled it tight against her neck, thrilling to his touch.

Cal's thrusts became stronger, harder, as he gave himself up to the passion and the hurt that had been embedded in him so long. The hurt he now tried to purge by embedding it into the woman who lay beneath him. He rode her hard, with no thoughts of anything but his desperate need.

His deep, hard movements sent her over the edge, and her cries became cries of ecstasy as her release came, but still he rode her, working up a perspiration that slicked their bodies.

When at last his own release came, Elizabeth's desire had flamed hot again, bursting in a flare of sensuous heat as he gripped her hard and sent his seed spilling into her.

He lay breathing heavy for a long time, then raised his head slowly, gazing deep into Elizabeth's eyes with a look of agony that chilled her heart.

"God forgive me for what I've done. I can never forgive myself."

Elizabeth couldn't believe his words. She had thought their lovemaking would make everything right. How could he regret what they had just shared? Tears filled her eyes, and she sobbed loudly, feeling betrayed once again by his rejection.

Cal groaned when he heard Elizabeth's sobs. He couldn't bear to hear the heartbreakingly sad sound. Rolling off her, he pulled himself unsteadily to his feet, the effects of the rum still working on him, and stood leaning against the wall for support. Memories flooded him of their earlier love, and of the place where they had made love so many years ago. A waterfall in the woods nearby.

They had been like children then, running naked through the woods, making love on the forest floor. How wild and exciting she had been. Then, unbidden, the image of Summer flashed through his head. He remembered his first glimpse of her in the river, and how boldly she had walked out of the water as he stood and watched. The two women were so much alike—not physically, but in their untamed, sensuous ways. He admired them both for their courageous spirit and independent manner. Funny, he had never realized before this moment, how much alike they truly were.

Now Elizabeth would use her body as a weapon. A weapon he found hard to defend himself against. But he must. For all their sakes. "It won't work, Elizabeth. Spare the tears. You sealed your fate when you married my brother. Now we must all live with the consequences."

"No, Cal. *You* sealed our fate when you chose to walk away from here. You condemned us all to a life without love."

Cal looked at her with blurred vision. It was true. He had caused the course of events that had separated two pairs of lovers. He and Elizabeth, and now, John and Summer. He knew they belonged together, as surely as he knew Elizabeth and he should have married five years ago; and he was helpless to change any of it. Divorce in Deerfield was near impossible. Divorce, plus marrying your brother's wife, was unspeakable. They were all condemned to the course already set.

Damn Elizabeth for seducing him, and damn Summer, too, for leaving him alone with her. She had known full well the aroused state he had been in, and how drunk he was. It was almost as if she had wanted him to make love to Elizabeth.

No, that was ridiculous. He had no one to blame but himself. He knew what he was doing. He hadn't been that drunk. He desired Elizabeth. Had always desired her, even though she was married to his brother. How could he face John after what he had done? How could he face Summer?

Downstairs in the parlor, Summer sat thinking about Cal and Elizabeth, and what they might be doing. She was a fool, an utter fool, for leaving them alone like that. But she couldn't help herself, they deserved a chance to work out what had been between them so long.

She heard the pounding of hooves and ran quickly to the window. John! She watched as he slid off Shadow and strode into the house, a grim look on his face. It became grimmer when he saw her. Her heart constricted. Something was very wrong. A feeling of helplessness swept over her, and she knew she didn't want to hear what he had to say. But he continued walking up to her and took her hand, his eyes glazed with sorrow.

"Summer, it's . . . Hannah, she and Charles, the Osbornes, too . . . They never made it back to the Osborne place. They were attacked by the French and Abenakis. Summer, they're all dead."

"No! It isn't true. Why are you lying to mè? Hannah can't be dead. Dear God, no. Please don't let it be true. Not Hannah, not Hannah, not Hannah."

John held her in his arms, as the tears gushed down her cheeks, and her voice rang out in anguish, "No, no, no."

The sound of her voice reached upstairs to Cal and Elizabeth, stirring them into action. They started down the stairs, stopping halfway down to stare at the scene below.

"What is it, John?" Cal cried out.

"Cal, it's Hannah and Charles, they've been murdered by the French. They never made it to the Osbornes. The Osbornes . . . they're dead, too. I'm sorry, I know how much Hannah and Charles meant to you."

Cal was numb with pain. Elizabeth reached out to comfort him, and he came alive. "No! Don't touch me. Don't ever touch me. I'm being punished for what we've done. Don't you see that? God is punishing me for our sin. Oh, God, how could you be so cruel? How could you take the most loving woman in your kingdom?"

Summer knew what punishment Cal meant. It was obvious he and Elizabeth had made love. Fresh tears rolled down her cheeks, and in a voice wrapped in sorrow, she said, "Cal, stop torturing yourself. God isn't punishing you by taking Hannah—" She could say no more, the sorrow overwhelmed her. How could that plump little woman, so full of love and life, be gone?

"Cal," John said. "It's not your fault she's dead. It's just a tragic consequence of the bloody war between the English and French. Put the blame where it belongs—on Robillard. This time we'll get him." Tilting Summer's head up, he gazed into her eyes. "I promise you this. Robillard is as good as dead. I'll not let Hannah's death go unavenged. I'm pulling all the militia out of here. We'll search every home, every farm, from here to Albany if we must, until we find where the bastard is hiding. And we'll hang anyone we find giving aid to the French. We must move fast. There'll be time for grieving later. Right now, we've got to get you women to town. We can ill afford to leave any men here to guard you."

Turning to Cal and Elizabeth, he continued. "Elizabeth, help Summer gather enough clothes to see her through. Cal, prepare Nenepownam for the trip to town. She can ride in the carriage. The rest of us will ride horseback. We'll stop at my place for clothing for Elizabeth and Alisha."

John's commanding voice sent the women into action. John was right. They would have time later to grieve.

When they were ready to go, they quickly mounted their horses and started toward town. Passing the pasture, Summer could see the militia making ready to move out, and for the first time in her life, she wished she had been born a man. She wanted to go with them, find Robillard and his murderous band, and wreak revenge on them.

They stopped at John's long enough to get their belongings, then continued toward town. Summer listened as John and Cal made plans as they rode along. John would leave only one unit of men behind to defend the town. It was chancy, but he was counting on the French to be caught off guard by their large force of men. They wouldn't be expecting so bold a move. But if John was wrong, if the French got wind of their plan and escaped, then the people in town would be at risk of their lives.

Jessica greeted them with grief etched into her pale face. She had always been fond of Hannah. And the Osbornes, Charity's parents, how could this have happened? They had all been so happy just one short day ago. Charity was upstairs in her room now, being comforted by Nat. Thank the Lord that Jessica had insisted on Charity staying in town with her, else she, too, would be dead now.

As soon as the men had unpacked the carriage, they made ready to leave with the militia. The troops were marching into town, forming a line the length of the street. Women and children gathered along the way, calling out encouragements and goodbyes to their husbands and sons, knowing it might be the last time they saw them alive.

Summer ached at the sight of John and Cal and Nat, riding side by side. They made an impressive sight, sitting tall and straight in their saddles. Tears flowed as she watched the men start down the road.

Watched as women had since time immemorial, as their men went off to battle.

Chapter Twenty-One

Days of sorrow followed nights of worry for the safety of the men. They had been gone much longer than anyone expected, almost a full month, and had to be running out of food and supplies by now. Summer pictured them starved and cold on some godforsaken mountain, struggling valiantly to survive. She tried hard not to think of that, tried not to show her anxiety in front of Jessica and Charity, but they knew.

Jessica tried to reassure her that the men could manage quite well living off the land, but Summer was still worried and Charity was, too. The young woman was afraid of losing Nat as she had her parents, and no amount of reassuring could take the scared look off her young face.

It was difficult for Summer, getting through the lonely days, grieving for the loved ones they had lost. How she missed Hannah's cheerful face. She had depended on her much more than she realized. Hannah had been a beacon that guided her through the rough waters of colonial life, and she didn't know how she could go on without her. It was hard to believe she would never hear her friendly voice calling her Lamby, or feel her warm presence in Cal's house.

Jessica tried to help Summer through her grief, but she had her hands full with Charity. Just a few short weeks ago, Charity had been a beautiful young woman with dancing eyes, full of life and hope and ready to marry the man she loved. How cruel life could be, and how precarious.

Everyone in the household was affected by the deaths in some way. Elizabeth had been strangely quiet ever since that terrible day, and whenever she looked at Summer, there was a puzzled expression on her face that Summer couldn't fathom. Elizabeth hardly spoke to anyone except her daughter, whom she clung to with a ferocity that frightened the little girl. Alisha wasn't used to seeing her mother act in such a strange manner.

Summer felt sorry for the child, caught up in the grief that had changed everyone so drastically. She was only five years old; how could she possibly comprehend all that was happening? It was only natural for the child to gravitate to the one person in the household unaffected by the deaths, Nenepownam.

The Indian woman sat outside each day, exposing her wound to the fresh cold air and the healing rays of November's midday sun. Alisha would sit at her feet and listen to the tales of the forest and of the creatures that roamed there. Nenepownam related the stories in a musical voice that kept the child enthralled. After the telling, Alisha, so like her mother, would go to the woods that bordered the house and play by herself. Summer overheard her tell Nenepownam that she played at being a Pocumtuck Indian just like Nenepownam, and it occurred to Summer that Alisha did have Pocumtuck blood running through her veins.

It pleased her to see the relationship developing between the small child and the Indian woman. Nenepownam was Alisha's grandmother, though she didn't know it. It was good that she of all people was there for Alisha, when the child needed her most.

A memorial service was planned for Hannah and Charles Stedman and the Osbornes that afternoon, weeks after they had died. The bodies had been buried at the site of the Osbornes' homestead, but the townfolk had been too busy—reinforcing their homes for an attack and stocking them with provisions—to hold a proper service until now.

Summer dreaded going. Her grief was a private thing. But she had promised Jessica that she would make an appearance with the rest of the Hawke women, to show a united front to the town.

She was glad Jessica had insisted. It made her feel she belonged to the Hawke family, if not by blood, then at least by love.

But it wouldn't be easy. She was still feeling nauseated every day, but now, instead of the afternoon, it hit her each morning. As she dressed in her plainest dress for the service, Summer noticed that the bodice was tighter than usual. She had noticed her breasts had been heavy and sore, but had been too busy to worry about it. She always had heavy breasts before her monthly flow.

Her period! When had she had her last one? Her mind raced back. No—it couldn't be! She couldn't be pregnant! But she knew she could. She had never been a day late in her whole life. She *was* pregnant. How did she think she could get away with making love without birth control, and not get caught?

The enormity of the situation hit her. What was she going to do? It wasn't enough that she was captive in the eighteenth century, in love with a man

227

she couldn't marry, now she must face the scorn of the townfolk when they found out that she was pregnant. She didn't know how the people of this century took to unmarried mothers, but she was sure it wouldn't be in a positive way; otherwise, Elizabeth wouldn't have had to marry John, when she became pregnant with Alisha.

How ironic. She was in the same predicament Elizabeth had been in! It was as if she was doomed to follow in her footsteps, only instead of marrying John, she would have to marry Cal to give her baby a name. But she couldn't think of that now. She couldn't handle more than one major problem at a time, and right now, she had a memorial service to get through.

All the way down the stairs, and then on the walk to the meetinghouse, her mind kept echoing the thought that she was pregnant with John's child. She knew it was John's, for she remembered back to when her nausea first started. It had been just before she made love with Cal. John's baby. She wanted it. Wanted it very much, no matter the hardship it would cause, and the complications it would add to her already complicated life.

The Hawke women walked into the meetinghouse and took their seats in the place reserved for members of the Hawke family. Jessica, Elizabeth, Alisha, Charity, and Summer sat side by side, the target of furtive glances as well as outright stares from the people gathered there. But they were oblivious to it all, taking comfort only from each other. The tragedy had brought them all closer together.

It was cold and damp in the room. The weather had turned bitterly cold over the past week, and though there was a small stove in the room, it was unlit. Summer wondered how cold it would have to get before these hardy New Englanders would turn on the heat.

The service droned on and on, and Summer found it hard to relate to what Daniel was saying about the people she had known. The service was an ordeal she had to get through, for appearances' sake, but it didn't console her in any way. She would mourn for Hannah and Charles in private.

Daniel stood at the tall, oaken pulpit, talking in a monotonous tone. She wished he would hurry up and get his never-ending speech over with. She wanted to get back to the comfort of Jessica's house.

Suddenly, the door to the meetinghouse was thrown open, and a small boy ran in crying, "Mama, Mama, Jacob fell into the river."

Pandemonium broke out as the congregation ran from the building, down to the river that flowed behind it. There was no sign of the child in the water. The surface was smooth as glass.

The child's mother stood by the river's edge crying, as two men—one of them likely the father—waded into the icy water and dove under. They came up twice without the child, and each time the mother's wail became louder. As they came up for the third time, everyone seemed to hold their breath, until they saw the child in one of the men's arms.

An audible gasp rang out, followed by a hush, when they saw that the child was not breathing. The small, limp body was laid on the riverbank, and the mother, Mattie, lifted his head into her lap, crying over and over, "Wake up, Jacob. Wake up."

The child's father took off his jacket and started to lay it over Jacob's small form, when Summer could bear it no longer. She cried, "No! Don't give up yet. Let me give him mouth-to-mouth." Running over to the child, she reached for him, but was held back.

229

"For God's sake, Mistress, let him alone." One of the men said. "Can you not see he's gone?"

Summer appealed to Mattie. "Let me try. It may not be too late." How could she explain to these primitive people about mouth-to-mouth resuscitation?

Mattie was desperate. She didn't know what Mistress Winslow planned on doing, but anything was better than covering Jacob's little body and giving up. She beckoned to Summer.

Summer broke loose and knelt by the child, feeling in his mouth for anything that might be obstructing his air passage. There was nothing in the way.

Pinching his small nostrils together, she put her mouth over Jacob and sent her life-giving breath into his mouth. The spectators gasped as one, and murmured among themselves at such inappropriate behavior. They had never seen such a sight before. Why was Mistress Winslow kissing the dead child in such an intimate way? Their voices rose in outrage.

Summer ignored the voices around her and worked feverishly on the child. She knew he couldn't have been under very long, and she knew how cold the water must be. She remembered seeing a news report on the diving syndrome in small children, and she remembered reading that it was especially effective in cold water. Many children had come back after being in the water for as long as forty-five minutes. Jacob could only have been under a fraction of that time. There was a chance.

The voices around her rose in angry unison, and rough hands pulled her from the child, but they stopped, suddenly, when the child began to cough. The crowd let out a cry, then edged back in amazement and fright. Mattie grabbed her son and cried out her thanks to God and to Summer, his handmaiden. The grateful words brought some people to their senses, and they, too, praised Summer, but a few more superstitious people stood in frozen-faced fear of the strange occurrence.

Summer heard the one word spoken that she had been afraid of hearing since her first night here. WITCH! Fear filled her as the word spread through the crowd, rising higher and higher until it became a chant.

Mattie's husband rose to her defense. "Is it witchcraft that brings a child back from the dead? You blaspheme God to say such things. He is the only one with such awesome power. Mistress Winslow's gift was bestowed upon her by God, not the devil."

Elizabeth had been standing there watching the strange scene with as much awe as everyone else. Who was Summer to have such powers? And what chance had she to win Caleb back against such a formidable foe? She listened to the cries of witchcraft, and for a brief moment let herself get caught up in it. Then reason prevailed, and a small voice inside her said, there but for the grace of God . . . How many times had she been close to being called a witch herself, simply because she acted so differently from the other women in town. And because she had the healing power, she had been considered an outsider. The only thing that saved *her* from being accused was the fact that she was married to John Hawke.

Summer was no witch, of that Elizabeth was sure. She couldn't stand by and see her accused. But without proof these superstitious people would go on silently accusing her. There was one way to end it now. She owed Summer that much, though she doubted Summer would thank her for what she was about to do. But Summer had left her alone with

Caleb that day they made love, and for that she would always be grateful to her.

"Listen. Summer Winslow is not in league with the devil. I know this, but you must know it, too. For your peace of mind, and to prove Summer's innocence, let her be looked upon to see if she bears the mark of the devil on her body. If she does not, then we will all breathe easier knowing her gift truly comes from the Lord."

Summer listened in frightened silence. What was Elizabeth trying to do?

Daniel's voice rose above the crowd. "Yes. It is just. Mistress Winslow will prove her innocence by examination."

The cry went up among the few who feared Summer. "Let her be tested."

Summer wasn't sure just what the examination was, but when she looked over to Jessica, the woman nodded to her. If Jessica thought it okay, surely she wouldn't be physically harmed.

"Seven women must be chosen to witness the examination and to undress you. One may be a member of your household, the others must be God-fearing women of the congregation." Daniel's eyes swept the crowd, and his fingers pointed to the women he selected. Elizabeth was chosen as the woman of her household; the others were all strangers to her.

Comprehending what was going to happen, Summer's fear grew. "Am I to take all my clothes off? Surely that isn't necessary. Surely there's no need for seven women. Won't one do?"

"It is prescribed by law that seven women must do the undressing, and the preacher the examination. Why do you object? Do you have reason to fear?" The words were spoken by one of the women who called her a witch. Summer's heart chilled with fear.

"No. Of course not. It just seems . . ." Summer decided it was best not to say anymore. She could be getting herself into deeper trouble. Did they say the preacher would do the exam? Oh, God, Daniel was going to be looking at her naked body. A surge of nausea swept over her at that thought.

Summer fought the sick feeling and forced her head high, as she made her way into the meeting-house. She mustn't let anyone see how frightened she was. Daniel and the seven women followed after her, while the rest of the congregation waited outside, murmuring amongst themselves in small, huddled groups.

Moving to the front of the meetinghouse, Summer stopped in front of the stained glass window, the light from it radiating behind her. She stood silently as the women formed a circle around her, hiding her from Daniel's view. She was grateful for that. Grateful, too, for the reassurances the women murmured as they worked at removing her clothing. Her hands shook, and she felt weak in the knees, but she was determined to be strong. To get through this with as much dignity as possible.

When she was completely naked, the women parted the circle, exposing her to Daniel's all too fervent stare. He had been waiting in eager anticipation for this moment, and was not disappointed.

Never had he seen so beautiful a sight. Summer Winslow stood naked as Eve, her body soft and curvaceous beyond belief. The vivid panels of the stained glass window behind her—depicting a scene from the Garden of Eden—surrounded her with a halo of colored light, in sharp contrast to her ivory body. It was a sight that would stay with him the rest of his life.

His eyes moved over her body, taking in every delicate curve, every shadowy recess. The pink of her nipples, the dark reddish gold of her venus mound, excited him beyond anything he had ever experienced before, and he was unaware of anything but the sight of her. He was unconscious, too, that his arousal was obvious to all the women in the room, in the tight breeches he wore. They smiled knowing smiles at each other, as he moved closer and closer to Summer.

Watching Daniel approach, Summer felt utterly and completely humiliated. The room was icy cold, but she was unaware of it, though her nipples were standing tautly from her heavy breasts. She was unaware of anything but the ordeal she was being subjected to, and of Daniel's lustful gaze. She hated the look she saw in his eyes, but she had to endure it, had to be proven unmarked. Her life and her child's depended on it.

Her flesh crawled as Daniel walked up the two steps to the altar, then over to where she stood. Slowly, his hands reached up and touched the top of her head, parting her hair to look through it. She was puzzled until she realized he was looking at her scalp. She breathed a little easier. That wasn't too bad. She could endure that.

When he finished her scalp, his gaze moved down to her face and neck, and behind her ears, then to her shoulder, lingering overly long at her breasts. She held her breath, waiting for him to touch her there, but instead, he lifted her arms, turning them to look at the undersides. She breathed a sigh of relief. This was bearable. She had nothing to worry about. Daniel was going to be a gentleman, just give her a casual perusal for appearances' sake.

Moving behind her, he lifted her long hair, and she

felt his eyes on her back and buttocks, making her feel very uneasy. Then, circling her as an animal circles its prey, he moved to the front of her again.

Sweat stood out on his forehead.

Her uneasiness grew as his face took on a strange look, and reaching out with both hands, he grabbed hold of her breast. Summer wanted to throw up, but she fought it down. She must get through this. She must survive. He lifted her breast and bent over to look at the underside, a thumb brushing lightly over her nipple. She wanted to scream, wanted to tear his hand away from her, but she stood silently, enduring his intimate touch. He repeated the procedure with her other breast, while his fingers dug into her delicate tissue. She wanted to slap him, scratch him, anything to get him to stop, but knew she could do nothing.

Daniel pulled his hands away from her breasts reluctantly, wanting to explore every inch of them, but knew if he did that Summer would do something violent. He could see it in her eyes.

Kneeling in front of her, his eyes lingered on the soft mound between her legs. With shaky fingers, he grasped her legs and parted her thighs.

Summer gritted her teeth as his hands moved up her legs to her knees, then pushed her legs even further apart. Was there no end to her humiliation?

Daniel wasn't finished. Still kneeling, he moved his head between her legs, gazing up inside her legs to her inner thighs. The female scent of her drifted to his nostrils, filling him with such lust he was afraid of spilling his seed right then. He bit down hard on his tongue, to keep from thrusting it into her delicate opening, but his self-control was not strong enough to keep one restless finger from moving into the hot wetness that only a lover should touch.

Summer gasped loudly, her body jerking at the terrible violation. Her sudden movement brought him to his senses, and he stood up, shakily. In a strange, hoarse voice, he said. "I declare Mistress Winslow to be free of the mark. She is no witch. Now. Get her dressed, before she dies of the cold."

Summer was relieved at his verdict, but enraged that he had dared to defile her body. She could still feel the alien touch of his finger inside her, and the nausea she had been experiencing rose again in her throat.

The women finished dressing her before Daniel spoke again, his voice still sounding strange. "Go— tell the people of my thorough examination and of its satisfactory conclusion. I want to speak to Mistress Winslow, alone."

After the women left, Summer faced Daniel, keeping her hands locked behind her back to keep from scratching his eyes out. She knew she must stay composed, not speak the words she ached to say to this despicable man for the unspeakable thing he had done. She knew now how much power he had in this town. She would have to be careful in her dealings with him, afraid of hearing chanting voices once again declare her a witch.

Daniel strode back to where she stood, the spot she had not moved from since she walked into the room.

"Summer, daughter of Eve, I'm compelled to tell you that I find you the most desirable of women. Do not be ashamed that I looked upon your nakedness. For as I gazed at you, I thought Eve herself could not have been more gloriously beautiful. I crave more fervently than ever that you consent to be my wife, else, I fear, I shall die of wanting you."

Summer's face never changed. *Then die, you horny bastard.* "Daniel, I beg of you not to speak so

236

intimately to me. You are my pastor, and I—"

Daniel stopped her from finishing the sentence. Pulling her up against his throbbing hardness, he moved his body in such a way as to push it between her legs. Summer struggled, trying to push him away. "Daniel. For God's sake, stop this!"

"Forgive me, Summer, it is just—"

Without waiting for him to finish, Summer ran toward the door, where Elizabeth stood watching.

Chapter Twenty-Two

Elizabeth caught Summer's arm, preventing her from running outside. "Compose yourself before you face these people. Do not let them see you like this."

Elizabeth was right. She couldn't face anyone as distraught as she was now. Forcing herself to be calm, Summer faced the throng of people, Elizabeth's steady grip on her arm.

A murmur went up among the crowd of people when Summer appeared in the doorway, and she smiled, timidly at first, then broadly when the people cried out their support and sympathy for what she had had to endure.

The two women who had been the most vocal at having her examined, now looked sheep-faced. They were obviously sisters, in their mid-fifties, she imagined, dressed in Puritan garb. Elizabeth whispered their names to her. Jemima and Hester Sheldon. Summer walked over to where they stood, vengeance in her eyes. Elizabeth grabbed her arm and steered her away. "Let it be."

A rider came pounding down the road, his clothes covered with dust. "The militia has had a triumphant victory, and will be home in time for evening meal," he shouted hoarsely. "So—ladies, start a-cooking!"

Whoops of joy filled the crisp air and the crowd dispersed, eager to prepare for their men's homecoming. Elizabeth and Summer exchanged glances. For one brief moment there had been a truce between them, but now John and Cal were returning, and the barrier between them was returning also.

"Elizabeth, thank you for your help back there. I was really upset, and I'm sure I would have made matters worse if I had faced the townfolk in that condition."

"Do not thank me. I would have done the same for any poor fool. Since you are feeling better, I take my leave of you. There are things I must do before the men return."

Summer watched as Elizabeth walked away, then looked around for Jessica. She was talking with Charity and Alisha. Jessica saw her and waved, beckoning her to join them, but before she could take a step, Daniel appeared beside her.

"Summer, I implore you to forgive my actions. I am made of flesh and blood, after all, and you are a most desirable woman. A man has needs—"

"A woman has needs also, Daniel, and right now, I have a need to be alone. So, if you'll excuse me." Summer moved away from Daniel and quickly joined Jessica.

Daniel Bradford seethed inside. He wanted Summer. Wanted her so much it hurt. Why must she continue to treat him so abominably? His groin ached with the relentless passion he had felt when he touched her rapturous body. A man could take just so much. He had to have a woman—now.

239

Making his way to his horse, he mounted it and rode toward his father's house, knowing he would find the Indian woman, Asperensah, more than willing to ease his aching loins. She had been swishing her tail in his face ever since she started working for his father.

Visions of Summer standing like Eve before the colored glass haunted him as he galloped down the road, increasing his desire, his need, for quick release.

When he reached the house, he jumped from his mount, not bothering to tether it, and with long strides made his way into the house. The Indian woman was bent over the fireplace, stirring a rabbit stew. Daniel moved up behind her, and grasping her hips, pulled them up against his hardened shaft.

Asperensah gave out a little cry, then realized it was the handsome young master instead of the wrinkled one. Before now, only the old one had poked at her with his swollen thing.

Daniel's hand moved up her sides, then reached around the front of her to grasp her small breasts, walking her into the pantry where he stood her up against the wall. He turned her around to face him, and impatiently raised her petticoats around her waist, tucking them behind her to keep them out of the way. He unbuckled his breeches and let them fall to the floor.

Asperensah stood wide-eyed and speechless, staring at this rutting male. Ah, yes, he was well equipped to give her what she wanted. She had known it was only a matter of time before he came around, but she never expected it to be like this. He must truly desire her to be in such a hurry.

Daniel pushed into her with great haste, and began

240

to move against her body in a frenzy. Asperensah was but a vessel to vent his frustration in, to release him from his torment. The heat of her brought him quickly to the point of release, and when his throbbing shaft plunged into the woman for the last time, he cried out the name of his tormentor. "Summer, Summer, Summer."

Preparing for the men's return was a happy chore for Jessica. The delicious aroma of venison drifted from the kitchen into every corner of the house. It would be a grand celebration tonight with the men safely returned. No sadness would be allowed in the house this day. They would have a respite from grieving, and enjoy the deer Otis had purchased from a huntsman.

Everything was ready. The house sparkled from Otis's scrubbing, and Elizabeth, Summer, and Charity were in their rooms, getting into their prettiest dresses. Thankfully, Charity had pulled herself from her despondency when she heard that Nat would soon be home. It was good to see the child smile again. Nat would help her forget her sorrow. Jessica hoped they wouldn't delay their marriage, for it would be the best medicine for them both.

Hearing the stairs creak, Jessica went out to the hall and peered up the stairs, eager to see how beautifully her girls were dressed. Elizabeth came down the stairs first, in a yellow silk that set off her raven hair to perfection. She hadn't seen Elizabeth dressed like that for a long time, and thought it a good sign that she and John would finally act like a man and wife should. What other reason could there be for Elizabeth's carefully chosen attire?

Following close behind Elizabeth, Charity made her way down in pale pink taffeta, which gave her wholesome beauty a touch of delicacy.

"My, my," Jessica declared. "How beautiful the two of you look. 'Twill be a fine homecoming for the men. They'll soon forget the weary days on the road, when they gaze at you."

Summer stood at the top of the staircase, looking down at Elizabeth and Charity. They really did look beautiful. Elizabeth's bright yellow dress was stunning. Yellow was the one color Summer had never been able to wear. It made her skin look sallow.

Lifting up her petticoats, she glided down the stairs.

Jessica stood at the bottom, taking in every detail of the gorgeous gown Summer wore. The color was a delicate pale blue, and the bodice was embroidered with cream-colored roses. "Summer, darling. Cal will not be able to take his eyes from you in that dress."

Jessica's words pierced Elizabeth's heart. She wanted Cal to have eyes for no one but her.

"Mother. Grandmother. They're coming, they're coming," Alisha shouted excitedly. "Hurrry, hurry, they're rounding the corner."

The women ran out the door as the three brothers rode up to the house. Summer looked at each of them anxiously, to see if they were injured, but they seemed fine. Then, before she knew it, Nat was climbing down from his horse and embracing a blushing Charity, twirling her around and around to Alisha's glee.

Summer smiled as she watched the spectacle, then looked up at Caleb and John astride their horses. The sight of them took her breath away. They looked so omnipotent, exuding strength and masculinity to a degree that set her heart beating out of control.

Her eyes moved from one handsome face to the other, drinking in the wonderful sight, then her gaze was drawn back to John's eyes, the same sensation sweeping over her that she felt whenever she looked at him. She wanted to feel his arms around her, and craved for the touch of him, the smell of him. She could see by the hungry way he looked at her, that he felt the same way.

John didn't stir from his saddle. He sat staring down at her, whilst Cal jumped from his horse and rushed over to her. With only a second's hesitation, he circled her waist with his sinewy arms and kissed her long and hard. When he released her, Summer looked over her shoulder to John, wishing with a terrible longing that it was his lips she had felt.

John's eyes narrowed slightly, and his cheek twitched as he sat watching his brother and Summer.

Elizabeth's voice broke the spell. "Cal. Welcome home."

Caleb heard Elizabeth's voice, and turned to stare at her with eyes that suddenly clouded. Boldly, Elizabeth moved up to him and embraced him. Caleb stiffened, and Elizabeth knew he was still upset with her. Knew it would not be easy winning him back.

John dismounted and greeted his mother and Alisha, who were clamoring for his attention. Then he moved toward Summer with long strides and kissed her chastely on the cheek. But the words he whispered in her ear sent her into a tailspin.

"Meet me at midnight, in the burial ground." He released her quickly, but his eyes implored her to heed his message.

Summer stood there, her mind swirling. She

243

wanted to meet him. Wanted to feel his arms around her once more. Just one more time. Just one more time, and she would content herself with memories.

"Summer, why are you standing there?" Alisha asked. "We're going to have supper now." Alisha grabbed her hand and began pulling her inside. The little girl looked happier than Summer had ever seen her. Poor little thing. She had been affected by all the sadness even more than Summer realized. Now, with the men back, perhaps she would begin to lead a normal, happy life.

Summer allowed herself to be swept inside into the dining room, where everyone was making their way to the table.

Cal, happy to see Nenepownam sitting at the table, embraced her warmly. "Mother, you're looking well. How fares the foot?"

"It grows better each day, thanks to Elizabeth's and Summer's tender care. But, enough of me, I want to hear of your brave adventures."

Everyone laughed, setting the mood at the table, and soon they were all talking at once.

The food was the best Summer had ever tasted, and she soon found herself ravenously hungry, a welcome change after all the nausea she had been experiencing.

Caleb and Nathaniel did most of the talking, telling of their successful campaign against the hated enemy, and then Nat announced, "You should all know that Cal is the hero of our venture. He wounded Major Robillard in the side with his sword. Unfortunately, the slippery eel got away once more. I swear that Frenchman has more lives than a cat. But he was bleeding heavily, so there's a chance we may yet find him lying dead somewhere."

"Nat. Please," Jessica pleaded. "The supper table is no place to be relating such gory details. Certain young ladies should not be hearing such things." She nodded her head toward Alisha.

Alisha had been listening with rapt attention to the exciting stories her uncles told, and thinking to add her own bit of excitement, announced, "Uncle Nat, we had an exciting time, too, just this day. You should have seen how Summer brought the Graysons' little boy back to life, after he drowned in the river."

Silence filled the room.

"Oh?" John's eyebrows raised. "Tell us about it, darling."

Alisha related the morning's events. The drowning, the limp body, the mother's crying, and Summer's miraculous kiss of life. She paused to catch her breath, and then continued, "And then, some of the people said Summer must be a witch. That she used witchcraft to bring Jacob back. But other people said she couldn't be a witch. But then, Mama settled it by telling them all that Summer should be tested to prove she wasn't a witch."

The glint of danger showed in John's eyes, his voice laced with steel. "Tested? How?"

"You know, Father, undressing her and looking to see if she has the mark of the devil hidden on her body."

Tension built in the room as John's voice took on a dangerous edge. "And did they test her, darling?" His eyes never left Summer's face, which was now beet red.

"Ask Mama. She was one of the women chosen to undress Summer, and there was Mistress Wells and—"

John interrupted her, his voice now low and strained. "Who did this testing?"

"Why, Pastor Bradford, of course. Who else?"

"Who else, indeed." John raised himself from his chair. "Did that bastard lay a hand on you, Summer? If he did—"

"John, calm down," Jessica said. "It was an unfortunate incident, but it's over, and as you can see, no harm has come to our Summer. She handled it with great dignity and pride."

"I repeat. Did that bastard touch you?"

Summer couldn't speak. She was too choked up and ready to burst into tears.

Elizabeth couldn't help herself. She spoke, knowing the fury her words would cause. "John, really. He barely touched her at all, except, of course, to lift her breasts and to spread her legs, to see where it was impossible to see any other way."

John's fists slammed down on the table, causing the food to spill and the tableware to rattle like a timber rattlesnake. "That bastard! I'll see him in hell!"

"John. You make too much of it," Cal said. "As you can see, no harm has come to Summer. It is all to the good. Now there'll be no lingering doubts in anyone's minds that Summer is a witch. The English make too much of nudity. My mother's people walk around half-naked all the time."

Nenepownam nodded in agreement.

John's fury was unabated, and he left the table before his anger became out of control.

"Nat," Jessica said. "Go after him. Make sure he stays away from the preacher."

Nat quickly left the table, following John out the door.

Caleb looked over at Summer, tears streaming down her cheeks. He remembered the first glimpse he had of her lush naked body, and almost pitied the preacher. The man would not easily forget her ripe body. A body the poor bastard would never possess. Not if Caleb had anything to say about it.

Elizabeth didn't miss the warm look Cal gave Summer and a pang of jealousy gripped her. Caleb had been avoiding her all through the meal. And when she had greeted him outside, his face had frozen when he looked at her, his kiss on her cheek cold and impersonal. Would he never get over his feelings of guilt?

With the meal ended, Cal stood up and addressed Jessica. "An excellent meal, Mother, but now, if you would dismiss Summer from kitchen duty, I have need of her company on a walk."

Jessica was more than happy for Cal and Summer to be alone. "Certainly, take your time. There's much for the two of you to talk of."

Elizabeth sat stone-faced, unable to deal with Cal's attention to Summer. She couldn't bear it if he married her, and she vowed she would find a way to make sure the marriage never took place.

Summer was glad to leave the house, the tension had been too much to bear. The air was cold, but felt good against her flushed face. Silently they walked down the street, lit only by candlelight seeping from the windows of the houses that lined the street.

They walked to a wooded lot, and Summer noticed it was the same spot where someday the museum that housed John's sword would stand. The nippy air made her shiver, and Cal, noticing, drew her into his arms, his expression becoming solemn. "Do you forgive me for the way I treated you when I was

247

drunk? I swear, it will never happen again."

She knew by the way he spoke that he meant more than just his drunken behavior toward her, but she felt it best that it remain unspoken. "Cal, I understand and, of course, I forgive you. I just pray you can forgive me."

"Enough talk of forgiveness. Let's put it behind us. There's a much more pleasant subject to speak of—our marriage. I want you for my wife, Summer. And I'll try to make you happy."

"Cal, before you say anymore, I have something to tell you. This morning . . . I found out . . . I'm pregnant."

After a long pause, Cal said quietly. "I'd like to think it is mine."

"I won't lie to you, Cal. In all likelihood, it's John's."

With a voice tight with emotion, he replied, "Well, then, in any case, it will be a Hawke." His face softened and he went on. "It seems there'll be a wedding after all. This long, lonely month without you, I had my doubts that you would marry me, but now there is no choice. You cannot walk around town with a swollen belly, and no man to call your husband."

Cal swooped her up into his arms, and twirled her around. "Let's tell the two mothers. Jessica and Nenepownam will be ecstatic. They have wanted this wedding since first they met you."

"Cal, think a moment. We can't barge in and announce our wedding. Think how it will hurt Elizabeth and John! We've got to go about this quietly. I'll talk to John, and you must talk to Elizabeth. Do you understand? It will be enough of a blow even then, without hearing it in front of the whole family."

"I agree, but I tell you, I don't relish telling Elizabeth."

"Who's afraid of the fearsome creature now?" she kidded.

"All right. I won't say anything to anyone, until John and Elizabeth have been told. But let's make it soon. Tonight, or tomorrow at the latest. We have a future to plan."

Reaching down, Cal lifted Summer's hand to his lips, then reaching into his pocket, took out a ring and sipped it on her finger.

"Oh!" Summer gazed at the ring with shiny eyes. The gold ring was set with a huge green stone. "It's breathtaking."

"It was my mother's—Nenepownam's—given to her by my father on the night I was conceived. She gave it to me the night you and I brought her home with her hurt foot. I've had it sized smaller to fit you. Now—there's but one thing more to do to make it official—this." His eyes sparkled with light as he gazed into her eyes, holding her head gently in his hands, he kissed her, lightly at first, then harder, as the love he felt for her and the new life she carried swelled his heart.

As midnight approached, Summer lay in bed agonizing over whether to meet John as he had implored, or to stay away from the temptation that always claimed her whenever he was near. In the end she gave in to her desire to be with him, rationalizing her decision by deciding it would be the best opportunity to tell him of her betrothal to Cal.

Her mind made up, she crept from the bed

hoping not to wake Elizabeth or Nenepownam, who slept in the same room. She didn't dress, fearful of making too much noise, but instead slipped into her shoes and grabbed a shawl to wrap around her shoulders.

The night air fanned her face as she walked the short distance to the cemetery, telling herself all the while that she would stay only long enough to tell John her decision.

It was eerie seeing the graveyard so late at night, and only the thought that John waited for her gave her the courage to open the wooden gate and enter.

The gate hinges squeaked ominously, setting her nerves on edge, and she moved faster, scanning the darkness as she walked. Where was he? Hadn't he come yet? Would he stand her up, as he had that day on the hill?

When she came to the center of the grounds, she stopped, straining her eyes to see him. What if some late straggler wandered down the road now, and saw her standing there? How could she ever explain her presence dressed only in a nightgown? She should have dressed.

Spying a large elm tree, she moved into the comforting shadow of its low hanging branches, relieved to be partially out of view from the road. Suddenly, a sound behind her made her whirl in fright. She gave out a little cry, as John's mouth covered hers in a hungry kiss.

Pushing him away while she still had the strength, she cried, "No! That's not why I'm here. I came to—"

His lips covered hers again, preventing further talk, and her own lips, traitor to her mind, responded.

Hearing the sound of hoofbeats on the road, John

250

pulled her into the shadowy recesses of the tree, his lips still locked on hers. "God's blood, but I've missed you. Wanted you. Tell me it's the same with you."

"It is, I can't deny it. But we can't—"

"Shhhh, darling." He kissed her again, his hands seeking out the remembered pleasure of her breasts. The flannel gown she wore hindered him, and he lifted it impatiently, sliding his hands up to cup the warm softness he craved. The feel of her hardened him like a rock, and he lifted her gown higher, lowering his head to take a stiffened nipple into his mouth.

Summer moaned as the wet heat of his mouth broke down any resolve to leave. She had a desperate need of him. A need that wouldn't be denied. With trembling hands, she reached down and unbuttoned his breeches. Her fingers curled around his solid manhood, pulling it free of his clothing. How could anything so hard feel so velvety, she wondered, reveling at the deep, sensuous sensation the touch of him ignited. It felt so good to touch him there. So right. He was hers—now—for this moment, the only moment that mattered, and she would feel him inside her one more time. Just one more time.

"Oh, God, Summer. I fear if you keep that up we'll both get very wet." Grabbing her around the waist, he lifted her up over his hardness, then eased her down on it.

Immediately, Summer's legs wound around him, locking behind his back as he buried himself in her. She wriggled her body, settled on him in just the right way, circled his neck with her arms, and held on tight.

His hips moved in a circular motion, grinding into

251

her, his need escalating to an intensity that made it impossible to continue standing. Sinking to his knees, he laid her down on the blanket he had laid on the ground, their bodies still joined together.

They made love, fiercely, intently, with a need that drove them higher and higher into a world of sensual pleasure, their whispered voices mingling with words of love.

And when it was over, John still felt a need to touch her. Using his mouth and teeth and tongue, he covered her cheeks and neck and breasts with tender little love bites and kisses, that sent the passion surging between them again.

Still inside her, John grew hard again. They moved together, this time with more leisure, until they were sated and lay exhausted in each other's arms.

"You're mine, Summer. Now and forever." His whispered words carried on the night wind, swirling around the lonely graveyard as if seeking something solid to become embedded in, like the epitaphs carved on the moonlit stones.

The words tore at her heart, filling her with incredible sorrow. Tears came to her eyes as she cried softly into her hands.

"Darling, what is it? Was I too rough? My need was so urgent, I didn't think."

Summer stopped his words with a salty kiss. "No, John, it's not that. You could never hurt me with your lovemaking. I was just thinking how much I love you, and how hopeless that love is."

"Never hopeless. We can move away. Go where no one knows us."

"John, this is where you belong. This is your land. Land you'll hand down to your sons, and they to theirs. It's the way it will be. There's no use fighting it."

"You and that confounded research of yours. Would you destroy our happiness for the sake of words written by some misinformed stranger?"

"Please, I don't want to argue with you. Not tonight. Let's not spoil this precious time together."

John wrapped the blanket around the two of them, and held Summer in his arms. "Nothing will, or ever can, spoil what we have, my darling. Have faith in our love. It's stronger than the will of mere mortals."

Hearing those poignant words, Summer knew she couldn't tell John of her betrothal tonight. She couldn't spoil the last time they would ever be together. She would tell him in the morning. But . . . where would she find the courage?

Chapter Twenty-Three

Next morning, Summer rose early, hoping to speak with Jessica before she had to face John. She needed advice desperately, and trusted the older woman's good sense. Otis was just bringing Jessica a breakfast tray.

"Mistress Jessica is feeling poorly. Asked to have a tray sent up. I'm worried 'bout her, Mistress. It's not like her to lay abed."

"Here. Let me take it, Otis. I'll see how she's doing." Summer rapped lightly on Jessica's door, then entered. Jessica was sitting up in bed, a shawl around her shoulders, a linen cap on her head. Summer smiled to herself. She could never get used to seeing people sleeping with a hat on.

"Good morning, Jessica. Otis tells me you're not feeling well. Is there anything I can do?"

"No, dear. 'Tis just an old ladies' complaint. I'm afraid I had an overly large amount of excitement yesterday. What with my sons coming home and all."

"Well, then, I must be getting old, too, because the excitement was too much for me as well. I'll just sit here and keep you company while you eat."

Summer sat quietly while Jessica ate her bread and

cheese, washing it down with a mug of mead. That was another thing she could never get used to, drinking spirited beverages for breakfast. But she drank herself, knowing from her research that the people of this time who abstained from drinking water lived far longer than the ones who did not.

When Jessica finished eating, Summer braced herself for the announcement she must make. "Aunt Jessica, I have news for you."

"Yes, I thought you might, looking at me with that soulful expression. It can't be all that bad now, can it, dear?"

Summer smiled wanly. "Actually, it's good news. Last night, Cal asked me to marry him, and I said I would."

"Summer. Child. That pleases me greatly. You know how much I've wanted you in the family. But why do I not see joy in your eyes? Is it not a happy occasion for you?"

"Oh, Aunt Jessica, I've made a terrible mess of things ever since I came to Deerfield. It would be better for everyone, if I had never set foot here."

"How can you say that? You're the best thing that has ever happened to this family. Before you came, John and Elizabeth were sleepwalking their way through life, but now, they're alive and feeling."

Summer was amazed Jessica should use sleepwalking to describe John and Elizabeth's life. The same word she herself had used to describe her own life, before she came to this century. Could it be true? Could it mean that she was meant to come here? Meant to live out her life here?

"As for Cal," Jessica continued. "He was a restless, rootless man, who would very probably have married some squaw and lived a dreary existence in the woods like a savage. Denying his Hawke blood, never coming to terms with the heartbreak that has been a part of his life since Elizabeth married John.''

Summer couldn't let Jessica go on talking in such a positive way. There was one more thing she had to tell her, and she dreaded it. But Jessica would find out soon anyway. She couldn't hide her pregnancy forever. "Jessica, please, there's something I must tell you, even though you'll probably hate me for it.''

Jessica touched Summer's hand lightly. "If you mean to tell me you are with child, I guessed that days ago.''

"But how? I don't show yet.''

"The signs are obvious. Your illness each morning. The tightness of your bodice. You forget, I have borne children myself. I'm well aware of the signs. Why did you think I would hate you for giving me a grandchild?''

"Because . . . because . . . the child is . . .''

"John's?''

"So, you guessed even that. Surely, now that you know, you must think me a harlot or—''

"Child. I have eyes in my head. I know you love my son, and I know your love is returned. The marriage between John and Elizabeth has been troublesome since first they said their vows. I had hoped—still hope—that somehow they'll accept each other and make their marriage work. Now that you'll marry Cal, it might finally happen. Elizabeth has always harbored the hope that somehow she and Cal would get back together. Now, with you as Cal's wife, she'll have to know that's impossible, and make the most of her life with John.''

Elizabeth walked into the room, stopping short when she saw Summer. "Jessica, Otis tells me you're not feeling well. Mayhap my herbal tea will help.''

"No need, my dear. Summer has just given me the

best medicine in the world." She patted Summer's hand in reassurance.

Elizabeth's face betrayed her as wariness crept into her eyes. "Oh? And what is this wonderful medicine?"

Summer couldn't speak. She wanted to disappear, wishing fervently that the sword was there right now to send her away from the scene that was sure to come.

Jessica spoke the words for her. "Summer will marry Caleb."

The words were said with a finality that struck Elizabeth's heart like a blow, turning her face ashen.

Summer wished the words could be called back. For some unexplainable reason, she felt fear. "Elizabeth, I . . . I'm pregnant." She blurted out the words hoping Elizabeth would understand her need to marry Cal.

The look of hatred Elizabeth bestowed upon her shook her, but the words she uttered were even more devastating. "What a coincidence. So am I."

Summer could barely get the words out. "But, how? Whose child?"

Elizabeth was gloating now, reveling in the anguish she saw on Summer's face. "Why, who else's, but my husband's?" Turning in triumph, she strolled out of the room, closing the door behind her. Once safely out of Summer's view, emotion overcame her, and she ran blindly down the stairs, brushing past John and Cal, as they made their way up to Jessica's room.

Elizabeth barely realized what she was doing when she left the house. Spotting Caleb's horse, she mounted it and rode away, her eyes blinded with tears. She rode furiously, unaware of where she was going until she found herself at the one place that had given her comfort through the years—the waterfall where she and Cal had made love. She stared at the rocky cliff with rushing water spilling over it into a small pool below, then threw herself off the horse to lay by the water, letting the tears flow freely. Her loud sobbing was blunted by the roar of the falling water.

Back at the house, Summer was stunned at the news of Elizabeth's pregnancy. Stunned at the knowledge that John had lied to her, had been sleeping with Elizabeth all along. But then, why should she be surprised? Wasn't it written that Elizabeth would have a son, Adam, in the same month, ironically, that she would give birth to her own child? How could she have forgotten that simple fact, and what difference did it really make? John was never hers.

But what a fool she had been to believe him. A fool to believe that any man who would keep her captive until he granted him sexual favors could be trusted. No. She was more than a fool, for she loved him still, despite everything.

"Are you all right, child? You look white as a ghost."

A light rap on the door kept Summer from answering. Cal walked in, followed by John. Summer's heart skipped a beat. Had Cal told John yet? No. He seemed too content. Her heart ached, knowing he had been intimate with Elizabeth.

"Summer, what's going on? Elizabeth passed us on the stairs, as if she didn't even see us. And you, why do you look so troubled?" John asked, suddenly afraid.

Jessica saw how upset Summer was, and said the words too hard for her to say. "I'm afraid the news of Summer's upcoming marriage to Cal was too upsetting for Elizabeth."

"What are you talking about, Mother? Summer isn't marrying Cal! Or anyone else, for that matter." John turned to look at his brother. He had wondered why Cal was dressed in his Sunday best, with John's own sword belted to his waist, and now he knew why.

"John," Cal said quietly. "Summer has agreed to marry me."

John's burning gaze turned to Summer. "Is this true?"

Summer's eyes pleaded for understanding. "Can't you see, John? This is the only way."

"My God!" John exploded. "I would rather send you back to your own time, than to see you married to my brother!"

Exasperated, Summer answered. "John. We wouldn't be standing here agonizing over this if that were possible. You know as well as I do that the sword has lost its power."

This was all too confusing for Cal. "John, are you talking about this sword?" He patted the sword sheathed at his waist. He wore it today to honor his father on his betrothal day. "The one you insisted on trading for mine a few weeks back? What has it to do with any of this?"

Summer had a hard time following the conversation. "Traded swords? But how? John's sword is very distinctive. I would know it anywhere."

"Our father presented all three of his sons with identical swords, Summer. Didn't you know? Nat and I usually don't wear ours, preferring to save them for our future sons."

Summer's rage was swift. She threw herself at John, pommeling his chest with her fists. "How could you do that to me? You—you knew how much I needed to leave here. How much I agonized over leaving my family. No wonder you let me touch the sword. You knew it would have no power to send me back."

John stood frozen, barely feeling her small fists. He let her vent her rage, and when she was done, he spoke in a low, hoarse voice. "Did you think I could ever let you go?"

Jessica and Caleb watched Summer and John in bewilderment. They didn't understand any of this strange turn of events.

"I'm mystified, Summer. What power does my brother's sword have? How could it possibly send you anywhere?"

Summer was beyond caring. She blurted out the truth. "The power to send me back to where I came from, Cal—your future. I'm sorry you had to learn this way. I had hoped to tell you about it someday, in a proper way."

Composing herself, she sat down on the edge of the bed and took Jessica's hand. "Jessica. Cal. I was propelled here from another time. Sent here, when I touched John's sword where it was kept in a museum in the year 1993. I know how incredible that sounds. It's just as incredible to me, but it's the truth."

Jessica was speechless. Had the poor child cracked under the strain of loving two men? "John, what kind of nonsense is this?" Cal asked. "Surely, you of all people don't believe such a fanciful story?"

"I can prove it to you, Cal." Summer moved swiftly, her hand reaching out for the sword at Cal's side.

Cal grabbed her wrist, preventing her from touching it.

Shocked, Summer cried. "Cal! Why did you stop me?"

Cal looked at her solemnly. "When I saw the fear in John's eyes as you reached for the sword, I knew it must be true."

Summer looked from Cal to John. "Well, then, gentlemen, it looks as if there's a way out of this dilemma after all. I'll go back to my own time, where unmarried mothers are common. No one will feel differently toward me for having a child without benefit of husband there."

A strangled sound escaped John's throat. "A child? Is it true? When in God's name were you going to tell me? After you married my brother? Will no one in this family learn from the mistakes of the past? Isn't this how it all started in the first place? Are we to repeat the same mistakes over and over again?"

"What's past is past, John. What use in bringing it up now? Summer is marrying me. It's useless to discuss it further."

"Cal, Summer came here by my sword, not yours. Doesn't that tell you she belongs with me and no other?"

Summer couldn't bear the angry words between two brothers who had always been so close. "Cal, let me touch the sword and be done with it. Let me end this conflict between you. I can't bear to see you like this."

"Would you take the cowardly way out, Summer?" Cal asked passionately. "Would you leave here forever? The child you carry is a Hawke. He belongs to this time. This family. If you won't stay for me, then stay for the child. Would you deny him his rightful heritage?"

"Cal, I can't believe you would stoop to John's level. You've always been so honest with me, so kind. I can't believe you would keep me here against my will."

Summer took a step toward the sword, and again Cal kept her from touching it.

261

"We'll talk of this, the three of us, when you've calmed down. You can't decide your future in such a distraught state. We'll find a solution, I promise."

Nathaniel came in then, excited and out of breath. "There's been another attack, closer to town. The Graysons were set upon in the field behind their house. All dead."

"The Graysons?" Summer asked. "Isn't that the family of the little boy from the river?"

"Yes," Nat answered. "It seems God intended the child to die after all. He couldn't escape his destiny."

John and Summer sought each other's eyes.

"Was it Robillard?" Cal asked.

"No. Mohawks. Young bloods out for one last raid on the English, before winter sets in."

"Bloodthirsty bastards!" Cal answered.

"Assemble the men, Nat. We ride after them," John said, tearing his gaze from Summer. "Do you ride with us, Cal?"

Cal strode to John's side and clasped him around the neck. "We're brothers, aren't we?"

John's face lit up with a brilliant smile. "'Til the end." Shifting his gaze to Summer, his eyes lingered on hers a moment, then moved down to the small waistline that would soon be large with his child. "It seems destiny can not be thwarted after all. Yours was decided long before you came to me. Think on that well, and you'll know what you must do." His eyes caressed her belly one last time, and then he strode out of the room.

Chapter Twenty-Four

At first the wounded man thought she was dead. Standing over the still form, he gazed down at the angelic beauty of her face, the delicate lines of her of her body, and saw the rise and fall of her small breasts through the taut material of her bodice. He wondered if he was hallucinating. He'd lost a lot of blood, was light-headed, in a dreamlike state he knew was close to unconsciousness. The sleeping woman sighed and moved her hand. It wasn't his imagination. She was truly there, lying beside the waterfall. The ringing in his ears grew louder, competing with the sound of rushing water; afraid of passing out, he sank to his knees.

Elizabeth felt, rather than heard the thud of something hitting the ground, and opened her eyes in fright. She drew in her breath at the sight of the man covered with blood. Quickly taking in the situation, she knew there was nothing to fear from this badly wounded man and knelt over him. "That's a fierce wound you have there, sir."

He looked up at her through a red haze, soothed by the sound of her low, throaty voice.

"I'll just have a look at it. Do not fear, I'm

practiced in the art of healing.

Using up most of his remaining strength, he spoke. "How providential . . . to . . . fall in the hands of . . . a healing angel."

Elizabeth could hear the pain in his voice, and wondered how he had been able to make it here from wherever he had been wounded. She noted his French accent and the patch over his eyes, and knew instantly who the man was. Major Phillipe Robillard. She should let him bleed to death, he deserved no better, but she had spent too many years healing to let a helpless man to die, no matter how vile he was.

Gently, she tore away the red, sticky shirt that clung to his wound. Tearing a piece of cloth from her petticoat, she dipped it into the pool and pressed it to the wound. Wiping it gently, she saw it was a clean cut from a knife or sword, not a musket ball. Good. She didn't relish digging for an iron ball.

"We must get this bleeding stopped before you perish. How long have you been wandering around like this?"

The man looked at her through a cloud of pain. "I don't know. Hours . . . I think . . . days . . . I don't know. I'm afraid I've been delirious. Mayhap I still am, and imagine you here."

"Major Robillard, I am going to try and find some oak leaves to staunch the flow of blood. Just lie here and keep the cloth pressed to your wound."

"You have the advantage of me, Mademoiselle." His voice was halting, slow, but seemed determined to speak. "You . . . know me, but I've never met you. I could never have forgotten so fair a face."

"Your reputation precedes you, Major. And that patch. How could I not have recognized you with so distinctive a calling card? As for my name, there's no need for you to know it."

"If you will not tell me, then I shall call you Angelique, for you are truly my angel—my angel of mercy, I pray."

Gazing at him, Elizabeth thought of all the pain and suffering this man had caused. He would dance at the end of a rope when he was strong enough to walk to the gallows. Or . . . or . . . would he? She suddenly thought of a reason to keep him alive. It was as if destiny had brought her to this spot to meet the one person in the world who could help her. But first she must make sure he lived to do her bidding.

Quickly she searched the forest floor, until she found what she needed, then, making a poultice, she placed it over the Major's wound, covering it with strips of cloth from her petticoat. Cupping her hands in water from the pool, she carried it to him. Awkwardly, he sucked the water from her hands, then demanded more. She repeated the process until he had his fill.

"Are you truly my angel of mercy? Or will you turn me over to Captain Hawke?" He spat out the name with venom.

So, he hates John. That could work to her advantage. "Why do you say the name with such hatred? Was it John Hawke who caused your wound?"

"Not this one, but the one that forces me to wear this accursed patch. It happened years ago, at a spot very near here."

"Well, then, it is obvious to me, sir, you well deserved your fate. For what would you be doing in these parts, if not bringing harm to the people here?"

Major Robillard ignored her question. "Tell me, how well do you know this John Hawke?"

"Deerfield is a small community. I know him as I do everyone in town." She felt it best to keep her true identity a secret, for her own protection. "As for my turning you over to Captain Hawke, I have a proposition to make to you, Major. One I think you will enjoy very much, since it involves someone that John Hawke loves above everyone else in this world."

What mischief was this beautiful woman up to? He could see the hatred shining in her eyes. "Please, I am your humble servant."

"I will nurse you back to health and agree not to turn you over to Hawke, if in return for that very large favor, you contrive to capture the woman of whom I spoke, and take her back to New France with you. She is quite a beauty in a vulgar sort of way, and would bring a good price, I am certain."

"Who is this woman to cause such hatred in your heart? Is she Hawke's wife, and you his mistress?"

Elizabeth almost laughed out loud. If he only knew. "If you must know, *she* is his mistress, and mistress also to the man I love. She's to marry him soon. I don't want that to happen."

"I envy this man you love with such fierceness. I pray he is worthy of all this attention. Very well, I agree. When I am well enough to travel, I shall take this woman with me, but you . . . you will have to lure her to me. I no longer have an army at my disposal, and must make my way north alone."

"That will be no problem. I'll tell you the day and time, and will deliver her to you, personally. Now, I must take leave of you. I've been here too long. It would not do to have a search party looking for me. I'll be back in the morning with food and clean clothes, and blankets to warm you. For tonight, my shawl will have to do. 'Tis large and warm. Try not to move too much. I don't want the bleeding to start again."

Elizabeth rode back to town in an euphoric state. She couldn't believe her luck at finding the Major. She would be rid of Summer, and no one would know of her complicity. It would be so easy to make up a story about being attacked by the French, once she lured Summer away from town. She would tell Caleb and John that Summer had been captured, but she had escaped. What could be simpler? All she needed to make it work was to make friends with Summer, a simple task, since she had expressed an interest in hawking. Summer would never again lay in Caleb's arms, and her bastard child would be born in New France and raised by some loathsome Frenchman.

The euphoria lasted until she returned to Jessica's and heard about the deaths of the poor Graysons. She was disturbed by the news, and felt guilty about aiding a man who more than likely was a cohort of the murderers. Robillard was a murderous dog. How could she nurse him back to health?

But when she stepped inside the house and saw Summer talking cozily to Nenepownam, her determination to be rid of her overrode her hatred of the French. Anyway, sooner or later, Robillard would get his just desserts. She was sure of it. She had to be. How else could she live with herself?

Two weeks later, all was set for the ambush. Elizabeth nervously reviewed the steps she had taken, as she rode down the path to the waterfall. She wanted to make certain she had not overlooked some important detail. She had but one chance to make it work, and there could be no mistakes.

Her first step had been the easiest—winning Summer's friendship—making her think she no longer cared about Caleb. The little fool. How could she have believed such a preposterous notion? She wanted to laugh out loud when she saw the look of relief in Summer's eyes when she told her. It had been so easy.

Jessica, however, was another matter. She had looked at Elizabeth in a funny way, as if she doubted her words. She would have to work harder at convincing that shrewd woman of her sincerity.

She had returned to the waterfall the next day to stitch up Robillard's wound, and was amused to see how surprised he was to see her. Evidently, he hadn't quite believed she would go through with her bargain.

Every morning since, she had slipped out of the house to bring him a basket of food and tend to his wound, and she was eminently satisfied at how fast the healing progressed. She often sat with him by the water awhile, talking of trivial things. Phillipe, she knew, was always happy to see her, not just for the food and medicine she brought him, but for the companionship as well. It was too bad he was the enemy, for he was a charming, good-looking, and intelligent man. And he looked at her in a way she found pleasing.

Surprisingly, she had gotten him to reveal the name of the person who had shielded him after each raid, the person he had been trying to reach after he was wounded.

"Why do you want to know?" he had asked her. "So that you can turn him in?"

"No, Phillipe. So we can use him, if there's a need. I don't want anything to hinder our plans."

"Unbelievable, the extent you would go to obtain your lover. Ah, *chèrie*, if only you could love me with such fierceness! All right. I shall tell you. There is one who could help. Asperensah, the preacher's housekeeper."

"Hmph," Elizabeth said, indignantly. "Wouldn't Daniel and his father be surprised to know they have a traitor in their midst?"

Robillard smiled to himself. "Here," he said, handing her a ring with a fleur-de-lis seal on it. "Tell her I am well, and will have need of her. Have her meet me here an hour before you get here with the woman. She will know what to do."

Getting the message to Asperensah had been easier than she dreamed. The Indian maid came to town often, on errands for Daniel and his father. Elizabeth simply approached her outside the meetinghouse, and handed her Phillipe's ring. Asperensah had been shocked to see it, and even more shocked at the bearer. Elizabeth smiled, thinking about the encounter. The stupid woman thought she was a traitor, but it didn't matter. Nothing mattered, but Summer gone from her life. Gone from Caleb's life, forever.

She had whispered Phillipe's name to the Indian, and where he was hidden. Elizabeth knew the woman was aware of the spot. She had seen her there many times when she made trips to the waterfall in search of herbs, and had always resented the Indian's intrusion at the place she considered her own.

She told Asperensah that Phillipe would have need of her very soon. Elizabeth had decided she could wait no longer than that to be rid of Summer.

The last and most important step had been undertaken successfully just this morning. Summer had agreed to go hawking with her in two days' time. That gave her enough time to set the rest of her trap.

Sliding off her horse, she gave her signal, and Robillard came out from behind a tree. Her eyes lit up with pleasure, seeing how much stronger he was.

Her careful nursing had paid off. And by the way he looked at her, as a man looks at a desirable woman, she knew he must be feeling good. He slid his arm around her waist, and pulled her to him affectionately.

"Ah, Angelique, what have you brought me this day? I fear I am growing fat from your excellent meals. Strong, too. My body desires more than nourishment for the stomach. I have other needs that wish to be fulfilled."

"Phillipe," she answered, pushing him away. "Don't get any ideas about me. You know where my heart lies."

"Ah, yes, to a man who would marry another. How much can he love you, *ma chérie,* if he wishes to wed another? Your efforts would be better spent on someone who can appreciate your feminine nature, and your soft, womanly body. Forget about this fool, and come with me. A woman such as yourself would be an asset to my camp, as well as to my bed. Your healing powers are miraculous, and the love that fills your heart would not be lost on me. What can this fool give you, but secondhand love? You deserve much more than that."

"Phillipe, your speech is pretty, but my feelings can not be so easily changed. I have loved this man since I was a child." A sudden suspicion crossed her mind, and she gave him a critical look. "You're not trying to back out of our agreement, are you? I did my part. I nursed you back to health. If you—"

"Do not fear, *chère.* You will have your man. But meanwhile, here am I, ready to give you pleasure of a sort you have only dreamed of."

He took her hand and placed it against his swollen manhood. "Feel my desire. Do not waste it, but share with me the carnal pleasure of the flesh."

Elizabeth felt the hardness, and a sliver of desire tightened her belly. She pulled her hand back. "Phillipe, you're incorrigible. But I am pleased, for it means you are getting stronger and will be able to carry out your end of the bargain."

Phillipe pretended to pout. "Is that all my hardness means to you? That I am well enough to do your bidding? Bah! You disappoint me."

"I leave you, then, to your disappointment. Now, listen carefully. It's all set. In two days I'll lure our little pigeon into the trap. I just pray the men stay away until it's over. They could ruin my plans."

"The captain has not returned yet? What is keeping him?"

"There's been an attack by the Mohawks. The militia is out hunting for them, and searching every homestead for you at the same time, Major. They're determined to find you, and hang the person that has been hiding you after every attack."

"Hah! And thanks to you, my angel, they shall not find me. Captain Hawke must be puzzled indeed, as to why he has not come across my dead body. For surely I would have died, if you hadn't found me. Did I tell you it was Hawke's half-breed brother who caused this wound? Damn him and damn John Hawke. It will give me great pleasure to cause them both grief. I relish the thought of taking this woman of John's, and when I part her thighs, and use her body for my pleasure, it will be doubly gratifying. I only wish he could be there to see it happen. I shall be sure to leave a calling card, so there'll be no doubt in his mind as to who has his beloved."

Elizabeth looked at Phillipe in shock. His hatred for John was stronger than she realized, and she couldn't help but feel remorse. She hadn't expected him to take his revenge out on Summer. She just

271

wanted the woman out of her way, out of her life. She had never wanted her raped or beaten. But she couldn't stop now. It was too late. The plan was set in motion. Her future—and Summer's—was now in the hands of an Indian squaw and a treacherous Frenchman. She shivered, and pulled her cloak around her body to block the sudden, icy wind.

Chapter Twenty-Five

Sgt. Josiah Davidson couldn't help admiring the contrasting beauty of the two women riding toward him. One so fair, atop a white mare, the dark one riding a black gelding. They made a breathtaking picture riding side by side, regal and serene. All the more so because of the hooded hawk Mistress Elizabeth carried on her shoulder. It put him in mind of the days of chivalry and knights errant to see such a splendid sight.

"Good morrow, Mistress Winslow, Mistress Hawke. I see you're going hawking. Do not wander far. Captain Hawke would have my hide if any harm befell either of you."

"Never, fear, Sergeant," Elizabeth said, smiling. "We'll be safe. I have walked these woods every day of my life, and know well where we may go. Is that not so? Have you not benefited greatly from my wanderings?"

"Aye, 'tis so. From your herbs and potions, not to mention the succulent meat your hawk has downed."

"Beauty is a prolific hunter. Mayhap we'll bring you back a plump pigeon for your stew tonight."

"That would be a welcome change from my usual

fare. But I would rather go hungry than have you harmed. It would do no harm to wait until the militia returns before you go a-hawking."

"You speak like an old lady, Sergeant." Elizabeth's heart raced at the mention of the militia. It would be most awkward if they returned now. "Have you news of their return?"

"Not a word, but do not fear, your husband is keeping his movements closely guarded. While most of his company is out hunting the Mohawks, he and a special handpicked troop are searching for the traitors who harbor the French major Robillard. 'Tis hard to believe anyone would protect a cur like Robillard."

Elizabeth blanched at his words. She was no traitor, at least, not in her heart. But the words echoed through her head accusingly once unleashed, and there was nothing she could do but hope Phillipe's neck would be stretched on the gallows some day soon. But not until he had accomplished his mission and taken Summer away.

Looking in Summer's direction, she noted how blissfully unaware the woman was of the danger that was rapidly closing in on her. Summer had accepted Elizabeth's feigned friendship and her offer to teach her hawking, without the slightest hesitation. The little fool! How could Summer possibly believe she could forget her love of Caleb so easily?

They were on their way to the waterfall even now, where soon her troubles would be over, Summer's just beginning. A smile crossed her face. Everything was working out just as she had planned.

Her thoughts were interrupted by the sound of a child's voice. Elizabeth looked over her shoulder and saw Alisha riding up on her pony. Her heart sank. Alisha could spoil everything.

"Mama, wait for me. I want to ride with you and Summer."

Elizabeth whipped her horse around to face her daughter. "Alisha, I want you to return to Grandmother's immediately. If I had wanted you to join us, I would have told you so."

Alisha's small face screwed up, ready to cry. She had never heard her mother speak so harshly before.

Elizabeth saw the hurt in Alisha's small face and softened her words. "Alisha, Mama is going to be very busy with Summer, teaching her ways of the hawk. It would not do to have you along. But, if you're a good, little girl, I'll take you out riding on the morrow. Now, go home. Mayhap you can convince Charity to ride with you, *in town*."

Elizabeth watched as Alisha started back home before continuing with Summer. She could ill afford to have a witness to what was about to take place.

Summer saw the anxious look on Elizabeth's face and wondered what was troubling her. Why hadn't she let Alisha join them? Usually, Elizabeth was very indulgent toward her daughter. But then, Elizabeth had been acting out of character all week. Summer wondered what had caused this sudden change. Whatever it was, she was grateful. It was a rare opportunity for her to learn hawking. In the twentieth century, not many were allowed that privilege.

Things had been much pleasanter these past few days. At first, she had been leery of living in Jessica's small house with Elizabeth, but with her sudden change of heart, it had not been difficult at all. And, thankfully, the morning sickness that had plagued her had all but disappeared, and her appetite returned. She felt stronger now, better able to cope with her problems. She would need that strength, for

275

soon John and Cal would be back, and she would be faced with the hardest decision of her life.

The baby she carried complicated an already tangled situation. If she stayed, she would have to marry. There was no getting out of that. But there was only one man she wanted, and she couldn't have him. If she touched the sword and returned to her own time, she could raise her child in comfort, and without the censure and condemnation she could expect here. But then, she would never see John again, and her child would never know its father. There had to be a solution she could live with, but so far it had escaped her.

They rode down the road a short while, before turning down a path so narrow they had to ride single file. It led to a clearing and a beautiful, pristine, storybook waterfall. Summer drank in the beauty of the peaceful scene, content at being in such a lovely setting. But she wondered what they were doing here. It was hardly the kind of place to go hawking. She didn't know much about the subject, but any fool would know a hawk needed room to move about in, unhindered by dense woods.

In a strange, tense voice, Elizabeth spoke to her. "We'll water the horses here, and then be on our way. I thought you might like to see the waterfall. A grand sight, is it not?"

"Yes, oh yes. I was just admiring the view. Thank you for bringing me here to see it."

Elizabeth seemed taken aback by her words, and Summer began to feel uneasy. "Do you come here often, Elizabeth?"

Elizabeth's face took on a dreamy quality when she spoke again. "In times past, this is where Cal and I met. Our own small patch of paradise, where Alisha was conceived."

Summer's uneasiness grew. Something was not right.

Summer watched as Elizabeth's silver eyes shifted to somewhere behind Summer's head, and the hair on the back of her neck stood on end. Gathering all her courage, she turned slowly in her saddle. A rugged-looking man with a patch over one eye straddled the narrow path. He stood, hands on hips, staring at her arrogantly, and beyond him stood three Indian braves and Asperensah. Summer's heart raced as realization hit her.

"Major Robillard!"

"At your service, Mademoiselle." He bowed deeply, sweeping his plumed hat from his head in a gallant gesture.

Summer whipped her head back to face Elizabeth, amazed to see her sitting serenely on the black horse. Didn't she realize the danger they were in? Didn't she know who Major Robillard was? "Elizabeth, this man is a French major. Get out of here, quick!"

Summer spun her horse around, she'd have to ride right by the major, there was nowhere else to go. She spurred her horse, but the major was too quick for her. He grabbed hold of the mare's bridle, preventing her from getting away.

Summer calmed her horse with a soothing voice, while her mind raced, trying to think of a way out of the danger she was in. She tried to sound confident and unafraid when she spoke, but her hands trembled and her voice shook. "Surely you do not do battle with two helpless women, Major Robillard?"

"One helpless woman," the major emphasized. "The other is quite able. It is she who commissioned me to take you captive, thereby removing you permanently from her lover's arms."

Summer looked at Elizabeth in disbelief, as she

moved the black gelding up next to Summer's mare. It couldn't be true. Elizabeth couldn't be that cruel. But Elizabeth sat calmly on her mount, stroking its sleek neck as if she were out for a pleasant afternoon's ride, the hawk still perched on her shoulder.

It was true! Elizabeth had only pretended to be her friend, so that she could lure Summer to the ambush. Summer remembered reading the accounts of women and children captives who had been marched to Canada. Many died along the way, because of the harsh conditions and forced marching.

Children had been bludgeoned to death, because they were too small to keep up. Those hardy enough to survive were sold to the French, or adopted into the Indian tribes. She remembered, too, what she had read of John Hawke rescuing his wife and daughter from the French, and how another unnamed woman had died before he could rescue her. A cold chill went through her. Was she that unnamed woman? No! This couldn't be the same incident. Alisha had been rescued, too, and Alisha wasn't here! But she could take no comfort in that, for a small voice inside her answered. *She would have been here, had not Elizabeth turned her away!* But then, what about Elizabeth herself? She was in no danger; she had instigated the whole thing!

The welcome sound of a horse moving along the narrow path gave Summer hope. John. Please let it be John. But the figure that burst through the opening was a small girl on a pony.

"Alisha!" Elizabeth called out in anguish. "Go back. Leave this place at once."

Alisha looked around in confusion, then, understanding she whirled her pony around.

Asperensah moved swiftly to block her way.

Phillipe was taken aback by the sight of the small

278

child. She looked so much like Angelique, there was no doubt in his mind who she was. Funny, he hadn't thought of his beautiful angel of mercy being married. Nothing she had said to him ever indicated that. "And what do we have here? Your name, young lady?"

Alisha bravely raised herself in the saddle and said, proudly, "Sir, I am Alisha Hawke."

Phillipe recoiled as if he had been struck a blow. That was the last name he expected to hear. His eyes narrowed to dangerous slits, and his voice took on an urgency. "Hawke, did you say? And who is your father?"

"Why, Captain Hawke, of course. Everyone knows that."

"No, my dear, not quite everyone." He turned to look at Elizabeth. "John Hawke's wife. How unkind of you not to tell me, and how fortunate for me your daughter happened along, just now."

Fear clutched Elizabeth's heart. "Do not look at me so. I have not betrayed you. I nursed you back to health. I gave you Summer Winslow. You'll still have your revenge on John. Nothing's changed."

"Ah, but you see, this puts an entirely different light on the situation. A most favorable one at that. What a coup! Not only do I have the good captain's mistress in my possession, but his wife and daughter as well. How tragic for the captain! I almost pity the man."

"You can't mean that. Surely you'll keep to our agreement. You would have died, if I hadn't helped you."

"Yes, *chèrie*, but you see, there are no rules of fair play in the game of war." Phillipe's face hardened as his hands moved up to caress the black patch over his eye. "And, as you have shown so aptly, no rules of fair play in the game of love either."

Wincing at his remark, she uttered, "Let my daughter go, at least. Surely, you have some compassion in you. She knows nothing that can cause you any harm."

"I am sorry, truly, but that is impossible. But, to show you I have some compassion, I will allow you to set your magnificent bird free."

A spark of hope flared in Elizabeth. If any townspeople saw Beauty flying overhead, they might recognize her, and realize that something was wrong. They would send out a rescue party. It was her only chance—Alisha's only chance.

Elizabeth removed the hood from the hawk's head before Phillipe could have second thoughts; the bird shook its head back and forth and ruffled its feathers. This was not the hill it soared from seeking prey. The golden eyes sought the reassurance of a familiar sight and locked onto Summer. It flew to her, landing on her shoulder.

Summer tried to push the bird away, knowing that if it stayed, it was in danger of being killed, but the hawk flew right back.

Elizabeth, seeing all eyes on the hawk, took the opportunity and struck out at Phillipe with her riding crop.

Robillard heard the swoosh of air and sidestepped the blow easily. Two Indians moved in quickly, forcing Elizabeth from her horse.

The hawk became riled over the aggressive behavior of the strange humans to its mistress. It flew at the Indians, its lethal claws extended, and the Indians let go of Elizabeth to fight off the fierce bird.

Elizabeth ran blindly down the path.

Phillipe mounted Elizabeth's horse and pursued her. Catching her up in his arms, he swept her into the saddle in front of him. "It seems you will be my escort after all. Resign yourself to that fate."

"Never, you bastard! I'll reap my revenge on you, be sure of that. And when John and Caleb catch up to you, we will see whose fate has been decided."

"Caleb? The brother to John? It is he that wounded me so gravely. Is he the lover you would betray your people for?" He saw by the look on her face that he had hit upon the truth. "Then it is fitting you were the one to heal me from his wound, is it not? Now, call off your hawk. I have need of those men, and would not see them stripped of their flesh."

Elizabeth looked at him defiantly.

"Now! Else I will kill your hawk with my bare hands, and make you eat every morsel of it."

Elizabeth knew he meant what he said. She whistled to the hawk, and it responded, climbing high into the sky.

The two Indians who had been fighting the hawk were covered with deep scratches on their faces and arms. They knelt by the pool and washed their wounds with cold water as the hawk climbed higher and higher, until it could be seen no more.

Taking off his hat, Phillipe removed the purple plume and watched as it floated to the ground. "My calling card. Would that I could see John Hawke's face, when he realizes it is I who have the ones he loves most in this world."

Gesturing to the Indians, he watched as they steered Summer and Alisha's mounts down the path toward the road. The Indians ran alongside the horses, holding tightly to the bridles, while Elizabeth, captive in Phillipe's arms, cried softly, ashamed that she was responsible for her daughter's capture.

Instead of going out to the road, the party veered down another path that wound through the dense woods. When they came off it, Summer was surprised to see that they were near the entrance to Daniel's place.

Asperensah moved ahead to see if the entrance road was clear, and when the signal came that it was, Phillipe rode into the yard as if he belonged there. And when Daniel walked over to greet Phillipe, Summer knew that indeed he did.

Major Robillard was the stranger she had seen talking to Daniel, the same man she had told John and Cal about. But they hadn't believed her, thinking him some harmless fur trader. She realized now that she should have tried harder to convince them.

Asperensah moved over to Daniel's side and, with a sly smile on her round face, stood looking at the captive women. She was happy to see these two beautiful whites in such a miserable state. She knew how Daniel felt about the fair-haired one, and was glad the woman would no longer be around to take up Daniel's attention. She would never forgive or forget the day he took her in the pantry like an animal, while he cried out the witch's name.

Daniel's gaze took in Summer, sitting forlornly on a white horse, and his eyes opened wide in shock. "You didn't tell me you would be abducting women, Robillard. I warned you once before I would not be a party to that!"

"Too bad, Bradford. This is a special occasion. One requested by the black-haired, black-hearted Mistress Hawke. Gentleman that I am, I could not refuse her."

"I don't know what you're babbling about, Robillard."

"It matters not. We pay you and your father well enough to do as we please. But, do not worry, we won't be imposing long. We stay only long enough to get the women properly clothed for the cold weather, and to pack provisions for the long journey ahead. I believe your father has furs enough to lend, and boots and snowshoes for their dainty feet."

"My God, Phillipe, you're not planning to take them to New France? I won't allow it. Summer Winslow stays with me."

Phillipe looked at Daniel in amazement. "My friend, the woman you are so concerned about was going to marry Hawke's half-breed brother. Surely you knew that? No? Tsk, tsk. It seems the beautiful Mistress Summer has not confided in you. You should be glad she will not be around to remind you of your ardor, once she has shared her bed with him."

Daniel looked at Summer, his face drained of color. "Is this true? Were you planning to marry the half-breed?"

He saw the truth in her eyes and paled. He had never had a chance with her. It had only been a dream. "Then, you have sealed your fate." Turning his back, he walked into the house.

"Mademoiselles, dismount and go into the house. You must clothe yourself for the arduous journey ahead."

Summer entered Daniel's house, her heart heavy with sorrow. Elizabeth's betrayal had shocked her and left her numb, and now Daniel, too, had betrayed her, leaving her to the ruthless Major Robillard.

How could she trek through hundreds of miles of wilderness in *her* condition? She could miscarry, and if she did, she would be in great danger of dying. Elizabeth was pregnant, too, and Alisha a small child. This would be a perilous journey for them all.

Her gaze focused on Daniel, standing by the staircase. "How do you live with yourself, knowing you have betrayed your friends and neighbors? What reward is worth the pain and suffering you have caused?"

Daniel winced at Summer's words. He hadn't wanted any of this to happen. Had never wanted anything to do with his father's dirty business. But he had been weak. Had given in to his father's stronger will. And for what? So his father could have a lucrative fur-trading business? He struggled for an answer Summer could understand, and knew it was hopeless. How could she understand what he could not?

"Daniel?"

He heard his mother call from upstairs, and was relieved to be able to turn from Summer's accusing eyes.

"Is that Summer I hear, son? Send her up to visit with me."

"Summer. You'll have to speak to her, but be careful of what you say. She's not involved in any of this."

"I understand too well. Don't worry. I'd never say anything to let her know what a despicable bastard you really are. It would kill her."

"I think not," Phillipe said. "Summer stays down here."

"Robillard, my mother will be suspicious if Summer doesn't visit with her. Why take the chance?"

"As you wish then. But listen well, Summer. I'll be in the room with you every minute. If you say anything to her of your predicament, if you show by any gesture that you are troubled, I will not hesitate to kill the old one. Do you understand?"

Summer looked at Daniel with contempt. "Is this the man you would betray your country for? A man who would slit your own mother's throat?"

Summer made her way up the stairs, followed closely by Daniel and Phillipe, while the Indians stood guard over Elizabeth and Alisha in the parlor.

Entering the darkened room, Summer walked over to Sarah's bed and leaned down to kiss her cheek. "Sarah," she said, trying to sound cheerful. "I was riding my horse nearby, and thought I'd stop in and see how you were doing. How are you feeling?"

Sarah gazed at the beautiful pale face before her, and then at the two men behind her. She knew who the one-eyed man was, and that his presence meant Summer was in grave danger. She knew very well the activities her husband and son were involved in, though they tried to keep her from knowing. She must try to help Summer. She couldn't bear it if Summer shared the same fate as her own beloved daughters, sold to wealthy Frenchmen in payment for her husband's thriving business. It had been two years since last she saw them, two long years that she had spent in this very bed.

"I would feel much better, my dear, if I could change into a clean shift. I fear I must smell like a goat. Would you mind helping me? That is, if the men would be so kind as to leave the room for a spell."

Daniel looked at Phillipe, but the man stood stone-faced. "I'll, ah, send Asperensah up, Mother. After Summer's visit."

"Is there some reason why Summer cannot help me now, son?" Sarah asked innocently, knowing her son would have a hard time refusing such a reasonable request.

"Why . . . no, Mother, of course not. Summer?"

"Certainly. Where do you keep your clean shifts?"

Sarah nodded her head in the direction of a chest of drawers against the wall, then looked pointedly at her son and Phillipe, who very reluctantly started out of the room.

"Summer cannot stay long, Mother," Daniel said, more for Summer's benefit than his mother's. He walked out of the room with Phillipe.

As soon as the door closed, Sarah grabbed Summer's hand, whispering, "I know you must be in terrible danger, dear, but there's no time to talk of it. They'll not leave us alone long. You can escape out my window, then walk around the roof to the back of the house. You will see it slopes enough for you to jump to the ground unharmed."

Summer looked in Sarah's pale eyes. "Thank you," she whispered, then quickly tiptoed to the window. She opened it quietly, easing it up slowly so as not to be heard; then bunching up her skirts, she climbed out onto the roof.

Making her way around to the back where the roof slanted steeply, she lay down and edged herself down the incline; her skirt rode up on her, catching on the rough surface as she moved. She was sorry now that she had chosen to wear her newly made riding outfit, instead of Nat's breeches. But she had thought Elizabeth would be too shocked if she went hawking dressed as a man. Thank goodness, the outfit was made to be worn without stays or hoops or corsets, or she'd really be in trouble now.

Reaching the edge of the roof, she looked down and saw that it was only one story high here. She could make the jump easily. Bracing herself, she jumped, landing on the flat of her feet.

A sharp pain shot up her feet and legs, paralyzing her for a second. But, afraid to linger, she ran in the direction of the water, the pain still severe, adrenaline pumping strongly through her veins. She would follow the river back to town, instead of taking the road, where she was sure of being caught by Robillard.

Running blind with fear, she stumbled through the trees and brush, holding her hands in front of her, to keep from being scratched by the sharp twigs that reached for her. She ran until she was winded and had a stitch in her side, but kept on, knowing this was her only chance to escape.

At last, exhausted and with a terrible pain in her lungs, she came to the river. Flinging herself down on the bank, she tried to catch her breath. She lay panting, listening for sounds of pursuit. But the wind had picked up, and blocked all other noises with its fierce howl.

She pushed herself up on her elbow, recovering enough to continue, and started to rise.

Robillard and Daniel stood looking down at her.

The sight of them jolted her, sending a shock wave of pain to the pit of her stomach, and she sank back in despair. She wanted to cry, to beg them to let her go, but knew it was hopeless. She wouldn't give them that satisfaction.

"I don't like being disobeyed, Mistress Winslow. I don't like it at all." Grabbing her arm, Robillard pulled her to her feet, then slapped her hard across the face.

Daniel stepped over to Phillipe and yanked on his arm. "Don't ever touch her again."

Phillipe pushed him away. "You fool! Do you realize the damage she could have done our cause, if she had escaped? She needs to be taught a lesson."

Grasping Summer by the hair, Robillard pulled her to him. "Perhaps a taste of leather on your bare skin will teach you to obey." Taking a riding crop from his belt, he drew it lightly across the exposed area of her breasts, then raised it as if to strike.

Enraged, Daniel pulled a knife from his waist, raising it high. "I told you not to touch her."

Robillard quickly pulled his own knife from his boot, and plunged it into Daniel's chest. Daniel slumped to the ground, clutching at his wound, his fingers turning red.

The sight of Daniel covered with blood sent Summer into shock. She gasped for air, but though she took in gulp after gulp, couldn't catch her breath.

"Do you see what you've made me do? This man is valuable to my cause. If he dies, it will set my efforts back many months—if not years! I should kill you right here and now, but I mean to gain something profitable from this venture. Help me get this romantic fool back to the house."

Phillipe's words brought Summer to her senses. Daniel needed immediate help, or he'd die. She grabbed one of his arms while Phillipe took the other, and struggled toward the house, each step causing Daniel to cry out in pain, and Summer to cringe.

As they got closer to the house, an Indian spotted them and gave assistance. They carried Daniel into the parlor, and laid him on a long bench by the fireplace.

The Indian woman ran toward Summer, a knife in her hand.

Phillipe stopped her before she could harm Summer. "Calm yourself, woman. You will be of little help to Daniel like this. Go to him. See what you can do."

"No. I cannot do this. The wound is too severe. There is but one person here who can help him." Asperensah ran to Elizabeth. "Help him or I will kill you!"

"There's nothing I can do. There's nothing

288

anyone can do. He's in God's hands now."

Asperensah cried out the anguish she felt, and the Indian brave put his arm around her and led her to a chair.

The emotional scene was too much for Summer. Tears streamed down her face and she sobbed, "Daniel, I'm so sorry—"

Daniel smiled through his pain. "Do not be . . . troubled. I . . . was lost . . . long ago."

Summer's sobs grew louder as she listened to Daniel's pain-filled words. He was a traitor, but he didn't deserve to die like this. He had only been trying to protect her.

"Better this way . . . I pray . . . Summer, you find a way out . . . marry Cal. He—he followed right path . . . though torn between two worlds . . . as I was."

The door was suddenly flung open, and Daniel's father strode over to where he lay. "You fool! You bloody fool—to be stabbed over a woman!"

Summer couldn't believe how heartless Martin Bradford was. How cold-blooded! Didn't he care that his son was dying?

"Martin." The tiny voice called from the stairs. "Is that you? What's happening?"

Martin looked at Summer with hatred. "Because of you, that woman up there will lose her only remaining child."

Summer put her hand over her mouth to keep from crying louder; she watched as Martin climbed the stairs to his wife's room.

Elizabeth worked on Daniel, knowing it was useless. She managed to stem the flow of blood, but it was too late. He was already deadly white.

Martin came down the stairs carrying his wife, and set her down near her son. Sarah knelt beside Daniel, her face wet with tears. "Daniel, my first born, my son . . ."

Summer's heart broke watching the tiny woman. She tried to go to her, but Asperensah held her back. "Haven't you done enough harm? Do not dare go near him. It's your fault he is lying there." Straining to pull free of Asperensah, Summer cried, "Sarah, oh, Sarah, I'm so sorry."

Sarah never lifted her head, oblivious to all but her dying son.

Martin turned away from the heartbreaking scene and walked over to Phillipe, talking to him in French. Summer watched, unbelieving; how could he be friendly with the man who murdered his son? Did Martin actually blame Daniel for getting stabbed? Or was it possible that he didn't want to ruin the profitable arrangement he had with the Frenchman? Could he be that unfeeling, that callous?

Phillipe nodded his head, then gave orders to the Indians in their language. They hurried from the room, returning in a short time with fur jackets, leggings, and boots for the women and Alisha. Phillipe ordered them to get dressed, and when they were ready, and the horses packed with provisions, they mounted their horses and rode away. Martin and Asperensah watched from the door.

Summer sat stiffly in the saddle, numbed by all that had happened in such a short span of time. She felt like she was in the middle of a bad dream, and couldn't wake up. Then, remembering she wasn't the only one held captive, she looked over to see how Alisha was doing. Alisha had been very quiet throughout the ordeal, but her eyes were wide with fear and shock. Poor little thing.

Thank goodness, the child had a great deal of

fortitude. It would help get her through what lay ahead. Elizabeth, on the other hand, looked ready to collapse. Hatred shone in her eyes for the man who had betrayed her, and Summer was sure that hatred was the only thing keeping her going. That and concern for her daughter.

Phillipe, the object of that hate, calmly led the small procession toward the Connecticut River. He and the three Indians rode horses borrowed from the Bradford place, and another horse laden with packs was led by one of the savages.

Deep in sorrow and shock, Summer relived the traumatic events of the day over and over in her mind, unaware of the scenery around her, until they came to the great river.

The Indians uncovered two canoes hidden skillfully under some brush, and unloaded the provisions, placing them in the center of each canoe. After they had all dismounted, the horses were sent galloping back toward the Bradford place.

Summer was guided into one of the canoes, manned by two Indians, and Elizabeth and Alisha into another, manned by Phillipe and the remaining Indian. The canoes were hollowed-out trees, still smelling of the fire used to carve them.

They pushed off, and the canoes headed upstream, the Indians paddling through the water with little effort. Their strong arms and shoulders seemed hardly to strain at the chore.

This was the first time Summer had ever been in a canoe, and she felt very precarious, barely moving for fear of upsetting the canoe and ending up in the icy water.

She looked up to the sky to determine what time it was, having long since lost track of time. Squinting at the sun, she guessed it to be early afternoon. A dark speck moved across her field of vision. A hawk. She thought she saw jesses trailing from its feet. No, it couldn't be Beauty. Those couldn't be leather jesses. But as the hawk swooped lower, she saw that they were. Beauty was following them.

The hawk had a calming influence on her, and a spark of hope ignited inside her. The hawk's presence symbolized the tenacity she knew John possessed, and she knew he and Cal would never give up until they were found.

The rhythmic movement of the paddles and the sound of water lapping against the canoe had a hypnotic effect on Alisha, and she was soon asleep. Elizabeth looked down at her, cradled in her lap, and hugged her close. What a fool she had been. It was her fault that her daughter was in grave danger. She had let her jealousy and hatred of Summer blind her to reason.

All these years she had told herself that it was John's fault for marrying her, and Caleb's fault for leaving her, that had caused them all such heartbreak, when all along it had been *her* fault and hers alone.

Tears welled in her eyes. She should have trusted in Cal's love and known that he would return for her. She could have left town until Alisha was born, but no, she had taken the easy way out, and married a man she could never love. She didn't deserve happiness. But Alisha was innocent, and had her whole life ahead of her. She couldn't bear it if anything happened to her daughter.

Phillipe watched Elizabeth holding her daughter, a morsel of compassion touching him. He had wanted her since he first saw her, and had grown to care for her throughout the days she had nursed him beside the waterfall. He had asked her then to accompany him, to be his companion and lover, but she had refused because of her blind love for the half-breed. He had another chance now to win her love, and he would use any means at his disposal.

He would use the child, if he must, as leverage. Elizabeth would do anything for her daughter, just as she would do anything for her lover. And someday she would love *him* with that same wonderful fierceness.

He wouldn't be in this bloody business much longer. Soon the French and English would make peace. It was inevitable. Then he could think of settling down and raising a family.

Summer's gaze moved to the other canoe, and saw the way Phillipe looked at Elizabeth. So, that was the way it was. He wouldn't be selling her to some fat Frenchman. Her forehead creased, remembering from her research that Elizabeth and Alisha would be rescued. Phillipe's scheme would fail. That left only *her* fate undecided.

Or did it? Since there were no other female captives, was Summer the unnamed woman who would be killed? Had she come through two hundred years of time to die on a lonely march to Canada?

Chapter Twenty-Six

An abrupt jarring woke Summer from a sound sleep. Her eyes flew open in fear, forgetting for the moment where she was. Then it all came back to her.

She watched as the Indians jumped out of the canoe, realizing that the jarring that woke her so rudely was the canoe being beached. Evidently, the Indians were weary from their relentless paddling and needed a rest. Looking up at the sun, she judged that they had been on the water at least three hours. She scanned the sky for the hawk. No sign of it. Had it turned back finally?

Major Robillard gestured to her to get out of the canoe, and she did so gladly. Her body ached from staying in the same position too long, and her bladder was about to burst.

"Major, I have to go behind the trees. Tell your Indian friends I'm not trying to escape."

With as much dignity as she could muster, she walked stiff-legged and sore to a stand of trees. She didn't know if the major would respect her privacy or not, but in any case, she couldn't wait any longer. She needn't have worried, the Frenchman and the

Indians were busy doing the same thing in plain view. No hiding behind bushes for them.

Obviously, Major Robillard wasn't worried about her escaping. And, after all, where could she go? She was completely helpless in this rugged landscape. She hated feeling that way, and was angry that her life was in somebody else's hands. Her very existence depended on the whims of a stranger.

She had to find a way to escape, no matter the odds. She wasn't the kind of person to just sit back and accept defeat. But if she was the unnamed woman destined to be killed, her efforts would be useless. Little Jacob Grayson proved that. She had brought him back to life, only to have him killed by the Mohawks.

Could it be true? Was she going to die? Her pregnancy was certainly a strike against her survival. If she miscarried during the physically exhausting journey, she could die from loss of blood or other complications. But, then, Elizabeth was pregnant, too, wasn't she? And Summer knew for a fact that she wouldn't miscarry. Adam Hawke would be born.

It was too much to think about. The thought of Elizabeth pregnant by John was enough to put her in a tailspin. Why had he lied to her about having marital relations with his wife? She could hardly condemn him for that, even though it hurt terribly. It didn't make sense. But she couldn't deal with that now.

Standing behind the trees, she started to undress, not an easy chore with all the heavy clothing she had on. She had to admit, though, she was grateful for the furs. The weather had turned bitterly cold, and she hadn't realized just how cold until now, bereft of her warm furs.

As soon as she finished, Elizabeth and Alisha availed themselves of the same spot, then all three walked around, stretching their cramped, aching muscles.

The Indians built a fire and prepared a meal of roasted squirrel and rabbit, while Summer sat by the roaring fire with Elizabeth and Alisha.

At the sight of the crisp, brown meat, Summer realized that she was starving. She made fast work of a squirrel haunch and a big chunk of bread. Feeling better, she relaxed and looked around the campfire at the rest of the group huddled there.

Her eyes rested on the three Indian braves, talking quietly amongst themselves. It was hard to believe them capable of tomahawking or scalping helpless women. But she knew these attractive young men could very well be the same ones who had killed Hannah and Charles and the Osbornes. A shiver went through her. What a harsh world she had been transported to.

She listened to the Indians' husky voices, knowing the huskiness was a part of the genetic makeup of Indians even in her own century. She had always enjoyed listening to the low timbre of their voices before. But now, the sound was ominous to her ears, frightening; for they could be speaking at this very moment of how they would kill her, or who would rape her first.

She tried not to think of that. So far there had been no indication that she or Elizabeth would be raped, another reason to be grateful for the bulky furs. They gave her a shapeless, unfeminine look that perhaps kept the men uninterested.

Summer's eyes shifted to Major Robillard. He was their leader; her fate was in his hands. Surely he didn't want to kill her. He said he wanted to make a profit from her capture, and he'd have to keep her alive for that.

The Frenchman sat by Elizabeth, talking in a low, intimate voice, while Alisha rested her head on her mother's lap. The little girl seemed in good spirits, considering what she had been through, and Summer's heart went out to her. She put on such a brave front for such a little thing. Elizabeth was lucky to have such a courageous daughter.

Every once in awhile, Elizabeth's gaze would drift Summer's way, but she didn't try to talk to her. That was fine with Summer, she wasn't about to make small talk with the woman who had caused this terrible travail.

It was true that Elizabeth was suffering, too—more so, because of her daughter—and it was hard not to pity her for that; but what about the child Summer carried in her womb? The child Elizabeth had been well aware of when she asked the major to abduct her. How could Elizabeth do that? What kind of a woman wàs she?

Summer's thoughts were interrupted by a small hand on her shoulder. Alisha stood looking at her, with silver eyes so much like her mother's. "Do not be sad, Summer. My daddy will rescue us." Alisha's arms wound around her neck, hugging her tightly. A lump came to Summer's throat.

"Yes, darling, your daddy will find us, and your Uncle Caleb, too. Before long we'll be safely home, and you'll be telling Nenepownam of your mighty adventure." Reaching out, she felt the child's face. "Are you warm enough, sweetheart?"

"Oh, yes. The furs keep me very warm. I've taken a fancy to them. Do you suppose I might keep them, after we're rescued?"

Summer laughed. "Yes, I suppose you may. I am certainly going to keep mine."

Elizabeth felt a touch of jealousy and . . . something else she couldn't quite put her finger on, when she saw Alisha talking so warmly to Summer. Could it be regret? No. Summer well deserved the fate that awaited her and her unborn child in New France. Hadn't she taken away everything that was dear to Elizabeth? Everything but her daughter. And even now, she tries to win Alisha's love.

Elizabeth knew in her heart that she was being unjust, but the guilt she felt was overpowering; and she couldn't handle it any other way. What would become of them? That thought nagged at her constantly; that, and the hatred she felt for Phillipe.

Her only consolation was knowing how attracted he was to her. She'd use that attraction anyway she could to save her daughter.

Phillipe signaled that it was time to go, and they resumed their same positions in the canoes. Robillard told them they would continue the journey in the dark, to put some distance between them and Deerfield. And they were certainly doing that. Summer figured they must be in New Hampshire by now.

She felt stronger now that she had eaten, and settled down for the ride. The winter scenery they glided by was breathtaking. The Connecticut River in 1744 was a beautiful waterway, clean and fragrant. There was an abundance of fish in the water, and strangely enough, though it was winter, waterfowl darted across the surface, unafraid of the humans who traveled the green waters. Tall, majestic oaks and elms bereft of leaves lined the river, along with weeping willows whose drooping branches reached down to form archways for the canoes to travel through. Dense woods by the side of the river gave way to meadows and rolling hills, and the air smelled pungent with earthy aromas.

The voices of the Indians echoed across the river as they called back and forth to each other along the way, speaking in French or Abenaki, the sound of camaraderie evident in their tones. They seemed not to mind the labor of paddling for hours on end, enjoying it, in fact, and she grudgingly admired their youthful, masculine strength.

As they progressed north, Summer noticed that ice was beginning to form along the river's edge, and the air was getting colder. Once the sun sank behind the thick forest infringing upon the water, the cold became more noticeable, even with the furs. Every muscle in her body was sore from the strain of sitting so still in the canoe, and her tailbone was numb.

They traveled for two more hours after dark, and the river took on a eerie glow from the light of the moon. They glided along silently now, until a command from Robillard sent them toward shore, where the canoes were beached.

Phillipe jumped out of his canoe, and walked over to Summer's. "We camp here for the night."

It was a relief to get out of the canoe once again and stretch. Summer walked around trying to get the kinks out of her body. She was apprehensive, wondering if she and Elizabeth would be raped by the men. She had seen no sign of sexual interest all day, but night could be another thing. Thinking back to her encounter with the two Frenchmen on the hill, she thought, *Please, dear God, don't let it happen.*

The men again prepared a meal, while the weary women sat by the fire. Summer relaxed. There was no sign of sexual interest. In fact, the evening was very domestic. Evidently, the Indians were making sure their valuable captives survived.

From a great distance, an eerie sound penetrated the night. A wolf's howl. The lonely sound drifted on the night wind, sending goose bumps across her skin. The call was answered by another wolf, and another and another, until the night air was filled with the haunting sound.

It was strange listening to animals extinct in the time she came from. Strange, but exciting. She was privileged to be hearing their plaintive call. Elizabeth and Alisha were affected by the sound, too, drawing closer together. The Abenakis and Robillard took little notice, but Summer noticed they piled more wood on the fire, presumably to keep the wolves away.

"Ladies, you will sleep in the canoes tonight. But do not get any foolish ideas of escaping. You will be well guarded at all times. And do not harbor any faint hope of being rescued. Your John Hawke will not find us. It was clever, was it not, traveling by water? No tracks to be followed. Hawke and his brother will search for us in vain, while we are safe as if in our mother's womb. Be grateful for that, otherwise, we could afford no fire and would eat our meal cold. Now try to sleep. Our journey begins in earnest on the morrow."

Summer didn't need to be told twice. She was dead tired, as were Elizabeth and Alisha. She watched as Elizabeth carried her daughter into the canoe, snuggling up against her in the bottom. Climbing into her own canoe, bone-weary, she lay listening to the water lapping against the canoe, the steady rhythm soon sending her to sleep.

A woman's screams woke her. Elizabeth!

Her nerves jangled hearing Elizabeth's terrible plea. "No, don't take my baby away. Please—"

Summer jumped from the canoe and ran over to Elizabeth. She was pulling on the sleeve of Phillipe's fur jacket, pleading with him. Looking out at the water, silvery in the morning light, Summer saw Alisha sitting forlornly in the center of a canoe, while it was being paddled from shore by one of the Indians.

"Elizabeth," Phillipe said calmly. "I do this for the child's own good. We will be traveling through very primitive territory. 'Twould be hard for your daughter's little legs to carry her. There's a family upriver who can take her in. She will be safe with them."

"No! I'll carry her if need be. Summer will carry her, too, won't you, Summer? Please, she won't be a burden. I'll do anything you want, I'll, I'll lie with you if you wish! Just don't take her away from me."

Phillipe's mouth curled into a smirk. Summer could see he had the response he wanted from Elizabeth. The bastard had no intentions of taking Alisha away. He just wanted Elizabeth to acquiesce to his desires.

Sure enough, the canoe turned back after Phillipe waved his arm, and Alisha crawled out and ran to her mother.

Almost in a whisper, Elizabeth said, "Thank you, Phillipe. You won't regret this." Pulling her daughter into her arms, she held her tightly.

The anger Summer had felt toward Elizabeth vanished completely, as she looked at mother and daughter clinging to each other. The days ahead would be hard on Elizabeth. She would have to watch over Alisha every step of the way. Keep the small child moving at the same pace as the rest of them, so Robillard would not kill her. Elizabeth was paying dearly for her betrayal.

After their morning meal, they continued once again in the canoes, the Indians paddling at the same steady beat that had them moving swiftly through the water.

By dusk, they came to white water. Would they be dashed against the rocks, or hurtled over some unseen waterfall? Gazing at the men's faces, she was reassured. They seemed to know what they were doing, and where they were going. Before long they turned the canoes toward shore, sliding them onto a sandy beach.

The men unloaded the provisions, and the same procedure was carried out as the night before, women sleeping in canoes, the men on shore.

In the morning, the canoes were carefully hidden behind thick reeds, and they began their journey over land, heading toward the northeast. That was a surprise to Summer. She had thought they would be heading toward Montreal, which was northwest of the river. Where was Phillipe taking them? How could John ever find them now? Surely, he must think they were heading toward Montreal.

The terrain was rough, but after an hour or so, they came to a small path worn into the landscape, evidence that it was a well-used trail. Good, if John did make it this far, it wouldn't be hard to find this trail.

As the path started winding upward through thick forest, it became apparent to Summer that the small path had been used many times. Could it possibly be the Appalachian Trail? She and her family had hiked and backpacked along small sections of the trail many times in her own century, and here she was, possibly treading on it, helping to establish with her feet and the feet of the others, the future famous trail.

Summer became winded as they climbed higher and higher, up the first of what could very well be many mountains. At least the pace was not brutal, nor the mountains very high. Most of New England's mountains were barely more than hills, and she was eternally grateful for that now. The men were moving at a leisurely pace the women had little trouble keeping up with. Had Phillipe decided to make the trip easy on them? Was there a spark of human decency in the man, after all? Or was it because of his wound? Maybe he hadn't regained his full strength yet.

The Indians suddenly signaled to stop. Something—or someone—was moving noisily through the trees to their right. Summer spotted them coming right at her. Deer! The Indians quickly drew arrows from their quivers and armed their bows. The deer came leaping across the trail, fear glazed in their beautiful eyes, and then they were gone. All except one. The men were on it in a second, pulling out a blood-soaked arrow and whooping their blood-curdling yell of victory.

In no time, they had the doe skinned and gutted, then hacked into pieces, while the female captives looked on in horror at the bloody scene.

Before long, the aroma of venison was thick in the air, stirring up the juices in Summer's stomach. She felt like a traitor to the deer, but she was hungry and eating for two now.

Sitting around the fire, they ate their fill. The rest of the meat was cut into manageable chunks, and wrapped in the deer's own skin to tote.

Continuing their trek, weighed down now by the heavy meal, the women were forced by the men to walk at a faster pace. Summer paid close attention to where they walked, keeping track of which shoulder the sun was over. She would need to know the direction to take if she escaped.

Elizabeth, too, paid attention to the direction. It was obvious they were not going to Montreal. That worried her. At least Montreal was civilized to a degree. She had no idea what to expect now.

As they climbed up the steep incline, Elizabeth and Summer helped Alisha. In some places where the mountain went straight up, they had to cling to roots and small trees to help pull themselves up. Their heavy clothing hindered their movements, making the climb all the more difficult.

At the top of the mountain, the icy wind chilled their faces and teared their eyes. Looking out at the view of the valley below and the mountains in the distance, Summer felt a deep loneliness. It was as if she were standing on the edge of the earth. How could John or Cal ever find them in all this vast wilderness?

She was exhausted by the hard climb and ached all over, and knew Elizabeth and Alisha must be feeling the same. She wanted to sink to the ground and never get up again, but Major Robillard pushed them onward, telling them if they stopped, they would be killed. The leisurely pace was ended. It had not been an act of compassion on Phillipe's part, but a way of conditioning their cramped muscles for the steep climb.

A shout from one of the braves drew Summer's attention. He pointed to a large lean-to hidden by thick bushes. Made from branches of trees and covered with dried leaves, it was large enough to hold them all. Evidently, it had been built by the Abenakis on their way to Deerfield.

Gratefully, the females collapsed on the pine needle floor. Soon a fire warmed them, and the venison, heated once more, filled their bellies. Summer had survived two days, and that made her hopeful. Exhausted and aching all over, she curled up next to Elizabeth and Alisha and slept.

Chapter Twenty-Seven

Few people could be seen on the mile-long stretch of the street, as John Hawke and his two brothers rode into town at the head of the militia unit.

Where was everyone? John had been expecting a hero's welcome, and was beginning to feel uneasy about the almost deserted street. Coming to a halt at the town common, he dismissed the troops, weary and dust-covered, and sent them home. He was bone-weary himself from the long hard campaign coming so soon after the last one, but well pleased. Those Mohawks who hadn't been killed or captured, were on their way home with their tails between their legs.

He would have been elated at the victory, except that the one person he had hoped to find was still missing. It could mean, of course, that when Cal wounded him, it had been a fatal wound, but until he actually saw Robillard's rotting corpse, he had to believe the man was still alive. If he was still among the living, at least he wouldn't be capable of doing much harm anymore; his forces had been mightily depleted, and it would be a long time before they could be amassed again.

John's gaze took in the near empty street, and his

uneasiness grew. Where were the cheering crowds eager to greet their victorious return? And where were the women of his own family? Surely word had spread of their return by now. Something was amiss.

A sinking feeling hit him, and a hard ball in the pit of his stomach grew. Summer! Something had happened to Summer. Dear God, no. Without saying a word, he spurred his horse into a canter. Cal and Nat followed closely behind, knowing, too, that something terrible had happened. Something so terrible the townfolk could not face them.

Reining in at Jessica's house, they jumped from the horses without bothering to secure them, and dashed into the house.

John was relieved to see his mother and Nenepownam standing in the parlor. Everything was all right. He'd been foolish to worry. As he moved closer to embrace his mother and saw her tear-stained face, his relief turned to cold fear.

"What is it? In God's name, what has happened?"

"Where's Charity?" Nat asked almost simultaneously.

"I'm here, Nat." Charity answered from the kitchen doorway. "Thank the Lord, you're home safe."

Nat ran to Charity, folding her in his arms. "Charity, sweeting, I was so afraid . . ."

Jessica looked at John and Cal through redrimmed eyes. "They . . . Elizabeth and Alisha . . . Summer, too. Gone . . . taken . . ."

The room became deadly quiet, as the men stood there stunned at Jessica's words. Words too hard to grasp. Cal came to his senses first. "How? When?"

"Yesterday morning. Elizabeth and Summer had gone hawking—"

"Hawking?" Cal couldn't believe what he heard.

"Why would they go hawking *now?* It doesn't make sense."

"I don't know, but they did go, and somehow, little Alisha followed them out there on her pony. They were captured at the waterfall."

"Waterfall? Why would they go there? I don't understand . . ."

"For God's sake, Cal, let Mother finish," Nat said, holding Charity close.

John still stood silently, hearing the conversation as if he were under water.

Jessica continued, her words spoken in deep sorrow. "I don't know why, all I know is Sergeant Davidson got worried when they didn't return, and went looking for them. He saw their tracks going down the path leading to the waterfall, and followed. He . . . he found Alisha's bonnet, and . . . and . . . bloodstained bandages made from a woman's petticoat. Elizabeth's. The bandages were days old. It seems someone was using the waterfall as a refuge, while they recuperated from a wound. Sergeant Davidson believes that someone else, most likely, Elizabeth, had been nursing the wounded man, but I cannot believe such a thing of her."

Cal digested the news. "Of course not. It's unthinkable. There must be some other explanation. Where are these bloody bandages?"

"Here," Jessica pointed to the fireplace, where the strips of cloth hung from a hook on the hearth.

Cal walked over to look at them. "The blood is days old, no doubt of that. I don't understand."

John looked at the bloodstained bandages and became suddenly ill, grabbing at the mantel for support and clutching his stomach as if he had been stabbed. "Robillard!"

Cal saw the state his brother was in and guided him

308

to a chair. "Mother, some brandy." Then, realizing the name John uttered, he cried, "John, we don't know that! There's no reason to believe the wounded man is Robillard."

Choked with emotion, John said, "My God, Cal, if Robillard has them—"

"We don't know that he does, and until we do, it's senseless to think about it. We have enough to worry about as it is. There's much to be done."

Nenepownam's heart went out to John and Cal. Sorrow was so clearly etched on their faces along with the fatigue of battle. "Do not fear. I have sent for my son, Pedajah. He is the best tracker of the Five Nations. He will be here soon and will find the women and child. They will be returned to us. You must believe."

John stood, saying, "I'm not waiting for Pedajah. I'm leaving now."

Cal pushed him back in the chair. "John, you're not thinking clearly. You're too exhausted. How far do you think you'll get in that condition? We rest first. Provision ourselves for the trip. Pedajah will be here by the time we've readied ourselves, and we'll go together, as we have always done before. Is that understood?"

"I go, too," Nat said.

John looked at Nat through blurred vision. "Nay, you are needed here with Mother and Nenepownam. And what of Charity? If something happens to Cal and me, you'll be the only remaining Hawke to carry on our father's name. Do you understand the importance of that?"

Nat felt a lump in his throat. "Yes, but . . . nothing will happen to either of you, and you may have need of me."

"John is right, Nat. My mother and yours, and

now your own sweet Charity, will have need of a man around here. 'Tis every bit as important as going on the search.''

Nat gave in reluctantly. He knew they spoke the truth.

"Marry Charity now, brother. Don't wait for our return. Take happiness while you . . ." John's voice trailed off, and Nat knew he was thinking about Summer.

Cal knew, too. He saw the pain in John's eyes. His brother's love for Summer was stronger, deeper, than he had ever imagined. If the women were found alive, something would have to be done about it. They couldn't continue like this. "I agree. Nat, when we return, I hope to see you and Charity married. And now, John, time to rest and regain our strength. Mother will wake us when Pedajah is here. Nat, will you see to our needs for the journey? Have the horses packed and waiting when we awake.''

"Gladly." Nat was pleased that he could be of immediate help.

"My God, Cal," John said. "Do you think I can sleep knowing that Summer is in that bastard's hands? And Elizabeth and Alisha? I won't sleep again until they are in my arms.''

"Son, I know it's not easy, but think of this. You will need your strength to find them. Elizabeth, Alisha, and Summer are depending on you. Sleep before you go. Take the brandy bottle upstairs with you. It'll help you relax.''

The women prepared provisions for John and Cal while they rested. Nat sought out Sergeant Davidson, eager for a firsthand account of what he had found. His brothers would have need of all the information they could obtain.

"I feel real bad about this, Nat. I should have

310

stopped them from going off like that, but Mistress Elizabeth always seemed to know how to take care of herself, and truthfully, I didn't think Indians would be around, what with the militia out hunting them.''

"I wish you had stopped them, too, but there's no use dwelling on that now. Captain Hawke and Caleb will be leaving at dawn, and when they set their minds to do something, it usually gets done. Now, can you think of anything that can help them?''

Josiah scratched his nose. "Well, when I went looking for the women, I followed their tracks to the waterfall. That's where I found the bloody bandages and scraps of food. It was clear someone had been using the place for a refuge. And, Nat, I didn't tell the women this, but I believe it was Robillard.''

Nat had been afraid of that. "What made you think so?''

"Found a purple plume just a-laying there by the water. Only one person I know of wears a purple plume in his hat, and that's Robillard. It's as much his hallmark as the patch over his eye. I believe he left it there deliberately. So as to let the captain know he has his loved ones.''

"I'm afraid you're right, Sergeant. When Cal wounded him, he was wearing a purple plume. Damn! I'm not eager to tell my brother that news. If Robillard knows who his captives are, it'll not bide well for them. He'd like nothing better than to slaughter the people John loves most in the world.''

"If there's anything I can do . . .''

"No, Sergeant. This is personal now. John and Cal want to handle it themselves. And I think they're right. They can travel a lot faster and quieter alone. If Robillard got wind of the militia, he'd slit the women's throats before they could get within a league of them.''

Nathaniel returned home to find Pedajah sitting at the table in the kitchen, his mother Nenepownam serving him a trencher of stew.

Pedajah rose from the table and clasped Nat's hand. "It is good to see you, Nathaniel. I am sorry it is for such a sorrowful reason."

"Good to see you, Pedajah. Been too long. I've just met with the man who discovered the women were missing. I'm afraid he had bad news. There's every reason to believe the man who took them is Major Robillard."

"That is not good. Robillard is a wily wolf. And he has good reason to hate the Hawkes. Even more so now, I understand. My blood brother Caleb is to be, ah, how do you say, ah yes, congratulated for that deed. And it may work to our advantage. The Frenchman may still be weak from the wound and travel at a slower pace. But we will see, yes?"

"Yes, and when my brothers are ready to leave, I'll ride with you as far as the waterfall."

"You look tired, Nathaniel. Rest. There is nothing more to be done here."

"There'll be plenty of time later for rest, after you and my brothers have left. Until then, I want to do as much as I can."

"It is good. Come then, help me carry the provisions to the horses."

At the first streak of pink in the sky, the men were on their way, after a bellyful of stew that Jessica and Nenepownam had stayed up to make for them. The women watched now from an upstairs window as the men departed. Each woman saying a prayer in her own way for the safety of her son.

Nat and Sergeant Davidson accompanied them as

far as the waterfall, where they searched for more clues. Nothing further could be found. The men followed the trail back to where it turned off at a small path leading north, and after a brief talk with Davidson, putting him in charge of the militia, they headed down the path.

Eventually the path led them back to the main road, near the entrance to Daniel's place, and they studied the ground for tracks. Most of the trail had been obliterated by the hooveprints of others using the road since the previous day, and it would have been impossible for them to follow—except for one thing. Alisha's pony. The small crescent hooveprints could be seen clearly amongst the jumble of horse's hooves that overlapped each other, and they led straight to the preacher's place.

Cal and John exchanged looks. "No wonder we've never been able to find that one-eyed bastard. The preacher's been hiding him all along." John was angry and it showed. "I've never trusted that slimy reptile. He was just too good to be true." Remembering that Daniel had explored Summer's naked body set his blood to boiling. If Daniel was responsible for this, he'd run him through with his sword.

Cal could see that John was about to explode. "Hold on. We don't know for sure Daniel and his family are involved in this. For all we know, they could be held captive, too. We'll just ride in as though nothing is amiss, and look over the situation."

"All right. But Pedajah stays out of sight. We don't want the Bradfords to see anything out of the ordinary."

Pedajah nodded his head and steered his horse into the trees to wait.

Cal and John rode into the clearing slowly, their

eyes taking in every detail. The place looked deserted. Strange, since business was generally brisk here. Warily, they moved up to the house and dismounted. Striding up to the house, hands on swords, they opened the door without knocking and stepped in.

Sarah Bradford sat on a bench, cradling her son's head in her lap. She looked up at the men through grief-filled eyes. "You won't find them here. All gone. Deserted. Even my husband. He left when he realized you would find out what he's been up to. Took that Indian woman with him, he did. Good riddance, I say. Left me here, alone, to bury my son. You'll help me, won't you? The ground is hard this time of year."

"Mistress Bradford, we can't spare the time. We've got to find our women." John's voice was edged in anger. "Tell us—"

"Mistress Bradford, we'll help you bury your son," Cal said, in a gentle voice. "And we're sorry for your loss. If there's anything else we can do to help?"

Sarah stood, taking Cal's hand in hers. "No, young man, there's nothing you can do for me. I'll be fine. You cannot tarry long. You've got a heap of traveling to do to find your womenfolk."

"Did you see them? Were they all right?"

"They were fine, John, just fine. Elizabeth tried to help my Daniel, but the wound was too bad. And that angel, Summer, she brought that boy back to life, but she couldn't save my son."

"Can you tell us anything? Did you hear where they were heading?" John's voice was softer now. Sarah Bradford wasn't his enemy.

"I'm sorry, no. But wait, they did mention canoes. I believe they're going up the great river."

"How many of them were there?" Cal asked. "Was Major Robillard one of them?"

"Yes," Sarah spat out. "He was one of them all right. It was him that killed my boy. Had three Abenaki with him. You find him and you kill them all. You find them before they sell your womenfolk, like my husband did my own poor sweet daughters."

Cal put his arm around the woman. "Mistress Bradford, let me take you up to your bed. I know you haven't been feeling well."

"No. No. I've spent too much time in bed. I'll be all right. But now, we must bury Daniel. We must bury my son."

Clutching a wet cloth in her hand, Sarah gently wiped her son's face.

Chapter Twenty-Eight

Two mornings later, the world looked a little brighter to Summer. The soreness in her body was still there, but it was bearable, and she slept each night unmolested. By the end of each day, they were all exhausted from the strenuous walk, and fell asleep as soon as they touched the ground. The men, too, for they had the extra burden of carrying heavy packs on their backs.

Summer was surprised that she and Elizabeth were spared that burden, taking it as a sign that Robillard indeed wanted to keep them alive. She knew, however, that she couldn't count on conditions staying as they were. Anything could happen. But at least Phillipe was not sexually interested in her. He had eyes for only Elizabeth, and surprisingly, seemed more interested in wooing her, than in forcing her to lay with him.

She joined the others for a breakfast of venison, washing it down with a pewter mug of water from a nearby brook. The brook was frozen, so the ice had to be melted over the fire, giving the water a smoky taste that was not very appealing. But she was surprised at how often she craved water on the long trek. The wind whipping across her face constantly dehydrated her quickly, and even though it was cold, she sweated under the warm furs.

As usual, the only conversation around the campfire was between the men. Summer had not spoken to Elizabeth since their capture. Even Alisha spoke little. But it was understandable. The walking used up every bit of energy they possessed.

As they started their journey once more, Summer's aching bones rebelled, but soon she limbered up, and the walk became more tolerable. It was amazing how much abuse the human body could withstand.

They crested a mountain and started down the other side, relieved to be going downhill, even though it meant using another whole set of muscles that would ache the next day. It seemed that each day she felt the pain in a different part of her body. The trip down was made quicker and easier than the last mountain, as the terrain was much easier to manage, having a more gradual descent. Before long they made it to the bottom, then traveled across a narrow valley after a short rest. Phillipe had set a faster pace, and it was beginning to take its toll.

Alisha felt the impact of their accelerated pace first, whimpering quietly to herself, afraid of attracting Robillard's attention.

Noticing that Elizabeth was unaware of Alisha's plight, walking ahead with the major, Summer scooped the little girl up and carried her on her back.

A grateful Alisha hugged Summer tightly around the neck, and reached down to kiss Summer's cheek. Before long she was sound asleep, her arms dangling over Summer's body, her head nestled on Summer's fur-clad shoulder. Summer hunched over some, so Alisha wouldn't fall off her back as she moved. She knew how hard the strenuous trek must be on the child's small legs. The added burden slowed Summer down, and soon there was a large gap between her and the others.

Elizabeth glanced back and saw Summer struggling to get over a large fallen tree that blocked the narrow path, and saw Alisha asleep on her back. Summer looked so small and frail framed by the tremendous woods that surrounded her; a pang of guilt knifed through Elizabeth's heart. She watched as Summer made it over the fallen tree—moving carefully so as not to wake Alisha—and waited for Summer to catch up to her.

"How long have you been carrying her like that? You should have called me. Here—let me take her."

"No," Summer whispered. "She's asleep now, and God knows she needs it. Let her sleep undisturbed, as long as she can."

Elizabeth kept pace with Summer, glancing furtively at her as they walked. She saw how tired Summer looked, thought about her pregnancy, and could hardly believe that she had taken on the burden of Alisha's dead weight without complaint. Her feelings of guilt became overpowering, and in a small voice she asked, "Can you ever forgive me?"

Summer's gaze stayed on the path ahead. "I don't know."

Elizabeth swallowed hard. "I understand, but promise me one thing. Promise me that if you get the chance to escape, you'll take Alisha with you."

Summer wondered what Elizabeth was getting at. She was acting very strangely. "If I get a chance to escape, surely you'll have the same chance."

Elizabeth's lips curled up into a bitter little smile. "I think not. You see, tonight you may have an opportunity. Phillipe has been making overtures to me all day. He has that look in his eye. Do you fathom my meaning? I think he's going to expect me to thank him properly for keeping Alisha with us, instead of sending her away. Do you know what I'm trying to say?"

Summer stopped walking and faced Elizabeth. "Of course, I do, but—"

"Do you not see? While he is occupied with me, you and Alisha can escape."

"Aren't you forgetting our three friends here?"

"They won't be a problem. Phillipe told me earlier that he was sending them out tonight, to backtrack a-ways. Says he wants to make sure we're not being followed, but I think the real reason is to get them out of the way while he is busy with me. It will be the perfect opportunity for you. I'll pretend to respond to him, and keep him occupied while you escape with Alisha."

"Elizabeth. I can't let you sacrifice yourself like that. There must be some other way."

"Don't be a fool. If there was another way, we would have taken it by now. And don't forget, if I don't go to him willingly, he'll take what he wants anyway, or send Alisha away. It's the only way."

"Elizabeth, how can I leave you behind?"

Elizabeth gave her a cool look. "The same way I arranged to have you taken, without thinking. You must do this for me, for my own salvation. How can I go on living with myself, if my daughter comes to harm? I got her into this nightmare, and I must get her out. Your taking her is the only way."

"But how? I don't know anything about surviving in the wilderness. I'll only get killed."

"Trust in yourself. I do. You're a very resourceful woman. I know you can do it. Do you think I would trust my daughter to you, if I didn't?"

"Shhh," Summer whispered. "Phillipe is heading our way."

Elizabeth grabbed Summer's sleeve. "Wait! There's one more thing I must tell you. I may never get the chance again. That morning, when you told me you were pregnant, I was blind with rage. I struck out at you in a way that I knew would hurt you. I told you I was pregnant, too, and I saw by your reaction that I had succeeded in hurting you. Summer. It was a lie. I'm not pregnant. It would be quite impossible, you see, since I have never slept with John."

Summer's eyes opened wide. *"But you have to be pregnant!"*

Elizabeth didn't understand Summer's insistence. She shook her head in denial.

Moving again, Summer's feet automatically stepped one foot in front of the other, but her mind was filled with but one thought. *John had been telling the truth. His marriage to Elizabeth had never been a real one.*

Oh John! If only she could see him one more time, feel his arms around her one more time! She had been such a fool to deny one minute of their precious time together. It had always felt so good, so right, when she was in his arms; she should have known they were meant to be together.

She had believed the future could not be changed. That what must be, would be, no matter what. But now, she no longer knew what to believe. There were forces at work much greater than she would ever understand.

If by some miracle she got out of this mess alive, she would go to him, declare her love, and be with him forever. The future be damned. The town be damned, too. She'd be a scarlet woman if she must, but she would be with John. And that was all she had

320

ever wanted or needed.

Summer's steps became lighter, and she felt stronger, knowing John's love for her was true.

Phillipe eyed the women curiously. "Well, beautiful ladies, I see by the smile on Summer's face that you have reconciled your differences. That is good. It will make the journey more tolerable. Do you not agree? Yes, yes, I think 'tis time we all became friendlier."

The look he gave Elizabeth left no doubt as to what he meant by that remark.

"I have a pleasant surprise for you ladies. Today's march will not be so long or hard as yesterday's. We have but a short distance to travel, before our next overnight resting place."

Summer looked up to the sky. There was at least another two hours of light left. Perhaps Elizabeth was right. Perhaps this would be her chance to escape. Her heart began to pound harder. If she did escape, the future would be changed irrevocably. It was written that Elizabeth and Alisha would be rescued by John, and that couldn't happen if Alisha was with her. So—she was already changing the future. Well, so be it.

An hour later, they reached their destination, a room-sized cave set in the side of the mountain.

"You see," Phillipe said, in a jovial mood, "I have provided a roof over your heads."

The women peered into the shelter, the dank smell assaulting their nostrils. Following the men, they entered cautiously, feeling uneasy about lodging in a dark cave. But it was warmer here, and when the Indians had a fire crackling in the center, its glow lighting up the darkness, it wasn't bad at all. In fact, it was quite cozy.

Supper was the last of the venison.

Phillipe kept gazing over at Elizabeth while they ate; she took off her fur jacket to further entice him. It was certainly warm enough by the fire to do so.

Summer kept hers on. She didn't want to give the Indians any ideas. She needn't have worried. After they had eaten their fill, the Abenakis said a few words to Phillipe, then left the cave. Elizabeth was right. Her heart started racing. This could be the only chance she would have to escape, and she had to take it.

Making a pretense of being tired, she curled up against Alisha, making sure they lay close to the cave entrance. Phillipe and Elizabeth sat on the other side of the fire, talking in low tones and gazing deep into each other's eyes. Summer wondered how Elizabeth could be so convincing. If she didn't know better, she would have believed her to be genuinely interested in that miserable snake.

No sooner had she closed her eyes, then Summer heard the rustle of clothing, and knew Phillipe was making his move. Summer's heart went out to Elizabeth, for what she had to do to save her daughter.

After a few moments, Summer opened an eye and saw Phillipe kissing Elizabeth's neck, while he fondled one of her breasts with his hand. He didn't waste any time. But then, he knew he had a woman who would do anything to keep her daughter. The beast!

Elizabeth played her part well, pretending that his touch excited her. It was strange watching the two of them; it made her feel like a voyeur. Phillipe's touches became more demanding, his breathing ragged; and she watched as he pushed Elizabeth backward onto the hard ground. He took off his fur leggings and then Elizabeth's, and unbuttoned his breeches. Suddenly, his head turned in Summer's direction. She closed her eyes quickly.

Hearing Phillipe's grunt as he climbed on top of Elizabeth, Summer opened her eyes again. She would have to wait for the right moment to make her move. She watched as he fumbled with Elizabeth's clothing, impatiently, guiding his swollen shaft inside her body with a satisfied grunt. When he started moving against Elizabeth, Summer knew it was now or never.

As quietly as she could, she picked up Alisha's sleeping form—praying she wouldn't wake up—and carried her out of the cave. As she walked out, she glanced back and saw that Phillipe was oblivious to all but the small woman beneath him.

It was dark now. Summer strained her eyes, peering into the dark shadowy forest that surrounded her. What now? Where to go? She couldn't go back toward Deerfield, that was the way the Indians had headed. If she headed north, she would be hopelessly lost. Instinctively, she decided her best bet would be to stay put until they gave up searching. Robillard would assume that she would try to get as far away from the cave as possible, and that assumption could save her and Alisha.

She remembered reading how well Indians of this time could track the white man. Every leaf, every twig she stepped upon would point them in her direction. She must be careful. But where could she hide?

Her eyes darted around the clearing, lighting on a gigantic evergreen with thickly carpeted branches that started low to the ground. It would be easy to climb, even for Alisha, and the heavy greenery would conceal them from their pursuers. It was worth a try. At least in the tree she wouldn't be making any tracks, or noise, for that matter, to give her away.

Stepping carefully to the tree, she woke Alisha,

explaining what they must do.

"What about Mama? We can't leave her with that bad man."

"I know, baby. But you must understand. Your Mama is making it possible for us to escape, and once we do, we'll bring your father back to rescue her. I promise, we'll come back."

Alisha, as young as she was, was quick to understand their plight. They climbed the tree easily, going up three quarters of the way before stopping, then sat on a huge limb in the crook of the tree, and leaned their backs up against the wide trunk for support. It would be a long cold wait until morning, and then . . . But they would cross that bridge when they came to it.

In a few minutes, Summer heard Phillipe curse, and then made out his form in the cave opening, backlighted by the soft glow from the fire. Elizabeth appeared in the opening, too, pretending to be upset that her daughter was missing. She started to cry, and Phillipe was taken in by her performance. Putting his arm around her, he held her tight. Alisha became upset at the sound of her mother crying, and would have cried out if Summer hadn't put her hand over the child's mouth, whispering that her mother was just pretending.

In a few minutes the two figures disappeared into the cave, and relief washed over Summer. They had passed their first hurdle.

An hour or so later, she heard the Indians return. By the sound of it, they weren't too pleased with the Major for letting her escape. It was too dark for them to search now, but she knew that at first light they would be out hunting for her, and she prayed there were no tracks leading to the tree.

It was impossible for Summer to sleep in the tree,

although, thankfully, Alisha could. Summer had wedged her in between her and the tree trunk, to keep her from falling in her sleep, and to help preserve the child's body heat.

To pass the interminably long hours until dawn, she tried to remember the landmarks they had passed, so she might retrace their journey back to Deerfield. It wouldn't be easy; there were places along the way where the trail was almost nonexistent.

Cramped and sore, with her tailbone numb, the backs of her thighs aching from hanging over the tree limb, she endured. And when she thought she could stand the pain and cold no longer, she opened her eyes and saw a streak of pink in the sky. It was dawn.

Before long, the Abenakis emerged from the cave and began to study the ground for tracks. Phillipe and Elizabeth stood at the cave entrance, watching.

Summer held her breath whenever they came close to the tree, and prayed Alisha would sleep through it. It soon became obvious that they could find no trace. She breathed a little easier.

Phillipe was angry and ordered the men off to search in different directions. Summer could see the smile that played across Elizabeth's face.

Alisha stirred, crying out, but the wind through the trees was so loud, Summer was sure no one heard. She woke Alisha and pointed below, making a sign to be quiet. For a second, Alisha became disoriented and lost her balance. She grabbed for a branch to steady herself. When she pulled back her hand, her mitten snagged on the rough bark, and pulled off her hand, falling through the air.

Summer watched in horror as the mitten floated to the ground, her eyes darting to Phillipe to see if he saw it fall. He hadn't, but Elizabeth had. She gasped out loud.

325

Phillipe looked at her. "What is it, *mon amour?*"

Composing herself, Elizabeth answered. "'Tis nothing. I have to piss so bad it hurts. I hope I make it to the tree in time."

Phillipe laughed. "Do you want company?"

Elizabeth made a face, and Phillipe gave her a playful shove in the direction of the big evergreen. She strode over to the tree and surreptitiously kicked the mitten. When she squatted to relieve herself—unencumbered by the fur leggings that still lay where they were dropped the night before—she picked up the mitten and stuffed it into the top of her fur boot.

Looking up at the tree from her squatting position, she could make out a piece of Summer's fur leggings. Her heart started to pound. She would have to get Phillipe away as soon as possible. How long could they sit in a tree in this terrible cold?

Making her way back to Phillipe, she pretended to be distraught over Alisha's disappearance. "We must find her soon, or she'll perish in the wilderness."

"My dear, I am doing all I can. My aboriginal friends will return soon, with your daughter safely in tow."

But that was not to be. One by one the Indians returned empty-handed. There was nothing to do but go on without Summer and Alisha. Phillipe felt certain they would die out there alone, or starve to death, and in that way he would still exact his revenge on John Hawke. The captain would never again hold his mistress in his arms, or hear his daughter's sweet little voice. And Elizabeth, his most valuable prize, was still his.

It pleased him well that he had made love to Hawke's wife. It made the coupling all the sweeter. Elizabeth had been a wild thing last night, quite unexpectedly. He had never known a woman to

326

respond in such an unabandoned manner. She had clung to him fiercely when he was finished with her, and had used her hands to harden him again. The little minx couldn't get enough of him. He wondered if she responded to her husband in the same eager way. It weighed on his mind. Elizabeth meant more to him than just a means of revenge. He had grown to care for her more each day. She was everything he could ever want in a woman, and he wanted to bring her back to his home, to live with him there. Her response last evening gave him hope it was possible.

The thought of spending uninterrupted nights with his wild beauty prompted him to send the Indians away. He had no further use of them, now that there was no one left to guard, and told them they could go home. The Abenakis were happy to oblige. It had been a long time since they had seen their wives and children, and they were still angry with the Frenchman for letting their captives get away. Doubling back, they headed toward Montreal and the Abenaki village at St. Francis.

"Well, my dear, it seems we're on our own. Mayhap we'll come across your daughter as we travel, or mayhap they will find refuge with some fur trader who happens upon them." He didn't really believe that, but he thought to make her happier. He didn't want a weeping woman on his hands. It would spoil the evenings he had planned.

"Take heart. We have but two more days of travel, before we reach our destination."

Elizabeth was shocked. "We can't possibly be so close to New France!"

"Is that where you thought we were heading? No, my dear, our destination is much closer than that. We go to a trading post, one of many, I might add, owned by the husbands of Martin Bradford's daughters.

They're his partners in business, and have made him a wealthy man. Mayhap Martin is there already. He travels much faster than we, and by a more direct route."

His hand moved under her fur jacket to fondle her breast and, looking up to the sky, he said. "It looks like we'll get there none too soon. There's a fierce storm brewing."

Chapter Twenty-Nine

It wasn't hard for Pedajah to spot the place where the canoes had been hidden. His trained eye detected a disturbance in the marshy grasses. John was elated. They were off to a good start. This was their second bit of good luck. The first had been finding canoes at the Bradford place. They had portaged them to the river. And so swiftly finding the spot where they had embarked was indeed lucky. It confirmed what Sarah had told them, and gave them reason to hope.

John shared a canoe with Cal, while Pedajah manned the other. At Pedajah's suggestion, each canoe hugged a different side of the river, to be sure they wouldn't miss the place where Robillard left the river. Robillard couldn't know that Sarah had overheard him mention the canoes, so he wouldn't be expecting John to follow the river. If he was the least bit careless, the tiniest bit oversure of himself, it would work to John's advantage.

On the other hand, Robillard had a two-day head start. That meant they would have to travel all the faster to catch up. But then, they had no women or children along to hold them back.

They paddled swiftly through the water, their

strong arms and backs pulling the paddles through the water in an ever-increasing rhythm, while their eyes scanned the river's edge carefully, looking for any sign of disturbance to the natural order of things.

They paddled unceasingly, an unspoken agreement among them not to stop for rest or food, until they found the spot where Robillard had disembarked. After several hours, Cal was beginning to wonder if they missed the spot, when he saw a corner of a canoe hidden in the tall grasses lining the bank. Now the hunt would begin in earnest.

With a couple of hours of daylight left, they decided to take advantage of it and continued their search on foot. Pedajah was glad of that, for he knew what John and Cal did not, that the signs were present for a major snowstorm within the next twenty-four hours. A storm that could wipe out any traces of footprints, and prevent them from finding the women. He kept this information to himself, not wanting to worry John or Caleb. Their minds were troubled enough over their loved ones.

Their diligence was rewarded with the discovery of the Indian path leading up the mountain, and they climbed, compelled to cover as much ground as they could before dark. Robillard couldn't possibly move at so fast a pace. With luck, they could overtake them by tomorrow evening. It grew dark, and still they followed the well-worn path in the moonlight, traversing the top of the mountain.

Almost by accident, Pedajah found the lean-to hidden behind brush. "This is where they camped last night. We'll rest here, and get a good start in the morning."

John entered the lean-to, his eyes raking every inch of the pine needle floor, as if to burn it into his brain.

Cal knew John was looking for any sign that the women or Alisha had been hurt. "Robillard will keep them alive, John. How else can he exact his punishment on you? He means to take them to New France, have no doubt of that. But it will never happen. We'll find him long before he breathes French air."

John's brow was still creased with worry. "But, if he discovers us closing in on him, he'll kill the women. Can you doubt that?"

"No, you're right about that. But we won't be so foolish as to let him see us. Pedajah is brother to me as much as you are, and I trust him implicitly. He'll get us close enough to take Robillard in whatever way we can. Dead or alive."

"It is so," Pedajah said, nodding his head solemnly.

John lay down on his bedroll and thought about Summer. It was the first time he had allowed himself that luxury, since he had returned and found her gone. As his mind moved through all his memories of her, he remembered the book of the future, and the entry Summer had made about Elizabeth and Alisha being captured, and of him rescuing them. There had been no date of the incident mentioned, so he had not given it much thought. So much of her research was distorted truth, half-truths, at best, but not, so it seemed, about their abduction.

His heart sank when he remembered that she had written of an unidentified woman, who had been killed somewhere along the march. If that was correct, there was only one person who could be killed, and that was Summer. He had to trust to blind faith that it couldn't happen. How could God be so cruel as to bring her to him through two hundred years of time, to tease him with her beloved presence, only to take her from him so cruelly? It was inconceivable to him that it could happen. Somehow, they would be together, he had to believe that. The love they shared was so strong, so powerful, that it had conquered time itself.

Caleb, too, lay on his bedroll and looked out at the black night. Not a star appeared in the sky. A storm was brewing. He had seen the signs earlier, but had hoped it would blow over. He still hoped for that, or at least that it would hold off long enough for them to find the women.

And when they did find them, then what? He knew Summer loved John with a passion that consumed her, and knowing that, he knew he could never marry her. Summer was fond of him. Of that he was certain. But she had turned to him only in desperation, trying to deny her love for John. But it was a love that could not be denied. He wanted to be loved in the same way Summer loved John. The way Elizabeth loved him. What a confusing situation. And if that wasn't enough, the incredible knowledge that she came from the future, the year 1993.

How could he believe such a preposterous thing? And yet, he did. His brother had good reason to believe it, and that was good enough for him. John had asked for his sword back before they started their journey. He said that if he found Summer in danger, he would let her touch the blade and send her back to her time. His voice had been deadly serious when he spoke, and Cal knew he meant what he said.

It was so hard to fathom. Why had Summer been transported here? Her coming had churned up feelings better left undisturbed. Before she came, he was unaware that Alisha was his child, unaware that

Elizabeth still loved him so passionately, and now he was in agony over the hopelessness of it all. Always before he had found a way out of any situation that confronted him, but he had never been faced with anything so extraordinary before. And yet, there had to be an answer.

It had all started with John's sword. Summer had come to this time by a touch of it, had been compelled to stay because of it. Robillard had been wounded by that same sword in Cal's own hands, and because of that wound, was put into Elizabeth's hands. And from that—this. They were all coming together now because of John's sword, and because of the powerful love between John and Summer.

He had to think carefully about this. There had to be a solution. Tomorrow they would catch up to Robillard. He must have an answer by then, for all their sakes.

Standing up, he crept out of the lean-to, trying not to disturb John or Pedajah, and walked to the edge of a cliff. He sat and looked up at the dark sky and the crescent moon, the only visible object in the sky. He had enough Indian blood in him to feel that there was a reason for everything that happened in this world. If he sat here long enough, mayhap the wisdom of his Pocumtuck ancestors would seep into his brain.

He stared transfixed at the silver shard glowing in the sky, putting himself into a heightened sense of awareness. The crescent moon symbolized new beginnings. New beginnings for whom? His brain started working faster and faster as new ideas were born, until, at dawn, he knew what must be done.

He watched the sun coming up over the mountain range, and at the moment when it emerged full and red over the tallest mountain, he heard the cry of a hawk.

Looking in the direction of the sound, he saw the hawk circling overhead, gliding on the air currents that dipped low over the mountains. Leather jesses dangled from the hawk's feet.

"Beauty!" It had to be Beauty, but what was the bird doing so far from home? Whom did the bird seek? He who had raised it? Elizabeth, who owned it? Or Summer, whom the bird had loved at first sight? Was it really here, or was it an hallucination brought on by his sleepless night, and by his desperate search for an answer that would bring happiness to them all?

John heard Cal cry out to the hawk and ran over to the cliff. "What is it? Do you see them?"

"No, John. It's Beauty! Can you see her up there? I don't understand how, but the hawk followed us here. You would think once it tasted freedom, it would fly away forever."

"I'll be damned. It *is* Beauty. I guess there's no accounting for the power of love, even in the heart of a hawk."

"The power of love, yes. That's it. That's what it's all about. I have spent a sleepless night pondering that very thing." Clasping his brother around the shoulders, he hugged him, then hit his arm playfully. "The power of love. How right you are. Powerful enough to defy time. Powerful enough to overcome wrong turns we have made in our lives, and powerful enough to correct them. Come, brother, the time grows near when we shall all fulfill our destinies. Beauty is here to see that we do. She is impatient with us foolish mortals, and would set us on the right path."

Cal ran back to the lean-to, shouting for Pedajah. "Brother, get off your lazy bones, else we'll leave you here to sprout branches like a willow tree."

John was astonished at Cal's strange behavior. He had never seen Cal so animated before. Was this his brother who stayed calm no matter the situation he was in? John glanced up at the hawk still circling overhead, and shook his head.

Chapter Thirty

Climbing down from the tree was not as easy as climbing up. Summer was stiff from the cold and from balancing on a tree limb all night long, and her fingers were numb from clinging tightly.

She waited a long time after Robillard left with Elizabeth before coming down, afraid he might double back for some reason and catch her. She was afraid, too, that it could be a trap. That he was waiting for her to come out of hiding. But she had to forget her fears and chance it. She had no choice. Alisha was starting to weaken, and so was she. If they stayed up there much longer, she would fall asleep and topple to the ground.

The hard ground under her feet felt good. She stretched her cramped muscles and did a few kneebends to limber up and get her circulation back. Then the next order of business was for her and Alisha to relieve their aching bladders.

After that was accomplished, she was reminded of their empty stomachs, and worried that Alisha might become dehydrated if she didn't get something to drink soon.

She searched the cave for any food or drink that

might have been left behind, but found nothing. But she couldn't let it get her down. They had survived a long, uncomfortable night in a tree. She wasn't going to be stopped now by hunger or thirst.

"We'll have to find a way to catch something to eat. If only I had a knife, I could whittle a spear."

Alisha, clinging to Summer's jacket as she had been since they came down from the tree, said timidly. "I have a knife, Summer. My kitchen knife. They searched you and Mama for knives, but they didn't think to search me."

Summer hugged Alisha. "Then we have nothing to fear. We shall be brave like Nenepownam's people, and become mighty warriors."

Alisha was joyful. "Oh, Summer, that's what I'd like more than anything. Even more than learning herbs and medicine like Mama! Shall we really become mighty warriors?"

"Yes, darling. Give me your knife and find me two sturdy branches to sharpen."

Alisha skipped away happily, forgetting her fear and her cold aching body. They were going to play mighty warrior. She was soon back with two straight branches seasoned just right.

Summer began whittling away at the end of the smaller one, honing it to sharp point. She handed it to Alisha and fashioned another one for herself.

"Now, we're ready." With great show at being a warrior, she started down the trail followed by the diminutive child, who strutted as she imagined a mighty warrior should.

Before long, they came across a snow hare, white and soft and beautiful. It looked up at Summer with fearful doe eyes. If she hadn't been so hungry, Summer would have admired its beauty and then walked on. But they needed food for energy, for their very survival, so she aimed the spear carefully, and caught the animal in the middle of a leap. It went down, and lay convulsing on the ground for a few seconds before becoming still.

Shocked that she had actually hit the hare, she ran to the small white creature with tears brimming her eyes. It wasn't dead yet. While Alisha looked on, her eyes as wet as her own at having to kill such a beautiful, gentle creature, Summer drew Alisha's knife across the fur-covered throat and put it out of its misery. Immediately, the first flakes of snow began to fall, landing softly in the puddle of red beneath the animal.

Alisha looked at the snowflakes in wonder, and whispered in reverent awe, "Summer, I do believe that killing the snow hare has caused it to snow. It is an omen. Nenepownam has told me of such as this."

Summer laughed. "Yes, mighty warrior, I believe you're right. It is a powerful omen, for now we will not go thirsty." Tilting her head to the sky, she opened her mouth and stuck out her tongue, collecting enough of the delicate snowflakes to swallow. Alisha followed suit, lapping up the flakes that melted on her tongue.

When they settled down from the excitement and sorrow of their first kill, Summer was faced with yet another problem. She skinned the hare and gutted it, then cut it into small chunks of meat, before she mentioned it to the child. "Alisha, we must be very brave. We cannot take the chance of anyone seeing smoke from a cook fire. So we must eat the meat raw."

Alisha's eyes widened.

"Here," she said, handing a piece of meat to Alisha. "Eat it while it's still warm. It'll go down easier."

Alisha looked with revulsion at the pink leg dripping with blood and shook her head. Summer knew she must set a good example. She bit into the leg and tore off a piece of meat. Reluctant to swallow it, she rolled it around in her mouth. Instantly, her stomach started rumbling, eager for nourishment, and she swallowed. It went down easier than she expected.

Alisha took her lead, bit off a piece of the meat, and her hunger took over. Before long she had made short work of the leg, nibbling every bit of meat off the bone, then sucking on the bone itself.

Summer was pleased to see Alisha eat. It could make the difference between survival and death, and it meant they would not starve and were not completely helpless in this harsh winter world. They had a chance.

Asperensah's stomach lurched as she rolled the dead man off her body. The old fool! Martin had insisted on having her while they waited for the snow to stop, sitting in a small refuge of overhanging rocks that formed a snug shelter. It wasn't her fault he was dead. She had resisted the idea, not wanting to expose any of her body to the frigid air. But lecherous pig that he was, he had demanded, and she had given in, helpless to do anything else. And now he was dead. She went over it again in her mind, needing the chance to sort it out.

"Woman, if you don't give it to me, I'll have to take it, and that could be most uncomfortable for you."

"All right, you pig. Take me, but I will lie like a dead woman, and you won't enjoy it very much."

"Methinks you lie. You like it as much as I, and now that we're far from my pious, mewling wife, we can enjoy the act more, free to do as we please. Free to cry out our pleasure without fear of being overheard. Here we are cozy in our little cocoon with the falling snow to keep us company. Yes, I think I'm going to like this very much."

Martin began untying her fur leggings.

"Pah! I will freeze, old man, and your pecker will fall off."

"If it displeases you so to undress, then do not. I can think of another way you may pleasure me." Undoing his breeches, he pulled out his swollen shaft.

Asperensah knew what he wanted, and took it in her mouth. Better that, than undressing in the cold. She moved her mouth and tongue in the way she knew he liked, concentrating on the most sensitive side, wanting to bring him to a fast conclusion.

"Suck on it, woman. Suck it right out of me."

She did as she was told, eager to be done with it, but try as she might, he still wouldn't come.

The cold was starting to get to Martin, and impatient to be finished, he rammed his member down her throat.

Asperensah spat the foul-tasting fluid on the ground, then swore at him in Abenaki for the brutal way he had treated her. Martin laughed, pulling her down on him. Reaching under her furs, he grasped her breasts, fondling them roughly.

"I like it when you get angry. It puts fire in my loins. Feel! It grows hard again." Rolling her over, he worked at removing her leggings. "I feel as strong and as lusty as a bull moose in musk here in the wilderness, and would hear your cries of pleasure when I give it to you. Passion should be expressed with the voice as well as the body."

He shoved his hardness into her. "Yes, yes, I want

340

to hear you cry out. If not from pleasure, than from pain."

His movements became rougher as he plunged in and out of her, his excitement mounting higher and higher.

Asperensah cursed under her breath. Would this never end? If he was waiting to hear her cries of pleasure, then she would give them to him. Anything to get this over with. She moaned softly at first, and when that didn't work, louder, until her voice escalated loud enough to rival the howl of the wind, blowing a few short feet away.

As her cries became louder, his movements became frenzied, and he worked up a sweat in the cold air. "Yes, yes, yes," he trumpeted, then suddenly slumped against her.

Asperensah stopped her caterwauling. "Get off me, you oxen. I cannot breathe."

Martin didn't move.

"Get off me, I say." She moved her head sideways to look at his face, now resting against her shoulder, and her heart stopped. Martin's eyes were wide open, his mouth gaping, and, she could not see his breath in the frosty air. "Ayahhhhh!"

And now, here she was alone with a dead man. What evil gods had caused this terrible thing to happen? Was she being punished for sleeping with both the father and the son? She must leave, get away from this evil place. It didn't matter that it was snowing harder now, she must get away.

She and Martin had been on their way to one of his outposts. The one where they would meet up with Robillard and his female captives. She knew the way from here. There was no reason for concern. She could make it on her own.

Picking up her pack, her hand reached for Martin's

pack. No, it would weigh her down too much to carry both. She crawled out of the shelter and shuddered, as if shaking off Martin's clawing hands, and moved quickly away. She would find another place to weather the storm, a place where the spirits of the dead did not linger.

Somehow the vast forests and never-ending mountains had not seemed quite so overwhelming, when Elizabeth and Phillipe had been accompanied by the Indians and Summer and Alisha. Now Elizabeth felt the eerie silence and endless miles, and knew the true meaning of loneliness.

Phillipe had been quiet ever since they left the cave this morning. He seemed to be sorting things out in his head, for every once in a while he would look over at her with a strange expression. She wondered if he was deciding her fate, and anger welled up. She would not go willingly to whatever fate he had decreed for her. She might not be able to use physical strength against him, but she could use her brain, and if she must, her body.

She flushed, thinking about Phillipe's fervent lovemaking in the cave, and of Summer's furtive glance over her shoulder when she carried Alisha out of the cave. It shamed her that Summer should see her in such an intimate act, but then, she had once seen Summer stand before a colored window without a stitch of clothing on, and had watched as the preacher ravished her with his eyes. When all was said and done, there was little difference between the two events.

And whatever possessed Summer to climb the tree with Alisha? It had been an anxious moment, watching while the mitten fell to the ground. A sudden shiver tingled through her thinking about it. It had really been quite clever of her to climb the tree. The Indians would have found Summer's tracks easily, since she had no training in forest lore. But it had been the only chance Alisha had of escaping, a chance Summer used to full advantage. Elizabeth felt a twinge of admiration for the woman who had won Caleb's love. Despite her lack of training, Summer had the same sense of survival, the same indomitable spirit that Elizabeth had prided herself on having. Alisha was in good hands.

Phillipe stopped walking, and she noticed that they were standing on the edge of a frozen pond. His eyes scanned the slick surface before making up his mind. He started walking around the edge.

"Phillipe, are we not going over there?" She pointed to the other side of the pond, where she could clearly see the trail continue.

"Yes, but do not think of taking the short way across it. The pond may not be sufficiently frozen to hold our weight. I do not relish the thought of getting wet in this weather. 'Twould be a fatal mistake, *mon amour.*"

"Fine. Then *you* walk around, but I'm crossing it. I mean to save as many steps as I can on this infernal march. I don't weigh nearly as much as you do. The ice will hold my weight."

Before he could stop her, Elizabeth started out onto the ice with a determined stride. She walked just a few feet before she heard the loud *CRACK*, and felt the ice give way. Instantly, she was plunged into the depths of the icy water.

The shock of cold went through her like a knife, paralyzing her, taking her breath away; her chest constricted in terrible pain. She panicked, thrashing around underwater until her feet touched bottom.

343

Pushing up hard, she rose in the water, her head breaking the surface; and Elizabeth gulped in air before going under again, pulled down by the heavy furs.

Phillipe looked on in horror as she plunged through the ice, his heart tight with fear. Lying down on the ice, he slowly inched his way to Elizabeth, fearful at any moment to be sharing her fate. Thank God, it had happened close to shore. When Elizabeth surfaced for the second time, his hand found hers. Holding tight, he tugged, backing up on the ice at the same time.

Elizabeth felt Phillipe's hand wrap around hers, and the feel of it gave her hope. Phillipe would save her.

The ominous sound of cracking ice sent Phillipe's heart racing. Backing up, he reached a spot where it was frozen enough to sustain his weight. The ice cracked again, as Elizabeth's weight was pulled up on it, and she fell back into the water. His tight grip kept her head from sinking under. Using all his strength, he pulled her up inch by inch, moving her up on the ice. With a final mighty tug, he heaved her out.

"Don't move, Elizabeth. Let me pull you across the ice."

Elizabeth lay flat on the ice, scarcely breathing, afraid of being sent to the bottom of the pond again. After a few tense moments, they were once again on solid ground; the cold wind that whipped at her as lethal as the icy water. It chilled her skin, making her body hurt as if pierced by a thousand, little, stabbing knives. Her teeth rattled, and her body began to shake violently.

"Phillipe—" She gasped for breath, clinging to Phillipe. "I—thank you."

Quickly, Phillipe pulled off her wet clothes and wrapped her in his own fur coat. Pulling off her water-filled boots, he saw a child's mitten tumble to the ground. Alisha's mitten. What was it doing in Elizabeth's boot? What did it matter? The only thing that mattered now was keeping Elizabeth alive.

Without saying a word, he set about starting a fire. It was crucial that Elizabeth get warmed as soon as possible. When the fire burned hot, he hung her wet clothing and boots over a branch of a tree to dry. They were already stiff as a board from the cold. When that was done, he lay next to Elizabeth, using his body to help warm her. He, too, felt the bitter cold without his warm fur coat, but he could tolerate it for a time. He still had his buckskin tunic on, and it protected him some.

After a while Elizabeth's violent shivers grew weaker and weaker, then stopped altogether. He knew that was not good. Her body was too weak to shiver anymore.

Realizing the danger she was in, Elizabeth looked into Phillipe's eyes for reassurance, and found fear glazed there. "Stop looking at me that way, Phillipe. I am not going to die. I have a daughter to raise."

She said it with such conviction that Phillipe took heart. Pulling her close, he said softly, "I know."

That was all she needed to hear. Closing her eyes, she let sleep take her.

Phillipe lay holding her close, his mind working swiftly to fathom the situation they were in. It wasn't wise to keep the fire going for such a long time. Not with the Hawkes on his tail. If they were anywhere in the vicinity, it would be a beacon to guide them. But if he didn't keep the fire going, Elizabeth's clothes would never dry in the icy air, and without the fire's warmth, she would stand no chance of surviving. To make matters worse, it had begun to snow.

Working swiftly, Phillipe built a lean-to around Elizabeth, encompassing the circle of fire. He covered the opening with his canvas bedroll. Soon it was warm enough for his muscles to relax some from the cold-tightened state they had been in, and he watched as the smoke from the fire rose, traveling through the opening in the top of the lean-to. The smell of musk emanating from the wet furs crinkled his nose with displeasure.

Elizabeth moaned in her sleep, and Phillipe knelt beside her to feel her forehead. It was cold. He slid his hand beneath the fur coat and felt her skin. It should have felt warm to the touch, protected by the fur, but it, too, was cold and clammy. Her body wasn't responding, and he knew that if she didn't improve quickly, she would die.

Rubbing her arms and legs, he tried to warm them, working at it until he was too tired to continue. He had seen strong, rugged men die of exposure, and wondered how her frail body could ever fight off what strong men could not.

The snow was coming down harder now, making it difficult to see. Summer tucked her long hair into the tricorn, so it wouldn't get wet and freeze into thin strands of icicles, and lowered the brim to just above her eyes to shield her against the bright glare of the snow. She glanced down at Alisha to see how she was faring, pleased to see her snug and warm. Alisha's fur jacket was hooded and kept her head warm, and her unmittened hand was pulled up into the shelter of her jacket's sleeve.

They walked down the trail carrying their spears, the leftover meat tied to a belt around Summer's waist. It was slippery now, and descending the mountain tricky. They held on to branches of trees and bushes to keep from sliding down too fast. The constant grabbing and pulling used all their energy, and Summer was grateful when they finally made it to the bottom.

If only it would stop snowing! The snow that had been so welcome a short time ago, now turned into a nuisance. But, oh, it was beautiful. The woods had been transformed into a crystal-laden forest, glittering and sparkling like diamonds.

Alisha's eyes reflected the magic world she gazed at. "To think we made this happen killing the snow hare. 'Tis most mystifying. But, Summer, how will we find our way home now? The trail is covered with snow."

"Darling, don't worry. It won't snow forever. When it stops, and we can use the sun again to guide us, we'll find our way home."

"But how?"

"How? Let's see. If I keep the sun over my left shoulder in the morning, and my right shoulder in the afternoon, we'll be heading in the right direction." It wasn't quite that easy, but there was no reason to worry Alisha. If Summer could keep the little girl in good spirits, she could keep her alive.

It would be fairly easy traveling for a while. There was a large valley to cross before they came to the next mountain, but with the snow becoming heavier all the time, she didn't know how long they could go on before they would have to seek shelter. And she was worried about food. God knew when they would be able to eat again, once the meat was gone. She would save it for later; right now they would have to fill their bellies with snow.

An hour later, the snow had made it impossible to

see where she was going. It whipped across her face, stinging her with its intensity.

Making her way to the side of the mountain, she searched for a ridge or overhang of some sort. There had to be one. They were plentiful in this rugged, boulder-ridden landscape. Yes. There. Ahead.

Summer started running, encouraging Alisha as she moved. The wind numbed her face, and she knew she had to get Alisha out of the snow if she was to keep her alive.

The overhang was formed in a way to offer them shelter on three sides and overhead, and was deep enough to protect them from the snow.

She crawled under the granite overhang, pulling Alisha in with her, and strained her eyes to see in the dim light. There was only one place where the snow seemed to be coming in heavily; a large mound filled one end of the shelter. But that was okay, there was still plenty of room for them to stretch out. A luxury Summer hadn't had for a long time.

Wearily, she lay down and stretched out, but something hard pressed against her hip. Feeling with her hand, she grasped the strange-feeling object, but could not move it. Was it a tree root? Brushing the snow away, she gasped in horror.

It was a man's hand!

Alisha heard Summer's gasp and whispered, "What is it, Summer?"

The little girl couldn't see the grisly sight, thank goodness; Summer's body blocked the view. Pulling herself together for the child's sake, she answered, her voice trembling with shock and fear, "It's nothing, darling. Just an uncomfortable spot to sit on. Could you move down a little? I'll join you as soon as I push some of this snow away." Making sure she continued to block Alisha's view, she worked at the mound of snow. She had to see who was buried there. Had to know it wasn't John or Caleb.

Cleaning the snow off the dead man's body, she rolled him over to look at his face. A shock of blond hair framed a pale, frozen face with ice blue eyes. Eyes that stared up at her with a blank stare. Martin Bradford!

She shuddered, revulsed by what she saw, and clasped her hand over her mouth to hold back the cry that threatened to escape. She had never seen a dead body before, not even in a funeral home. She had always averted her eyes, unable and unwilling to look.

And now, here she was in close proximity to one, and it was more horrible than she could ever have imagined. She tore her gaze from his face, unsettled by his staring, unseeing eyes, and saw his unbuttoned breeches and a glimpse of white flesh. Would the horror never end? What was he doing with his breeches unbuttoned? What was he doing here at all? It didn't make sense, or . . . maybe it did. Martin would have had to flee Deerfield after Robillard brought her and Elizabeth to the Bradford place. What with his son Daniel dead and Sarah left to talk about it. He was probably on his way to join Robillard, when he had a heart attack and crawled in here to die.

She wanted to leave this horrible place now, but how could she? They would die out there in the blizzard. She would have to stay until the storm ended. But how could she bear to spend the night with the body of a man a few inches away?

Clenching her teeth, she covered Martin with snow again, and scooted down close to Alisha, as far from the mound of snow as she could get. But it wasn't far enough to suit her. He was still barely more than a foot away.

Forcing a smile on her face for Alisha, she pulled her into her lap. The poor little girl had been through enough already. She wasn't going to add to her trauma. She could feel Alisha's heart beating like a trap drum, and knew the child suspected something was wrong. She would have to take her mind off of their plight.

"Darling, you know what it looks like out there all covered with snow, those sparkling icicles hanging from the trees? A crystal castle. Yes, a crystal castle. Did you ever hear the story about the princess in the castle made of ice?"

Alisha's eyes lit up, reflecting the icy scene outside. "No. Tell me, please?"

"Well, once upon a time, there was a beautiful princess named Alisha. She . . ." Summer told Alisha the story, trying to keep her own mind off of sightless eyes and frozen flesh, holding the child tightly throughout. By the time she finished, it was dark. Still her voice droned on and on, about Cinderella, and Snow White, Rapunzel, and Beauty and the Beast, all through the long, lonely night.

Her voice grew hoarse and dry, but she kept on long after Alisha fell asleep, compelled to do so, afraid if she stopped, she would break down, thinking about what lay just a few inches away from her in the dark. Afraid she would give in to the despair that hovered at the corners of her mind.

Chapter Thirty-One

The snow blew in the men's faces, blinding them with its fury as they made their way up the rugged trail. They moved swiftly, trying to cover as much ground as they could before all traces of the women's tracks were obliterated by the ever-increasing snow. They kept on, defying the elements, knowing they wouldn't be traveling much farther this day. The darkness would come early.

A shout rang through the air, reverberating against the mountain walls. Pedajah had found a cave.

Exhausted and bone cold, they laid their bedrolls in the welcome shelter, too tired even to eat.

After a while, John moved to the opening, and looked out at the snow swirling in a frenzy. He wondered how the women were weathering the below freezing temperatures. Had they found a haven? Or were they still out there somewhere, slowly freezing to death in the bitter cold? It was maddening to think of, yet he could think of nothing else.

Cal saw how troubled John was, and tried to steer him into conversation of a happier note. For the first time John told Cal the incredible story of Summer's first appearance by the river, and how he had captured her that night in his bedchamber. He told Cal about the book of the future, and all that it held, and of the foretelling of Elizabeth's and Alisha's rescue by him, and of the unknown woman destined to die.

Cal reassured him as best he could, and after a while John lay back down on his bedroll and fell into a restless sleep. Cal lay awake thinking about what John had said, the story reaffirming the decision he had come to the night before as he stared up at the crescent moon by the side of the cliff. Once the women had been found, he would implement his plan, and if it worked, they would all live the life they were meant to live.

In the morning, Pedajah was the first to rise. Looking out at the valley below, he saw something that filled his heart with hope.

"John. Cal. Look! Smoke. They are near."

"If that don't beat all," Cal said, scrambling from the cave. "Who would have thought the Frenchman would be stupid enough to have a fire going in broad daylight?"

John thought it was peculiar, too. "Something isn't right. It's not like that wily fox to do something so stupid."

"The gods are with us, brother," Pedajah said. "Nothing more. Think of this. The trail we followed is buried under snow now. We had no way to continue our pursuit, and yet now there is another trail to follow in the sky."

"I don't understand it," John pondered. "Why would they be tarrying so long? Something has happened."

"Never question the gods. Pedajah is right. Major

352

Robillard's black heart awaits the piercing of my sword." Laughing, Cal picked up his pack and, without waiting for the others, walked to the edge of the mountain looking for a way down.

"I think we can make it down here," he said, pointing to a narrow depression in the rock. It ran down to the bottom of the mountain. The others followed, and soon they were walking along the foot of the incline, skirting the wide-open places where they could be seen by unfriendly eyes. They circled around the spot the smoke came from, approaching the site from the north. Robillard wouldn't be expecting any visitors from that direction, and by midday they reached the source of the smoke.

The fire blazed inside a makeshift lean-to, covered by snow. Tracks were visible all around it, but traveled no further. Whoever had built the lean-to, was still inside. By the looks of it, they had been there awhile.

The men advanced as quietly as they could, their swords at the ready. They hoped the wind through the trees would shield the sound of snow crunching under their feet, but knew they couldn't count on it.

Suddenly, the canvas flap covering the opening was flung open, and they came face to face with Major Phillipe Robillard standing defiantly, sword in hand.

John watched Robillard through narrowed eyes. This was his hated enemy. The man who had taken his loved ones. A rage filled him, but he knew he must control it if he would conquer his enemy.

Robillard faced the men in a crouch, ready to do battle. He knew who they were. His blood had flown freely from wounds inflicted by two of them. This time it would be their blood that flowed. He raised his sword.

"Don't be a fool, Robillard. Give up. You cannot hope to get out of this alive."

"Give up, Captain Hawke? And end up in a dark dungeon? Or even worse, hanging from a rope? No! I'd rather die like a man and take some of you with me."

"No!" Elizabeth appeared next to Phillipe, her body weaving back and forth. With blurred vision and unsteady feet, she took a step forward, then collapsed at Phillipe's feet.

Without thinking, Phillipe knelt and took her into his arms, his sword dropping from his hand as he reached for her.

Cal watched, stunned at seeing Elizabeth so weak and frail. "What have you done to her, you bastard!"

Phillipe looked up at him, an anxious look on his face. "I have done nothing. She fell through the ice. The reason for the fire. At first she could not warm up at all, and now she burns with fever." Picking her up, he carried her to the bedroll inside and laid her on it.

Pedajah took the opportunity and picked up Phillipe's sword. There would be no killing this day.

Moving quickly to Elizabeth's side, Cal took her hand in his. The heat of it jolted him. Looking at John, he shook his head.

John was confused. He had thought Summer would be the one lying here with a fever. Elizabeth was dying . . . and Summer and Alisha were missing.

"Major Robillard, where is Summer Winslow and my daughter? I promise you, if you've laid one slimy hand on them, I'll run you through right here. You won't have to worry about being hung."

With malice dripping from every word, Phillipe told them of Summer's escape. "You'll never see your lover again, or hold her in your arms. And your daughter is lost to you forever. If they are not lying

354

frozen somewhere, it is because the wolves have already gnawed at their bones. I can die now, knowing I have been avenged."

John struck Phillipe in the face, his fist doubled hard.

"John, don't. The important thing now is to find Summer and Alisha as soon as we can. You can take care of him later. He won't be going anywhere." Cal held John's arm, calming him with his words. "The snow is a blessing. Summer and Alisha will be setting down tracks that will be easy to follow. If we can find the place they escaped from, we will have fresh tracks."

"The cave." Elizabeth whispered the words hoarsely. "They hid in a tree near the cave. Alisha . . . bring her . . ."

John was bewildered. "The cave? They escaped from the cave? Damn! By the time we reached the cave last night, the snow had covered all traces of them. Cal, you and Pedajah had better get started right away. Find them before they perish in the cold."

"John," Cal said quietly. "You go. I'll stay with Elizabeth and keep watch over Robillard."

John longed to start out after Summer, but he knew that as Elizabeth's husband, it was his place to stay with her. "Are you sure? Elizabeth is my wife. It . . ."

"This is no time to start acting like a husband. Go! Elizabeth will get more comfort from me than she could ever get from you." The words were harsh, but the tone was not.

John realized the truth of it. He kissed Elizabeth's hand, wincing at the heat emanating from it. "I'll bring Alisha to you before this very day is ended."

After John and Pedajah left, Cal turned to the Frenchman. "Will you give me your word as a gentleman that you will not try to escape, or must I bind you to a tree?"

Robillard laughed bitterly, knowing what he must do. "Would you trust my word, Hawke? I think not. I will endure no bonds, and I will be no prisoner to the Hawkes." He made a move toward the opening, knowing the futility of it. Cal held Phillipe's own sword to his stomach.

"Halt! Major Robillard. It's futile to try and escape. You are my prisoner."

Phillipe looked down at the sword nudging his stomach, then up to Caleb's face. A strange light flickered in his eyes. Without a moment of hesitation, he walked right into the sword, impaling himself on the blade.

Cal sucked in his breath in shock, and watched as Phillipe fell over, clutching the sword between his bloody hands.

"What is it?" Elizabeth called out weakly, unaware of what had just transpired. "What's happening?"

"Nothing, Elizabeth. Close your eyes and rest. Everything will be all right. I promise you."

Caleb knelt by the major. "You bloody, bloody fool." A lump came to his throat. Whatever else Robillard was, he was a brave man.

Cal felt the futility of war at that moment, and the waste of human lives. He would welcome living with his mother's people, and their simple way of life. He would relish living deep within the forest, where this useless war could not reach him. Picking up the lifeless body, he carried it from the lean-to and laid it down in a cradle of fallen branches, then set the major's sword on his chest. When he was done, he returned to Elizabeth.

Kneeling beside her, he whispered, "Darling, open your eyes and look at me." As he said the words, he recalled almost the same words spoken by Elizabeth as she stood naked in the bedroom. He remembered the sight of her beautiful, petite body, and how vulnerable she had been at that moment.

Elizabeth turned her head toward him, as he had once turned toward her, and opened her eyes.

"Darling Elizabeth. You must get well. You must get your strength back. I've worked out a way that we may be together; a way John and Summer can be together, too. I promise you it's true."

Elizabeth knew that she must be very close to death for him to say such things to her, such things as she had waited five long years to hear.

Cal saw the disbelief in her eyes. "It's true. We will be together. Look in my eyes and believe."

Elizabeth gazed into his eyes, and a spark of life ignited in her. She must live. Live to feel Cal's arms around her again, live to feel his lips on hers, and know he would be hers forever. If only it could be.

Caleb saw the struggle for life in Elizabeth's eyes and kissed her feverish lips, knowing it would be a miracle if she lasted the night.

Chapter Thirty-Two

Alisha tugged at Summer's sleeve. "Wake up, Summer. Look what I found. Do you think the fairy godmother left it for us?"

Summer smiled sleepily. Alisha was still thinking about the fairy tales she had heard. Opening her eyes, she saw the canvas bag in Alisha's arms. She knew immediately what it was, and turned to look at the snow-covered mound. She was fully awake now.

"My goodness, Alisha. I think you're right. Let's look. See what goodies the fairy godmother left for us."

Summer rummaged through the bag, pulling out cheese, hardtack, some sort of dried meat, and dried apples. Enough food to last for several days, if they were careful. Thank you, Martin Bradford, you miserable old man. This is probably the only good thing you've ever done for anyone, and you had to die to do it.

She hadn't noticed the pack last night, but then it had been on Alisha's side of the shelter. She had been too occupied with the grisly discovery on her own side to notice much of anything.

"Alisha, do you know what that means? Thanks to

our fairy godmother, we can have a delicious breakfast and enough food to last for days. The snow hares will be safe from the mighty hunters for a while."

Laughing, she gathered the child into her arms. "You see, we are doing fine. In no time at all, we'll be back at your grandmother's house, and she and Otis will cook us a grand banquet of all our favorite foods."

"And then, Father and Uncle Cal will find Mama and bring her back to us; and we'll live happily ever after, just like in the fairy stories you told me."

Summer felt a lump in her throat. Even if by some miracle they made it back, she doubted they would live happily ever after. But it wouldn't do to think about that now. She needed the courage that could only come from believing that everything would turn out fine.

Once they had eaten, Summer hefted Martin's pack onto her back, satisfied it wasn't too heavy, and crawled out of the shelter. She looked around warily. Thank goodness it had stopped snowing during the night. The sun was out, and she could feel its warmth on her face and deep in her soul. The bright rays gave her hope, and feeling better than she had since she was captured, they began the long journey home.

In a short time they came to a clearing, where she could look down at a wide meadow below. With the trail now buried a foot under snow, she would have to follow her instincts, and her instincts told her the meadow was a good place to cross. She would be heading in the right direction, and walking across the clear stretch of land would be a welcome relief from having to fight through dense forest or rocky slopes that taxed her energy.

Her gaze took in a depressed area free of trees and

brush. Why not slide down? It wasn't far to the bottom, and the snow was packed hard, perfect for sliding.

"Alisha, the mighty warriors are going to slide down the hill. Do you think you can do it?"

Alisha nodded, her eyes wide with fear, or was it from the excitement of sliding down the slope? "Follow behind me in my trail, and do exactly as I do."

Sitting down, Summer pushed off and started down the slope. The heavy fur leggings she wore protected her well and kept her from sliding too fast. The ride was bumpy, but not unlike tobogganing. Moving down the slope, she steered her body by leaning from side to side, exhilarated that she didn't have to use up valuable energy walking. She landed in a tumble at the bottom of the slope, Alisha plowing into her. Her joyful cries echoed against the hill. Pulling her into her arms, she hugged Alisha, rolling over and over with her and laughing as joyously as the child.

"Summer, being a mighty warrior is fun. Can we slide down another hill? Wait until Mama and Grandmother hear about this!"

"Darling, when we get home, I'll take you tobogganing if I have to make the toboggan myself. And I just might have to, since I'm not sure they've been invented yet."

Asperensah cursed. What a fool she had been to leave the other pack with Martin's body. It contained most of the food. She had been so frightened after his sudden death, she hadn't been thinking straight, and had sought another shelter as fast as she could. But now the storm was over, and it was but a short

360

distance to the place where the pack lay. She would retrieve it, and be on her way to the outpost.

When she drew close to the shelter, she saw the tracks. Someone had been there. More than one person, too, by the look of it. Kneeling for closer inspection, she discovered one of the tracks was that of a small child and the other a woman. Could it be possible? Had one of the Hawke women escaped with the child? That could be the only explanation. But which woman? She checked the woman's track, then smiled. Yes, the sunset-haired one. It could be only she. Summer's foot was much larger than tiny Elizabeth's.

The tracks led away from the shelter. Why hadn't she come sooner? Crawling under the overhang, she looked around. Martin was buried under snow, but as she feared, the pack was missing. Summer had found it. But she wouldn't have it very long. She would track the white woman and take it from her, and then . . . then, she would take her revenge—kill her for causing Daniel's death. She had been prevented from doing so once before, but now, there was no one to stop her.

Coming to the spot where Summer and the child slid down the hill, her gaze scanned the scenery below. She quickly made out the two figures just starting across the meadow. Patting her knife at her waist, she clutched Martin's flintlock and followed them down.

The two men strode through the high timber, never slaking their pace, hoping at any second to catch sight of Summer's fair hair. Their trail had not been easy to follow at first, covered with snow, but once they found the shelter they had stayed in during the storm, the tracks became easier. It had been a shock to John to see the third set of footprints, and to know that someone was stalking Summer and Alisha. It had been a shock, too, finding Martin Bradford's body under the mound of snow.

Pedajah saw the concern in John's eyes. "Fear not. The tracks we follow now were made but moments ago. Soon you will hold your daughter in your arms."

"Pedajah, I had hoped to find a more suitable time to tell you this, but now, with circumstances being what they are, you need to know that Alisha is not my daughter, but Cal's. I tell you this to forewarn you. As soon as Summer and Alisha are found, things will be changing. Think on this, meanwhile. Alisha has as much of your blood, as she has of mine. We are both uncles to her, and it's a bond I gladly share with you."

Pedajah never changed his placid expression. "The way of the whites is strange, and has ever been so. But it is not for me to say. I am happy that Caleb has a daughter, and I such a beautiful niece. I have always been fond of the little one; her spirit is good, like her mother and my own mother, Nenepownam. It is good that she is of my people."

Pedajah stopped suddenly. He had almost missed the marks going down the hill. Striding to the edge, he examined the slide marks that marred the otherwise undisturbed snow cover.

John saw them, too. With eyes red and tearing from the cold and brilliant glare of the sun on snow, he scanned the scenery below. Something moved in the snow-covered valley. Shading his eyes with his hands, he looked again, and saw the form of a hunched-over figure trudging slowly across the broad valley.

It wasn't a hunched-over person. It was someone carrying a child on their back. Could it be? Yes, yes, it was Summer and Alisha. Joy swept over him as he watched Summer put the small child down, then straighten up. He laughed when he saw the spears carried in their hands.

Pedajah shared his joy, thumping him soundly on the back. "You see, they have managed quite well without our help. Our search is—" Pedajah's words froze in his throat, seeing a third figure advancing on Summer and Alisha in a furtive manner.

John saw it, too, and his heart constricted with fear. The figure carried a flintlock. As they watched in horror, the figure stopped walking and slowly raised the rifle into firing position.

"Nooooooo," John shouted in rage. But the distance was too great, and the wind too strong to be heard over. He was helpless to stop the tragedy unfolding below.

But wait—Alisha was tugging at Summer, pointing behind her. Summer was turning now. She saw her assailant. But what could she do against a lead ball?

Summer turned toward the fur-clad figure pointing a rifle at her, and at the same time heard the fierce cry of a hawk. Beauty dove toward the assailant, her lethal talons extended.

The Indian woman's shot went wild and she dropped the rifle, clutching at her bleeding face.

The sound of the shot frightened Beauty, and the bird climbed back to the safety of the skies, circling restlessly overhead, calling out a warning to the bleeding figure below.

Summer ran for the rifle. She had to reach it before her assailant could load again. But instead of reaching for the rifle, the person pulled a knife from her belt. Summer was close enough now to see that it was Asperensah.

Crouching in a defensive position, Summer clutched her spear tightly, ready to defend herself if she must. She wasn't going to be defeated, not after she had come so far.

Asperensah saw the determination in Summer's eyes, and knew Summer would use her weapon. What use was her small knife against a spear? She turned and ran. She would deal with Summer another time.

John and Pedajah slid down the hill and advanced toward Summer, calling out to her as they ran. She didn't hear them, still too far away to hear over the howling wind.

Alisha saw them first. Crying out a warning, she ran up to Summer. Fear overpowered Summer. Was it the French? Or Abenakis? There was no use running. There was nowhere to run to, and no one to turn to for help. She was on her own with nothing between her and the two men, but a stick she had carved with a child's knife.

Alisha watched as Summer took a defensive stance and held her own small spear in the same position. "We are mighty warriors. Like Nenepownam's people. We will show no fear."

Summer glanced down at the brave little girl, ready to do battle against grown men and, in a voice choked with emotion, said, "Yes, we are brave warriors. Nenepownam would be very proud of us."

John saw the defensive position Summer had taken, and realized she didn't recognize him bundled up as he was. Taking his sword from its sheath, he waved it over his head. The sun caught the shiny steel and sent an iridescent circle of light radiating from the blade.

Instantly, Summer knew who it was. Never had she seen a more welcome sight. Dropping her spear in the snow, she took off her tricorn hat and waved it triumphantly over her head. Was he really here? Was the nightmare truly over? She burst into tears of relief and joy. She had made it. Against great odds. She was alive. John was here. She could face anything now.

John saw all that glorious hair come spilling out of the hat. It caught the light from the sun and shone like a welcome beacon. His throat constricted at the enchanting sight, and he knew he would remember this moment the rest of his life.

Alisha and Summer were running toward him, but he held his ground. What he did now would determine his future, his happiness, his very life. When Summer drew close, he suddenly lowered his sword and pointed it directly at her. "Stop! Don't come any closer."

Summer stopped, astounded. What was the matter with John? Why was he telling her to stop, when all she wanted in this world was to be in his arms?

Alisha paid no attention to the demand and ran up to her father, throwing her arm around his leg. John hugged her to him without taking his eyes off Summer.

Summer started moving again, and again he held his sword up to her. "I repeat, don't come any closer."

Summer was stunned. This was no time to be playing games.

Looking down at Alisha, John patted her back with his hand. "Sweeting, go to Pedajah. There is something that must be settled between Summer and me."

Alisha was confused, but did as she was told. Her father was here. Everything would be all right now.

Scooping her up in his arms, Pedajah waited to see what was about to happen between these two strange-acting whites. Alisha's little arms closed around his neck, holding tight, and the Indian brave held his niece against his chest crooning words of reassurance.

"John, what is it? Why are you acting so strangely? Do you mean to run me through with your sword?"

"No, Summer. I mean for you to touch it, here and now, and return to your own time."

John's words went through her like a knife. "John, you can't mean that. This is no time to joke."

"But I do mean it . . . and Summer . . . this time it *is* my sword. Be sure of that. Touch it and leave me forever, or . . . vow this moment to be mine forever. No more doubts, no more ideas of marrying my brother, no—"

"God's blood, John. Do you have to do this now? Can't it wait until we get back home? I've been captured by a crazed Frenchman, marched through icy wilderness, climbed mountains that would break a mountain goat's spirit, and now, now, I'm confronted by a madman who threatens to skewer me with his sword! A madman whose arms I desperately need to be in! Oh, John, I've prayed for this moment, prayed I would see you again, to feel your arms around me just one more time."

John's voice never wavered as he said, "Decide your destiny, Summer."

Chapter Thirty-Three

John stood his ground on the frozen meadow and repeated the words. "Decide your destiny, Summer, before a touch of my blade decides it for you."

The hawk circling overhead emphasized his words with a raucous sound that startled Summer, but her eyes never left John or the sword clenched in his fist. The shiny blade reflected the rays of the sun, sending shafts of light dancing in the frigid air. Summer thought King Arthur himself, with his sword Excalibur, could not have looked so appealing or more masculine than this eighteenth-century knight she loved so much.

John took a step closer.

She flinched and jumped back, the tip of the blade almost touching her fur jacket.

"What is your answer, Summer?"

Staring into his eyes, she thought, *How can he be so calm?* How can he be so cold? Doesn't it matter to him whether she chose to stay or leave? Slowly her hand moved tantalizingly close to the sword. She was testing him and he knew it.

He held the sword steady, not moving an inch, as she moved her hand even closer. Would he let her touch it?

He stood like a rock, his face expressionless—except for his eyes. She saw the familiar glint there and something more . . . she saw the love that burned deep. The love that defied even time.

"Throw the sword away, John Hawke."

Opening his fist, the sword dropped to the snow. Tears sprang to his eyes, and an animal sound escaped his throat as he pulled her into his arms. "I was so afraid . . . if you had touched . . . I . . ."

Summer saw the tears and began to cry, too. "How could I ever leave you? I'm captive still, to your heart."

Her tears once started, could not be stopped. They escalated into a full-blown crying jag, and she let it all out. All the hurt and fright and weariness she had experienced. All the worry that she would die without ever seeing him again.

John held her tightly throughout, soothing her with words of love, and when the sobbing subsided, his lips came down on hers in a kiss so tender, so sweet, tears came to both sets of eyes again.

She inhaled the sweet smell of his breath in the icy air when his lips drew near, and breathed deeply of him, needing his scent as well as his touch. She could never, would never, get enough of him. The feel of his arms around her was the only home she would ever need.

When the kiss ended, John held her at arm's length. "That damn book of yours. The first thing we do when we return to Deerfield is to burn it! I've been worried sick I'd find you dead. I was so afraid you were the woman who would die."

"John, forget about it. I'm here. We're together. Right now, we've got to find Elizabeth. Robillard has her. She sacrificed herself to give me and Alisha a chance to escape."

"Calm down, darling. Cal and I found her. He's with her now. But I'm afraid it isn't good. It seems your book is partially right. A woman will die— Elizabeth. She fell into a pond and has a raging fever. I can hear the death rattle in her chest."

"Oh no! Where is she?"

"Not far from here. The other side of the mountain. I promised I'd bring Alisha back to her today. I fear that's all the time she has. Are you up to it? I know how tired you must be."

"I'm fine. But Alisha—I don't know."

"Pedajah and I can take turns carrying her."

"Then I'll carry our vagabond hawk. She deserves a rest after what she's done for me today."

Summer signaled the hawk as she had seen Elizabeth do, and it flew down, landing on her outstretched arm. Then suddenly it gave out a wild cry and flew off again, climbing high into the sky before diving once again, swooping low to the ground then climbing again. A lonely mournful sound emanated from the hawk, stirring Summer's heart, then it was gone. She knew it wouldn't be back.

"Why did it do that?"

John pulled her into his arms. "Beauty's job is done. You're safe now, safe in the care of the only Hawke you'll need from now on."

It was almost dark when they came to the lean-to. Alisha ran ahead, eager to see her mother. Summer held her breath when she opened the canvas flap, afraid Elizabeth would be dead. But it was all right. Alisha was hugging her mother, and Elizabeth, pale and wan, was patting her daughter's head.

Elizabeth's gaze turned to Summer as she entered,

and spoke to her in a weak and raspy voice. "I asked you once before if you could ever forgive me, and you didn't know. I ask you again."

Summer choked back a sob, shocked at the sight of Elizabeth so pale and weak. "I forgive you. We'll talk it all out when we are safely home, and you are stronger."

A small smile played across Elizabeth's blue-tinged lips, and she turned her attention back to her daughter.

John looked around for Robillard, giving Cal a questioning glance. Cal motioned for him and Pedajah to follow him outside. There, he told them of Phillipe's shocking suicide.

When they reentered the lean-to, Summer looked at Cal for the first time. His clear blue eyes gazed back at her lovingly. Walking over to him, she put her arms around his neck and embraced him tenderly.

"I know," he said quietly. "There's no need to speak of it. You have always belonged to my brother."

Tears welled in her eyes as she gazed at Caleb. He was such an honorable man. She wished she could take back all the hurt she had caused him, then thought of one thing she could do.

Slipping the ornate green-stoned ring from her finger—the ring Cal had given to her such a short time ago—she knelt beside Elizabeth. Taking her burning hand in hers, she slipped the ring on Elizabeth's finger.

"This ring was always meant to be yours. I give it to you now."

Elizabeth looked down at the ring, and tears came to her eyes. She looked up at Cal, who nodded his head in agreement. It was true! Caleb would be hers, if only she could get well.

Alisha watched her mother and Summer with a puzzled expression. "Mama, why are you wearing Uncle Caleb's ring?"

Elizabeth looked at her daughter, then up to Cal. "Darling, there's something you must know."

John smiled, content with the world for the first time in his life. He sat with Caleb, talking in low tones, while Alisha filled Elizabeth in on her exciting adventure. Pedajah returned with two snow hares he had shot for supper.

"Uh, oh," Alisha exclaimed. "I fear it will snow again."

Everyone laughed when she told her story of the snow hare she and Summer had killed, and of the following fierce snowstorm.

An hour later, bellies full of roasted hare, they lay down to sleep, except for Pedajah, who had first watch.

It was a tight fit, but there was room enough for them all in the lean-to curling up against each other, taking comfort from the closeness and warmth. When John left to take his turn at watch in the middle of the night, Summer barely stirred.

In the morning, Elizabeth's breathing was still labored. Summer could hear the fluid in her lungs, and wondered how the frail little woman had held on so long. She wanted to stay, do whatever she could for her, but all three men ganged up on her, and Elizabeth agreed with them.

"It's important you get my daughter back home safely. She has gone through enough. I entrusted her to your care at the cave, and you proved worthy of that trust. Now I ask you once again to take care of her."

371

"I'll take good care of her, you know that. Just get better and come back to us."

Elizabeth smiled. "The men have not told you of their plan for our future, I see. I will not see you again in this life, but however it works out, whether I live or die, you will be with John."

"What do you mean? What plan have the men worked out?"

John put his arm on Summer's shoulder. "You'll find out soon enough. 'Tis a long walk home. Time enough to fill you in on all the details."

Summer's inquisitive eyes moved from Elizabeth to John to Cal. What did it mean? Surely there was no way to make everything turn out right. But she wouldn't push it, not with Alisha listening intently to every word.

After a tearful goodbye, the small party was on its way. Caleb waved goodbye to them from the opening of the lean-to, then went inside to care for Elizabeth.

The miles, which had seemed endless before, now flew as John, Summer, Pedajah, and Alisha made their way southward. Pedajah would stay with them until they got to Deerfield, and then would join his own people at winter camp.

Summer felt safe in John's company. Nothing could harm her as long as he was only an arm's distance away. He still had not told her of Caleb's plan, but she was content for now, knowing they were on their way back to civilization.

But it was puzzling. She—not Elizabeth—was on her way home. The book had been wrong! If Elizabeth died, everything would be greatly changed. And what of the child she herself would be giving birth to in June? The future would be changed even more when he or she was born. How could its presence be accounted for? Its very existence in the world would cause untold changes in the future. If Cal had a way out of this mess, she was anxious to hear it.

At dusk the next day, they were surprised and pleased to see the smoke of a huge campfire in the distance. John knew it must be his militia. They would not be content to sit and wait for him to return. His steps became lighter, as he and Pedajah guided Summer and Alisha toward the camp.

They trudged through the dusky twilight and into the night guided by the amber glow, until, at last, they made their way into the camp. They were immediately surrounded by John's men. Whoops of victory filled the air.

Sgt. Josiah Davidson greeted John enthusiastically, patting him on the back, repeatedly, "Sir, glad to see you safely returned! I took the liberty to assemble a small party to meet you. Figured your womenfolk would have need of hot food and warm blankets."

"Small party, Davidson? It looks like half the regiment is camped here. But I'm not complaining. It's good to see you, Sergeant. Now, where's this hot food you mentioned? I'm starved."

Weary from the long day's journey, Summer and Alisha paid scant attention to the activity around the campfire. They filled their bellies with stew and endured the attentions of the men for a short time, then wrapped themselves in blankets and curled up by the fire and slept.

John gazed down at his loved ones, studying the face of the woman who meant more to him than life itself. She had been through so much in this century, and yet she still chose to stay with him. His heart filled with pride.

Sergeant Davidson walked over to where he stood.

"It's mighty happy I am, seeing those two sleeping so peacefully. I never doubted you'd find them, sir. I just wish your wife had survived, too. Would it be too painful to tell me what happened?"

John hesitated for only a second. His answer to the sergeant would be the first step toward making their future together a reality.

"It's quite all right. Sergeant. My wife fell through some ice and caught the fever. It was too much for her in her weakened condition. She . . . she didn't make it."

"Sorry to hear that, sir. She was an uncommonly beautiful woman. She'll be sorely missed."

"Thank you, Sergeant. You're right. She will be sorely missed."

"I was wondering, sir, what you'll be doing about the uh, remains?"

"It's being taken care of. My brother Caleb stayed to . . . handle that."

"I see. Will we be waiting here for him then?"

"No. Cal has decided not to return to Deerfield. He'll be joining his mother's people at their winter camp. He's chosen to live with them from now on."

"But his mother, isn't she staying with your folks right now?"

"Yes. Nenepownam will stay the winter with us. Cal will return for her in the spring, so she may join her people."

"Seems to me this isn't the first time he's chosen to live with them Injuns. 'Tis strange, the lure their way of life has on some folk. He's not the first white man, or woman, for that matter, to choose that way of life over our own civilized way."

"That's a fact." John thought about Elizabeth and her wild ways. She would have been much happier if she had been born an Indian. And if, by some

374

miracle, she survived, she would be living that way from now on.

"Praise be, your daughter is alive and Mistress Winslow, too." Sergeant Davidson looked down at the sleeping forms. "Amazing how well they've come through this. The Hawkes have strong blood in their veins. That's a fact."

"Aye, Sergeant, that's a fact."

With the militia escorting them the final miles home, the tension and anxiety Summer had been feeling ever since she had been taken at the waterfall, had blown away with the icy winds. The weather turned warmer and the snow began to melt. And, thanks to the men of the militia, Alisha's tiny feet never touched the ground. They carried her on their backs, happy for the burden.

With the snow melting, snowshoes became useless. Trudging through snow on foot was difficult and tiring. By the end of the next day's march, Summer's shins were cut and bleeding from the sharp edges of the snow drifts. She began to envy Alisha's mode of transportation.

That night, as she sat by the fire, John explained to her what Caleb had told him that morning by the cliff.

"If Elizabeth lives, Cal will take her back with him to his mother's people. They'll live together there, as they should have five years ago. You know how much Elizabeth loves the woods. She'd rather wander through them then do just about anything, and her wild spirit is well suited for that way of life."

"John, I'm the last person you need to explain to. I know how much Elizabeth loves the forest, but what does that have to do with any of this?"

"Simply this. We'll tell the townfolk that Elizabeth died, whether she actually does or not. That way, there'll be nothing to keep us from marrying. The historians of the future will never know the truth."

"John, I pray Elizabeth lives. She and Cal deserve to be happy after being separated so long, and maybe, under Cal's loving care, she will. But I don't see how Elizabeth and Cal living with the Indians can solve *our* problem."

"Don't you see? We can be married now."

"How can you say that? You know the town will never accept our marrying so soon after Elizabeth's death, real or imaginary, and—"

"We'll make it acceptable. We'll tell everyone Elizabeth urged us to marry right away, so that you could be a mother to Alisha. They'll understand that. Alisha will need you. Even if by some miracle Elizabeth does survive—and we know the chances of that are slim—Alisha won't be able to see her until spring. We would have the same arrangement with her that Cal had with Nenepownam. The child would be brought to summer camp each year. Though, in this case, we would have to keep her visits to Elizabeth a secret from the townfolk. You see, Cal and I have it all worked out. No matter what happens to Elizabeth, you and I can marry."

"But, John. There's an even more important thing to consider. The future. It doesn't show another marriage for you. How can we marry, knowing it would change the future? How can we marry, knowing that our being together would have terrible repercussions on generations of people?"

"Summer, you've been so distraught these past weeks, you've forgotten a very important aspect of this situation. The book says Adam Hawke will be orn June 21, 1745. Is that not so?"

"Yes . . . but . . . Oh, John, with Elizabeth gone, hat can never happen now! The future has already hanged, and it's all my fault!"

"You're not thinking clearly. Didn't Elizabeth dmit to you that she wasn't really pregnant?"

"Yes . . . she did, but, but . . . Oh John!"

"Exactly, my sweet little idiot. Since Elizabeth vasn't pregnant in the first place, she could never ave given birth to Adam. Your being here had othing to do with that. Elizabeth and I never slept ogether, but, my darling, you and I have. *You* will be iving birth. Don't you see? The Adam Hawke estined to be born in June will be *your* son!"

Chapter Thirty-Four

Summer listened, absorbing what John told her in amazement. If what he said was true, then her being here had been preordained. For she knew without a doubt that Adam would be born, and Aaron Hawke as well, two years later. Somehow, she would be living Elizabeth's life. But, no, there were still too many loose ends. It would never work.

John anticipated her questions. "We'll marry in Boston. That way, our marriage will be recorded there, not in Deerfield. The future historians won' know that, of course. They'll assume Adam's mother is Elizabeth. We'll make sure no record of Elizabeth': death is recorded."

"But, John, Adam's mother is on record, in 1993 as being Elizabeth Hawke, not Summer Hawke. You can't alter that."

"Ah, ha! That's where you're wrong, my sweet. We'll let it be known that your proper name is *Elizabeth* Summer Winslow, that you simply prefer to be called by your middle name. 'Tis not uncommon to be called by your middle name now, is it? That way, when we're married, your name will become Elizabeth Hawke. Don't you see? It will work."

Summer's eyes opened wide in shock as she realized the full meaning of his words. She clutched at John for support. "My God! Do you know what that means? When I die, I'll be buried in Elizabeth's grave! Now I understand . . . all the strange, eerie feelings I had whenever I stood on her grave were because *I was actually standing on my own grave!*"

Summer started laughing. It escalated out of control until tears ran down her cheeks. The men who sat nearby looked at her with sympathy, thinking she had finally broken under the strain of her terrible ordeal.

Sergeant Davidson walked over to where she sat. "Is there anything I can do for her, Captain?"

"No, Sergeant. She'll be fine. It's just hit her that she has a long happy life ahead of her."

Sergeant Davidson studied Summer's face. The tiredness was gone and something else replaced it. He wasn't sure, but he thought it was pure joy.

Later, when everyone had settled down for the night, Summer worked it all out in her mind, as she gazed at the starry sky. The people of Deerfield would accept her sudden marriage to John because of the power of the Hawke name, and because it was true that Alisha would have need of a mother. And when the baby came, well, it was true that tongues would wag, but in time it would be forgotten.

The child would be named Adam, and that name would be officially recorded. The mother's name would be recorded as Elizabeth Hawke, and so, in years to come, no one would know that Summer wasn't the original Elizabeth.

Even the unknown woman who had died in the wilderness could be explained. Since Summer would be recorded as Adam's mother under Elizabeth's name, it would confuse historians when they read

379

accounts of Elizabeth's death or disappearance in the wilderness. Accounts that were sure to be passed down through letter, or diaries, or family tradition.

Historians would assume it was an error, and that some unnamed woman had died in the wilderness. Errors such as those were common. Historians took them as part of their lot in life. They might even assume that it was another Elizabeth Hawke. Summer had seen that name used throughout the genealogy book, but since they wouldn't know for sure who the woman in the wilderness was, she would stay unnamed. Records from the 1700s were sketchy at best, and some facts were impossible to track down.

Yes, it would work. It was meant to work. Her excitement rose as it all sank in. She would have John and would actually become his wife! Never in her wildest imaginings had she dared to dream such an impossible dream.

She thought back to her first glimpse of his portrait. How she had yearned for him even then, so much so, that she felt a need, an absolute need to touch something that belonged to him. His sword. His sword! Oh, no! They had forgotten about his sword!

Reaching over to John, she shook his shoulder. "John, wake up, we've forgotten something important. How can your sword end up in a glass case in Memorial Hall, when it's buried in the snow in a mountain meadow?"

John pulled her into his arms. "Have you no faith, woman? Hasn't everything turned out right so far? That sword brought you to me through two hundred years of time. It kept you here with me, despite your determination to leave. Its destiny is entwined with our own. I doubt not that at the proper moment it will show up. Mayhap some wandering fur trader will stumble over it, recognize its distinctive markings and return it to me. Though, God knows, I never want to lay eyes on it again. 'Twould be too easy for you to disappear on me whenever we have an argument. No. I am content for it to stay exactly where it is."

Summer laughed softly, picturing the scene in her mind. "Come to think of it, I just might turn back and find it. It would certainly come in handy keeping you under control."

"You hold my heart in your hands even now, what more control can you want? Ask me to bleed and I will. Ask me to love you forever, and I must. You are my life, my love, my destiny, my—"

Summer stopped him with her mouth.

"I'm telling you for the last time, John, Summer will not be sleeping under any roof but mine, until you are legally wed. Propriety must be upheld. 'Tis strange enough that Summer, so recently betrothed to Cal, should up and decide to marry you, with your wife not cold in her grave yet. If indeed there be a grave out there in the frozen wilderness. But to flaunt the fact that you are lovers by having her live with you, is too much! There's just so much people will accept, even from a Hawke. She stays with me."

"Damn it all, Mother. We've not been alone since I found her a week ago. A whole company of militia accompanied us back here, and you grabbed her from me as soon as we set foot in this house. I have a need to be alone with her."

"Yes, and I'm not too old to remember just what that need is. No. Propriety must be upheld."

"Propriety be damned! Since when have you cared

about such things?"

"Since an unmarried woman has been put in my care. Thanks be that Charity is safely married to Nat, or I'd have two rutting bucks at my door. Your wedding will be soon enough, what with a pregnant bride and all, though I don't understand the need to go all the way to Boston to marry. We shall all be half dead by the time we get there. Oh dear, there I go again, interfering with your life. Forgive me. Despite my complaints, I know it will be exciting to go to Boston. I haven't been there since *I* was a bride."

"And now that that is settled, Mother, be done with all the griping and be satisfied that finally all your children are happy."

John leaned down to kiss his mother's cheek, then swatted her on the behind. "Now, if you'll excuse us, Summer and I are taking a walk. You can accompany us if you insist, but we intend to walk very fast, and I doubt your legs can keep up with us."

"Be off with you then, but mind you don't stop at any bushes along the way to use as a love's nest."

John laughed, then grabbed Summer's hand, pulling her out of the room.

In the hallway, Summer said, "If you think you're going to make love to me out in the cold somewhere, you are sadly mistaken. I've endured lying in a spooky graveyard and on a windy hilltop, while you planted apple trees and had your way with me, but enough is enough. The next time we make love will be in a feather bed."

Without saying a word, John opened the outside door, then slammed it shut again.

"What the—" Summer was interrupted by a hand over her mouth.

"Shh," John whispered. Taking her hand, he led her up the stairs to her bedroom. Closing the door behind him, he gazed at her with such desire that Summer felt suddenly weak in the knees.

She looked over to the feather bed, and back to John's face, then, wrapping her arms around his neck, molded her body to his in a passionate kiss.

Slowly the clothes fell to the floor. They undressed, never taking their eyes from each other. And when they were naked, their gazes traveled leisurely over each other's body, enjoying the unrushed luxury.

John kissed her gently on the lips, then neck and shoulders, before his lips moved down to her breasts. They lingered there awhile, enjoying the taste of her cherry nipples. Continuing their journey, his lips moved down to the delicate swelling of her belly, and kissed it fervently, knowing the roundness was caused by his child growing there. How he loved this woman and the child she carried. She was his mate in every sense of the word, and he would cherish her forever.

His lips moved down to the hot moistness between her legs, needing to taste the nectar that belonged to him alone, and he thrust his tongue inside her, paving the way for what was to come.

Summer moaned at the touch of his hot tongue inside her, and at the exquisite pleasure it brought her. How could anything feel so good? Grasping his head, she pushed him away, afraid of becoming satisfied before he even entered her; but then she pulled him closer, lost in the ecstasy of his touch.

When she could stand the intense feeling no longer, he pulled her down to the floor and covered her body with his own. As she felt him slide into her, and as her body encompassed him, closing tightly around him, she heard him say, "The feather bed will have to wait 'til our wedding night."

Epilogue

The silence of the frozen wilderness was broken by the crunching of fur boots in the crusty snow. A man and a woman walked hand and hand across the wide expanse, alone but for the hawk that glided overhead.

Ahead, something glinted in the snow, catching the afternoon rays of the winter sun. A beam of light, bright and compelling, drew the couple closer and closer, curious to see what treasure glittered there.

Kneeling, the woman gasped in surprise as her small feminine hand, adorned with an ornate green-stoned ring, reached down . . .

. . . to touch the half-buried sword.